DIS

She stared into his eyes, eyes that were blacker than the night. He lifted the heavy weight of her hair, letting it slide across his hand, then ran his fingers almost wonderingly over her cheekbone and along the side of her face. His thumb traced the shape of her lips. With a soft sound that could have been a sigh, he leaned down, his lips captured hers, and both of them were caught in the moment's wonderment.

Intoxicated with sensation, she slid her hands under his jacket and over the hard planes of his chest. She whispered his name, and he echoed hers, each syllable becoming part of the rhythm of desire. Together they swayed on the riverbank, her breath coming so fast it seemed to deplete rather than supply air. Almost instantly she was caught up by a need that made her clutch him in a longing for something her mind didn't recognize—but her body knew. . . .

THRILL TO THE DARK PASSIONS OF SIGNET'S HISTORICAL ROMANTIC GOTHICS

The
Captive Heart

by

Barbara Keller

AN ONYX BOOK

NEW AMERICAN LIBRARY

NAL BOOKS ARE AVAILABLE AT QUANTITY DISCOUNTS
WHEN USED TO PROMOTE PRODUCTS OR SERVICES.
FOR INFORMATION PLEASE WRITE TO PREMIUM MARKETING DIVISION,
NEW AMERICAN LIBRARY, 1633 BROADWAY,
NEW YORK, NEW YORK 10019.

Onyx is a registered trademark of New American Library.

SIGNET, SIGNET CLASSIC, MENTOR, ONYX, PLUME, MERIDIAN
and NAL BOOKS are published by NAL PENGUIN, INC.,
1633 Broadway, New York, New York 10019

First Printing, June, 1987

1 2 3 4 5 6 7 8 9

PRINTED IN THE UNITED STATES OF AMERICA

To my family,
whose pride and encouragement
are one of my greatest rewards

1

MARGARIDA Ross reined in the sorrel mare at the top of the rise. She pushed back her straw hat, and the wind caught her thick curls, so dark brown they looked almost black. Excitement widened her dark eyes as she looked down through the pine trees at a small shack in the sunlit clearing below, and her heart began to beat rapidly. The deserted hitching rail and the midday stillness told her no one was in the building—she'd arrived in time.

At a sudden chirp in the nearby brush, the mare skittered sideways, and Margarida patted the horse's neck. "Easy, Dolly," she murmured, realizing the horse may have sensed her nervousness. Her green riding habit suddenly felt too tight, and her muscles tensed, almost trembling, in anticipation of what lay ahead.

Her plan was scandalous; if her parents knew, she'd be in the greatest trouble of her life, even more than she had been in three years ago. But she was nineteen, she reminded herself, and this was 1885. In New Mexico women didn't have to be meek and timid, afraid to do anything their mothers wouldn't. And Brant Curtis was worth the risk.

Ignoring the flutters in her stomach, she nudged her mare down the slope and across a small stream. Overhead two red-tailed hawks soared and swooped. Ordinarily Margarida would have stopped to watch, for she was drawn to all wild things, but today she gave the hawks only a glance. When she reached the line shack, she dismounted and tied the reins to the hitching rail. She hadn't used her own horse; Brant would recognize it and might ride on. But he hadn't seen her mother's new mare.

For a moment she hesitated, her hands still clenched around the strips of leather. An inner voice, not her usual assured one but a fragment of uncertainty she ordinarily kept well hidden, asked her—could she really do what she'd planned? Unwillingly she remembered the party her parents had given three weeks ago in early July to celebrate her return home. People from the surrounding valleys had come, and she'd received their welcomes—all except the one she wanted.

Excitement had wakened her that day at dawn. Long before it was time for guests to arrive, she had dressed in a yellow lace gown with a bodice high enough for modesty, yet tight enough to show the fullness of her breasts. The skirt fell from her waist in ruffled tiers that floated with every movement. It complimented her dark hair and eyes and made her feel like a butterfly.

Everyone on the Ross ranch was ready for a day of festivities. In the large *sala*, paper flowers, their crimson and orange and yellow blossoms brilliant against the whitewashed walls, festooned the foot-deep window enclosures. Outside, the ranch hands clustered by the corral to smoke and gossip, looking unfamiliar in their holiday finery. Lobo, Margarida's large malamute dog, had been banished to the stables.

Finally the laggard time reached noon, and Margarida stood with her family in the *sala* as the first guests arrived. The sound of "Welcome home, Margarida" mingled with the softer "*Bienvenido*." She curtsied to women in black silk and men in formal frock coats. Girls in rustling pastel taffeta embraced her, and the eyes of young men told her they would like to do the same. The *mariachi* band began to play in the patio, brushed smooth for dancing, and the Spanish music Margarida loved filled the adobe house.

She floated among the company, her anticipation giving everything a special enchantment. But before long her excitement gave way to an anxiety that she barely managed to conceal. Brant Curtis had not appeared.

His father arrived in the early afternoon. As he came through the wide entrance doors, Margarida looked beyond him, but Rupert Curtis was alone. She tried to ignore the disappointment that made a hard lump in her throat as he bowed formally over her hand. "I trust you had a pleasant trip home," he said, his stiff manner making his British accent more pronounced than usual.

"Yes, thank you, Mr. Curtis," she responded. He gave his frosty smile and walked past the leather sofas and chairs of the *sala*, as if he would have to unbend too much if he sat down. She wanted to shout at him, make him tell her why his son wasn't with him. But knowing how much Rupert Curtis disapproved of her, she couldn't bring herself to ask about Brant.

When the elaborate midafternoon meal was served, her stomach was in knots and she was barely able to eat. At sunset, he still hadn't come. Her smile felt frozen in place, as unnatural as the one Brant's father had given her.

She'd counted so much on this first meeting with Brant after her three-year exile at the eastern school, with not even a vacation at home. Now that she was nineteen, the nine-year difference in their ages wouldn't seem so great. She must find out why he wasn't here; waiting was too painful. Maybe her brother would know.

Across the *sala* she saw J.J. Despite being two years younger than Margarida, he was tall and easy to find. She made her way to him and pulled him aside where no one could hear. "J.J., is Brant away from the valley today?"

Under a tumbled lock of sandy hair his mischievous blue eyes for once looked sympathetic. "No—he's home. Maybe he'll still show up."

Margarida wanted to believe J.J., but her hands felt cold and her smile numb. Her festive yellow dress seemed like a hypocritical disguise.

"Margarida, it's time for the dancing to begin," Jesse Ross said, his erect stance disguising his sixty years.

"Yes, Papa," she said, and took his arm to go to the patio where the musicians were playing. She gave one last glance back at the entrance—and saw Brant.

She'd thought she remembered everything about him, but now air felt trapped in her chest at the sight of him—his blue-black hair, the legacy of his Indian grandmother, the eyes to match, the tall, lean figure and hawkish face. And above all, his masculinity—making all other men seem soft and pallid. Her breath returned, and she felt more alive than she'd been in three years. With him was Walt, his half-brother, who was as blond and amiable-appearing as Brant looked dark and self-controlled. She released her father's arm. "Just a minute, Papa. Brant and Walt have arrived, and I must greet them."

"Margarida, you're not going to start that again." Her father's voice was low, meant to be heard only by her, and a frown deepened the lines around his blue eyes. She smiled up at her father, knowing her determination matched his. She'd loved Brant for as long as she could remember, and she'd waited forever to see him again. "Papa, it would be rude not to speak."

Brant, with Walt close behind, was covering the room with his long strides. Margarida thought everyone must be able to hear her heart pounding as he reached her and stopped. He stood, so elegantly attractive in his black Mexican-style jacket and pants, and his smile almost destroyed her self-control.

"Good afternoon, Mr. Ross." His voice was just as she remembered—deep and resonant. "Welcome home, Margarida." She held out her hand to him. His touch sent a rush of excitement through her that was too much to bear in front of all the people—and yet, not nearly enough.

"Thank you, Brant. It's wonderful to be here again." Amazed by her contained tone, she turned to Walt.

His childlike smile, with its betrayal of the illness-damaged mind in the grown man, offered uncompli-cated warmth. In a different way she loved him almost as much as Brant. Though Walt was just her age, she'd always mothered him, even when they had played together as children. He pulled her into an exuberant embrace. "Margarida, where have you been so long?"

She hugged him in return. "Away at school. Re-member?"

"No. I thought you were never coming back."

She laughed, hearing her own joy. "No one would go fishing with me in Connecticut, so I had to come home."

His gray eyes sparkled. "Yes, let's go fishing."

Margarida felt her father's hand on her arm, and his voice was polite but restrained. "We must start the dancing now. I'm sure Brant and Walt will excuse us."

Walt's face lost its smile and his mouth drooped as if he might cry. "Are you going away again, Margarida?"

Brant took his arm and said gently, "No, we'll see Margarida later. Maybe she'll save each of us a dance."

"Of course," Margarida said, suppressing her desire to begin a wild dance all by herself right there.

"Then we'll be waiting," Brant said as Jesse Ross strengthened his hold on her arm and led her outside.

On that promise Margarida floated through the first dance with her father and the next with J.J. "Are you happy now that your hero's here?" he teased.

In answer, she flashed him a gleeful smile, a smile that lasted after he surrendered her for the obligatory dances with the heads of the families gathered to welcome her. When the young men began to claim her, some of her earlier anxiety seeped back. It didn't surprise her that Walt hadn't returned; he was easily diverted and was probably outside with the ranch hands, but she'd expected Brant to come for a dance as soon as possible.

The evening light had vanished and servants had lit lanterns before he appeared. By then the more strenuous waltzes had given way to slower tempos. Brant bowed formally. "May I have the honor of this dance?"

He hardly waited for her "Yes" before he swung her into his arms. Margarida felt as if the ground were swaying in time to the music. Though they had to maintain a proper decorum, she longed to close the distance between them.

They danced for a few minutes without speaking, an unexpected shyness silencing her, until he finally said, "You're looking very grown-up. Did you like the school?"

Her head barely came to his shoulder, so she leaned back far enough to look up into his eyes. "The school wasn't bad. When they let me take literature and history, it was fun. But I hated being away from . . . New Mexico. What about you? Have you been happy the last three years?"

She wanted him to say he'd missed her too much. He only grinned. "I've been too busy to notice."

Almost jealously she asked, "Doing what?"

"Working on the ranch and building up the herd. Setting aside land for hunting. Visiting with *shiwóyé.*"

She remembered that he'd always used the Apache word for "grandmother" when he meant his mother's mother, as if he had to distinguish her sharply from any English relative. "How has she been?" she asked, more out of politeness than any desire to talk about his grandmother.

For a moment he looked grim. "How well do any of my people get along?"

Margarida felt uncomfortable, as she always did when he spoke of the Apache as his people. She never thought of Brant as Indian—after all, he was mostly white. To her relief he smiled again and said, "But things are improving. *Shiwóyé* and her band have a camp in one of our valleys."

Startled, she almost asked why his father would allow Indians, even Brant's relatives, to stay. But she didn't want to remind Brant of his father's dislikes.

The music ended, and the restraint she'd managed so far suddenly seemed impossible. When he started to escort her toward the swarm of waiting young men, she put her hand on his arm, thrilling at the feel of the hard muscles under the smooth cloth. "Did you miss me?"

He paused, and the corners of his mouth quirked into an expression she recognized. She'd seen it many times before; it meant he wanted to laugh but was trying not to. "I did notice that life seemed simpler," he said.

Again he moved toward the side of the patio, but she resisted, holding fast to him. "Oh, Brant. It's been so long. Couldn't we go outside—"

Abruptly he removed her hand from his arm and stepped back. "Now, that would make your father very unhappy." His black eyes looked distant but still amused as he said, "Margarida, you're not grown up yet, in spite of your eastern airs." Taking her elbow, he steered her firmly across the patio to where several men stood talking to her father.

"Thank you for the dance, Margarida," he said, bowing. With a nod to the others, he left.

Stunned by Brant's refusal of her overture, she hardly noticed the identity of her next partner. That Brant might not feel as she did hadn't seriously occurred to her; she'd been so sure he would recognize they belonged together. Choking with frustration, she watched as Brant had the gall to dance five dances—she counted every one, seething inside—with the hardware merchant's daughter. He couldn't really like that shallow flirt, with her blond hair and careful curls and too-plump figure, she told herself. He'd only been protecting her from her father's disapproval. But she didn't escape the pain from having her dreams of their reunion shattered.

The rest of the party passed in a blur during which she felt like a doll wound up to say and do the correct things with nothing inside her except sawdust. Exhaustion put her to sleep that night, but the next morning the pain of Brant's dismissal returned.

Goaded by the memory of his blond dancing partner, she tried to think objectively about her own face and figure. Her dark wavy hair was thick and lustrous, but her face wasn't beautiful like the women pictured in magazines. It was wide, her cheekbones prominent, her nose upturned, and her mouth generous. But men seemed to like her eyes, with their long, thick lashes. And her figure, with full breasts, tiny waist, and rounded yet slender hips, had provoked attention she'd had to fight off all too often.

Not from Brant, though. Reluctantly she remembered he'd never done more than give her a brief, teasing kiss. She'd been sure he was just waiting for her to grow up.

Had she done something wrong in the way she spoke to Brant last night? she wondered. Or was she undesirable in some way? She knew of only one person she could ask. Not her mother—Elena Ross was moody and intense, her reactions unpredictable, and Margarida had learned long ago not to try to confide in her or ask advice. It would have to be Adela Ramírez, the foreman's wife. For years Adela, with unusual candor, had been Margarida's source of worldly information that, in Margarida's limited testing so far, had proved true. If anyone could tell her how to excite a man enough to think about marriage, Adela could.

After breakfast Margarida crossed the yard to the small adobe house where Miguel and Adela Ramírez lived. As she knocked, she could hear Adela's melodious voice singing a cheerful Mexican folk tune. The song stopped; Adela opened the door and swept Margarida inside with a welcoming hug.

Adela was plump, with full breasts and hips that swayed with obvious sensuality when she walked. Her dark eyes usually danced with enjoyment of life. "Margarida—I'm so happy to see you. Sit down, sit down. Did you enjoy the party? You looked beautiful."

Margarida stopped and said intensely, "Did I really? Am I beautiful?"

Adela smiled, her black eyes sympathetic. "Surely you don't have to ask me. But I see you do." She patted Margarida's cheek and said, "You're beautiful. Besides, you have something better than beauty—you're a passionate female, and it shows. Remember, '*La mujer y las tortillas, calientes han de ser.*' Women and tortillas should be hot. Don't worry—men will go mad for you."

Margarida wanted only one man mad for her, but she couldn't tell even Adela about her failure with Brant. "But how do you . . . get a man to propose to you?"

Adela laughed, but with a warmth that put her on Margarida's side. "I'm not sure about marrying, but it's easy to get one to make love to you."

For a moment Margarida felt startled—that hadn't been what she wanted to know. Adela went on. "Men are so simple. All you do is show a little this and a little more that and they can't wait." She touched her breast and hips, making clear what "this" and "that" meant.

Margarida laughed, her embarrassment vanishing under Adela's infectious good nature. She stayed and visited, enjoying Adela's gossip. When Margarida left, she hadn't received the advice she wanted, but she felt happier.

Lying in her bed that night, Margarida indulged her favorite daydream: she and Brant were married, living in the two-story Curtis ranch house. In this fantasy Rupert Curtis, Brant's father, was conveniently absent, but Walt, his half-brother, lived with them. Because of the illness that had damaged his mind, he needed their help.

The discouraging memory of Brant's reaction to her at the party intruded into her illusion. How could she get him to marry her if he insisted on keeping his distance? She thought again of how Adela had told her it would be easy to persuade a man to make love to her. In the school in Connecticut, she'd heard stories about girls who'd been "ruined" and had to marry.

She remembered, too, the previous Christmas, which she'd spent with the family of her closest school friend. Charlotte's older brother, Palmer, had pursued Margarida unobtrusively but persistently. He was handsome and very sophisticated. She'd been flattered and curious, and once, after several passionate kisses, she'd let him touch her breasts. It had been exciting and scary, and the effect on him had been startling. His assured air had disintegrated, and he'd acted as if he'd do almost anything to touch her again. She'd had difficulty stopping him.

Her pulse began to pound erratically at the idea forming in her head. If she could entice Brant into making love to her, his sense of honor would force him to marry her.

Shocked at her thoughts, yet filled with growing excitement, she got out of bed and went ot the window. She'd have to arrange an opportunity to be alone with him someplace where a seduction was possible.

Then she remembered the small shack that was close to the dividing line between Ross and Curtis property. After the time three years ago when she'd gone to the Curtis home and accidentally seen Brant bathing, she'd been forbidden to cross the boundary from Ross land onto the Curtis ranch. At the memory she felt a twinge of old resentment; her parents never believed her explanations and had hurried her off to school. But before that, during the years she and J.J. and Walt had followed Brant around, she'd been at the shack often. It was isolated; Brant had regularly made a noon stop there when he went to that particular section of land, and he always rode out alone. She could coax J.J. into finding out Brant's schedule, and if she went there and were waiting for him one day—she could put Adela's words into practice.

She went back to bed that night, resolved to consider her plans carefully before doing anything. She'd been in trouble too many times because she didn't stop to think. Even as she vowed to practice a caution which didn't come easily, she'd known she would go ahead; she loved Brant too much to falter at the risk.

Now, shading her eyes from the July sun, she stared at the bleached pine building with her determination renewed. If she had to seduce Brant to get him, she would. This was a chance she wouldn't be cowardly enough to waste.

Resolutely she took a bundle from one of her saddlebags, untied a blanket from behind the saddle, and went into the one-room shack. It was dusty, but not really dirty. She propped open the shutter over the one small window. From the pocket of her long skirt she took a cloth and wiped the rough table and chairs and the shelf that held the few eating utensils. Ashes choked the small iron stove, but she didn't expect to use it. The rope bed looked narrow. She wasn't sure how much room two people needed to make love.

After she spread out the blanket, she opened her
bundle and set out a corked jug of wine, a fresh loaf of
sourdough bread, and a wedge of yellow cheese. Outside by the stream she found delicate purple-blue irises
and white daisies. The daisies especially pleased her
since her name was also the Portuguese word for that
white flower. An empty jar made a vase to go on the
table. The sunlight seemed too bright, so she closed
the shutter partway, leaving what she hoped was a
romantic half-light.

Satisfied with the room, she undid the rest of her
bundle and shook out a navy cotton cape and a sheer
muslin gown of pale blue she'd found in an old trunk.
After her boots came off, her green top and full skirt
followed, then the pants she wore underneath the skirt
so she could ride astride. The air felt cool on her arms
and legs, and she debated about her chemise and
drawers. Before doubts could weaken her resolve, she
slipped out of her undergarments and stockings and
into the gown.

She was glad she didn't have a mirror, because the
dress only veiled but didn't conceal any part of her
body. Over the dress she fastened the cape, tying it
closed at her throat. Its dark blue folds hung to the
floor. She put her arms through the slits in the side
and belted it around her waist. Taking out her brush,
she worked on her hair until it felt like silk, then
refastened it in a fall at the back of her neck.

A sound outside startled her, but she realized it was
only a sudden whine of wind through the pine trees.
Her heart slowed a little, but her skin felt cold with
tension. She moved the chair so that she could see out
of the one small window. When Brant came, she would
be ready.

Brant, his denim pants and shirt dampened with
sweat, stopped his horse in the shade of a tall ponderosa
pine. He could smell the resinous fragrance of the

pine-needle duff. The day was hot for this part of southwestern New Mexico, and he looked forward to his noon stop at the shack. In this mountain valley the temperature rarely got above eighty-five degrees, even in midsummer. No wonder his Apache relatives had resisted so fiercely when the government tried to settle them in the Arizona desert.

He touched the side of his brown gelding and rode on slowly, savoring the feeling of well-being that the events of the last months had given him. The spring roundup had been the most successful in years. As a result, his father had agreed to Brant's plans to set aside more land for the Indians to use for hunting. Even with the troubles last spring, *shiwóyé*'s band had been safe.

It still rankled Brant that his father's attitude toward Indians was almost as intolerant as that of most of the American ranchers in New Mexico. Years ago Brant had concluded that his father married his half-Indian wife because he couldn't resist his desire for her. But he'd been ashamed of her Apache blood—and of his quarter-Indian son. When she died of a fever, Rupert had returned to England to choose a second wife who was untainted white. Then, tragically, she died in childbirth, and her son suffered a childhood illness that left his mind damaged.

Walt's illness had changed Brant's life too. With his restless nature, he probably wouldn't have stayed on his father's land. As a seventeen-year-old he'd left, planning never to come back. But when he'd visited at the end of five years, he'd recognized his half-brother's difficulties. With encouragement and care, Walt got along well, and Brant provided both, as no one else did. Because he'd stayed, he'd been here when his mother's people needed help. Since then he'd worked to improve their lot. And now his father was reluctantly aiding that effort.

As he reached the rise leading to his noon stop, he

saw a black-and-yellow butterfly fluttering above the brush. It reminded Brant of Margarida in her yellow dress. At her parents' party she'd looked immensely attractive, but he didn't welcome her return to New Mexico. His plans were going well, and he didn't need the kind of trouble she'd made in the past.

Her pursuit of him three years ago, and that farce when she'd walked in on him bathing, had angered both his father and hers. She'd been sent away—the first time, Brant suspected, Jesse Ross had ever resisted his daughter. The Ross lands adjoined the Curtis holdings, and Jesse could help or hinder Brant's plans for his Indian relatives. Jesse already disliked Indians; an involvement between a "breed" and his daughter would destroy any chance that he might go along with Brant's aims.

Jesse had been honest enough to say so directly, soon after Margarida left for school. He'd come to the Curtis ranch and sought Brant out. "I hope you won't be offended," he'd said bluntly. "I respect you and your father, but I don't believe in mixing blood. Margarida is obstinate, and she'll come back a woman. I'll appreciate it if you'll discourage any foolish ideas she may still have."

Then Brant had only said, "I understand," thinking Margarida would change in three years away. But he'd been wrong. Now, Brant decided, she was even more dangerous than she'd been at sixteen. Jesse Ross had spoiled her all her life, and she was undoubtedly just as headstrong as ever, but now she had the lush body and sensual attributes of a woman. Her behavior at the party made it clear she still imagined she was in love with him.

Desirable as Margarida was, he didn't intend to get involved with her. While he admired her spirit and her audaciousness, he wasn't even sure he wanted a wife, and certainly not one as impulsive and unsettled as she.

Brant halted at the sight of an unfamiliar sorrel mare hitched to the rail in front of the line shack. He frowned; no one else should be here today. A glance at the shack confirmed that the door was closed as usual, but the shutter over the window was open.

Tying his horse next to the mare, he examined the saddle. Something about it looked suspiciously familiar—a Ross saddle, he concluded. Only one Ross would have any reason to come here today.

Momentarily he considered ignoring her and leaving, but instead he headed for the shack. Grimly he decided that Margarida's childish fixation on him must stop, now, before she could disrupt what he'd worked so hard to achieve. He opened the door and stepped inside.

When she heard Brant come in, Margarida was standing beside the small table with her back to the door. She had to concentrate all her attention on keeping her hands from trembling as she poured wine into two pottery cups. Turning toward him, she smiled brightly and held one cup out to him. "Hello, Brant."

Noon sunlight from the open door turned him into a silhouette, outlining his black hair but concealing his expression. He made no move to take the wine from her. "What are you doing here, Margarida?" She could hear the hostility in his voice.

She swallowed, her mouth suddenly dry. This wasn't going the way she'd imagined. She put up her head defiantly, stretching her less-than-impressive height as much as possible. "I was waiting for you. I persuaded J.J. to find out what day you'd be here because I wanted a chance to talk to you. Is that so terrible?"

Brant, watching her large eyes, saw a flicker of what looked like uncertainty, and despite his resolution, he spoke more gently. "You shouldn't be out here. You know how your father feels about me."

She flushed slightly. "That was just because I was only sixteen. He really likes you."

"As a fellow rancher, yes," Brant responded, "but he doesn't want you, now that you're grown-up, having anything to do with a man who's part Indian. You know that."

Her dark eyes flashed rebelliously, then crinkled as she laughed, and dimples appeared in her cheeks. "But he's not here, and I am. So we might as well visit—just for a little while." At that moment, Brant thought, she resembled the harum-scarum tomboy who'd trailed after him on hunting and fishing expeditions years ago. Her face was made for laughter, and as Brant watched her eyes begin to sparkle, he knew he couldn't be as harsh with her as he should.

He grinned and took the cup of wine. "I see you have some bread and cheese that look better than what's in my saddlebags. We'll share the food, and then off you go."

As he walked behind her to the table, he noticed her cape. "That's a strange get-up for riding."

Margarida felt her pulse begin to race again; now that he'd relaxed she didn't want to put him on guard. Deciding candor would amuse him, she gave him an impudent smile. "Just trying to impress you with how exotic I can look."

He laughed in turn, the fierce lines of his face softening. "Sorry to disappoint you, but it doesn't suit you, Margarida."

We'll see, she thought, and busied herself in arranging the bread and cheese. "Tell me about the roundup," she suggested as he sat down at the table.

"The cattle herd has built up very well," he replied. An enthusiastic smile took away the last of his disapproving expression. "My father is convinced now that we can raise plenty of cattle and have land left over."

While he ate and she pretended to, he continued to talk about the ranch work, and she refilled their wine cups several times. She had difficulty attending to what he was saying, only partly listening as she tried to disguise her agitation and to plan just when she would remove her cape. Reaching that point was proving harder than she'd thought.

A silence made her realize that Brant had stopped talking, and his face looked closed and distant. She tried to remember what he had been saying—something about lands and Indians and hunting. A blush heated her face. "I'm sorry. What did you say?"

He rose and responded, his voice cool, "It doesn't matter. I think it's time for you to go."

A feeling close to panic made her stomach shrink into a tight ball. "But . . . we still have wine. Let me pour you some." Her fingers could barely hold on to the jug.

Brant put his hand over the top of the pottery container. "No more wine. You can hardly manage now. In fact, you could probably use some coffee. We'll take time for that. You can start the fire while I get water and the coffee from my saddlebags."

When he took the coffeepot and disappeared out the door, Margarida raised shaky hands to the fastenings of her cape. Now, she thought—it must be now.

Brant glanced up at the sky as he carried water and the bag of coffee back to the shack. Clouds, white on top but blue-gray underneath, were piling up to the west. Margarida should be on her way, he decided. Maybe they wouldn't take time for coffee after all. He should have prevented her from drinking the wine, but she was an excellent rider. She'd get along all right on her way home.

He opened the door and said, "I think you should—" The sight of her stopped him. For a moment he could only stare at a Margarida who made his heart beat faster and his groin tighten.

She stood facing him, her dark brown curls cascading over her shoulders and down her back. The cape was gone; instead a blue dress clung to her body, and through its sheer material it was evident that she wore nothing underneath. Against the thin fabric her breasts thrust forward, the dark rose of her nipples looking purple through the blue. The gathered skirt concealed her legs only slightly more, and he could see the dark shadow of hair at the top of her thighs.

Shock and anger brought the blood to his face but didn't destroy the desire he could feel rising through him, making his penis swell against the heavy fabric of his pants. In the dress her body was more arousing than it would have been nude. In two strides he reached the table and put down the water and coffee. When he looked at her again, he forced himself to concentrate on her face and found relief by letting his feelings turn into rage.

Margarida saw Brant's shoulders stiffen and his body take on an angry stance, and her pulse raced even faster. She held her hand out to him. "Brant, I've been waiting for years." Her voice faltered at the fury she saw in his face.

"So this is the reason for the flowers and wine. My God, is this what you've learned at school? To dress up like a whore?" His voice deepened with contempt. "Or maybe you're demonstrating what some man has taught you."

She felt as if he had hit her—he wasn't supposed to react this way. "No," she protested, "how can you say that? I love you, Brant. I've always loved you, and I want you to . . . make love to me."

His hand clenched in a fist at his side. "You're a child in a woman's body. Did you think you could just parade your charms and I'd fall into bed with you?"

Brant could tell from her white face that she'd had exactly that expectation, and he steeled himself not to let her know how close she was to succeeding. Then deliberately he relaxed his stance and let her see his arousal. He laughed in cold and mocking derision. "Yes—you look desirable, but I know you, Margarida, and I won't be caught in your trap. You're wasting your time with me."

Margarida felt humiliation swell her throat until she feared she would choke. The tension of the sleepless nights of planning, the uncertainty and shyness she'd denied to bring herself here, exploded into rage. She launched herself at him, wanting to hit him, to hurt him as badly as he was hurting her. She managed to raise one hand toward his face before he caught her wrists. Through the thin dress the buttons of his shirt rasped painfully against her breasts, but she was so enraged that she hardly felt it. Twisting, she tried to kick his legs, but he held her away.

His voice sounded harsh and implacable. "You're going to get dressed properly now and get on that horse and ride back to your own house."

"No! No! I won't!" she screamed. "You bastard. You bastard half-breed. You can't tell me what to do."

His face became a mask, and he spoke with a cold sarcasm that erected a barrier more insurmountable than anger. "Apparently you acquired some unpleasant words in that eastern school. But I'm only a quarter-breed, not worth your display. You seem also to have forgotten very quickly how much you love me. In any case, Margarida, you *are* going home, even if I have to tie you to the saddle."

He gripped her arm so tightly that she would have screamed from the pain if she hadn't already been overwhelmed by hurt and fury. He almost snarled, "You must have other clothes here. Where are they?" In answer she tried to jerk away from his hold. He looked around, then dragged her to the bed, reached under it for the bundle that held her riding clothes, and thrust it at her. "You have five minutes to put these on."

"God damn you, I won't," she hissed, "and you can't make me." Glaring at him, she added fiercely,

"Unless you want to dress me yourself. But then you'd
have to touch me, and I see I was mistaken. You're
not man enough for that."

"You really think so?" He still held one arm, but
with his other hand he gripped her chin, holding her
face immovable. His fingers seared her, and she trembled with a confusion of anger, fear, and quaking
anticipation. For years she'd waited for Brant's first
kiss. Now his lips were above hers, but no love softened his face. Instead his eyes looked like obsidian as
he lowered his head and kissed her imprisoned mouth.

Fire raced through her veins at the feel of his hard
lips against hers. She'd dreamed of the tenderness and
excitement of his mouth passionately seeking hers. For
a moment she wanted to lean against him, to savor his
masculinity. But this fierce kiss was an insult that
lacerated her, fueling her anger, as his rejection seared
her spirit. Wrenching her face away, she pushed at
him, freeing herself.

He laughed, a mirthless, cruel sound. "Don't think I
wouldn't enjoy fucking you. But don't think I would
marry you if I did. You have a beautiful body, but I'd
be insane to tie myself to you because of it."

"No more insane than I was to imagine I was in love
with you," she spat, knowing from the choking sensation in her chest that if she let down her anger, tears
would follow. For him to see her cry now would be the
final humiliation. "Get out and leave me alone. All I
want is never to see you again."

She stood facing him, hating him at this moment
and clinging to that feeling. His eyes flickered, and
briefly she thought she saw something else in his face—
pain or regret. Then he swung on his heel and went
out the door.

With hands that seemed to fumble endlessly, she
stripped off the blue gown and pulled on her riding
clothes. She gathered up her hairbrush and cape and
folded the dress with them. The jug and remnants of

food were still on the table, but she left them where
they were. When the moment came for her to leave,
she stared at the door, trying to decide if Brant was
waiting outside. Facing him as she left would be a
fearsome task.

Then she stiffened her back and clamped her jaw
shut. Her arms would be bruised where he'd gripped
her, but she had more painful bruises inside her that
her pride wouldn't let him see. Resolutely she opened
the door and walked to her horse.

Brant stood beside his gelding, but she looked through
him as if he weren't there. She fastened her bundle
behind the saddle, untied the reins of the mare, and
swung up onto her horse. Without a backward glance,
she rode off through the trees.

As Brant watched her proud figure ride away, a
pain he hadn't expected surprised him. Margarida had
an outrageous spirit, one he reluctantly admired: He'd
treated her brutally, and he hadn't liked hurting her.
She probably had no idea what she'd put him through
that afternoon—how desirable she'd looked, and how
much he'd wanted to do exactly what she'd planned. If
she ever learned to discipline herself, she'd be a magnificent wife for some man. But, he thought as he
mounted his horse, not for him. He had too much at
stake with her father's land. Besides, this afternoon's
encounter had settled that there'd be nothing between
Margarida and him.

2

BY the time Margarida reached the cluster of adobe buildings at the center of the Ross ranch, the sunset was turning the underbellies of the clouds crimson and gold. Her head ached and her stomach threatened to lose everything she had eaten that day. An afternoon shower had caught her away from any sheltering trees, and her wet hair hung down her drenched back. The wind penetrated her clothing; she felt as if she would never be warm again.

As she approached the corral, her brother walked through the gate. J.J. had blond hair and blue eyes like their father, while Margarida got her coloring from their mother, but his spirit was as unruly as hers. He grinned up at her now. "Well, did you find Brant?"

She answered his grin with a glare. "I don't want to talk about Brant Curtis—or ever see him again." She walked her horse to the stable, where she dismounted and let a ranch hand take the mare. Lobo bounded out to greet her, his tongue washing her hand with kisses. But she pushed him away; not even his affection could soothe her now.

When she passed the corral, carrying her wet bundle, J.J. was waiting for her, barely concealing his amusement. "What's the matter? Couldn't you get him to propose?"

To her horror, Margarida felt tears gathering. "Let me alone!" Lifting her bedraggled skirt with her free hand, she ran to the house. Its familiar whitewashed

adobe walls and wide shaded veranda seemed like a
sanctuary. She jerked open the double doors and hurried through the *sala* to the covered walk that ran
around the patio. Behind her a plaintive voice called,
"Margarida, where have you been?"

Turning reluctantly, she forced herself to respond
normally. "Out riding, Mother."

Elena stood in the doorway to the *sala*. At thirty-six
her hair was a glossy brown and her figure trim. Now
her mouth was pinched and her dark eyes frowning.
"But you're all wet. It's almost time for supper. Where
were you?"

'Riding. I don't want any supper, thank you." Knowing her mother wouldn't persist, Margarida continued
around the patio. When she reached her room, she
slammed the heavy wood door closed and dropped her
blanket roll on the floor. She stood, her hands pressed
behind her against the door, then gave up the struggle
and let her tears flow.

When she had regained control, she threw herself
down on her bed and stared at the bleached boards of
the ceiling. She must have been crazy, she thought
bitterly, to have convinced herself she loved Brant. It
had been a habit, left from days when she and J.J. and
Walt had trekked after him. He'd let them do things
their parents tried to prohibit—swimming in the stream
when the spring snow made it a river, climbing trees,
shooting his pistol, riding horses that were too wild.
Until he was seventeen, he'd looked out for them,
treated them like real people instead of two eight-year-
olds and a six-year-old.

Then he left, and when he came back five years
later, he seemed different, harder and impatient with
everyone except Walt, but she'd still looked at Brant
with love-clouded eyes. She rolled over on the bed
and buried her face when she remembered the next
three years. She'd followed Brant around until, at
sixteen, she'd made so many visits to the Curtis ranch

that Brant's father came to see her father. With all the
frosty dignity of his upper-class English background,
Rupert Curtis had asked Jesse Ross to keep her away
from his son.

After the scolding from her father, Margarida had
stayed away for a while. But one day she couldn't
resist the desire to see Brant and went to the Curtis
ranch house. Even now she could close her eyes and
see the events as if they were happening again.

J.J. had mentioned that Brant was going to Silver
City. That meant he would likely be at home that June
afternoon, getting ready to leave. It had always been
easy for her to escape her mother's supervision, so
she'd announced she was going riding, and left.

The day was almost summer warm, with thin elongated clouds trailing across a blossom-blue sky. When
she reached the Curtis ranch house, she tethered her
horse to a tree in a small grove of pines slightly uphill
from the cedar frame house. Seeing no one around,
she looked into the stable. Brant's favorite horse was
in his stall.

Outside the two-story frame house she paused and
listened. No voices disturbed the quiet, but she decided to go to the back and through the kitchen. The
cook would be taking her midafternoon *siesta*. The
windows were too high for Margarida to look in, but
at the back she listened again. She heard nothing.

The screen door creaked as she opened it, and she
peered inside. No one was nearby. She backed into
the room, inching the door closed. Just as it fastened,
she heard a laugh and whirled to see Brant in the
opposite corner of the large room. He was naked,
standing beside a large oval tub. In the first startled
moment she noticed only that water was running down
his body.

His body! She felt a queer, squeezed sensation in
her stomach. Not since she and J.J. and Walt had
gone swimming as children had she seen a male com-

pletely undressed. She'd sneaked looks whenever she could, but she'd never really seen a naked adult man.

Brant's body was magnificent. The broad chest, bronzed even darker than his natural olive skin, narrowed to a flat waist and straight hips above long, muscular legs. The bush of black hair around his penis drew her eyes with a fascination she couldn't resist.

"This is a surprise," Brant said, his amusement obvious. Margarida found that her voice wouldn't come out of her dry mouth. As casually as if she were an elderly relative, he picked up a towel and began to dry his arms, but he didn't conceal the rest of his body.

Behind her the kitchen door creaked, and she turned to see Brant's father. His narrow face was at first astonished and then flaming red. "You!" he shouted. It was the only time Margarida had ever seen him lose his aristocratic composure.

Rupert Curtis had escorted her the five miles home himself. When he informed her father, Jesse Ross had been furious. For the first time in her life, he had been as hard on her as he was about his business. Off she'd gone to school, where she'd spent three years with the conviction she still loved Brant and had only to see him again for him to realize he loved her.

Now she sat up on the bed, determined to have no more regrets or weeping. Picking up her wet blanket, she went to the door and opened it. One of the maids was sweeping the porch. "María," she called. "Please tell my mother that I will be at supper after all. And please see that this blanket is hung up outside."

When María took the blanket and gave a soft *"Sí, señorita,"* Margarida closed her door and pulled off her wet clothes. After hanging them and the sodden cape and gown over a rack, she began to towel her heavy hair. Obviously, she thought, she hadn't really known Brant at all; she couldn't be in love with the unfeeling man he'd become. And she wouldn't forget so quickly how he'd humiliated her. Abandoning the towel, she shook loose her hair and chose a peach-colored voile dress from the wardrobe.

As she dressed, she cringed to remember she'd called him a bastard half-breed. She'd never cared whether he had Indian blood—he'd never even seemed Indian to her. Though she'd heard stories about how barbarous the Apache were and how brutally they murdered whites, the few Indians she'd seen around the towns had looked only poor. Nothing like Brant. In her hurt and rage she'd repeated a term of contempt she'd heard often from her father and other men.

Anger replaced shame as she recalled Brant's words to her—desirable, but not enough for him to want to marry her. She decided she did want to see him again after all—for one more time. Then she'd make him regret his statement, and she'd be the one to reject him.

Half an hour later she entered the *sala*. Elena sat with her inevitable embroidery on the low leather-covered couch. Her father and J.J. were standing beside the large oval curve of the fireplace, having a glass of whiskey. J.J. winked at Margarida, and she knew he wouldn't say anything about where she'd been that afternoon. They were too loyal to each other for that.

Jesse Ross, his white hair falling over his forehead, pulled her close and kissed the top of her head. "So, you rode too long and got wet," he scolded fondly.

She returned his kiss and hugged him affectionately. "Yes, Papa, but I'm fine now." She smiled around him at her brother and repeated, "Just fine."

After kissing Elena on her offered cheek, Margarida sat on the sofa next to her mother. Looking carefully innocent, J.J. said, "Please go on with what you were telling us, Papa, about the Curtis ranch."

Jesse frowned, his bushy white eyebrows emphasizing his look of displeasure. "Damned fool business. Curtis let that son of his talk him into running cattle only on the lower grasslands. And I heard some bunch of Apache has set up a permanent camp in one of the side valleys. Rupert's letting them hunt in the mountains. That arrangement is Brant's doing."

Before she realized what she was saying, Margarida found herself defending Brant. "But what's so bad about that, Papa? The Indians have to live too."

Jesse's face became even more flushed. "That question shows how little you know, Margarida. You weren't home last May. Chihuahua and his Chiricahuas killed six whites over by Alma and five more near Silver City before they ran for Mexico. We're just lucky they didn't come here. If Rupert weren't so wealthy, people wouldn't put up with Brant's Apaches living on Curtis land. This country won't be safe for decent people until those savages are gone—or at least shut up where they can't kill or rob."

"But, Papa—" Margarida began.

Her father ignored her. "Rupert Curtis just doesn't seem like himself anymore—doesn't look well. But even so, he should know better than to listen to Brant. One of these days Brant will marry some Apache woman and bring her and a bunch of Indian brats to the ranch. Then Rupert will wish he'd kept a tighter rein on his affairs."

Margarida felt a sharp pain just below her breastbone, as if her father's words had hit her in a vulnerable spot. She sat up straighter on the sofa. Brant could marry a dozen Apache women, and it wouldn't matter to her. Any foolish pang she felt now was just habit. After she repaid his rejection with her own, she wouldn't even think about him anymore.

In the middle of the night Lobo's growl and the thump of his paws hitting the floor wakened Margarida. He was allowed in her room only at night, when he slept on one side of her bed. She sat up, still dazed from sleep, and heard a woman's scream. She scram-

bled to the window and looked out. In the small house
across the compound where Adela and Miguel Ramírez
lived, light shone dimly through the lace curtains of
the bedroom. A man, unrecognizable in the dark, ran
across the yard toward the foreman's house.

Pulling a robe over her nightgown, Margarida ran
around the dark patio and through the *sala*. Lobo
bounded ahead of her to the door of the foreman's
house. When she reached him, she heard shouts. She
pushed open the door and called, "Adela!" Light came
from the entrance to the bedroom; she ran across to
the open door and then stopped, horrified.

In the center of the room Miguel wrestled with
Carlos García, a man who had worked on the ranch
for years. Behind them Adela huddled against the
wall. Her hair streamed over her shoulders, and she
held her right arm with her left. Blood stained her arm
and the front of her white nightgown.

From behind Margarida Lobo rushed at the struggling men. Under the dog's assault, the two men broke
apart. "Lobo!" Margarida screamed, and grabbed his
collar. As she dragged Lobo backward, she saw that
Miguel's bare chest and white pants had blood on
them.

"What's going on here?" The voice was her father's.
He stood in the bedroom door with J.J. just behind
him, holding a lantern; both men wore only pants and
boots.

"Margarida," Jesse ordered, "take that dog and get
back to your room."

Holding Lobo, she protested, "But Adela's hurt."

Jesse scowled. "This doesn't concern you. Now, go
back to the house."

"But, Papa . . ." she began, and then gave up. She
looked atAdela, who seemed frozen against the wall.

"I'll let you know," J.J. promised as she led Lobo
past him and outside.

Back in her room, she stayed by the window, from

where she could see the Ramírez house and hear muffled voices. Once she thought she heard Adela crying,
and she bit her knuckles in anxiety. Something terrible
had happened.

All through her childhood Adela had been the one
she'd gone to for uncritical comfort and advice. Elena
was moody and often short-tempered; Margarida had
never been sure what to expect from her mother. But
Adela, with her happy, loving nature, had welcomed
and soothed Margarida and candidly answered all her
questions. She'd mended torn dresses so cleverly that
no one knew Margarida had been climbing forbidden
trees. When all the mothers had maintained a conspir-
acy of silence, Adela had told Margarida how babies
were conceived. At thirteen Margarida—wishing it were
Brant—had let a boy give her her first kiss behind the
church after a social. Afterward she'd gone guiltily to
Adela, who'd laughed gently at the story.

Tonight, Margarida thought, Papa should have let
her stay to help; he'd made her leave just because she
was a woman. Brant wouldn't have treated her that
way, she fumed, and then caught herself, horrified
that she was still holding Brant up as the model of
masculine behavior.

Finally two men came out of the house. One was
Carlos, and she couldn't tell who the other was. They
were half-carrying Miguel between them and disappeared in the direction of the bunkhouse. A few minutes later Jesse and J.J. appeared and crossed to the
house.

By the time they were inside, Margarida was in the
sala. "What happened?" she demanded.

"I told you to go to bed," was all her father said.

"Papa, Adela's my friend. I must know if she's all
right."

Real anger made his voice harsh. "I don't want you
to have anything to do with her." He stomped past her.

Indignant, she began, "But—"

J.J.'s hand on her arm stopped her. He pulled her head close to his and whispered, "Adela's hurt, but she'll be all right. I'll tell you tomorrow."

With that promise Margarida had to be content, but she was awake early the next morning. She found her father in the breakfast room off the kitchen. He sat at the round table finishing his breakfast of beef and beans and strong coffee. Her mother wasn't there; Elena always slept late.

Seeing Jesse's gloomy face, Margarida kissed his cheek and took her seat with only a "Good morning, Papa" and busied herself with a peach from the fruit bowl.

When she looked up, Jesse tried to frown, but she could see what an effort it took for him not to smile at her. She didn't try to hide her own smile. Whatever else was wrong, she knew he loved her; their relationship was back on the old indulgent footing.

"I guess I might as well tell you," he said. "You're old enought to know about such things. But," he admonished, "you must realize that Adela Ramírez is not the sort of person you should have for a friend."

"Papa! Please, just tell me what happened."

He put down his coffee cup, his anger genuine now. "Miguel got drunk last night and beat up one of the hands, then took a knife to Adela. Apparently he was aiming for her face, but he cut up her arm when she tried to defend herself. So we had to lock him up in one end of the bunkhouse—not that he didn't have reasons for what he did."

"But what about Adela?" Margarida interrupted. "How badly hurt is she? Who's taking care of her?"

"She has a bad cut on one arm. One of the maids is looking after her until we can get her to the doctor in town. We'll have to take Miguel to the sheriff at the same time." Jesse scowled, even his white mustache bristling. "Now I'm without a foreman. Guess that's what I deserve for hiring a Mexican. Almost as bad as

Indians. Never can tell when they'll get liquored up and start something, though with that . . . wife of his, I'm not surprised."

Outraged, Margarida stared at her father. "Miguel Ramírez has been an excellent foreman; you've said so yourself. Besides, he *is* an American—Hispano-American. Even if he weren't, Mexicans are no worse than Americans. What about those cowboys up on the San Francisco River last fall? I heard what they did to some man—the same thing you do when you geld a horse. And they shot someone who tried to stop them."

"Margarida!" Jesse's shocked face turned red as he rose, almost knocking over his chair. "No lady would listen to a story like that," he blustered, "and I don't have time to argue with you. I have to find a new foreman." He stormed out of the room as J.J. entered.

"I could hear you and Papa all the way down the hall," her brother commented as he helped himself to coffee from the sideboard and sat down. "You might as well give up. Papa will never change his mind about Mexicans or Hispanos or Indians, no matter how much you argue with him. Even if you got Brant to propose," he added, "Papa would never let you marry a man who's even a quarter Indian."

"Jesse Ross, Junior," Margarida snapped, deliberately using the name he hated, "don't mention Brant Curtis."

"That bad?" he teased. As she jumped up to leave the room, he leaned from his chair and caught her arm. "Sorry, Margarida, that was mean. I won't bring him up again. Stay, and I'll tell you about Adela."

Sitting down, she waited as he filled his plate with beans, slices of fried beef, and a slab of cornbread. He took several bites, then put down his fork. "Did Papa tell you that Miguel tried to carve up Adela and got her arm instead of her face?"

Margarida shuddered. "Yes, he told me that much.

But I don't understand why. Was it because Miguel was drunk?"

"I guess you don't know about Adela's reputation," J.J. said with a superior air that made Margarida fume. At seventeen he was more a man than a boy, but she didn't appreciate his forgetting that she was two years older. "From what I've heard around the bunkhouse," he went on between bites, "Adela has a wandering eye for men. My guess is Miguel must have heard about one man too many, and last night his patience ran out."

Shocked and sobered, Margarida waited while J.J. heaped more food on his plate. For years she'd admired Adela and tried to be like her—carefree and sparkling. But if what J.J. said were true, the pleasures that Adela made sound so lighthearted had led to violence. Even so, Margarida couldn't believe that someone so warm and loving as Adela could be bad. Confused, she leaned on her elbows, watching J.J. finish his third cup of coffee.

Lupe, one of the maids, came into the room and spoke to J.J. "Señor Ross wants you outside right away."

J.J. slumped in his chair, his face rebellious, and muttered, "Ranching!"

"Thank you, Lupe," Margarida said before the young girl left. "J.J.," she admonished, "you were rude to her."

"Yes, it's not her fault I have to go out with Papa," he said sullenly, and finally rose.

Astonished, Margarida watched him walk slowly to the door. "Don't you like working on the ranch?"

"God, no," he almost shouted as he left.

Margarida took some coffee and sat at the table, feeling she could hardly recognize her world. She was back on the old footing with Papa, but nothing else seemed the same. She couldn't—wouldn't—love Brant.

Adela, her admired model, had a life Margarida hadn't imagined. And now her brother sounded like a stranger.

Pushing her confusion aside, she decided she would visit Adela before the injured woman could be taken to the doctor. Despite Papa's prohibitions, she wouldn't give up her friend so easily.

When Margarida knocked on the door of the foreman's house, Rosa, one of the oldest maids, let her in. Adela lay in the bedroom, her right arm bandaged, her eyes looking drowsy, as if she'd had some of the laudanum kept for emergencies. A braid of her straight black hair rested over one shoulder. Her normally olive skin looked pale, but she smiled and held out her good hand. "Thank you for coming, Margarida," she whispered in a slurred voice.

Margarida took the hand in her own and sat beside the bed, feeling increasingly distressed at the lines of pain in the older woman's face. "How are you feeling?"

"Not too bad," Adela responded. Then she spoke more clearly. "I'm sorry you saw that last night."

"It doesn't matter. I wish Papa had let me help you."

Adela managed a pale smile. "Rosa's been taking good care of me. Can you tell me what's happened to Miguel?"

"Papa said he's locked in the bunkhouse." Margarida hesitated, then added, "Someone's going to take him into town to the sheriff."

Tears began to trickle down Adela's cheek and onto the pillow. "Poor Miguel."

"But he tried to disfigure you," Margarida protested, "maybe kill you."

"He's never hurt me before, and this was my fault too." She tried to smile, but the tears still seeped from her dark eyes. "I was careless. I know you have to pay for pleasures in this life. I forgot that God would punish me, and now Miguel's being punished too."

Margarida could only sit silently. Was Adela right?

she wondered. Maybe she should be glad Adela's advice about seduction hadn't worked with Brant yesterday; so far she'd had none of those pleasures that had cost Adela so much. Would she ever have to pay a high and painful price for something she wanted? No, she wouldn't believe that. Her life would be sweet and joyful, she was sure.

3

"SEÑORITA, this one is very pretty." Lupe held up a turquoise silk dress from among the heap on the bed. It was the first one Margarida had tried on. "I hear Señor Ross going to the living room now," she warned, "and Señora Ross is waiting for me to pack the dresses for you both."

Standing in her chemise and petticoats, Margarida frowned in vexation. Every gown looked wrong. A wedding was a big social event in the little town of Rio Torcido; everyone in the area would attend today. Brant would certainly be there, so this was her chance to carry out the retaliation she'd brooded about for two weeks. Soon her father would be roaring that they would be late, and she hadn't decided what to wear for the evening's dancing.

"The color is lovely." Lupe sounded harried.

Exasperated with her own indecision, Margarida smiled at the maid. "You're probably right. I'll try it again."

When the silk settled around her, she looked in the mirror. She'd purchased the dress impulsively in the East, because it made her feel grown-up, but she hadn't been sure she'd dare wear it. The scooped neckline revealed the tops of her breasts, and short puffed sleeves barely covered her shoulders. The bodice clung to her high breasts, accenting their fullness. A panel of silk lay flat across her stomach; below it rows of ruffles curved around to the back, giving the effect of a small bustle.

The way the skirt showed the shape of her legs when she moved, as well as the low neckline, would shock her father. It would be obvious she wasn't wearing a corset. She hated corsets and refused to wear one, insisting that fashionable girls in the East cared about activity, not their waist measurements. The words "fashion" and "East" had great power with her mother, but not her father. At least he wouldn't see her until she'd emerged from the room where the women changed their clothes. By then it would be too late for him to object. Her mother, with her volatile swings of mood, might be either upset or indifferent— Margarida couldn't anticipate which. But even if Elena were angry, she'd probably abandon her protests when Margarida ignored them.

In New York this dress would only look fashionable, but here it would attract the attention of men at the wedding reception, including that insufferable black-haired man she now detested. According to feminine lore from boarding school, he'd be jealous and regret his treatment of her.

"Yes, Lupe," she said, "please help me out of this dress and pack it for me." When the maid left, Margarida put on a ruffled ivory blouse and brown cotton jacket and skirt and fastened a large square of lace around her hair.

Only her father, in his tan riding clothes, was waiting when she entered the *sala*. "Margarida, I want to talk to you before we leave. Let's go into my office."

"Have you decided anything about a new foreman?" she asked when they were in the cluttered room off the patio.

He sighed and rubbed his head, mussing his thick white hair. "I thought of Carlos García, but he's having trouble with his eyes. I'll have to look around for someone, maybe go to Silver City."

Margarida considered pointing out that Carlos García, like Miguel Ramírez, was Hispano, but she didn't want to provoke her father today. Jesse sat and leaned back in his worn leather chair, and Margarida perched on the edge of a wooden bench. "What did you want to talk to me about?"

Jesse looked uncomfortable but determined. "Brant Curtis will probably be at the wedding. I was glad to see that you spent so little time with him at your party, and I want you to stay away from him today."

Margarida felt her temper begin to rise. Her father's admonishing tone revived her old resentment that he hadn't believed her explanation of what happened three years ago. "Oh, Papa, can't you forget that stupid business?"

His face flushed, and he let his chair legs down with a thump. "We won't talk about that again. I just don't want you to have anything to do with him."

Though she had the same ultimate intention, Margarida didn't choose to tell her father that, and she wasn't going to promise not to speak to Brant today. Instead she said, "I don't understand why you dislike Brant so much, or why his father always used to act so cold toward him."

Jesse looked relieved that Margarida wasn't arguing, and he answered amiably, "I don't dislike Brant; he's done very well, considering his Indian blood. But that's the point as far as you're concerned. He *is* part Indian, and you're a white woman. Indians and whites are different. They shouldn't mix. Even if he was a childhood friend, you're too old to have anything to do with him now."

She had to tighten her lips to keep from lashing out at his peremptory manner. "As to Rupert Curtis' feelings," he continued, "I know he was upset when Brant refused to join the Guards when Victorio's Apache were raiding in seventy-nine. I guess that seemed cowardly to Rupert. He and Brant seem to get along all right now. At least well enough that Rupert lets Brant try out some of his wild ideas about Indians. With poor Walt's handicap, Rupert pretty well has only one son who can take over his land."

At Jesse's slighting reference to Walt, Margarida lost control of her temper. "Don't say 'poor Walt' like that. He's a wonderful person—no one has a better disposition."

Frowning again, Jesse said in an exasperated voice, "That's what worries me about you. When it comes to people you think are friends, you don't face facts. Walt's mind is like a child's. Someday he's bound to get into situations he can't handle, and I pity him. Anyway, I don't want to talk about him. Just you remember to stay away from Brant."

Still angry, Margarida left the office and returned to the *sala*, where she found J.J. looking bored, and her mother waiting in her blue traveling suit. Margarida was relieved to see that Elena's eyes glowed with anticipation and pleasure—it was one of her mother's good days. Jesse came in a moment later, and they all went outside, where Margarida and Elena climbed into the surrey behind Pedro, the middle-aged ranch hand who often served as their driver. J.J. and Jesse rode ahead on horseback.

During the three-hour trip, Elena talked about the people who would be at the wedding. She discussed the ranch and mine owners and their families first, starting with the most prosperous ones, and then the merchants and businessmen of the small town. The miners and the hired men and women who worked on the ranches she ignored, evaluating in her indirect way the social position of everyone who lived near the valley the Ross and Curtis families shared.

Listening to the gossip, Margarida wondered why her mother needed to assign friends and neighbors definite social places, with the Ross family at the top. Papa had come from a very poor Texas family. He'd led an adventurous life before he made his first fortune from mining. Later he'd met Elena in California, where her Portuguese grandparents had settled. Though her mother had always refused to discuss her childhood, Margarida suspected that her mother's family had once had money and position that had been lost, and that was why she seemed to care about her own social situation with an almost unnatural intensity.

While her mother talked, Margarida watched for familiar signs along the road—the huge gray boulder with one side splitting off, a trickle of water in a gully that came from a spring above, a snow-bent pine that formed an arch. The translucent azure of the sky and the unpopulated distances that she could see when the road topped a rise exhilarated her; she had missed New Mexico dreadfully.

It was almost three o'clock when they crested the last hill and looked down on the town of Rio Torcido. Through the pines and box elders, silver flashes revealed the course of the twisted river that gave the town its name. As they reached the first buildings clustered in the widest part of the valley, Margarida thought how much the small town was a mixture of its Mexican past and American present. Flat-roofed adobe buildings ran along the main street. Scattered among them were frame buildings, one with the steep roof appropriate for a New England winter. Next to the Catholic mission, a white picket fence outlined the new two-story courthouse and jail.

The Ross surrey turned up one of the steep side streets to the small Protestant church. Its white wood siding and slender bell tower glistened in the afternoon sun; carriages and tethered horses already crowded the yard. After Jesse helped Elena down and they started for the church, Margarida climbed out of the surrey and took J.J.'s arm.

J.J. looked teasingly at his sister. "Did Papa warn you to stay away from the terrible Brant Curtis today?"

She stopped, the peace of the ride through the countryside destroyed. "How did you know that?"

He laughed like the boy he sometimes still was. "Just a good guess. Now, Margarida, don't be mad. I like Brant, and I wish Papa weren't so opposed to him."

"Don't waste your wishes." Margarida jerked on J.J.'s arm. "Come on. Papa and Mama are already inside."

They found their parents seated on one of the pine-wood benches toward the back of the church. The bride had grown up in Rio Torcido, where her father ran a local grocery and dry-goods store. She knew everyone in the valleys the town served, so people filled the church. The groom was the oldest of seven boys from a modest ranch.

Margarida, her heart beginning to beat faster despite her efforts to be calm, looked for a black head taller than those around it. At the far end of one of the rows she saw the thick blue-black hair she'd been searching for. After that, she spent the service in a daydream in which Brant, probably on his knees, begged her for just one kiss, which she haughtily refused as she turned to another man.

Unfortunately she couldn't think of a candidate for that other man; several ranchers' sons had called on her before she went to school, but she'd been so enamored of Brant that she'd discouraged them all. She would have to look around, she decided, and choose a few men whom she would allow to court her. Somehow, that idea seemed flat after the excitement of yearning for Brant. Having him on her mind was a habit she must break, she reminded herself.

She was startled when music from the tiny organ interrupted her thoughts, and the bride and groom, flushed and happy-looking, came back along the aisle. Margarida followed her family to the receiving line and then out to their surrey.

She didn't look for Brant; the churchyard, crowded with people, wasn't the right place to reduce him to the status of rejected suitor. The reception, in the large meeting hall behind the courthouse, would be more suitable. It had a large yard with walks and several hidden corners, and somehow she would maneuver Brant into one of those places. He would be jealous from all the attention she was getting from other men, and . . . well, she wasn't sure just what she'd do, but she would manage something.

As the surrey jostled its way along the dusty road behind other horses and vehicles, they passed the two-room adobe, surrounded by a fence of mesquite poles, where Adela was living now. Jesse had offered to keep her on the ranch until she was well, but he didn't conceal his severe disapproval of her, and she had moved into town.

Margarida wished they could stop, but she knew Jesse wouldn't allow it. She'd ridden into town with J.J. once and visited Adela, but she hadn't told her father. Miguel was in jail, waiting for the circuit judge to arrive, and Adela had seemed sad and distraught. Margarida had left a little money where Adela would find it and wished she knew of some way to do more.

They soon reached a grassy area between the courthouse and the meeting hall where large cottonwoods provided shade. Men were setting up planks on sawhorses. Women waited with tablecloths, steaming bowls of spicy stew, and platters of beef, venison, and turkey to arrange on the improvised tables. Margarida climbed down while Pedro assisted Elena; he followed the two women inside the hall, carrying the heavy basket that had been filled in the Ross kitchen that morning. Soon their peach pies were added to the cakes and cookies on one end of a table.

Although Margarida enjoyed food, the time devoted to the dinner seemed interminable. She tried to visit with young women she'd known when she'd lived in

Rio Torcido two winters to go to the town school, but
their conversation bored her more than usual. Three
of the young men who had once tried to court her
joined them, but none roused her interest. She pretended great interest in a new bride's gingerbread
recipe and then eagerly helped clear the tables so that
the dancing could begin.

The sun had set when the men and women from
outlying areas went to the houses reserved for changing their clothes. The boxes containing the finery for
the evening had been taken to the women's house,
and Margarida found a corner in one bedroom where
she could put on her turquoise silk away from her
mother's eyes.

Taking special care, Margarida arranged her hair in
curls at the back of her head, anchoring them with
shell-trimmed combs, leaving only a few careful wisps
to soften her face. Twisting, she checked in the mirror
to see that the shining fall down her back ended just
above the deep scoop of the dress. Satisfied, she rubbed
her cheeks to bring out their color and wished she
dared use the eye makeup she'd tried once at school.

As she finished, she heard her mother say in a
shocked tone, "Margarida!" When she turned around,
Elena was standing in the doorway, her face flushed
an angry pink. The other girls stopped their preparations and stared curiously. Glancing uncomfortably at
the spectators, Elena said in a strained voice, "Margarida, please come with me."

When they were outside, Elena stopped far enough
from the house that no one could hear and said, "Where
did you get that disgraceful dress?" Without pausing
for an answer, she put both hands to her head. "I
don't now what makes you act the way you do. You've
been taught better. What will your father say?"

"I bought this in New York on my way home. It's
the latest fashion there."

Elena offered no more objections, and Margarida,

taking her mother's arm, gently started them both along the lantern-edged path to the meeting room. She knew her father's disapproval couldn't be turned aside so easily, but she didn't intend for him to see her until she was already dancing, and he wouldn't embarrass himself or her by saying anything then. For a moment she felt guilty; it wasn't really fair to take advantage of her father's good manners. But she thought of her purpose—for just this night she'd make Brant Curtis sorry he'd spurned her.

Inside the room she slipped away from her mother and circled around until she saw J.J., elegant now in a black suit. On each side startled faces turned toward her. J.J. was talking to Lee Hansen, one of the best-looking men in the area. Lee's blond hair and tall build made him look like a Viking; he would suit her very well as her first dance partner. She made her way to J.J. and took his arm.

Her brother looked at her dress, and for almost the first time she could remember, appeared shocked. Then, with a glint in his eyes, he said, "I think you want me to find Mama and calm her down."

'Would you, J.J.? She'll listen to you about anything." Margarida smiled at Lee, who looked as if he could hardly believe his good fortune. With a grin and a nod, J.J. vanished into the crowd.

"May I have the pleasure, Miss Ross, of sharing the first dance with you?" Lee asked, obviously trying not to stare at her neckline.

"That would be delightful, Mr. Hansen," Margarida responded, and took the arm Lee offered her. They stood beside the cleared area in the center of the room, watching the five musicians tune their instruments and waiting for the bride and groom to begin the evening's dancing.

Overhead lanterns, decorated with streamers of colored cloth, made rainbow patterns on the polished pinewood floor. As Lee talked about his father's ranch,

Margarida remembered why his handsome looks hadn't
appealed to her. The Vikings, she thought, would
never have conquered much of Europe if they'd all
been as dull as their descendant. Fortunately the bride
and groom soon appeared, and Margarida discovered
that Lee was at least a graceful dancer.

As he whirled her around, she caught a glimpse
through the other people of Brant's black head next to
a blond one. For a moment she thought he was dancing with the hardware merchant's daughter again, and
she could feel anger welling up like bubbles from the
bottom of a spring. Determined not to let her feelings
show, she smiled at Lee and was rewarded by a glazed
look in his eyes. At the next whirl she saw that Brant's
partner was Harriet Bodmer, the daughter of a wealthy
rancher, an unattractive woman whom men danced
with only to be polite. Relieved, and at the same time
ashamed that she'd reacted so strongly, Margarida
decided she would keep better control of herself.

Her father was across the room, engrossed in a
conversation with another man, and didn't see her. He
disappeared into a side room, and she concluded gratefully that he had gone to play cards, an activity he
greatly preferred to dancing. Though she was prepared to brazen out his disapproval of her dress, she'd
rather avoid him now.

For the next two hours she danced with men she'd
known before she went to school and several newcom-
ers who solicited introductions from her brother. Their
faces became a blur of light and dark eyes, high and
low voices, smooth skin and carefully trimmed mus-
taches and beards. Conversation seemed to deterio-
rate under the strain of ignoring her low-cut gown;
only one slight man with heavily tanned skin managed
to entertain her with stories of his adventures guarding
wagon trains traveling to Arizona. Another tall, shy
redhead who looked about J.J.'s age turned out to be
a marvelous dancer. Otherwise none of her partners

captured her attention enough to divert her from keeping track of Brant's whereabouts.

During the dancing, Brant found himself watching Margarida when he didn't intend to. Her dress showed just how well-developed her breasts were, something he wanted to forget. All too vividly he could picture how she'd looked that day at the line shack. As he tried to concentrate on his own partners, he found he was angry. Dammit, he thought, she's become a flirt, giving her partners seductive glances under those thick lashes, tilting her head back and laughing up at them. But maybe he wasn't being fair. She'd always loved a good time and treated most people with warmth and charm. He'd once liked that quality in her.

As he whirled his partner around, he caught a glimpse of Margarida, with Lee Hansen again, looking up at Lee as if he were the world's most magnificent man. That unreasonable feeling of anger returned. No, Brant decided, he wasn't wrong—she'd learned about the power a woman could have over men, and she was using it.

Suddenly he craved fresh air and a chance to be alone. When the music ended, he returned his latest partner to her husband and made his way around the edge of the room.

Margarida saw Brant leave the hall through one of the side doors. Though he hadn't approached her all evening, she thought she'd caught him watching her once. Now her chest began to tighten as she realized that this was probably her chance. Turning to Lee, she explained hastily, "Please excuse me, Mr. Hansen, I must . . ."

At her hesitation, he blushed and nodded. "Of course, Miss Ross. I hope you'll save me a dance later."

"Yes, later," she said, and hurried to a side door. When she stepped outside, she saw two men under a nearby tree, cigars glowing in their hands, but no one else.

Disappointment dropped like lead into her stomach. Straining her eyes for other figures, she walked along the path that led away from the light. Near one of the shadowy cottonwoods she saw a movement, and her heart almost jumped out from under its silk cover. Then she heard a laugh and recognized Priscilla Welles, a girl Magarida disliked for her mindless pursuit of any male who would notice her. She was leaning against the redhead who was such a good dancer.

Margarida drew back and hurriedly walked off to her right, farther into the darkness. Her heart still pounded, but growing uncertainty increased the cold knot in her stomach. Chasing after Brant suddenly seemed futile and, even worse, made her feel tawdry and scheming—no better than the silly girl back by the tree. Even if she found him, she thought miserably, her experience with him at the line shack told her that she wouldn't know how to reduce him to the pleading man of her fantasies.

The music echoed behind her, but she didn't want to return to the dance. Instead of elegant and attractive, she felt naked and exposed in her turquoise dress, the air chilly on her bare skin. The men she'd flirted with seemed stale and uninteresting and her use of them distasteful. All she wanted was to be alone, and she walked farther away from the lights until she could see the Milky Way spread across the sky. She was standing, her head tilted back, when she heard a voice that she recognized, and all the anticipation and anxiety of the day gripped her again.

"Margarida?" Brant appeared, only faintly visible in the half-darkness. "What are you doing out here? Are you all right?"

At the concern in his voice, longing swept over her, not for the lover she'd so foolishly counted on, but for the Brant she'd followed all the years she'd been growing up. She might hate the man who'd rejected her, but she still missed the friend. Disguising her agitation under a cheerfulness she hoped sounded natural, she said, "I'm fine—just tired of dancing and of all the people."

"You've attracted lots of attention tonight." He sounded casual, but she thought she detected an irritated note, and hope surged in her. He *had* noticed her this evening—maybe been jealous. Then she stopped herself; no, she decided, she wouldn't try to flirt with him again. Her plans for retaliation had been childish.

She managed a laugh. "That's what I wanted to do."

Brant heard a wistfulness in Margarida's voice that kept him from walking away as promptly as he'd intended when he found she was all right. It made her seem more of a child and less the woman whose allure threatened to upset his life. The night and the shadowy trees isolated them, and he felt the pull of all their shared memories.

"Are you pleased with your results?" he asked.

She turned away from him, looking up toward the sky. A moon that would soon be full had appeared over the top of a faraway bluff. When she looked back, her voice sounded sad. "I don't know. Sometimes I'm not sure what I really want anymore. I guess you know what you want. Papa says you and your father are letting Indians stay on your land."

It was obvious, Brant thought, that she hadn't listened to his explanation of his plans that day at the line shack. Half-irritated and half-amused, he only said, "Yes, we are."

"Why are you so interested in Indians, Brant? Of course you have your grandmother who's Indian, but you're mostly white; you were raised as a white."

"Not entirely." His few early memories of his half-Apache mother were of warmth and love and of soothing lullabies that were part song and part chant. But

his father—that was different. Brant thought of the
many times his father had punished him when as a
child he'd gotten into some kind of mischief. His
father's accompanying reprimand had invariably been
that Brant was acting like an Apache, said in a tone
which made clear his father's distaste. "My father
always thought of my mother and me as Indians."

"Is that why your father disapproved of you, and
not because you wouldn't fight with the Shakespeare
Guards?"

"You're full of questions tonight." She began to walk
farther along the path that led away from the hall. He
knew he shouldn't walk with her, but her mood seemed
different from the day at the line shack, and no one
was around to notice. "Maybe he thought I was a
coward. I don't know. But those years when I wandered around, I saw how most soldiers treated Indians, and the volunteers were sometimes worse."

Brant remembered the first time he'd seen an Indian camp after a raid on it. Braves lay dead, but also
bayoneted babies and raped and mutilated women.
He'd seen whites after Apaches had brutally killed
them, but he knew that first memory still seared him.
It wasn't something he could talk about, so he only
said, "I'll never fight in any army, regular or volunteer."

"I've heard gruesome stories about the things the
Apaches do to whites," she protested. "That isn't your
way either."

"Yes, Indians can be terribly cruel, but most whites
don't try to understand how they live. When I came
home in seventy-nine, all my mother's people had
been sent to San Carlos. I went there to find my
grandmother. I'll never forget what things were like in
that place."

"San Carlos?"

"It's the big reservation in Arizona, near Fort
Apache, in the desert west of here. The army had
promised Cochise that the Mimbres Apache would

have a permanent home at Ojo Caliente, in the mountains north of here. It was their hunting grounds where they'd always lived. But they were sent to San Carlos, which is mostly desolate flatland with no place to hunt. All the different Apache tribes were crowded in there, with Yavapai and Pima, groups that had never gotten along with the Apache or each other."

He stopped, remembering the men reduced to idleness and charity, and the women struggling to raise a few plants in the hot, barren lands. The proud warriors he'd admired were angry, bitter men, trapped in a useless existence. "I begged *shiwóyé* to leave with me, but she wouldn't. But last year, she and her band came to me—only thirty of them left. I've been trying to look out for them since. So, you're right that I didn't grow up in the Apache way, but I have Apache blood, and I'm proud of it."

Margarida felt an ache in her throat as if she had tears inside that wanted to come out. Why couldn't things be as uncomplicated as they had seemed when she was a child? she wondered. "Sometimes I wish I could go back and be happy just fishing or wading in one of the creeks."

Brant heard the sad note in her voice. Her wistfulness reached out to him, carrying him with her to simpler, more irresponsible times when he'd enjoyed her adventurous spirit—before he became its target. He spoke softly. "You've always loved any kind of water."

"Yes." Suddenly she laughed as if just remembering something joyful. Her eyes seemed to have captured some of the moonlight as she spoke. "The side creek that comes into town behind the livery stable—does it still have that little waterfall in the middle of the willows?"

Drawn in by her enthusiasm, he laughed with her. "It did the last time I noticed, but that's been a long time." He hesitated, but the nostalgia created by her mood overcame his caution. "Shall we go see?"

She clapped her hands, transforming herself even more into a young girl. "Oh, yes. Let's do." With one hand she picked up her skirts and held the other out to him.

When Brant took her hand, Margarida felt a ripple of excitement along her skin, but she was too caught up in the moment to worry about what it meant. He was her friend again, and that was enough. Laughing, she pulled him away from the meeting hall and along the dusty road to the dark shape which was the livery stable. As they skirted it, she could smell the familiar odor of the horses and hear their soft snorts. Then she and Brant were crossing behind the corrals, finding the path that led down past the cottonwoods and through the thick willows to where a small stream splashed its way down to join the river.

They stopped and listened. Suddenly too conscious of the pressure of Brant's muscular hand on hers, Margarida pulled away. To their left she heard a louder sound. "I think it's this way," she urged, and took the lead, pushing through the willows. She felt her carefully arranged hair catch on the branches, but she didn't care.

About twenty feet upstream they came to a bend where a combination of an old log and several large rocks had created a tiny waterfall. Margarida stopped, entranced by the sound of the water and the dancing reflection of moonlight on its whirls and ripples. Between the willows and the water a tongue of grassy bank reached out into the pool created by the falls. She crouched down and dangled her hand in the water. As she leaned over, the curls that had torn loose in the willows fell over her face. She released the combs, freeing the rest of her hair. Rising, she turned and found Brant immediately behind her.

Startled by his unexpected closeness, she stepped back onto the edge of the bank and felt herself slipping. He grabbed her, pulling her away from the stream and up against him. Clinging to him for support, she felt his hard body against hers, and all the tension of the day rushed back.

Frozen, she looked up at him. It seemed as if they had stepped outside of time, no longer playing at being in the past, but not in the present either. They were a man and a woman with all the attraction between them that had ever drawn a male and female together. She stared at the hawklike features of his face, at the eyes that were blacker than the night. He lifted the heavy weight of her hair, letting it slide across his hand, then ran his fingers almost wonderingly over her cheekbone and along the side of her face. His thumb traced the shape of her lips. With a soft sound that could have been a sigh, he leaned down, his lips captured hers, and both of them were caught in the moment's web.

Gently he kissed her and gently she responded, but underneath the first tenderness, urgency began to claim them. His mouth moved over hers, exploring, becoming more insistent, and hers responded, following his lips greedily. Their tongues met as well, discovering the harsh sweetness of passion. They broke apart, staring, before their mouths reclaimed each other. Kisses were not enough, and his hands, which had held her face, now sought her shoulders, the side of her neck, and finally her breast, freeing it from the moonlight-silvered silk. Gently he lifted the soft weight, warming it in his palm, his fingers teasing the crest to hardness. As his mouth followed his hands, she felt fire shoot through her at his touch. He kissed the nipple, then pulled at it with his lips, exciting her to pleasure so intense it almost resembled pain.

Intoxicated with sensation, she slid her hands under his jacket and over the hard planes of his chest. She whispered his name and he echoed hers, each syllable becoming part of the rhythm of desire. Her legs trembled, and she clung to him for support. Together they swayed on the bank; then he lowered her to the soft grass. She lay beside him, her breath coming so fast it seemed to deplete rather than supply air. Through her clothes she felt the stiff thrust of his erection, and she was caught up by a new and terrible need that made her clutch him to her in longing for something her mind didn't recognize but her body knew.

His harsh breathing sounded as rapid as her own. She barely recognized his voice—urgent, questioning, "Margarida?" Trembling with tension that rippled through her abdomen, unable to speak, she could only wait. He lowered his face to her naked breasts, kissing them again, while she buried her hands in the rough silk of his hair. Again his lips found her nipples, first one, then the other, sending waves of sensation rippling through her, blotting out thought. She felt his hand under her skirt, stroking her calf, then moving up her leg. His fingers were warm on the inside of her thigh, finding the opening in her clothes, brushing against the triangle of soft hair. The unfamiliar gesture, where no man had touched before, caught her unprepared, making her stiffen and gasp.

To Brant, Margarida's sharp breath sounded like a warning shout in his head. At that same moment a burst of wind whipped the willow branches overhead, letting the moonlight illuminate her face. He could see her eyes and her trembling mouth, passionate, yet fearful.

My God! What was he doing? Shocked, he drew back his hand. Margarida clutched at him, but he rolled away and lay on the grass. His heart pounded erratically and a painful ache began in his groin. She sat up and leaned over him; her hair fell in a shadowed cloud around her face and trailed across his chest.

He couldn't see her expression, but he heard distress in her bewildered whisper. "Why did you . . . what's wrong?"

Self-contempt choked him, so that his voice came out harsh and rasping. "I'm wrong. This is wrong. It's no good for either of us."

For a moment she stared at him, as if not sure what he'd said. Then she scrambled to her feet, covering her breasts and pulling down her skirt. He rose also, as appalled as she looked. In the touch and feel of her, in the passion she aroused, he'd forgotten everything but desire. Because of his weakness he'd almost dishonored her—and jeopardized all that was so important to him. He'd thought himself hardened against her appeal, but his nostalgia for a child had made him vulnerable to the danger of the woman. And, he recognized grimly, he'd let her conquests at the dance bother him.

"Margarida, I'm sorry. I don't want to hurt you. I should never have touched you. It's just that . . ." He stopped, not sure how to explain that she attracted him but that he mustn't give in—must not let himself want her.

Margarida could hear the disgust in Brant's voice, and it filled her with humiliation. She stared at him, trying to control her shivering, stunned by an inescapable question. After all he'd said to her, why had she let him touch her so intimately? If he hadn't stopped, in another moment she would have let him make love to her. Awareness flooded over her, and she knew why. In spite of her determination to hate him, she loved him. That knowledge and his rejection shocked and shamed her.

In her distress she could only think he'd scorned her again and that she must conceal her feelings from him. She welcomed the protection of anger and lashed out at him. "Don't worry that you hurt me. I only wanted to see how far you'd go after your pronouncements about being too smart to *fuck* me." She'd never used that word before, but in it she spewed out her pain and fury.

At her words, Brant felt first shock, then anger with her almost as great as with himself. He responded as cruelly as she. "At least we're well matched. I'm a degenerate and you're a tease." He watched her pick up her skirts and plunge back into the willow bushes, the pounding in his head matching the pain in his groin.

So filled with rage she felt as if she would explode, Margarida fled back along the path she'd followed so happily—so stupidly—before. As she neared the hall, she stopped, realizing that her hair and clothes were disheveled. She turned and hurried to the house where she'd changed earlier. A glance told her no one was inside.

When she reached the bedroom where she'd dressed, she stopped and leaned against the wall, her hands clenched over her stomach, determined she wouldn't be sick. Finally she was able to move and found her clothes box. Her first impulse was to change to her traveling dress and go to the surrey. Later she'd say she hadn't felt well. But she knew she couldn't do that. She might still be in love with Brant, but pride wouldn't let her hide from him.

With hands she forced under control, she brushed and refastened her hair and straightened her dress. After she rubbed some color back into her cheeks, she started back for the dance.

She'd made a terrible mistake tonight, but at least he didn't know how she felt. And she would forget Brant Curtis. He wouldn't have a chance to humiliate her again.

4

RETURNING to the dance was more difficult than Margarida had expected. At the edge of the light coming from the hall, she stopped. Her skin felt cold in spite of the black lace shawl she'd put around her shoulders. Coward! she accused herself, and walked to the door.

Inside she paused, searching quickly to see whether Brant were there. At a touch on her arm she turned to face Walt Curtis.

The pleasure on his face was medicine to her lacerated feelings. "Margarida, I've been looking for you. You're pretty tonight," he said, his gray eyes bright with unself-conscious admiration.

"Thank you for that compliment. It's the nicest I've received."

Walt wore a dark blue frock coat and trousers. His blond hair and even features, combined with broad shoulders and muscular body, made him an unusually handsome man. Ordinarily females would have tried to charm him, but his impaired intelligence was well known. No girl except Margarida had ever acted more than polite toward him.

"Do you want to dance?" he asked.

Walt loved music and was a good dancer, though quite unrestrained in his movements. Margarida had danced with him often, but now she shrank from calling more attention to herself. "Why don't we get some punch instead?" She tucked her hand through his elbow. "Then we can visit, and maybe plan a day to go fishing."

"Fishing!" He gave a delighted laugh. "All right."

They skirted the dancing area to the lace-covered table that held a punch bowl and glasses. Walt carefully ladled out a portion of the punch, apple cider with precious orange and lemon juice added. They started toward the row of wooden benches along one wall, when Margarida saw her father staring at her from across the room.

Even at that distance she could see that his face was flushed, his mouth drawn down in a scowl. He'd shared enough flasks that he might well choose to chastise her in spite of the onlookers, she decided. The shawl gave her a little modesty, but not much. After what had happened with Brant, she couldn't face her father's disapproval just now.

Quickly she turned to Walt. "Would you like to go outside to drink our punch?"

"Sure." He hesitated, looking at her dress. "Are you cold?"

She smiled affectionately at him, pulling him toward the door. "I'll be fine. We can find a bench, and I'll sit close to you to keep warm."

He'd always done whatever she wanted; now he laughed and hurried with her to the door. She glanced back over her shoulder and saw that her father was still standing where he had been. Apparently he didn't mean to follow her. Relieved, she held Walt's arm and walked close beside him as they went outside.

From a corner at the far end of the room Brant watched Margarida leave with Walt. The anger and disgust he'd felt with himself flared again, this time at her. Now she was turning her seductive ways on Walt, he concluded grimly, and that was something he wouldn't allow.

He thought about her earlier words to him, that she'd only wanted to see how far she could make him want to go. She'd spoken in anger and might not have meant what she said, but he couldn't be sure. She was headstrong and impulsive, careless of consequences; he knew that from the past. Her dress and her behavior with the men who'd flocked around her tonight showed how casually she flirted.

Walt, whatever his limitations, had all the desires of any other man, though he wasn't aware of them himself. And he had an even greater vulnerability because he didn't understand the need to control his impulses. Margarida probably didn't realize this, and she could carelessly provoke Walt into an action that would ruin his life.

Brant threaded his way toward the door. He regretted his own behavior with her and wished he could avoid hurting her, but he had to protect his brother first.

Margarida shivered in the night air as she sat beside Walt on a bench under one of the cottonwoods. A breeze penetrated the shawl, and she moved closer to him, letting his large body block the wind.

As if just remembering a grievance, Walt said in an accusing tone, "Why did you go away? You stayed a long time. I didn't like that."

"I didn't like it either," Margarida assured him. "But Papa said I had to go to school."

"Why?"

"Because he thought I needed to learn to act like a lady." Or to pretend to, she added to herself.

"You won't let him send you away again, will you?" he asked anxiously.

Margarida laughed. "No—I'm going to stay home now." She took Walt's punch glass and set it and hers on the ground. Then she gave Walt a hug. "I miss you too much to go away again." Impulsively she pulled his head down and kissed his cheek.

Behind her a cold voice said, "Walt. I've been looking for you." When she pulled away from Walt, she saw Brant.

He looked furious, and the rigid stance of his shoulders and legs told her he was barely controlling his feelings. Walt started to rise, but resentment and anger, as intense as what she saw in Brant's fierce eyes, made Margarida grip Walt's arm, holding him back. Why should he have to jump at his brother's words? she thought stormily.

Before Walt could respond, she said, as rudely as she could, "Walt and I are visiting. Can't you wait?"

Walt loosened her hold and scrambled to his feet, all his attention on his brother. "Did I do something wrong? Are you mad at me?"

Brant's voice sounded more gentle now. "No. Of course not. But we're going to leave soon. I need you to find our horses and calm down Chid. You know how restless he gets when he's tied up with strange horses this long."

"Yes, that's right." Walt's distress vanished, and he gave a pleased chortle. "Nobody can take care of Chid the way I do." He turned back to Margarida, and his smile wavered. "Are you mad at me?"

"No, of course not. We'll visit again soon." Sorry that she'd added to Walt's distress, Margarida watched as he hurried toward the stable. He'd always been extremely sensitive to other people's moods. The same sensitivity made him so good at handling all kinds of animals. But she wasn't the one who had upset Walt to begin with.

Angrily she turned back to Brant. Before she could speak, he said in a voice which could have frozen boiling water, "I want you to stay away from Walt."

Margarida had always had trouble controlling her temper. Now she not only didn't want to; she welcomed the flare of anger which made her heart pump furiously. "Why, Brant? Are you jealous?"

He stepped forward. At the suddenness of his gesture she moved instinctively backward, but he seized her shoulders, gripping her so tightly she couldn't move. His deep voice sounded almost toneless, like a whisper. "For all I care, you can screw every man in town and all the valleys around. Except Walt. Leave him alone."

Margarida felt as if she were choking. Rage at his presumption boiled inside her, and the pain that he would think she cared so little for Walt's feelings was like a match to kerosene. "You're insane. I love Walt—I wouldn't hurt him." She could her her voice shake. "You don't understand anything about me."

He released her shoulders, and she took another step backward, holding her hands clenched at her sides. He let out a long breath, but his voice still sounded implacable as he said, "You're the one who doesn't understand. Walt is a man, with all the needs you seem to know so much about now. You may not intend to hurt him, but those careless little games you think are harmless could wreck his life. I won't let you take any chances with Walt. I'll say it just one more time—*stay away from him.*"

Games! In that moment Margarida felt that if she had a weapon, she would use it. She swung her hand and hit him as hard as she could across the side of his face. "You don't even know what decent feelings are. I hate you. I—" She choked on her own rage. Brant's face suddenly looked blurred, and the lighted windows behind him tilted crazily. She pushed past him and fled around the corner of the meeting hall.

Brant watched Margarida disappear into the dark. His face stung, and he felt hollow, as if all the memories he cherished of her were disappearing too. He'd deliberately used the most ugly words he could think of to hurt her. Grimly he reminded himself what was at stake—his brother's happiness. And the survival of his grandmother's people, the people he'd come to think

of as his. These were the things that were important to
him. The child Margarida was part of the past—behind
him now and best forgotten.

He started toward the stable, carefully concentrating on Walt. Maybe it was past time to take his brother
to the local *bagnio*. Brant had never cared to patron-
ize the "girls" who took customers to their rooms
upstairs over the largest of the town's three saloons.
The one or two "fast" girls from good families he'd
avoided; taking them to bed could too easily result in
entanglements. He preferred a night with a lonesome
widow or with one of the Apache women who was
divorced or widowed, and available, if she chose, to
the unmarried men of the group. These women were
respectable, not like white prostitutes.

Walt, however, presented a different problem. Brant
couldn't take him to one of the Apache women. Despite Walt's amiability and good looks, he'd have to
pay someone to bed him. Maybe, Brant decided as he
reached the road, a woman could be found who needed
the money but didn't work regularly as a prostitute.

Walt was waiting with the horses, murmuring softly
as he stroked the neck of Brant's horse. Chid's raven-
black coat glistened in the moonlight; the narrow
white blaze on his face caught the light as he tossed his
head nervously, apparently having detected Brant's
scent. The horse, a cross between a quarter horse and
an Indian pony, had been a gift from Brant's grandmother. When he got to know the horse's temperament, he'd named him *ch'iidn binant'a'*, which meant
"devil" in Apache, and then shortened it to Chid. He
and Walt were the only ones Chid would allow to ride
him, though he let Margarida stroke him.

"Are you ready to go home?" Brant asked Walt.

"We're going all the way to the ranch tonight?"
Walt said hopefully. He'd always rather ride than sleep.

"Yes, there's plenty of moonlight," Brant replied,
and took Chid's reins. Seeing Walt's delight made up

for some of the pain of the encounters with Margarida. Brant swung up into his saddle, then quieted his dancing horse as Walt mounted.

Margarida stopped at the edge of the courthouse, not wanting to see anyone until she calmed herself. She heard horses and saw Brant and Walt ride past on the moonlit road. Bitterly she stared after them until they were gone.

She couldn't remember ever feeling so angry. If she hadn't hated Brant Curtis before tonight, she told herself fiercely, she did now. His actions at the line shack and tonight at the stream had wounded her. Now his command to leave Walt alone added another insult. Never, *never* would she yearn after Brant Curtis again. That was finished.

"Margarida. I've been looking for you." The slightly slurred voice was Jesse's. "That dress is disgraceful."

The familiar accusing tones loosened her locked-up tears. She began to cry, letting out sobs that had been waiting ever since she and Brant parted at the stream.

"Margarida, what's the matter?" She could barely hear her father, but she felt his arms enfold her. "There, there. Don't cry. You never cry."

"Oh, Papa!" was all she could manage. She put her head against his chest and clung to him.

He patted her hair as if she were still a small child. His voice sounded bewildered. "About the dress—I don't like it, but it isn't important enough to cry about."

While he continued to caress her, Margarida controlled her voice enough for a muffled "It isn't the dress."

"What then?" His hand stilled, and he said suspiciously, "Has anybody said anything to you?"

Her father's comfort and a kind of healing irony began to soothe Margarida's pain. He might rail at her, but no one else had better do the same. She wiped away her tears. "No, Papa," she lied, "nobody said anything bad to me," then added truthfully, "about the dress."

"Too much dancing," he grumbled. "Party's breaking up now, and it's about time. We'll find your mother and get our things. We're going to stay with the Welleses tonight."

The Welleses—Priscilla's family. "Why aren't we staying with the Franklins as usual?" Margarida protested. During her two school winters in town, she'd boarded with the Franklins, and she felt at home with them.

Jesse took her arm and started back. "Mrs. Frankin's been sick, and Nat Welles offered to put us up. Come on—the music's stopped."

What terrible luck, Margarida brooded. The last person she wanted to see or listen to was Priscilla Welles. They'd never gotten along, and Margarida didn't want to be reminded of how much she'd acted like Priscilla tonight.

When they reached the entrance of the hall, people were already pouring out, following the bride and groom. The place where the newlyweds would stay was supposed to be a secret to prevent a shivaree but from the high-spirited calls as the bridal buggy drove away, Margarida guessed the bride and groom would have a disturbed night. Jesse soon found Elena, but J.J. had disappeared, probably with the other young men.

Margarida groaned to herself when their surrey reached the modest Welles house, one of the older adobes. She had to smother even more dismay when she found she was to share a room and a bed with Priscilla. The tall, slightly overweight girl seemed pleased with the arrangement. Her rather pale face, surrounded by light brown curls, looked more animated and prettier than usual.

Silently Margarida followed the other girl to a small

bedroom. The three older daughters of the family no longer lived at home, which left one bedroom for Jesse and Elena and this one for her and Priscilla. J.J., if he ever showed up, would bunk with the hired man in a room off the stable.

The bed, with a patchwork quilt, took up one corner of the room. Under the single window an elaborate walnut washstand looked like a rich aunt disdainful of its simple surroundings. A lantern stood on a lace scarf on a dresser. Dresses hung on a row of pegs on the wall.

As Margarida removed her clothes and slipped into a chemise, she half-listened to Priscilla's chatter about the dance and dancers, providing only a "yes" or "no" when necessary. She had just climbed into the far side of the bed when a name caught her attention. "Funny you didn't dance at all with Brant Curtis," Priscilla was saying. "I danced with him twice."

Margarida pulled the cover over her head, but that didn't shut out Priscilla's high and penetrating voice. "He's such a good dancer. He's so . . ." Priscilla gave a suggestive giggle. "So exciting."

Under the covers, Margarida put her hands over her ears. She wanted to scream, "Don't talk about him— don't even say his name again," but she clamped her lips shut.

When Margarida didn't respond, Priscilla pulled at the blanket. Her voice had a sly edge. "Tell me about him. You know him really well. What's he like?"

Realizing the futility of hiding, Margarida sat up slowly. She could feel the flush on her face, but she was proud of how indifferent she sounded. "I've hardly seen him for three years. I don't know him at all anymore." Determinedly she lay down again and turned her back to Priscilla. What she'd said was true—she didn't know this Brant anymore, and she didn't want to.

She heard Priscilla's huffy "Well!" Then the lantern

light went out, and the bed sagged as Priscilla joined her. Hoping Priscilla would think she'd gone to sleep, Margarida tried to make her breathing even. But in the darkness she heard Priscilla whisper, "You don't like me, do you?"

Startled, Margarida lay still, unable to think of an answer. Priscilla's words rushed on, her voice soft but unmistakably bitter. "I know you've never liked me. But then, why should you bother? You have everything."

Margarida turned over, no longer pretending to be asleep. "I don't understand what you mean."

"Your father does anything you want. Buys you things. Sent you to a fancy school." Priscilla's voice began to tremble. "My father hates me. All he wanted was a boy, and he got three girls, and then me. He was sure God had promised him a boy when I was born. So he hates me."

Distressed, Margarida found Priscilla's hand and squeezed it gently, wanting to comfort the other girl. "You must be mistaken."

"No, I'm not. He's told me so, lots of times."

"Maybe he just gets mad at you," Margarida offered. "My father gets angry at me often. He can sound terrible when he does, but he doesn't really mean it."

Priscilla laughed, but with bitterness, not amusement. Though she was a year younger than Margarida, her voice could have been a decade older. "It doesn't matter, because I'm getting out of here as soon as I can. I'll go away. Someone will take me."

She didn't seem to expect any further comment, and Margarida turned over again. She lay quietly, glad to think about Priscilla instead of her own lacerated feelings. How mistaken she'd been about Priscilla. What had seemed artificial and forward was probably a desperate effort to escape from a father she was convinced hated her. Margarida could hardly imagine what that would be like, and she felt sympathy for Priscilla.

How many more people were different from the way she'd thought they were? she wondered. It was a long time before she could go to sleep.

When Margarida woke, the house was quiet. Beside her Priscilla snored faintly. Judging by the gray light seeping through the window, Margarida decided it must be very early. Everyone would sleep later than usual this morning. This was her chance to sneak away and see Adela.

As soon as the thought entered Margarida's mind, she slid out from the covers and down over the end of the bed. It had always been her way to act on impulse; she hated putting off anything. Besides, she reasoned as she pulled on her traveling dress, she could be out and back before anyone else was awake.

No one appeared when she tiptoed through the kitchen and ran softly out to the stable. J.J.'s horse stood in one of the stalls, with his saddle and blanket hung nearby. In a few minutes she had the mare saddled and outside by the fence. Hiking up her skirt and petticoat, she mounted, then pulled the full skirt down as far as she could so that only her high boots showed.

The dawn air was cool but not uncomfortable. Birds called softly from the cottonwoods beside the river. The dew-wet grass smelled fresh and sharp. At Adela's house Margarida dismounted and tied her horse to a post in back.

She went around to the side and tapped on the bedroom window. Adela's sleepy face appeared, first surprised, then pleased, before vanishing. Margarida went to the back entrance, and in a moment Adela opened the door.

"Whatever are you doing here?" she asked as she drew Margarida inside the room that was both kitchen and living room.

"We came to the wedding yesterday afternoon and stayed over. I woke early and came to see you."

"Does your father know?" Adela began to stir up a fire on the hearth.

"No, I left before anyone else was awake." Margarida hugged Adela and then sat down on a wooden bench beside a scarred table.

Adela put a pot of water over the fire and shook her head at Margarida. "*El pez que busca anzuelo, busca su duelo.*"

The fish that looks for the hook, looks for his funeral. Margarida had heard that warning before about not looking for trouble. "I'll go back before anyone knows I'm gone. I just had to find out how you are."

"Well, you can see." Adela laughed and spread her arms wide. "Good as ever."

Adela did look almost as she used to. Her face had lost most of the strained lines, and the scar on her arm was already less noticeable. Margarida waited while Adela ground coffee and chocolate and added them, along with a cinnamon stick, to the boiling water. She got out cups and poured sweetened milk into them, then filled them with the chocolate-and-coffee mixture. She gave a steaming cup to Margarida and then sat on the opposite bench. "How are you getting along, Margarida?"

"Oh, just as usual." For once, Margarida couldn't confide in Adela. The wounds Brant had left were still too fresh. "What are you doing now?"

"I have a job at the Imperial Saloon."

"The Imperial!"

"Yes, serving drinks in the bar."

Shocked, Margarida stared down at her cup. She'd heard about the women who worked in the saloon— bad women, who also worked in the bedrooms upstairs. Would Adela do that?

Adela laughed. "Margarida, you should see your face. I know what you're thinking." Her laugh faded, and she added, "I need the money, but not so much I'd sell myself."

Margarida, ashamed of her moment of suspicion, could feel the heat rising from under her collar up to her ears. "It sounds like an interesting job," she said loyally. Curiosity prompted a question. "What's it like?"

"Not too bad." Adela's eyes sparkled with a familiar warmth, one which Margarida had always admired. "A few of the men try to take liberties, but most of them just joke with me. And it pays good money."

Her face sobered and she looked at Margarida as if trying to decide about something. Finally she said, "It's a good thing you're not chasing after Brant Curtis anymore."

In spite of her determination not to talk about Brant, Margarida couldn't help asking, "Why do you say that?"

"At the Imperial I hear all the town gossip. Some people think that the last few years he's been acting too much like an Indian."

"But he's mostly white," Margarida protested. "Except for the color of his hair, he hardly looks Indian." She didn't know why it seemed so important, but she didn't want to think of Brant as Apache.

Adela looked unconvinced. "People have heard about what he's doing on his father's land, letting the Apache stay there. Anyway, I'm glad you haven't seen him lately. Men around here don't like white girls who act interested in Indian men. I've heard talk about a girl who lives just outside town. Maybe you know her. Mabel something."

"Mabel Webster. Yes, I remember her."

"According to gossip in the bar, she's taken up with a half-breed Indian who works for some horse traders. Some men have been threatening to do something about it."

"That's terrible," Margarida said indignantly. "They have no right to interfere in someone else's life, no matter what Mabel's doing."

Even as she protested, she remembered a time when she was ten or eleven. She'd gone with her father to one of the large trading fairs in Santa Fe and had seen lots of Indians. Many of them looked dirty and ignorant, and some of the men had been drunk in the middle of the day. Of course, they were humans with rights, not animals as some whites said. She believed they should be treated fairly. But they were certainly unattractive, nothing like Brant. She wondered how Mabel Webster could have anything to do with a man like them.

The light from the window beside the fireplace was growing stronger and she realized she couldn't stay much longer. "When is Miguel's trial?"

"Not for another month."

"I'll come into town and go to court with you that day," Margarida decided. "Can you let me know when you find out the date?"

"Yes," Adela said doubtfully, "but your father won't—"

"I don't care!" Margarida rose and embraced her friend, leaning her head against the tangled black hair. "I must leave now, but I *will* be with you for the trial." Before Adela could protest again, Margarida kissed her quickly and left.

Adela was right, Margarida thought as she mounted, that Papa would oppose her attending Miguel's trial. He'd be even more disapproving of Adela now that she worked in a saloon. He didn't know Margarida still saw Adela, so it wouldn't occur to him that Margarida would go to the trial. If he did, he'd certainly forbid it, but he wouldn't know. He'd see her there that day and be furious, but then it would be too late to stop her, only punish her.

As she rode toward the Welleses' house, she saw people stirring. A man in ragged overalls ambled toward a stable, and a woman carried milk pails across another yard. Margarida nudged J.J.'s roan to a faster pace, hoping no one was up at the Welleses'. When she arrived, the house was still. She unsaddled the horse and was back in the living room without hearing or seeing anyone.

Through the window she watched the clouds in the eastern sky turn from pink to salmon and finally to gold. It made her think of mornings when she and J.J. had ridden out early on expeditions of all kinds. Halfway to the Curtis ranch, Walt would be waiting for them beside a boulder that had a pine tree growing from its center—their special meeting place.

She almost wanted to cry again, and she realized she was feeling both wounded by Brant's accusation and grieved at the thought of losing Walt. Just because Brant told her to stay away from his brother, she reminded herself, didn't mean she had to. Walt was still her friend. She'd never flirted with him, and she'd be careful not to.

From years of observing Brant, she knew once he decided on a course of action, he seldom changed his mind. Probably he wouldn't relent about not wanting Walt to see her, but she wouldn't give in either.

Low voices from another room told her others were awake, and she returned to the bedroom she'd shared with Priscilla. Opening the door quietly, she saw that the younger girl was dressed and standing by the chest of drawers, brushing her hair. Priscilla glanced up, then quickly looked away, her pale face flushing pink.

"Good morning," Margarida said. "I've been outside."

Priscilla continued brushing silently before she finally turned toward Margarida. Her voice trembled, but her eyes looked defiant. "I guess you think I'm stupid, saying those things to you last night."

"No, I don't think that at all. It just . . . makes me feel I know you better."

A tentative smile softened the girl's anxious face, and Margarida found herself genuinely smiling in return and giving Priscilla an impulsive hug. "Maybe you can ride out to the ranch sometime to visit."

Priscilla's smile faded. "Papa wouldn't let me."

"Then I'll come here."

The smile returned and Priscilla's eyes sparkled. "Oh, yes. I'd love that."

Later, as Margarida observed Nat Welles during breakfast, she noticed that his broad face had a look of irritation whenever he glanced at Priscilla. His voice, when he spoke to his daughter, sounded contemptuous, and once when she dropped a serving spoon he said angrily, "Drat it, girl, can't you do anything right?"

When the Ross family was leaving, Margarida gave Priscilla a last hug. "I'll visit you soon."

As Margarida took a seat beside her mother in the surrey, she thought that Priscilla and Lee Hansen might suit each other. At the dance Lee had been eager to see Margarida again. She'd have to arrange a meeting and include Priscilla. And visiting Priscilla, Margarida suddenly realized, would also provide a reason to be in Rio Torcido for Miguel's trial. She laughed aloud.

"How can you be so cheerful this early?" Elena grumbled.

"Sorry, Mama." Remembering her mother's habit of sleeping late, Margarida settled back in the wagon, still smiling to herself. She'd get back for Miguel's trial, and somehow, she felt sure, she'd see Walt again.

Her smile faded as she thought of Brant. The memory she'd been denying flooded over her—of his face above hers last night beside the creek. The shivery feeling returned, and her breasts tingled as they had when he'd caressed her. She felt again the warm excitement deep in her belly.

She sat up straighter. No—she wouldn't think of last night. Instead she concentrated on Adela's comments. Margarida still didn't understand why Brant insisted on calling himself an Indian. He didn't look anything like the Indians in Santa Fe. Most of them were

Comanches from the eastern plains or Pueblos from the pueblos along the Rio Grande, but they looked almost the same to her. Probably his Apache relatives looked like them too. Certainly the few Indians she'd seen occasionally around Rio Torcido were poor and shabby. Brant said he admired them; maybe they'd lived a better life a long time ago, but from what she'd seen, they didn't live a good life now.

Well, Adela needn't worry about her and Brant. Even if he hadn't been so hateful to her, she told herself, she'd been foolish to think she wanted to marry a man who cared more about the Apache than anything else.

5

BRANT knelt beside the naked body of the dead man. For a moment he feared he would be sick. The corpse lay sprawled beside a creosote bush in the September sun, arms and legs twisted at grotesque angles. Cuts crossed bloody lash marks on the chest. Blows had crushed the face. Only a gaping wound remained where the genitals had once been.

He rose and stumbled to one side, leaning against Chid's flank, forcing his churning stomach to subside. He'd seen mutilated bodies before, but he'd never become used to that kind of cruelty.

The buzzards which had attracted his attention to the body circled overhead. "Get away, you bloody bastards," he screamed. A rock lay at his feet. He picked it up and hurled it at the birds in a futile effort to rid himself of his horror.

From behind him he heard hoofbeats and then Walt's alarmed voice. "Brant! What's the matter?"

Brant slowly turned back to the mutilated body. Walt dismounted and joined him. "What is it?"

"It was a man—once."

"What happened to him?" Walt sounded more curious than upset, and for once Brant was grateful for his brother's limited understanding.

"I don't know." He knelt again, forcing himself to examine the body more closely. The black hair was coarse, the skin bronze. Indian hair and skin. Brant could taste the bitter anger that filled him.

"Do you know him?" Walt asked.

Brant saw something he recognized. One torn ear still held an earring—silver with three turquoise chips in a triangular pattern. He remembered where he'd seen it—on a young half-breed who'd drifted into Rio Torcido a few months ago. "He worked at the stable on the south side of town near Dale Webster's place."

There was no blood on the ground near the body, so he'd been killed elsewhere. Questions churned in Brant's mind. Whoever tortured and killed this man had brought the body out to Curtis land. Near the road to town, but beyond the "Curtis Ranch" sign. Why had this poor Indian, who'd always seemed harmless, been so brutally murdered? And then left here?

Walt stared at the body. "What are you going to do, Brant? Are you going to take him to the doctor?"

'No, Walt. He's dead, and the doctor can't help him." And it wouldn't do any good to tell the sheriff, Brant thought bitterly. The death of an Indian never got any attention. No one would question what had happened to him, or even care. Rage gripped Brant so strongly that he had to hold himself stiff to keep from shaking. "We'll dig a grave and bury him."

"Can I do it?" Walt loved digging holes. At Brant's nod, he went to his horse and was soon back with a shovel. They carried the body up the hillside, to a spot where the grave would face east.

While Walt dug in the claylike soil, Brant went back to the place where the body had been and studied the surrounding area. He could see hoofprints from five different horses. Almost buried in the dirt he found a piece of leather, the end of a cinch strap which had apparently broken. It had a tooled design of interweaving lines with "CB" in the center. Brant felt his stomach clench again, this time with fury. Carl Bodmer, a rancher who owned large holdings south of Rio Torcido, had the most expensive and showy equipment around. Where his saddles weren't encrusted with silver, he used leather decorated with his brand, even for straps such as these.

Brant stood holding the piece of leather and forced himself to think rationally. Then he remembered something he'd overheard at the wedding dance a month ago. Willis Henderson, an elderly, excitable man, had been talking. He was a good friend of Carl Bodmer's and thought whatever Bodmer told him to think. Brant had been walking past just when Willis said to a group of men, "If Dale Webster can't keep his girl in line, we'll see to it. No half-breed Indian's going to—" Then Willis had seen Brant, and he'd stopped abruptly.

"Brant, I'm finished."

At Walt's call Brant started up the hill, his black rage building until he could hardly draw air into his lungs. Everything in him cried out to kill the men who'd done this.

Why had they dumped the body here? The answer caught him in mid-stride. A warning to him! To let him see how even a part-Indian could be treated. A warning to act like the white man he was supposed to be.

He'd say nothing to his father about the murder. They'd never been able to talk about the things that were most important to him, and the last few months Rupert hadn't been well. In any case, this was a problem Brant would take care of himself.

It wouldn't be hard to find out who the murderers were, especially since he had an idea about two of them. When he did, they'd learn that he might look white, but part of his soul was Indian.

A week later Brant squatted beside his grandmother in the customary position of Apache men that enabled them to jump up instantly in case of danger. Since he was alone with her in her wickiup, he'd persuaded her to sit on the one stool. Usually she insisted on giving it to him and sitting on the hides spread on the ground.

He wanted to supply more comforts for her, but she refused.

He studied her strong face affectionately; it looked impossibly old and wrinkled, though she couldn't be over sixty now. He'd been six when his father had left him with a family in Socorro and gone to England. Later Brant had realized his father hadn't wanted his family to see his part-Indian son. Until he was eight and his father returned with his new wife, Brant had spent summers with his grandmother. She'd looked the same then.

Her Apache name, Ha-na-sba ekaiye, meant "She-Returns-From-War-With-Her-Children." It was given to her after she and her two daughters had been recaptured from her Mexican husband and returned to the band, but Brant always thought of her just as *shiwóyé*, "grandmother." She seemed more fragile than usual to him today, perhaps because her black eyes appeared uneasy.

He asked, "Does something trouble you today?"

She touched his cheek tenderly. "You see too well, my daughter's son. Yes, I worry about your brothers."

Brant wondered what the sons of his aunt had been doing. They were only fourteen and fifteen, and he'd noticed that they'd been sullen and reluctant to talk to him recently. "Please tell me of your worries."

Her worn-looking fingers tapped restlessly against the folds of her calico skirt. "They do not want to hunt within the area you have decreed. They say the best game is on what you call Ross land. The husband of your mother's sister lets them wander too far."

Then they must resent me, Brant thought. They probably considered him a white who shouldn't be able to dictate their activities. They were old enough to be hotheaded but too young to appreciate the realities of white power. "I understand your worry, and I know you will help them to be wise," was all the reassurance he could offer.

He must approach Jesse Ross, try to make him understand that it would be to his ultimate benefit to allot a place in these valleys for Indians to live. They were excellent hunters and kept down the bear and mountain lions that preyed on the cattle. Thank God, Brant thought, he'd resisted Margarida. At least Jesse had nothing personal against him now.

"And you, my daughter's son—I can see that you also have troubles."

Startled, he avoided looking directly at her. The young murdered Indian had been on his mind even more vividly since he'd come to this mountain camp today. He wouldn't tell her about the murder; she had enough worries already.

After three nights in the saloons of Rio Torcido, Brant was sure that Carl Bodmer and Willis Henderson had been two of the murderers and Bodmer undoubtedly the leader. Two of the others were men who worked for Bodmer. He hadn't been able to learn the identity of the fifth.

Brant tried to put those thoughts from his mind and searched for an answer for his grandmother. "I have lost my sweetheart, so I am sad."

His unplanned words surprised him, as did the vivid image of Margarida's face which came to his mind at the same time. Good God, why had he said that? He could feel heat flush his face, and he knew from his grandmother's laughter that it showed.

"Oh, ho," she teased, "finally you are thinking of a wife and children. But don't worry, even with your ugly looks you can get another sweetheart."

"Maybe an Apache wife," he said.

Her face sobered. "No—not for you. You are a good man, but not Apache. You are too much white."

Brant rose, more wounded by her words than he wanted her to know. Even after he told her good-bye and left, the hurt remained, although he knew she loved him and said only what she thought best for him. Perhaps she was right that he wouldn't get along with an Apache wife; he'd been raised as a white, not an Apache. But he was enough Indian to avenge the murdered man who'd been left on Curtis land.

When Margarida and J.J. rode their horses out of the corral, a peach-colored glow in the sky promised that the sun would soon be up. As they started along the trail for Rio Torcido, a breeze lifted the edge of her sombrero. Because of a mid-September hot spell, she'd soon have to unbutton the cuffs of her long-sleeved white blouse, then adjust her skirt for more air around her legs. How inconvenient, she thought impatiently, to have to be a "lady." Around the ranch she often wore pants under her skirt so she could ride astride.

After their horses settled into a smooth gait, J.J. said, "How did you persuade Papa to agree to this trip?"

"I'm going to visit Priscilla Welles. When we were at the wedding last month, I told her I'd come to see her."

"Not Willing Welles?" J.J. looked astonished. "But you've never liked her."

"I found out she's nicer than I thought. And what do you mean, Willing Welles?"

A flush spread over J.J.'s fair skin. "Sorry. That just slipped out. You know how she is—any man around can get his hand inside her dress."

Margarida glared at J.J. "How do you know?" She was irritated at his unkindness and ashamed that she'd recently been uncharitable enough to think the same thing.

"I haven't tried anything with her," he responded huffily, "but I hear the talk."

"That's so unfair. A man can do what he likes. If a girl encourages him at all, then she gets blamed."

"All right—I'm sorry. Why are you her champion now?"

Partly mollified, she explained, "Priscilla needs a friend, and I like her. And Lee Hansen's going to call on me at her house this afternoon."

"Lee Hansen!" J.J. nudged his horse over beside Margarida and peered into her face. "You must be sick."

She had to laugh at the mock concern on his face. "Stop it. You'll upset Halcon." As if to confirm her warning, the ears of her chestnut gelding rose and he shied away from J.J.'s roan.

Margarida snapped the reins, and Halcon broke into a gallop. She let him run to the top of the next rise to calm his high spirits. His name was the Spanish word for "hawk" because when she rode him at top speed, she seemed to be soaring like the red-tailed hawks she admired. Brant, with his fierce independence, also reminded her of one of those birds, and it was he who'd been patient with her first efforts at riding. So in a way Halcon was named for Brant.

When they pulled back to a slower pace, J.J. said, "So that's why Papa agreed to let you come—he hopes you're interested in somebody besides Brant. Why Lee Hansen? You never had any use for him before."

She didn't need to warn him not to say anything to Papa. They'd never told on each other, even when one of them was punished for what the other had done. "I hope Lee will like Priscilla. I don't want him for myself, but Papa doesn't know that. And I want to see Adela before I go to the Welleses'."

"Well, good luck, but even Lee's probably heard about Priscilla. Sorry—I won't say that again. Any reason to get off the ranch suits me."

Margarida remembered the morning he'd slammed out of the breakfast room complaining about the work. It was hard for her to believe he wouldn't love the ranch. "Don't you like working on the ranch anymore, J.J.?"

He usually looked boyish, but now the set of his mouth showed an adult determination. "What fun is there in that? It's always the same thing. Papa had plenty of adventures in Texas and California, but he thinks I should just stay around here. Well, someday I'm leaving."

Though Margarida couldn't imagine anywhere she'd love as much as right where she was, she understood J.J.'s desire to see other places. If she hadn't gone east to school, she'd probably feel the same. "Where would you like to go?"

"California. You can still find plenty of gold there. After a while I'd be rich. Then I'd go everywhere."

A wild turkey flew clumsily up from the brush at the side of the trail, and Margarida had to keep her attention on Halcon. She didn't like the idea of J.J.'s going away, and she didn't want to talk about it longer.

She thought of what he'd said about Priscilla and about Adela's reputation. It reminded her of last Christmas in Connecticut when she'd let her friend's brother touch her breasts, and she wondered whether he'd bragged about it afterward. Did all men discuss girls freely?

No—not all men. No matter how much she hated Brant, she was sure he wouldn't ever say anything about her to anyone else. Her face still burned when she remembered how stupidly she'd behaved with him, but at least she didn't fear the humiliation of people whispering about her.

J.J. and Margarida arrived at the edge of Rio Torcido well before noon and stopped in front of Adela's house, but no one was home. "Adela must be at work," Margarida said, dismayed, "and I need to know the date of Miguel's trial. Please, J.J., will you go to the Imperial and ask her?"

"So she's working there! Why do you want to know?"

"I'm going to the trial with her."

J.J. whistled. "You better think that over, Margarida. Papa would be furious, and for once I agree with him."

His reproach shocked Margarida. "But Adela's been my friend for years!"

"That was when she was hired help on our ranch. Her reputation was bad enough then, but now she's working in a saloon—it'll be worse. I can go along with a visit at her house, but if you're seen with her at the courthouse, it looks bad for you too."

Angrily she retorted, "I know all that, but it doesn't matter. I have to go anyway."

He shrugged. "All right. I'll ask Adela and meet you at the Welleses' later." He put his horse into a lope in the direction of the saloon.

As she rode on, Margarida felt flat with disappointment. She missed Adela's love and cheerful spirits on the ranch, and had looked forward to seeing her. Also she resented J.J.'s scolding when she'd expected his support. Uncomfortably, she recognized he was right that people in Rio Torcido would disapprove of her association with a saloon woman with a loose reputation. But friendship meant more to her than that.

When Margarida reached the Welleses' house, she greeted Mrs. Welles, then took off her jacket and settled in a wicker chair in the deliciously cool living room. Priscilla welcomed her as if they'd always been friends.

As soon as Mrs. Welles left the room, Priscilla asked, "Did you hear about Mabel Webster?"

Margarida remembered that Mabel was the girl Adela had mentioned, the one who'd been interested in a mixed-blood Indian man. Not sure she wanted to hear more, Margarida said only, "No."

"Her parents had to send her away, back to Alabama to stay with relatives. They found out she'd been secretly meeting an Indian man. A half-breed. Imagine that."

At the disapproval in Priscilla's expression, Margarida felt uncomfortable that she'd had similar thoughts about Indians herself. Her irritation made her voice sharp. "Maybe he's a good man. And it's not our business."

"Well!" Priscilla looked startled. "Other people don't think so. And I guess the Indian must have known it wasn't right, because he's disappeared."

Margarida reminded herself Priscilla was only saying what most whites thought, but she preferred to change the subject. "Lee Hansen would like to call here this afternoon. Would that be all right?"

Pleasure and envy struggled for expression on Priscilla's face. "Of course. What are you going to wear? Did you bring something else?"

Margarida looked down at her white cotton blouse and untrimmed blue skirt. It was plain, but she didn't want to outdo Priscilla today. "No, I didn't."

Priscilla's excitement was too great for her to contain; she jumped up. "Come help me decide."

Margarida helped Priscilla choose a white muslin with blue and brown flowers which made her pale blue eyes and light brown hair seem an extension of the dress. Then she arranged Priscilla's hair in soft curls at the sides. By the time Lee Hansen arrived, Priscilla was flushed with color and looked prettier than usual.

Soon Margarida's hopes for Lee and Priscilla began to fade. Lee's conversation hadn't improved, and he kept his cow-eyed look firmly on Margarida. Priscilla's mouth took on a resigned sadness. Even Mrs. Welles, whose initial excitement had resulted in a pitcher of lemonade and an overflowing plate of molasses cookies, seemed discouraged.

Margarida knew that J.J. would arrive soon and decided she must do something. Taking her half-full glass of lemonade, she let her hand wobble so that the sugary liquid tipped over into her lap. She sprang up, the shock of the cold dousing lending realism to her actions, almost precipitating a "Damn!" that she barely managed to turn into "Dear me!"

Lee was on his feet immediately, his hand holding out a napkin, then frozen in midair by the impropriety of offering to wipe that particular portion of Margarida's clothing. "Oh, how careless of me," Margarida exclaimed. "Mrs. Welles, I'm so sorry. Could you help me, please?"

Holding her dripping skirt away from her legs, Margarida went into the bedroom and took off her skirt and petticoat. "Would you like to wear one of Priscilla's dresses?" Mrs. Welles asked. "It would be too large for you, but you'd be welcome."

"Thank you. I'm sure I can manage if I can just get this a little dry." Margarida smiled at Mrs. Welles; she looked as if a beetle could frighten her, but she probably did the best she could with Nat Welles for a husband.

Margarida was pleased that it took a long time to rinse and then blot her skirt dry enough to put on. When she and Mrs. Welles returned to the living room, Priscilla was showing Lee pictures in an album and looking pretty again.

When J.J. came for Margarida, Lee insisted on leaving also, but he sounded reluctant, and he smiled encouragingly at Priscilla. Margarida felt hopeful that a romance might develop.

She barely waited until she and J.J. had started to ask, "Did you talk to Adela?"

"Yes. The circuit judge will be here in two weeks, and since Miguel has been in jail almost two months, his case will be on the first day."

J.J. began to hum, and Margarida decided from his flushed face that he'd been drinking. "You sound pretty happy," she remarked.

"Had a few drinks after I talked to Adela. I met a man who just got back from California. You should have seen the nugget he had on his watch chain—as big as your thumb. Plenty more there, for anyone to go and find. Mines aren't all grabbed up, like the ones here."

Her pleasure in the day disappeared. She wanted to hold on to him and shout "No," but restrained herself to saying, "Men also die out there looking for gold." His silly grin told her he wasn't going to listen.

Since she had come back from school, everything had changed. Walt was the only real friend from her growing-up years who was the same. She needed him— his friendship and the good feelings she had when she was with him. She couldn't give him up too.

Getting back to Rio Torcido for Miguel's trial turned out to be simple. Three *comancheros*, men who traded with the Comanche of eastern New Mexico, were bringing horses to town to sell the same Monday the circuit-court session opened. Jesse Ross was going, and he agreed to take Margarida with him so she could see the horses. They would go to town the Sunday afternoon before the sale and court opening and stay overnight, her father with the Franklins, and Margarida with the Welleses.

"You want to stay with the Welleses again?" Papa asked.

'Yes—Lee's going to call there in the evening."

Her father gave her a perplexed look as he said, "Well, the Hansens are a good family."

Margarida guessed Brant and Walt would be in town also, and she would probably have a chance to talk to Walt. He was crazy about horses, and Brant wouldn't let him go to the sale alone. She would avoid Brant and watch for Walt and arrange a meeting with him. Brant couldn't guard his brother every moment. As she thought about the possibility, her excitement grew. She'd seldom been able to resist the challenge of doing something forbidden. That Brant had done the forbidding only increased her anticipation.

She decided to wear a russet dress on the ride to town and pack a green sprigged muslin and a straw hat with a green ribbon for the following day. The hat had a becoming droop to the front of its wide brim. The muslin had puffed sleeves, a flowing skirt, and ruffles around the high neckline. It enhanced her dark coloring and made her look proper but very feminine. That seemed important when she would accompany Adela and also . . . if she met anyone.

When Margarida thought about her promise to be with Adela at the trial, she felt her skin tighten with apprehension. Facing the disapproval of the townspeople didn't worry her; she'd resigned herself to that. But Papa could get violently angry. She'd seen him once whip a ranch hand who'd mistreated a horse. The worst he'd done to her, she reassured herself, was send her away to school, and he couldn't do that again. Papa would be in court to testify, and he'd see her there, but she'd face his anger then.

Elena didn't want to go into Rio Torcido, and she insisted that J.J. stay home while her husband was away. The new foreman wasn't used to his job, and she didn't believe she'd be safe without one of the Ross men near. J.J. protested, but Elena became almost hysterical, and he had to stay behind. Margarida felt sorry for him. She'd always known that J.J. was more special to their mother than she was, but she'd been glad not to be the focus of her mother's concern. The intensity of her mother's feelings made Margarida uneasy. Besides, she'd also known she was her father's favorite.

On the trip to town Margarida and her father rode companionably together, and she enjoyed the feeling of closeness with him. "Papa, tell me about your early life, before you and Mama married." She'd heard some of his stories before, but she liked to hear them again. "J.J. says you had lots of adventures."

Jesse snorted. "J.J. thinks it was all glory, but it wasn't. My father was killed in an Indian raid in Texas. After that it was poor farming and no fun."

Margarida knew that part. "But how did you come here?"

"In 1841 I figured I'd done my duty at home and I joined a bunch of Texans who were headed for New Mexico to do some trading."

"Were you a trader, Papa?"

He flashed her his handsome grin which reminded her so of J.J. "I wanted money and adventure. I was eighteen years old, and I hadn't had enough of either one." His grin disappeared, and he rode silently, as if remembering things he preferred to forget.

"What happened when you got here?"

"Maybe it would be good for you to know," he said, more to himself than to her. "Some men surprised us on the trail. Mostly half-breeds, and led by a half-breed. He persuaded one of our so-called leaders that if we threw in with them he'd show us where to find the best goods. Waited until he got the drop on us and took our guns."

A grim look matched his bitter-sounding voice. "Those breeds weren't happy just to kill. They loved torture. The breed in charge laughed all the while. They got drunk and decided to save me for the next day's fun. One man was still sober. He was halfway decent and tired of the rest. I had some money hidden, and I bribed him to let me go."

Margarida felt almost sick. "Papa! How horrible!"

"It's what I've tried to tell you, Margarida. Breeds are the worst of both races."

She realized his experience had scarred him, but she couldn't accept his conclusion. "Brant's not like that."

"Brant's all right as a neighbor. Maybe Rupert was lucky. But it was a fluke. Blood shouldn't mix."

Margarida wanted to protest again, but she saw it would be useless. "What did you do after that?"

"I met Rupert. We did some mining together. I went on to California and made out all right. Got rich and got married. After you were born, we came here to settle."

Margarida was glad J.J. wasn't along to hear the part about California. "How did you get rich, Papa?"

His face stiffened. "You ask too many questions," he said and urged his horse abruptly forward. Surprised, Margarida followed. She was curious, but she knew he wouldn't say more.

By the time they reached Rio Torcido, late-afternoon clouds were piling up on the western horizon, threatening a sudden evening shower. As they rode toward the Welleses' house, her father paused to speak to several friends. She watched the men passing, wondering whether Brant and Walt were already in town, and trying not to notice that her heart was beating faster as she looked for them.

"Miss Ross, I'm very pleased to see you," someone said in a southern drawl.

She turned to face a young man smiling at her from the saddle of a rangy gray horse. He wore the blue shirt, red kerchief, and denim pants of a cowboy. His light brown hair was thick and tousled, falling forward over a face that was too bony to be handsome, but looked as if he laughed a lot.

He laughed now as he said, "I do believe you don't remember me. I'm Enoch Springer."

Now she did. He had a small ranch south of town and was several years older than she. They'd danced at parties before she went away to school. His name had never seemed to fit him; he was just medium height, and somehow she expected an "Enoch" to be tall.

"Good afternoon, Mr. Ross." After her father's nod, he looked at her. "May I ride along with you?"

She smiled warmly at him; he'd always been light-hearted and fun. "Yes, of course, Enoch. Now I remember, but it's been a long time since we saw each other."

"Not a good excuse," he said as he turned his horse to walk beside hers. "I couldn't forget you. I was sorry I didn't get to the wedding here in town last month. I heard you were there." His admiring glance lingered a fraction of a moment on her breasts.

Margarida felt her face flushing at the thought that her dress might have been discussed afterward. Hastily she said, "Yes, I'm sorry too. How is your ranch?"

"Too small to count as a ranch around here," he said. His pride showed as he added, "I manage, though. You in town to see the horses?"

They had reached the Welleses' house. "Yes, I am. I'm staying here, so I'll have to say good-bye now."

He looked disappointed. "I would surely enjoy seeing you again, Miss Ross."

Impulsively she said, "Perhaps you might like to call on us this evening. I'm sure Mrs. Welles would be pleased to have you." She knew she should ask Mrs. Welles first, but the prospect of having a more animated companion than Lee was irresistible.

"Miss Ross, I would be delighted." He turned to Jesse, who looked a little surprised. "If that would be agreeable with you, sir."

"Why, yes." Jesse waited until Enoch had ridden on to say, "I thought you were seeing Lee Hansen."

"Nothing serious about that, and Enoch Springer is pleasant." Her father shook his head, as if to protest that he didn't understand her.

Margarida kissed him warmly. "I'll be ready early to go to see the horses with you," she promised, and watched him ride off. She was lucky, she decided, to have a father like him instead of Nat Welles, even if Papa had sent her away to school. And if he weren't too angry tomorrow.

As Margarida had supposed, Mrs. Welles approved of having Enoch Springer come to call. Priscilla was

delighted to see Margarida and was prettier than before. Her skin had a flush that made her pale eyes
sparkle, and she'd arranged her hair in soft curls around
her face. Even her figure looked more slender and
graceful.

Lee Hansen arrived soon after supper and Enoch
Springer immediately after him. To Margarida's relief,
the looks Lee gave Priscilla suggested her scheme for
them had already worked. No need for a lapful of
lemonade tonight.

Enoch entertained them with stories about becoming entangled in his own lariat or running from an
insulted bull. Margarida didn't believe he could be so
inept and manage even a small ranch. He didn't make
her heart beat faster or her skin tingle, but she enjoyed his company and almost managed to avoid com-
parisons with Brant. When Enoch left, she wished him
a warm good-bye.

Priscilla and Lee lingered outside the front door of
the house, so Margarida was already in bed before
Priscilla came to undress and slip in beside her. She
was almost asleep when Priscilla whispered, "Are you
awake?"

"Yes, I'm awake."

"Do you like Lee?"

"Well—he's pleasant," Margarida evaded, "but I
don't *like* him in the way I think you mean."

Priscilla bounced up, dislodging the light cover over
them. "Oh, Margarida, I'm so glad. Because I like
him a lot. He came to see me once after you were here."

Margarida sat up and hugged the other girl. "That's
wonderful." She plumped her pillow and lay back to
listen to a description of Lee's marvelous attributes,
happy that this time she'd done something that turned
out right.

"Please, Brant, I want to go with you." Walt stood
beside the door of the boardinghouse room; the lan-

tern light showed an expression wavering between anxiety and hope.

Brant sat on the edge of the hard bed and stamped his foot into his boot, considering his alternatives. It was almost nine, late enough after supper for the saloons of Rio Torcido to be full. When he found the men he was looking for, he didn't want to have to worry about Walt. But he also hesitated to leave his brother behind alone, and the two Curtis ranch hands who'd come to town had disappeared.

"All right." He stood up and fastened on his gun belt. "You'll have to do exactly as I say," he warned.

"Yes, yes. I will." Walt's pleased face was rewarding if not reassuring. "Where are we going?"

"To the saloons, until we find the people I'm after," said Brant as he checked his gun. He didn't intend to use it, but he didn't want to be without a gun.

Brant's first impulse had been to kill Bodmer and Henderson. When he calmed down, he realized he couldn't risk being killed or going to prison. His people would be turned off the land, and Walt would be left on his own. So the confrontation with the killers had to stop at a beating, and had to seem to be provoked by the other man in case the man died from his injuries.

Willis Henderson was frail and old. It didn't exonerate him, but it made fighting him unpalatable. In his own mind Brant was sure that Carl Bodmer was the leader, so he would begin there. Bodmer outweighed Brant by fifty pounds, but he was twenty years older, and on his side Brant had three weeks of accumulated rage.

"Are we looking for friends?" Walt asked as he followed Brant down the hall and through the deserted room which served as lobby and dining room.

Brant stepped out into the dusty street. "No, Walt. The men I want to talk to aren't friends. That's why you must do whatever I tell you."

Walt looked perplexed, but he nodded.

Rose's Palace, a ramshackle old adobe whose appearance belied its name, was the closest saloon to the boardinghouse, so they stopped there first. Mostly the poorer cowboys and miners drank and gambled here. Brant didn't see Carl Bodmer or Willis Henderson, so he and Walt went on.

The Silver Lode proved similarly disappointing. Brant felt rage waiting in his stomach as he pushed open the frosted glass doors of the Imperial. He stepped inside and looked first along the bar at the left. Its solid cherry top, polished dark red, reflected scattered glasses and bottles. Three tall mirrors behind the bar held the faces of men leaning there, but not of the men he sought.

Beyond an arch to the right, groups of men sat drinking and gambling. Brant strolled through the arch as casually as if every muscle in his body were not as tight as stretched rawhide. Across the smoky room he saw the thick neck and bald head of Carl Bodmer. At the table with him were Willis Henderson and Jesse Ross.

Brant stopped as if someone had dropped a lariat over him. He felt the jar of Walt bumping into him, but his thoughts churned too fast to respond to Walt's "Sorry."

He felt almost as sick as when he'd found the young Indian's body. Could Margarida's father be the fifth murderer? No—Brant refused to believe that. Jesse Ross might not want his daughter paired with anyone with Indian blood, but he wasn't capable of that kind of torture. He just happened to be sitting with Bodmer and Henderson.

As Brant walked forward, every muscle in his legs felt ready to snap. He'd soon know about Jesse's participation.

"Good evening, Mr. Ross, Mr. Bodmer, Mr. Henderson." Brant hated to accord the courtesy of even the "Mr." to the two men he'd been looking for, but he needed to begin with the appearance of amiability.

Bodmer turned. His heavy face whitened and his neck muscles went rigid. Willis Henderson's head jerked up. His mouth thinned to a narrow line, and a muscle twitched just below his left eye.

"Brant, Walt, glad to see you. Pull up a chair and join us." Jesse sounded at ease, and his face held his usual smile.

Brant felt his muscles relax a fraction. Jesse hadn't been involved. "Thanks." He found two empty chairs nearby and positioned them so he sat directly across from Bodmer.

Adela came by, and Brant ordered whiskey for himself and Walt, knowing she would put mostly water in Walt's drink. When the drinks arrived, Brant took a sip, then let his glass stand in front of him. Tonight he didn't want his reactions clouded by alcohol.

Willis Henderson looked nervously at Carl Bodmer, but the heavier man didn't return the look. After a minute of uncomfortable silence, Jesse asked Brant, "You here for the court session or to buy horses?"

Brant felt his stomach tighten. He looked directly at Carl Bodmer. "To buy horses. I don't need to go to court for any justice I want done." Bodmer shifted uncomfortably in his chair, and his face flushed. His eyes showed he knew Brant was talking about the murdered Indian.

Jesse gave Brant a quizzical look, but only said, "Is Rupert with you? We need to talk about the fall roundup."

"No. My father hasn't been feeling well lately."

"Sorry to hear that. Tell him I'll be over."

Carl Bodmer spoke abruptly, his voice hoarse, as if he usually shouted. "I hear you have a bunch of hostiles living in one of those canyons, Curtis."

Brant looked steadily into the other man's eyes, taking his time about answering. He could see a mix-

ture of anger and fear in Bodmer's face, and it filled
him with a fierce elation. This was going to work out
as he'd planned.

Over the years he'd been in fights; a few he'd started.
He preferred to keep his temper and respond with
violence only when he couldn't avoid it. But he'd seen
men who had so much anger inside them that they
would explode over anything. He guessed that Carl
Bodmer was that way. Bodmer was already nervous.
It wouldn't take much to set him off.

Brant chose his answer carefully. "Yes, there are
Indians living on Curtis land, living peacefully, without bothering their neighbors." Before anyone else
could speak, he asked, "How are Mrs. Bodmer and
Harriet?"

As he expected, Bodmer's eyes narrowed and his
face flushed again at Brant's use of his daughter's
given name. He had to know he was being baited and
why, but Brant was counting on Bodmer's lack of
control. Brant continued smoothly, "I'd like to call on
your daughter if I may. When I saw her recently, she
indicated she wouldn't object."

Bodmer's face turned dark red. He stood up, knocking his chair over behind him, and lunged across the
table at Brant, scattering glasses and bottles to one
side. Brant felt a wild surge of joy as he shouted,
"Walt. Stay back," and braced himself for the assault.

He staggered back under Bodmer's weight, and then
released his fury. Each blow to Bodmer's face and
body avenged that mutilated corpse. The pain of bone
against bone was nothing compared to the savage exhilaration of seeing blood spurt from the face in front
of him.

A chair caught against the back of his legs. He
heard shouts, but he saw only Bodmer. He felt the
bones of Bodmer's nose crack against his fist. Blows
landed on his own face and body, but they only fueled
his lust for revenge. Bodmer slipped and fell to one
knee.

"Come on, Bodmer," Brant taunted. "Get up. We're not finished."

Through the haze of his own rage he saw fear and defeat in Bodmer's eyes, and wild exultation seized him. Bodmer struggled to his feet and lunged at Brant again, but he was ready and sank his fist into Bodmer's stomach.

Everything narrowed to a whirlwind of violence—of blows received but more given—until the heavy man slumped to the floor between the overturned chairs. Bodmer moaned, "No more. No more," and covered his head with his mangled hands.

Gasping for breath, Brant stepped backward and felt a piercing pain in his side—probably a cracked rib. He stared down at the crumpled man, and his rage began to subside. Blood covered Bodmer's almost unrecognizable face, oozing from his smashed nose onto his stained shirt. He lay doubled over, then vomited onto the floor. He would feel his injuries for a long time.

Brant had just grasped the tilted edge of a table to steady himself when he heard a shout and a sharp whoosh of air behind him. Painfully he swung around. Walt had his arms clamped around Willis Henderson, immobilizing him. Through an eye that was beginning to swell shut, Brant could see that Henderson was grasping his gun by its barrel.

Walt looked at Brant, distress plain in his eyes. "I'm sorry. You told me to stay back. But he was gonna hit you with his gun. And you always said never to hit from behind. I hope you aren't mad."

Brant took Henderson's gun and handed it to one of the spectators in the gaping ring of men around them. He almost wanted to laugh, but it would be too painful. "Thanks, Walt. I'm not mad at you. You can let go of him now."

Someone helped Carl Bodmer to a sitting position. He was struggling to breathe, and his bloodstained mouth showed gaps from newly missing teeth. Finally he mumbled, "God damn you, Curtis . . . son-of-a-bitch. You and your dummy brother . . . better keep . . . out of the way."

With his hand Brant wiped a trickle of blood from the side of his face and turned to Jesse. "Sorry to break up your evening, Mr. Ross."

Jesse looked a little dazed; then he grinned. "I was leaving anyway."

Brant forced his legs into motion. "Come on, Walt. Let's go." As he walked to the door, he heard murmurs of "Good fight, Curtis." Walt and Jesse followed him outside.

The cold night air stung Brant's face, and he stopped, knowing exhaustion was close. Beside him Jesse said, "You gave Carl a terrible beating, but he started it. It was a fair fight." He scowled, and his voice sounded grim. "Fair until Willis Henderson tried to interfere. You need any help?"

Brant managed to shake his head. "Thanks. I'm all right."

When Jesse left, Walt said anxiously, "Did I do right, Brant?"

Brant found he could smile in spite of his painful face. "You did just right, brother. And now you're going to have to help me, or I may not make it back to the boardinghouse."

Walt put a gentle arm around Brant. "Are you feeling bad?"

"No," said Brant. The pain in his body made him want to fold up into a ball right there. But the sweetness of revenge would keep him going. "I feel wonderful."

6

THE sun was barely up the next morning when Margarida and her father rode away from the Welleses' house. He looked at her frilly green dress and hat and raised an eyebrow. "Expecting to see your beau?"

"I don't have a beau, Papa. Why do you think I only dress up to attract a man?"

"Hold your temper," Jesse said good-naturedly. "I'll admit I'm glad you aren't interested in Lee Hansen. He's not smart enough for you. Enoch Springer's not the man for you either. You need someone who'll keep you in line. Not spoil you the way I've done."

Her father's good humor banished Margarida's annoyance. "I can look after myself."

He only grinned. "Wait and see."

"What did you do last night, Papa? Since Mama wasn't along, I'll bet you didn't just stay at the Franklins'."

Jesse looked uncomfortable. "I went to the Imperial. I guess I might as well tell you what happened. Brant got into a fight with Carl Bodmer."

Margarida felt a jolt that spread from her stomach up into her chest. "Was . . . was Brant hurt?"

"He was still walking when he left. Carl had to be carried out."

"But why? Brant hardly ever gets in fights."

He frowned. "I'm not sure. Carl started it. He and Willis Henderson both began acting touchy when Brant came in. The three of them were like a bunch of suspicious dogs. Then Brant said he wanted to call on Carl's daughter, and Carl jumped Brant."

Margarida thought she'd heard incorrectly. "You mean Brant was fighting over Harriet Bodmer?"

"That's the way it seems."

Margarida hardly noticed where they were riding. Brant—fighting over Harriet Bodmer. It couldn't be. He barely knew her. Unwillingly Margarida remembered that Brant had danced with Harriet at least once at the wedding party. But Harriet Bodmer was old, twenty-three at least, and not even pretty. She was so stuck-up about her father's money that she didn't have any suitors except ones who obviously wanted to marry the Bodmer ranch.

The satisfaction of thinking how undesirable Harriet was didn't make Margarida feel better. You're a fool, she berated herself. If Brant Curtis was stupid enough to get into fights, it didn't concern her.

She was startled to realize they had reached the corral on the south side of town where the *comancheros* had arranged to show their horses. Jesse dismounted, then helped her down. "You upset?"

"Of course not. I was just surprised."

"You looked a mite pale when I told you about Brant's fight. You're not still thinking you have a fancy for him?"

"No, Papa," she said, glad to have a positive answer. "You don't have to worry about that."

His expression relaxed. "I'm glad you're over that nonsense. You understand, I like Brant, and I admire the way he handled himself last night. It's just—"

"Yes, I understand," she interrupted. She didn't want to hear his lecture again about not mixing races.

He started to lead their horses to the already crowded hitching rail, when she caught his arm. "Was Walt with Brant last night?"

"Yes." Jesse looked grim. "And it was a good thing. After Carl was down, Willis Henderson started to hit

Brant from behind. Walt grabbed Willis and saved Brant from a nasty blow. I don't know why Willis would do that."

After Jesse tied up their two mounts, he went to look over the animals for sale. The jingle of spurs and creak of saddles punctuated shouts and jocular greetings. Cowboys and ranchers surrounded the large corral, waiting to examine the horses and try out the ones that were already broken. Dust boiled up from restless hooves; its smell mingled with the odors of stable and corral.

Margarida wandered behind her father, looking at the stock, but without her usual eagerness. Finally she caught Jesse between conversations. "It's so warm, Papa. I'm going to find some shade." He looked surprised, but nodded. She walked over to a large cottonwood tree and stood underneath it, watching the men gathered by the corral.

Neither Brant nor Walt was in sight. Disappointment dimmed the brightness of the morning more than the clouds that were beginning to collect. She hadn't seen Brant or Walt since the disastrous night of the wedding party a month and a half ago, but surely they were here. She was determined to talk to Walt and plan a "secret" meeting with him. They'd done it as children; he loved secrets and would remember them when he forgot other things.

In the distance beyond the corral she saw three horsemen approaching. When they came closer, her pulse leapt as she recognized Brant and Walt, mounted on strange horses. The grimy hat and clothes of the third man suggested he was one of the *comancheros*.

Brant rode awkwardly, sitting stiffly in the saddle and holding the reins with his left hand. His right hand was bandaged. She'd never seen him look so ungraceful, and her own muscles tightened in unwilling sympathy at each motion of his horse.

When they reached the corral, Walt and the *coman-*

chero dismounted first; Walt hovered nearby as Brant carefully slid from his mount and gave the reins to a young boy. Brant took off his hat and wiped his hand across his forehead. Walt, standing beside his brother, immediately did the same. The *comanchero* pointed toward the horses they'd been riding, talking excitedly.

Brant stood, leaning against the fence of the corral, his bandaged right hand held close to his body. The *comanchero* made sweeping gestures, his body straining, pantomiming a horse responding to a cowboy's directions. Though Margarida couldn't hear what they were saying, she could tell that Brant was alternately listening and talking. Finally with his left hand he slapped the *comanchero* on the back in a friendly gesture. Walt did the same, and the three men disappeared into the dilapidated shed that the *comancheros* were using as an office.

Margarida found her fingers were clenched. Disgusted, she reminded herself Brant had not only rejected her; he considered a nonentity like Harriet Bodmer worth fighting over. At the thought, she breathed with liberating anger.

Walt came out of the shed and crossed to the corral. He stood apart from the other men, watching the horses. Margarida waited, but Brant didn't appear. And when he did, she thought uncharitably, he wouldn't be able to move very fast. Now was her chance.

She hurried across to Walt and touched his arm. He gave her a delighted smile. "Walt, I don't have much time to talk now," she said. "Can we have a secret meeting?"

"Secret meeting?"

"Yes—a secret meeting just between you and me. We used to do that sometimes. Do you remember?"

"I don't know." Then he laughed, uncertainty gone. "Yes, I remember. It was a secret, and we had a good time. And I didn't tell anyone."

Quickly she glanced at the stable, but Brant was still

out of sight. "Tomorrow morning. We'll meet at the big rock with the pine tree in the middle."

He nodded vigorously. "The rock with the pine tree in the middle."

"And it's a secret. We can't tell *anyone* else."

"Yes, yes. I don't tell secrets." He looked proud and assured as he said this.

She started to leave, but he caught her arm. "Brant was in a fight, and I helped him. He said I did the right thing."

"I'm glad you did. You can tell me about it tomorrow." She squeezed his hand and then hurried over to where her father was standing. Slipping in beside him, she stared at the horses as if her only interest was in them and waited for her breathing to return to normal.

One of the quarter horses was resisting a cowboy's efforts to mount him. Margarida tried to keep her attention on their struggle until she heard her father say, "Good God, Brant, what are you doing out here this morning?"

She turned to see Brant, with Walt beside him, standing just beyond her father. A cut showed along one side of his cheek, and his left eye was swollen. The injuries, instead of lessening his good looks, made him look more powerful—and dangerously attractive. In spite of her determination to be indifferent to him, a treacherous memory swept over her. Of the night beside the stream and his face resting against her naked breasts. Of the excitement she'd felt when he'd touched her so intimately. Shocked by thoughts so vivid she feared her expression would betray her, she pulled down the brim of her hat so that it shaded her face more.

Brant nodded to Jesse. "I couldn't let you have all the good horses."

"And wanted to prove you could still get around," Jesse responded admiringly. He frowned. "I'm disgusted with Willis Henderson. Good thing Walt was beside him."

Brant put his hand affectionately on Walt's arm. "Yes, Walt's a good man to have around."

Walt beamed. "I did the right thing. And Brant said I could ride the rest of the horses we might buy."

Jesse looked at Brant with concern. "You aren't going to ride any more strange horses today, are you? I tell you what—I want to try out a few." He turned to Margarida. "What are you going to do now?" She could see a warning in his eyes not to talk long to Brant.

"I'm going back into town in a few minutes. I'll meet you at the Franklins' later."

"Good. Remember, I may be a while. I have to go to the court session."

Nervous with the reminder, she said, "Yes, Papa."

Jesse turned back to Brant. "Suppose Walt and I go out together. That all right with you?"

Walt looked at Brant questioningly. At Brant's "Yes, thanks, Mr. Ross," he happily followed Jesse to the corral.

Reluctantly Brant turned back toward Margarida. He didn't feel up to a confrontation this morning. She looked too beautiful in the ruffled dress and drooping hat which partly concealed her face. But it didn't obscure the moist red lips which were just right for kissing. Unwillingly he noticed how the tight bodice emphasized her breasts and small waist and the way the soft skirt suggested the roundness of her hips.

Though he'd tried to forget how she'd looked that day at the line shack and in the moonlight beside the stream, when he saw the way her breasts filled out the dress, he couldn't help remembering. Too many nights he'd imagined what it would be like to make love to her—undress her, uncovering the satiny skin and soft breasts, touch those nipples again, feel the brush of pubic hair against his fingers, see her shiver and her eyes glow with pleasure. And finally to spend himself inside her. He felt the beginning of an erection and turned toward the fence, concentrating on subduing his unruly body.

He should have gone with Walt. But even with his chest tightly taped, riding this morning had been painful. Jesse was right—it was determination to prove he hadn't been hurt badly last night that had brought him here. Seeing Margarida didn't help the pain. God damn—with that figure, it would be better for him if she had three warts and a hooked nose.

Margarida's voice was frosty. "I understand you've been brawling."

His concentration worked, and he faced her again. "Yes, I'm afraid that's obvious."

"Over . . . your interest in Harriet Bodmer."

He wondered if the hesitation in her words meant she was upset that he'd supposedly fought over a woman. He could explain he wasn't interested in Harriet, but it might protect him if Margarida thought he was seriously attracted to another woman. He tried to grin, decided it wasn't worth the pain, and said, "Yes, but I doubt that she'd welcome any attention from me now."

Margarida felt her anger rising to an explosive level. So he was brazen enough to admit he'd been fighting over that ridiculous woman. True, Margarida thought furiously, she'd brought it up, but if he had any honor, he'd have denied it. She'd been foolish enough to wince at the bruises she saw on his face. He undoubtedly deserved them.

"I was surprised to hear about your brawl," she said, making her voice indifferent. "You don't usually get into fights. I thought nothing was worth that much to you." She knew she was unfair. He'd often taken up for someone who was being bullied. It was something she used to admire, but she didn't want to think anything kind about him today.

The skin of his face suddenly looked pale. His voice sounded as if his words had steel shafts in them. "I save my efforts for what's really important."

She felt caught in the intensity of his look. For a moment it seemed as if he were so close he might touch her and . . . But she didn't know what. Her heart began to beat painfully fast, as if Brant, using some power he could exert without moving, had trapped her.

The air between them seemed to be compressed so that nothing separated the accelerated beating of her heart from his. She almost felt the hardness of his body as it had once pressed against her. Deep inside her, excitement began to build. Tension from the juncture of her thighs crept up into her chest, spreading out to her skin until it was alive with sensations, but whether hot or cold, she couldn't tell.

Though she knew that Brant had not moved, her lips remembered every kiss—the punishing one at the line shack and the tender, passionate ones beside the moonlit stream. She could taste again the sweet freshness of his mouth and smell the fragrance of his skin. Her breasts responded to the memory of his hands caressing them, his mouth wakening her nipples to an existence of their own. The image burned in her, of his hands parting her thighs, brushing against her vulnerable center, sending waves of desire radiating through her.

"Miss Ross, I thought I'd find you here this morning." The voice behind her released her. She turned to find Enoch. "Excuse me," he said to Brant, "I hope I'm not interrupting."

She felt as if she'd been in danger of drowning and a rescuer had appeared. "Oh, no," she said before Brant could reply. "Mr. Curtis and I have finished our conversation. Good-bye, Brant." She smiled at Enoch and put her hand through his elbow. "Enoch, I thought we agreed last night you would call me Margarida."

They hadn't, but Enoch seemed too delighted to remember that. "Yes, of course. Margarida, you're looking even more beautiful than you did last evening."

She steered him away from Brant and tried to smile vivaciously. "Are you planning to purchase horses?"

"No, I don't have money for that. I really came in the hope I might see you."

Now she regretted that they'd moved far enough from Brant that he probably hadn't heard that compliment. "Unfortunately, I can't stay longer. There's something I must do in town."

"May I escort you there?"

"Yes, I'd like that." It wouldn't hurt for Brant to see her leave with another man, thought Margarida.

Brant watched Margarida walk away with Enoch Springer and couldn't prevent a disconcerting surge of jealousy. Deliberately he focused his attention on the activities in the corral. For too many years, he thought ruefully, she'd been his adoring admirer. He'd been used to all that adoration, like too much liquor. He guessed it would take a while for him to get used to doing without.

Margarida was glad Enoch was there to help her mount; her legs felt strangely shaky. When Halcon moved off, she had to grip the reins to keep her hands from trembling, as if she'd just been through an exhausting ordeal.

As they left the trading area, she glanced back. Brant was still beside the corral, but he didn't look her way. It didn't matter, though, she told herself. She'd accomplished what she wanted—a romance for Priscilla, a meeting arranged with Walt, and now she was on her way to go with Adela to Miguel's trial. She had a right to congratulate herself.

It wasn't quite nine-thirty by the time Margarida said good-bye to Enoch and reached Adela's house. She found Adela sitting nervously in the living room, looking strange in a very proper black taffeta dress. "Do I look all right?" she asked Margarida anxiously.

"Yes, fine." Margarida hugged Adela and sat beside her. "Are you worried about the trial?"

"A little." Adela studied Margarida's face. "But what's happened to you? You look so unhappy."

To her intense surprise, Margarida felt her throat tighten. The morning's tension rushed back—the news of the fight, seeing Brant's bruises, the conversation with him. Before she could stop herself, sobs began to shudder upward.

"Margarida, what's wrong?" Adela opened her arms and enfolded Margarida in a loving embrace.

The choked words finally erupted. "It's . . . Brant. He was in a terrible fight . . . over a woman."

"Ah, poor little one." Adela's hands smoothed Margarida's hair, and her voice was a sympathetic melody. "So you still care about him."

"No. I don't. I won't. He's hateful," Margarida gasped, trying to stifle her tears.

"*Amor y aborrecimiento no quitan conocimiento.* Love and hatred have nothing to do with reasoning. Go ahead and cry," Adela comforted her. "It's your nature to love ferociously. And hate that way too."

Margarida pulled away and found her handkerchief. "This is silly. You're the one who's supposed to cry."

Adela laughed. "You remind me of old times, when you used to come rushing to see me after something terrible happened. Which was usually your own fault."

Margarida smiled and put away her handkerchief. "Isn't it time to go?"

Two hours later, a stunned Margarida watched Adela follow Miguel from the courtroom. Miguel's trial had lasted only a few minutes. He'd pled guilty, been sentenced to time served and fined twenty dollars, then released. When Miguel spoke to Adela, she rose and left with him as if nothing had happened.

As her surprise faded, Margarida felt foolish; she'd shocked the townspeople and enraged her father to do something that suddenly seemed as if it hardly mattered. No, that wasn't true. It mattered to her to stand by Adela, as part repayment for the many times the warm-hearted woman had helped her. But now she had to face Papa.

When he'd entered with Brant and Walt and seen her, his furious face told her she'd underestimated the storm that would follow his finding her here. She stiffened her back, preparing for the inevitable clash with her father.

Standing in the back of the room next to Jesse Ross, Brant studied the wisps of dark brown curls which trickled down the back of Margarida's neck. He saw the infuriated expression on Jesse's face and noticed that his scarred hands were clenched at his side, the veins standing out. How typical of Margarida, Brant thought, to disregard what people thought of her and anger her father over loyalty to a friend. Probably without stopping to decide if it were wise or worthwhile. Margarida's way—act first, think later. Or not at all. Her impulses were often generous, but that didn't keep her out of trouble.

He saw Margarida turn and look at her father, her chin fixed in a defiant angle. But her eyes, dark and soft, betrayed her uncertainty. Slowly she started to walk back toward them. For a moment Brant had an insane impulse to scoop her up and whisk her away—to shield her from Jesse's wrath. And insane it was. There was nothing between him and Margarida, not even the friendship they used to have.

In the aftermath of last night's fight, Jesse had been relaxed and friendly, asking Brant to come along to court with him. This was no time, Brant reminded himself, to jeopardize the goodwill he'd been hoping for.

Before she could reach them, Brant said, "Walt and

I will be leaving, Mr. Ross. I'll tell my father you'll talk to him about the roundup. Or I'll be over to see you."

"Yes, certainly," Jesse said tightly. "Tell Rupert I'm sorry he's not well."

"Yes, I will." Brant tapped Walt's arm. "Let's go." Walt followed, and they escaped to the anteroom to retrieve Brant's gun.

Margarida saw Brant and Walt depart with a feeling of relief. As always when faced with a disagreeable confrontation, she wanted to get it over as soon as possible. Resolutely she joined her waiting father.

"Where is your horse, Margarida?" Papa said in a controlled tone.

"At Adela's house."

"You stay here. I'll collect Halcon and come back for you." He took her arm and propelled her to a chair in the gloomy entrance hall before he left. As men passed her, a few looked at her curiously, but most ignored her, their faces unfriendly.

While she waited, Margarida thought again about Adela and Miguel. She didn't understand why Adela would be willing to forgive Miguel and go with him so meekly. Was love so strong?

She hoped her plans for Priscilla and Lee, and for meeting Walt, would turn out better than the trial had. As her usual optimistic spirits began to return, she decided they surely would.

Jesse reappeared in the doorway. His face looked calmer, so she tried to smile. At least he didn't seem any angrier as they went outside. Halcon and her father's bay were at the hitching rail. Jesse strode toward the horses, and she followed, swallowing nervously at the thought of waiting until they were out of town to learn her punishment.

When they reached the horses, no one was anywhere near them. Impulsively she put her hand on her father's arm. "Papa, I know you're very angry with me, and I'm sorry. I don't like to make you unhappy, but I couldn't call myself any kind of friend if I hadn't gone with Adela today."

He looked at her, and his eyes were no longer so angry. Instead the lines of his face sagged, as if he were sad or discouraged. "Did you do any good?" he asked.

She felt herself flushing. "I don't know, Papa. I thought I would. What . . . will my punishment be?"

He helped her mount and swung up into his saddle before he answered. "You're too old for punishments, Margarida. I haven't been able to teach you that you can't have your own way all the time. You're determined to make mistakes, and you'll have to take the consequences."

She sat, her hands frozen on the reins. A strange feeling grew in her, like disappointment, or maybe dread. Papa had always punished her—it was part of her life.

He started off, then turned and snapped, "But don't expect to dash into Rio Torcido any time you feel like it."

With a sharp breath of relief, she nudged Halcon to follow her father's stiff back. He wasn't going to abandon her completely after all. The day felt as if it had turned upside down but then partly righted itself again.

From under a tree across from the courthouse, Brant watched Margarida and her father ride away. He'd lingered here, not quite able to go until he saw them leave. Not that he thought Jesse would start beating her in the middle of town—Jesse would never beat her anyway. But he'd been extremely angry in the courtroom. Brant had seen from his stance when he returned, riding his horse and leading Halcon, that some of his anger had cooled.

Walt, who'd been tossing pebbles across a gully, came back to Brant. "Are we going home?" he asked.

"Yes." Brant, moving stiffly, headed for the hitching rail. The image of Margarida as she'd faced her father in the courtroom came back to him, followed by other pictures—in her too-feminine dress this morning, and the most persistent vision, of her in the sheer gown that concealed nothing. Dammit—he wanted to forget that!

The trouble was, he decided, he'd been without a woman too long. During his last visit to the camp, he'd been too preoccupied with the murdered Indian to visit the Apache widow he enjoyed. That was probably why Margarida aroused his desire so easily.

Walt walked with his usual long stride, and when Brant kept up, he felt his bruises. No woman would be much use to him today, but as soon as he could, he'd see the widow.

He realized he'd also forgotten about Walt's needs. One of the ranch hands had mentioned a woman here in town who took a few paying customers. Maybe he should try to locate her before they left. She might be good for Walt.

He stopped. "Hold up, Walt. We aren't going to the ranch now. I think we'll stay another night in town."

Walt turned, frowning. "Does that mean we won't be home tomorrow morning?"

"That's right. Not until the afternoon."

"Then I want to go home now."

Surprised, Brant studied his brother. Walt almost never opposed any decision of Brant's. "Why don't you want to stay here?"

Pink color rose into Walt's fair-skinned face, and he stared down at the ground. "I can't tell you."

Puzzled by Walt's obvious distress, Brant made his voice gentle. "Why can't you tell me?"

Walt looked up now, his eyes almost tearful. "I can't tell you," he repeated. "It's a secret."

"A secret about tomorrow morning?"

Walt nodded, and a suspicion began forming in Brant's mind. While he'd been negotiating with the *comanchero* about the sale of the first horse, Walt had gone outside alone. Margarida had been there too. Years ago she and Walt had both loved secret meetings.

"Walt, I know what happened. You saw Margarida at the horse sale, and she asked you to meet her tomorrow morning."

His brother's unhappy face was Brant's confirmation. "But I'm not supposed to tell, because it's a secret."

Brant put his left arm reassuringly around Walt. "You didn't tell me. I guessed. So you did keep the secret."

A smile erased the dismay from Walt's eyes. "Then we can go home?"

"Yes. We'll leave now."

They started for the hitching rail again as Walt said happily, "And in the morning I'll go to the secret place and see Margarida."

Brant knew where that would be. They always met beside the rock with the pine tree in the middle, and she wouldn't choose an unfamiliar location. Tomorrow morning Margarida wouldn't be left waiting. Someone would meet her, but it wouldn't be Walt.

7

WHEN Margarida saddled Halcon the next morning, darkness still clung inside the stable. The only human sound was the faint humming of a Mexican tune from the cookhouse, where the cook would be building the morning fire. Lobo betrayed his doggy impatience by the soft thumping of his tail on the ground. She swung up into the saddle, taking pleasure from the freedom of wearing pants, which would be convenient for fishing or swimming.

The previous night when she and Papa returned from Rio Torcido, she'd told him she was going for an early-morning ride. He'd given her a tight-lipped look, but said nothing. His refusal even to acknowledge her plans made the lost feeling of yesterday return. Even more than before, Walt seemed the only familiar person in a confusing world.

She rode out of the corral, her spirits brightening with the sky as it changed from gray to gold to blue. She loved the early morning, when the sage smelled damp and heavy, reluctant to release its hold on the dew-wet night. Bird calls sounded almost sleepy; the jays and nutcrackers hadn't shown up to dominate the air with their scolding. Lobo bounded ahead of her, not yet freed from silence, but expressing his exuberance in zigzag bursts of speed.

Halcon climbed the sloping valley side, where pinyons gave way to tall ponderosas, and juniper to cedars. A cluster of aspen showed autumn gold against the dark evergreens. Margarida called, "All right, Lobo," and the dog lifted his gray-and-white muzzle in one joyous bark.

Sun began to penetrate the forested hills as Halcon reached the top of the ridge, and she turned him to follow its crest. Soon the land to her right would level off, and she'd be at the huge tan rock, where a small pine stubbornly thrust its roots down through the rock's core. The irony of that always pleased her, that something as seemingly impenetrable as the boulder was so vulnerable.

On the hillside overlooking the rock, Brant stretched, working the stiffness from his sore muscles. The ride this morning had been easier than yesterday and his right hand had only tape on it. He'd tethered Chid several yards back in the trees so that he would see Margarida before she realized he and not Walt had come to meet her.

He saw movement below; Margarida was riding Halcon toward the meeting place. In spite of his determination not to let her affect him, he felt his pulse respond to the sheer pleasure of seeing her. She was riding astride, and as he noticed her easy grace on horseback, a surge of old pride surprised him. He'd taught her to ride, and he'd always admired his results.

A gray-and-white streak up the slope meant Lobo had found him. The huge dog, aptly named for the wolf his size and heavy fur suggested, gave whimpers of pleasure. Brant ruffled the heavy fur, then sent Lobo racing back to his mistress.

He watched Margarida dismount. She pushed back her hat and brushed at wisps of dark brown hair that clung to the side of her face. A sheen of perspiration highlighted her wide cheekbones and upturned nose. The denim hugged her small waist and rounded hips and showed the outline of her slender thighs. With her large dark eyes, their thick lashes almost meeting as she peered into the slanting sun, her face looked intensely alive.

Pressure began to build in his groin. Hold on! he cautioned himself, and managed to will his excitement away.

She tethered Halcon and stood beside the rock. Lobo circled, checking all the scents around his mistress, then started back toward the old pine, and Brant knew it was time to go down the slope.

Margarida heard the crunch of pine needles underfoot and expectantly turned toward the sound. To her shock, she saw, not Walt's burly shoulders and blond hair, but Brant. To her startled eyes the tall, lean man with the coal-black hair suddnely looked completely Indian. The early-morning sun darkened his skin to burnished copper. His straight nose and high cheekbones emphasized his hawklike features.

As he came toward her, her heart began to pound. His graceful, almost fluid walk and the power of his broad shoulders suddenly seemed threatening, as if he were stalking her—as an Apache, and her enemy. He stopped, his intense gaze heightening his appearance as a dangerous stranger. The fading marks of his fight with Carl Bodmer completed it.

"Sorry, Margarida. Walt's not coming." The familiar deep tones of his voice let her breathe again, and the vision of the Indian warrior faded.

Her disappointment mixed with anger. "How did you find out what we planned? Walt doesn't tell secrets."

Brant leaned against the rock and looked at her almost casually, as if indifferent to her vehemence, or even indulgently amused. "He's too honest to conceal much."

She felt the sting of accusation. "I didn't promise to stay away from him. You tricked him or he'd be here."

His smile suggested an arrogance that raised her

temper further. "Remember how much Walt likes to play cards? He and I had a card game last night—and quite a few drinks. So he's sleeping late this morning, and he probably won't feel like getting out when he wakes up."

"You deliberately got him drunk? That's disgusting."

Brant straightened up, his casual pose gone. "This way he has only a bad headache. If he met you, it could mean something worse than a hangover."

Margarida's hurt and anger flared together. "Why can't you understand that I'm Walt's friend? I wouldn't flirt with him or harm him in any way."

For a moment Brant looked tired. "I believe that you don't intend to hurt Walt. But you can't help flirting, Margarida. You flirt with a man just by smiling at him. Just by the way you move."

"That's not true."

He went on as if he hadn't heard her. "Walt can get as excited as any other man from being kissed or touched. Or from what he sees. And he doesn't know how strong he is."

"But he's so gentle. He always does anything I ask."

"Margarida, you don't know how men are made. After a certain point, not much matters to a man except what he wants. If Walt go so worked up he tried to rape you, you couldn't stop him."

The bluntness of Brant's words shocked Margarida. It hadn't occurred to her that anything as innocent as the kiss she'd given Walt could affect him. Uneasily she remembered she'd planned that she and Walt might go swimming together today. Lobo bounded up and nudged against her hand, and she was glad to rub his head instead of look at Brant.

"Besides, Margarida," Brant continued relentlessly, "you know your father doesn't want you coming around to Curtis land." His voice mocked her now. "If you're with Walt, you might run into me, out here by ourselves, like this morning, and Jesse would be very unhappy about that."

She hated his composure. "I hadn't realized you worried so much about what Papa might think. You were willing to fight Carl Bodmer over his daughter. He must have hurt you enough to make you scared of fathers."

"That fight with Bodmer had nothing to do with his daughter," he snapped, and stopped, as if he'd said more than he intended.

Surprised, she asked, "What do you mean? Then what did you fight about?"

His posture eased, and he gave her a half-humorous look. "You have a remarkable ability to upset me, Margarida. Come on, get back on Halcon. I'll ride partway back with you and explain."

"But what about Walt?"

"Margarida, do you understand what I was saying?"

"Yes," she said reluctantly, "I think so. But you make me sound so dangerous. I can't believe that."

"Believe me—you are."

Something in his tone made her breath come faster, and she felt her cheeks grow warm. Stubbornly she argued, "You're expecting me to give up one of my dearest friends."

"I know. And I'm sorry." His voice softened and became almost gentle, but he looked as determined as ever. "You can't go back to the way you and Walt were as children. That kind of freedom is over."

"You can't keep him away from all women."

"I'll look after that problem. Come on—I'll help you mount."

"But if I'm not here later, Walt will think I just didn't bother to come. I don't want that."

"I'll tell him I saw you and that you couldn't meet him after all."

She stared at him, searching for some softening of his judgment. Then slowly she nodded. She couldn't doubt any longer that it was possible Walt might rape—no, she couldn't think that word in connection with him—that Walt might not be able to control himself. Brant's manner as well as his harsh words had convinced her. Sadness settled over her, and pressure in her chest and throat warned her that tears waited just below the surface.

Brant untied Halcon, put out his hands for her to mount, and went for Chid. When he rode back, they started through the trees with Lobo bounding alongside.

She asked, "What about the fight in Rio Torcido? You said you'd explain."

A white line appeared around Brant's mouth, and his face looked more hawklike than ever. She imagined she could see his Apache great-grandfather peering out from his eyes. "Two weeks ago someone killed a man and left him beside the Curtis sign for me to find. He'd been tortured."

The sun suddenly felt cold instead of hot, and Margarida's stomach clenched. "Why? Who was it?"

"An Indian who worked in Rio Torcido."

With a lurch of her stomach she remembered Adela's warning and Priscilla's gossip. "Near the Websters'?"

Abruptly Brant pulled up Chid and caught Halcon's bridle. Halcon danced sideways, but Brant held firm. "What have you heard about that?" His eyes glittered.

"Adela told me she'd heard gossip in the Imperial, that some men were angry because Mabel Webster had taken up with a half-breed Indian who worked near her father's place. Priscilla Welles said the Websters sent Mabel away because of it and that the Indian disappeared."

The tension in Brant's face relaxed, and he released Halcon. His voice sounded grim but more normal when he said, "The Indian disappeared because he was murdered. I'm sure Carl Bodmer instigated the murder, and probably decided to bring the body out here. Willis Henderson and a couple of men who work for Bodmer helped. There was a fifth man, but I don't know who he was. Yet."

Already afraid of what Brant would answer, Margarida still had to ask. "Why out here?"

"As a warning to me. To tell me to act like a white man. If they're examples of white men, thank God I'm not."

Over Brant's bitter voice, Margarida heard the cawing of a jay, like a warning that terrible things could happen in these mountains. She had to moisten her lips before she could ask, "And that's why you were in the fight? Papa said Carl Bodmer started it because of his daughter."

"That was just an excuse. Bodmer knew what we were fighting about."

"Are you going to fight all the others?"

"Henderson's too old and small. Bodmer's men were doing what he told them. So I don't know. I'll decide when I find out who the fifth man was."

Margarida's thoughts confused her; horror at Brant's story of the tortured Indian mixed with an almost shameful relief that he hadn't been fighting over Harrier Bodmer.

Brant reined in Chid. "I won't ride any farther with you," he said.

Upset at herself for feeling jealous of Harriet Bodmer, she retorted, "Yes—Papa might see you, and it wouldn't do to offend him."

Brant looked at her. Tiny lines were tight around his mouth, and his nostrils flared slightly. She could see the muscles of his arms tensing under his cotton shirt. "No, it wouldn't do. I hope your father will allow *shiwóyé*'s band to hunt over his land. If he knows there's nothing between you and me, he's more likely to agree."

Margarida felt as if Brant had given her a blow that would be terribly painful when she let herself feel it—worse than thinking he preferred Harriet Bodmer.

"And your Indian relatives are more important to you than anything else?" After she'd asked the question, she realized she needn't have. She knew his answer.

"Yes."

To her amazement, she managed a careless laugh. "Well, you shouldn't have to worry about Walt. Just give him a few lessons in how to be indifferent, and he'll be safe. You ought to be a good teacher. Come on, Lobo."

Brant watched her until she was out of sight. Indifferent! God—he was anything but. His body responded to her like resin-soaked kindling to a match.

As he rode back up to the crest and over to the Curtis ranch, he decided he had finally convinced Margarida of the futility of trying to start anything between them. She'd accepted his explanations, both about Walt's feelings and his own. He probably should have talked about Jesse and the Indians before, but it was hard for him to admit his most secret hopes. It was almost as if talking about them would jeopardize them.

He'd also given her a weapon she could use against him if she wished. She could say she was still interested, and that would finish his chances with Jesse. Margarida wouldn't do that though, he was sure. She was capable of acting on outrageous impulses, but she was never devious.

Damp patches of sweat clung to his shirt by the time he was within three miles of the ranch house. He thought of skipping his usual footrace with Chid because of his taped ribs. That way he'd reach home sooner to look after Walt. But he remembered he'd asked Luisa, their cook and housekeeper, to take care of Walt if he wakened before he returned. He knew from experience that Luisa's remedy for a hangover— goat's milk with honey and whiskey—was as effective as anything he'd ever tried.

He dismounted, took off his shirt, and changed his

boots for high moccasins. After putting the clothing in his saddlebags, he slapped Chid lightly on his rump. The horse swung into a lope, and Brant started after him.

During his two childhood summers with *shiwóyé*, he'd admired the running ability and endurance of the Apache boys and girls. Though his life probably would never depend on his capacity to outrun his enemies, his pride wouldn't let others his age outdo him for long. Ever since then he'd continued to run, ordinarily much farther than this distance today, and had taught Chid to keep pace with him.

By the time he reached the frame house, his heart was pounding hard, but the soreness had almost disappeared from his muscles. He led Chid to the stable and stood for a moment, letting his breathing slow to protect his painful chest. From the deep shadow under the eaves of the stable, a voice said in Apache, "So, you are getting soft."

Brant whirled, and saw the huge man squatting beside the stable wall. "My brother," Brant exclaimed with delight. As the man rose to his full height of six feet, seven inches, Brant was reminded of how appropriate his name, Ndè-ze, was. He truly was a Tall Man. His size and smallpox-pitted face gave him a ferocious appearance.

Ndè-ze's grandmother and Brant's grandmother were cousins. During Brant's two summers with the Apache, he and Ndè-ze had formed a close friendship that lasted throughout the years when they rarely saw each other.

"Where have you been, my brother?" Brant asked. "It has been four years since I last saw you."

"In Mexico, in the Sierra Madre."

Brant knew not to ask more. The Mexican mountains had sheltered the Apache who had fought under Geronimo. The whites considered those fighters renegades, to be captured or killed. Ndè-ze might not be safe even here on the Curtis ranch if he were thought to be one of Geronimo's followers.

"Will you be in this area for a while? I suppose you know that *shiwóyé* and what's left of the band are living here. And we could certainly use someone who's good with cattle on the ranch. I'd like for you to stay here."

"Perhaps. I am tired of hiding. But I do not want to live at San Carlos. That's a devil's place."

Brant wondered what had happened to Ndè-ze's wife and son, but that was another forbidden question. If they were dead, his cousin wouldn't want to speak of them; no Apache spoke of the dead if it could be avoided.

"Have you heard of Jaspers?" Ndè-ze asked.

"The scalp hunter?"

"The one who killed our relatives twelve years ago."

"No. I haven't heard of him." Brant wasn't surprised that Ndè-ze hadn't given up his vengeance. "After I unsaddle Chid, let's go into the house and get breakfast. Cornbread and beans, and we have a new supply of honey."

Ndè-ze scrutinized Brant with shrewd eyes. "The bruises on your face and the way you move tell me you have been arguing with someone recently."

Brant grinned ruefully. "Yes—a fight in town."

His cousin's face mirrored his grin. "I hope you won. Let me take care of the horse."

"I don't think Chid will take kindly to that," said Brant, and was immediately proved wrong when Chid docilely submitted to Ndè-ze's care. When the horse was stabled, Brant retrieved his clothes and put on his shirt. Then the two men went to the house. As they reached the kitchen door, Brant said, "We'd better speak English or Spanish inside. With your ugly face, your Apache words might frighten Luisa so much she couldn't cook breakfast for us."

Ndè-ze grinned and nodded; references to his appearance amused him.

Luisa was short and round, about half the size of Ndè-ze. She greeted the new arrival calmly; life in the same household with Brant had accustomed her to surprises.

"Luisa, this is my friend and cousin, Tall Man. Can you give us something to eat?"

"Breakfast is still hot, but I have little time today." She gave Brant a reproachful look. "What did you do to your poor brother last night? All he can do is groan."

"I'll look after him, if you will feed Tall Man."

"And with your papa not well either," grumbled Luisa, but she turned to fill a plate for Ndè-ze. "Put a new cold cloth on Walt's head," she ordered over her shoulder.

Brant found his brother sitting on the side of the bed, holding a cloth to his head. He looked up at Brant's entrance and said forlornly, "I feel sick. And I have to go to the secret place."

Gently Brant pushed his brother back down. "No you don't. Margarida sent a message—she can't meet you."

Walt was either too sick to care or didn't wonder how Brant knew Margarida wouldn't meet him. He groaned, but gave a trusting smile when Brant dipped the cloth in water and put it back on Walt's head. "Thank you, Brant."

Brant looked down at the unhappy face. Would Walt thank him if he could understand what he'd done? Brant wondered. That Walt couldn't understand was his tragedy and Brant's responsibility.

Margarida stopped before she reached home, wanting the solitude of the forest to sort out her jumbled thoughts and feelings. She slid off Halcon and tethered him to a small tree. Sitting on the ground in the shade of a tall ponderosa, she drew her knees up and leaned her chin on them, thinking of the morning.

Why didn't she feel relieved? Brant had been so cold to her, not because her charms were deficient, but because of his commitment to his Apache heritage. Sadly she realized that made the rift between them even more final. If she were still so foolish as to hang on to her girlhood infatuation, it would really be hopeless. There was no way she could be Indian, even if she wanted to. And obviously that was all that mattered to him.

Maybe Papa was right—Brant would end up with an Apache wife. Someone stupid and ugly, Margarida hoped.

Lobo pushed his nose under her hand, demanding to be petted. She scratched the heavy fur behind his ears, and the ecstatic look on his face brought a little pleasure to her battered spirit. "Lobo, are you my only friend?"

She thought sadly of Walt, and tears began to run down her face and drip into Lobo's fur. She would still see Walt at church or parties, but it wouldn't be the same. Her tears flowed faster. Lobo whined and licked at her face, his rough tongue feeling almost tender.

Resolutely she sat up and pushed the dog away. Crying solved nothing; it just made her feel more sorry for herself. She remembered one of Adela's favorite proverbs, offered each time Margarida came protesting that she was suffering some terrible injustice. "*Cuando el sol sale, para todos sale.*" When the sun rises, it rises for everyone. For me too, Margarida thought, though it didn't feel so just then.

As she mounted Halcon and started toward the ranch, she thought of Enoch Springer. He'd turned out to be a pleasant companion. Probably, Margarida decided, she could like lots of men besides Brant if she just gave herself the chance. Really, she was lucky to be so thoroughly rid of him. Just now she didn't feel lucky, but she would.

Toward the end of the second week of the October roundup, Margarida took Lobo and went to watch the branding. She hadn't seen Brant or Walt since that day by the rock, a month ago, and knew they might be there, but she wasn't going to stay away to avoid them.

As she approached the branding pens, she recognized the smell of the singed hair and hide that filled the air around the corral. She disliked the actual marking of the animals with the hot iron, but the calves kicked up so much dust, she couldn't see that anyway. She loved to watch the *vaqueros* display their skills with their rawhide lariats, two men working together until the calf was pinned down, one rope stretched taut from around its neck and the other holding its hind legs.

Brant and Walt were there, with an enormous man who looked Indian. Rather than following Brant constantly, Walt dogged the stranger's footsteps, imitating all the large man's gestures, just as he did with his brother. The man seemed pleased with Walt and gave him patient attention. Walt had an unusual skill with difficult horses, knowing just how to approach them, and his help was valuable in handling the colts to be gelded.

Walt was by himself, leaning against the corral fence, when Margarida went over to him. Sweat dripped from his sunburned face, and dust rimmed his happy eyes. He ruffled Lobo's ears while the dog gave small cries of pleasure.

"Walt, how are you?" she asked.

His smile told her how delighted he was to see her. "Margarida, you came back from where you went away."

"Yes—I came home pretty soon after the last

roundup." She knew he didn't have much sense of time, but he recognized the interval between roundups.

"Did you see me with the sorrel colt? He was really wild, but Tall Man said I did a good job."

"Tall Man?"

"Yes." Walt pointed proudly to the large stranger at the branding fire. "He's my new cousin. He's Brant's cousin, so he's my cousin too. I can't say his Apache name, but he told me to call him Tall Man."

An Apache cousin—that must make Brant happy, Margarida thought. And apparently Walt as well. She felt a flash of jealousy. She had been the one Walt had admired so much until Brant put a stop to their friendship. She was glad the man liked Walt, but right now it just seemed that someone else was taking her place with him.

"Look, he's coming now."

Tall Man was walking toward them, and Margarida didn't know if she wanted to meet him. His face was scarred with deep lines—almost frightening. Then he smiled, and she recognized intelligence and humor in his expression.

"Good afternoon, Miss Ross."

"This is Margarida," Walt offered unnecessarily.

"Yes—I remember you from the last time I visited Brant," Tall Man said.

Margarida didn't remember him, and she was sure she would have; it made her slightly uncomfortable. "Walt tells me you're called Tall Man. I see why."

He laughed, and she found she liked his easy way. Her discomfort disappeared. "Yes. My people gave me that name when I was barely fourteen, but it fits."

"And this is Lobo," Walt said. Tall Man held out his hand to the dog. Contrary to his usual suspicious ways, Lobo gave his greeting bark, as if he'd always known this tall Indian.

Margarida saw Brant coming toward them, and at the sight of his graceful walk her breath caught. Furious with herself for still reacting to him, she smiled at Walt and Tall Man and said, "I must go."

"It was my pleasure to meet you," Tall Man said politely.

"Mine also," she responded, and felt surprised that it was true. He looked nothing like the Indians she remembered from Santa Fe. Once she had become used to his scarred appearance, she sensed his grace and dignity. Perhaps she'd been wrong about what Brant's Apache relatives were like.

As she walked away, she glanced back and saw that Walt seemed undisturbed by her departure. He was laughing and looking admiringly from Tall Man to Brant. Again the curious jealousy made her uncomfortable. The three men seemed so close and happy together, and she felt alone.

The next day was the last one of the roundup, and Margarida stayed at the ranch house. She was in the small room off the kitchen, enduring the boredom of hemming napkins, when J.J. came in at midafternoon. He threw his hat on the floor and went to the cupboard where the liquor was kept. Glowering like their father in one of his tempers, J.J. poured a liberal amount of whiskey into a glass and swallowed half of it in one gulp. Holding his drink, he sat down next to her.

"What's wrong, J.J.?"

"Everything." He drained the glass and got up and filled it again.

"I can see what's going to be wrong pretty soon, but what's the matter now?"

"Don't act smart with me, Margarida."

He sounded so much like Papa that Margarida laughed. His face flaming purple, J.J. threw the half-full glass against the wall. It smashed, splattering whiskey over the tiled floor and the bottom of Margarida's orange skirt.

The sound seemed to shock J.J. out of his rage. He stared at the golden-brown liquid draining down the wall, then sank to a chair and leaned on the table, covering his face with his hands. "God, I can't stand it anymore."

Alarmed, she rose and stood beside him, rubbing his shoulder. "Tell me what's wrong."

He dropped his hands and looked at her, his face sullen and unhappy. "He's impossible. Nothing I do is right, according to him."

"That's just Papa's way—to talk cross and lecture a lot. He doesn't really mean it."

"Maybe not to you, but—"

The roar of their father's voice from the front room interrupted. "J.J., I want you in my office. Right now."

J.J. sat stubbornly, his face white and his hands clenched. Margarida pulled at him. "Go on, J.J., please. At least find out what he wants."

"I know," he ground out. "He'll tell me what I did wrong today."

"J.J.!" Papa's voice boomed through the hallway.

Margarida pulled more insistently. "Please go, J.J. I'll clean up the mess, and we'll talk later."

Finally J.J. picked up his hat and stalked out of the room. Margarida heard the door of her father's office slam. As she swept up the shards of wet glass and then mopped the wall and floor, she listened. She could hear angry voices, but not the words. Just when she finished, the door of the office slammed again; she heard J.J.'s footsteps cross the living room and then the shudder of the front door.

She started to follow him, but her father came out of his office and called to her. "No, Margarida, let him be. He didn't finish a job I gave him today, and he has to go back and do it."

"Oh, Papa. He was so upset and angry."

"Just a headstrong kid. Thinks he's a man and doesn't have to listen anymore. He'll get over it." Papa's words sounded confident, but his eyes looked unhappy.

Dinner that evening was miserable. J.J. came to the table but barely ate and refused to join the strained conversation. When Elena tried to ask him questions, he responded with single words. She looked suspiciously at her husband, who became more animated and talked about the roundup as if nothing were wrong. But Margarida noticed that he didn't eat with his usual appetite.

As soon as the meal was over, J.J. disappeared in the direction of the bunkhouse. Margarida, saying she was tired, soon went to her room, but she paced restlessly near the window, hoping to hear J.J. returning. For a while Lobo paced with her, but he finally jumped up on the foot of her bed and went to sleep.

She read until midnight, then gave up and began brushing her hair, when she heard a soft tap on her door. She hurried to answer it and found her brother. He came inside and closed the door, then spoke hurriedly. "I'm leaving, Margarida."

Fear for him chilled her. "Oh no, J.J. When?"

"Tonight. I already have a few things together. I just came to tell you good-bye."

Frantically she tried to think of something to say that would keep him here. "Can't you wait a little, J.J.? Papa will get over this."

"But I won't. I've stayed here too long now. And don't call me J.J. From now on I'm Jesse Ross—not Junior any longer."

"Where are you going?"

"To California. Remember the man I told you I met a month or so ago in the Imperial? I saw him when I was in town last week. That man and a couple of others are leaving for California tomorrow. I'm going with them."

A sick feeling burned in her throat. This was her brother, whom she'd played with, fought with, loved for all her life. He couldn't go. She wanted to grab him and hold on, or scream until he agreed not to

leave. But she couldn't do either one. She took a
shaky breath and forced down her despair. "Do you
have any money?"

"A little. But I can work—even if Papa doesn't
believe it. I'll get along."

In the lantern light his thin face looked so young to
her that the tears she wouldn't allow to surface almost
choked her. Quickly she turned to her wardrobe and
pulled out the bottom drawer. Inside she found a
leather pouch, not so heavy with coins as she wished.
She held it out to her brother. "Here. Take this. It
will help a little."

"No, Margarida. I can't take your money."

She opened his hand and poured the coins into it.
"You have to. I couldn't stand it if you left without
it." She tried to sound teasing. "If you didn't get to
California and become rich, then I'd think it was all
my fault."

He closed his hand over the money, and then hugged
her in a long embrace. His voice, muffled in her hair,
sounded as shaky as she felt. "Good-bye, Margarida.
I'll write to you—send a letter with someone coming
this way."

"You'd better," she said fiercely, then stepped back
before she could give in and cry.

"I'm leaving a note saying I've gone hunting with
Henry Franklin. Papa will think I'm just being irresponsible—the way he thinks I always am. He won't
like it, but he'll be too busy organizing the cattle drive
to Fort Bayard to check up on me until it's too late.
I'm taking my horse, because it belongs to me."

He went to the door of her room and looked out.
He turned and gave her one last grin. "Wish me luck,
Margarida, that I come back a rich man."

Her spoken words as he softly disappeared into the
dark patio were "Good luck, I hope you come back
rich," but her silent prayer was simpler—just for him
to come back.

She tried to tell herself he was only off on an adventure, but she felt frozen with apprehension. A morbid conviction filled her—that she might never see him again, and that his going would profoundly change her life as well.

8

"J.J.'s gone. He left last week."

At the sound of her father's voice, Margarida thrust the book she'd been trying to read onto the *sala* table and rushed out onto the veranda. Elena stood in front of the house, staring up at Jesse, still mounted on his sweat-lathered horse. She had been pacing the veranda the past two hours, waiting for him to return from Rio Torcido.

"What do you mean?" Elena's shrill tone revealed the beginning of hysteria. Dreading her father's answer, Margarida walked slowly down the steps of the veranda.

Jesse dismounted and handed his reins to Carlos García, who led the two horses toward the stables. Taking his wife's arm, he started for the veranda. "I'll tell you what I know when we're inside."

Margarida followed them into the *sala;* their strained faces added to her distress. Her father slumped into one of the leather chairs, then looked up at her mother. "J.J.'s gone to California," he said.

"California!"

"Yes—he went with a man named Charlie Fiske, someone who'd been hanging around Rio Torcido all summer."

Elena's voice rose another notch. "Then why are you here? Why didn't you go after him?"

Jesse stood, as if he didn't want to face her onslaught sitting down. "J.J.'s been gone five days. Even if I knew just what route he took, I couldn't catch up with him."

She was screaming now. "I told you! You should have gone after him the morning he left."

He kept his voice low and his anger controlled. "You know I had to take the cattle to Fort Bayard."

"A cattle contract is more important to you than your son." She began to weep, her hands clutched together.

Appalled, Margarida couldn't stand the hurt look on her father's face. "Papa couldn't have known where J.J. had gone. He wrote you he'd be off hunting."

Her mother swung around to Margarida. "*You* knew," she accused hysterically. "You knew he was going away."

Margarida stiffened her back, preparing for her mother's attack. "Yes. He told me the night he left."

"And you didn't tell us!" Elena screamed.

"I couldn't." Margarida tried to keep her own voice calm. "J.J. depended on that. He wouldn't have told me anything otherwise."

Elena's face contorted almost out of recognition. She slapped Margarida hard across the mouth.

Margarida jerked back, tasting blood where the blow had cut the inside of her lip against a tooth. Her left cheek felt fiery, and pain radiated into her eye.

"Elena!" Papa grabbed Mama's arm. "Stop that!"

She turned on her fiercely. "Go after him. Today."

"You know California's a big place. And I have responsibilities here."

Shakily Margarida said, "Papa, maybe I can help. I can do some of J.J.'s jobs."

Her mother rounded on her again, sobbing and screaming, "That's why you didn't say anything. You wanted J.J. to leave so you could take his place. You never were happy doing what you're supposed to do. You're an unnatural daughter."

"Elena! You're talking crazy," Jesse thundered. Elena

put her hands over her mouth, as if she were going to be sick, and stumbled toward the patio. Papa followed and put his arm around her, helping her from the room.

Stricken, Margarida stared after them. Could her mother's words be true? No—no, Margarida thought. She hadn't wanted J.J. to leave. She'd kept silent out of loyalty. But her mother's words lodged in her head.

Her father returned, his walk heavy and discouraged. She looked at him, fearing that she would see the same accusation in his eyes. "Papa, I hope you don't think I wanted J.J. to go away. But I couldn't tell you."

He patted her shoulder. "I wish you had, but I understand. You mustn't take what your mother said too hard, Margarida. She doesn't really mean it."

Margarida held back tears; she didn't want to upset her father more by crying. "Mama does mean it, Papa."

"You'd have to know the old Portuguese ways of her family," he said somberly. "Sons are more important than husbands. Elena's mother and father died in a fire, and she and her grandmother almost starved. Her grandmother harped on all her troubles being from losing her son."

"Mama never told me any of that."

Jesse sighed. "She doesn't talk about it."

"I always did like doing things outside better than in the house," Margarida admitted. "Mama's right about that."

"That will change when you have a husband and babies."

Margarida didn't think so, but she felt grateful for her father's words. "I could help you around the ranch."

"No—that's not work for a woman." Papa turned to leave, but she caught his arm.

"Some women do. Mrs. Fales ran a ranch west of town."

He shook his head. "She was a widow who'd learned about ranching from her husband."

"I already know some, and I could learn more from you."

A hint of a smile lightened his unhappy face. "Widow Fales was old and ugly, Margarida. Not young and pretty like you. The *vaqueros* wouldn't keep their minds on their jobs. They'd start showing off, and we'd have accidents."

Margarida decided Papa was too upset for her to press him now, but she wouldn't give up, only wait a little.

Her father was halfway through the door when he stopped. "I almost forgot to tell you. I saw Enoch Springer in town, and he asked if he could call on you. Fernando Reyes asked me the same thing. I told Enoch and Fernando both they could ride out once, and then we'd see."

After he disappeared, Margarida thought about what he'd said. Enoch—yes, she'd enjoy his company. Fernando Reyes she remembered as a plump, shy boy about her own age. His father owned land here and had a large grant just north of Silver City, near Piños Altos. She hadn't seen Fernando since before she went east to school.

None of this seemed important now, compared with thoughts of J.J. and her mother. Reluctantly she crossed the patio to her parents' bedroom, and then stopped outside the door. The side of her face still throbbed, and her lip stung. Even so, the blow hadn't hurt as much as her mother's venomous words. She dreaded facing Mama, but she would remember what Papa said about her mother's early life and try to offer comfort. She couldn't apologize for not having told her parents J.J.'s plans. It would be hypocritical, when she knew she'd do the same thing again.

When she knocked and entered, she found her mother lying on the bed with her eyes closed. "Can I get you something, Mama?" she asked.

"No."

Margarida tried again. "I'm sorry you're so upset. I'll do whatever I can to help."

Her mother's voice sounded subdued and indifferent. "I don't care what you do. It won't make any difference now."

When Margarida reached her own room, she took out a snake skull which J.J. years ago had put on her dresser, trying to scare her. She stared at it, thinking of J.J., and also of herself. He'd gone on an adventure, but what had she done? For years she'd planned her future around Brant. Now that was over. Since August she'd just been drifting through the days. No more, she resolved. She would decide what she wanted, and then do it.

Help Papa. She'd start in the stable, where J.J. had been responsible for the care of the family's horses. And she'd learn about the household. Eventually she'd marry, and she'd need to know more about a woman's jobs.

In the next few days, Elena made no more accusations, seeming almost numb as she stayed mostly in her bedroom. Margarida quietly began with her plans. She took over the household management and found, to her surprise, that it was harder than she'd realized. Planning the servants' jobs, helping with illness, seeing that food and supplies were ordered from town—all that required organizing that she found she enjoyed. She even liked doing some of the cooking. Her mother accepted Margarida's efforts without comment, apparently hardly noticing what her daughter did.

The work in the stable was easy, because it meant overseeing for all the horses what she'd always done for Halcon. She was sure her father realized what she was doing, but he said nothing. His silence encouraged her to accompany Carlos on forays out to check the barbed-wire fence, which her father had installed the previous year at the northern end of their valley.

The first Sunday of November was clear and crisp, with a gusty wind which scattered the remaining aspen leaves. In midafternoon Enoch Springer came to visit, his denim pants and workshirt replaced by a suit and a white shirt with an embroidered collar. The sparkle in his light brown eyes and his pleased smile made him more attractive than Margarida had remembered. He amused her with his lighthearted stories, and she enjoyed his admiration.

On his third visit, they took a picnic up on a nearby ridge which had a view of the valleys in three directions. At Jesse's insistence, Elena went along as an uninterested chaperon. After they ate, she got on her horse and started for home, not waiting for Enoch and Margarida.

As Enoch stood beside Margarida to help her mount, she could see that he wanted to kiss her. Deliberately she turned her face toward him. He said, "Margarida?" and then pulled her close and kissed her. It seemed strange to be held by someone not much taller than she, but his kiss was pleasant, even faintly exciting. She liked to think that meant she was forgetting Brant.

Fernando Reyes appeared the last Sunday in November. He'd lost his plumpness and looked handsome with his tight black curls above what Margarida suspected were deliberately soulful eyes. He'd also lost his shyness, as she discovered when she walked with him out to the stable to retrieve his horse. As soon as they were out of sight of the house, he grabbed her, twisting her around to kiss her and trying to put his hand inside her blouse.

She hit him in the stomach, and his shocked look was so funny that Margarida couldn't stay angry. He returned the following week, seemingly unperturbed by her rejection and acting the perfect gentlemen. Enoch arrived the same day. Margarida was amused by the way they competed to tell outrageous stories

and decided to let Fernando stay. It interfered with
any more of Enoch's kisses, but she didn't mind that
too much. Both men came regularly on Sundays after
that, subtly squaring off at each other.

Periodically Elena railed at Jesse because he hadn't
left for California. At first he repeated his explanations, but soon he listened silently. Margarida wondered what they said to each other in their room; she
couldn't imagine loving words. But because of her
mother's indifference to running the household, Margarida was too busy to worry.

Brant watched as the pale December sun slanted
through the bedroom window and touched his father's
waxen face. Luisa sat weeping beside the bed. It jolted
him that his father's death seemed to grieve her more
than it did him. He and this tall, austere man had
shared little throughout their lives until last year, when
his father had agreed to let Brant's Apache relatives
settle on Curtis land.

Though he'd seen his father's increasing illness, Brant
hadn't realized how serious it was. But from what the
doctor said earlier, Rupert had known he was dying.
He'd kept his knowledge to himself, never complaining, showing a self-disciplined reserve that Brant admired. Yet at the same time he felt shut out; his father
hadn't shared even this last suffering.

What would it have been like, Brant wondered, to
have a father he loved and who felt that way about
him? Tears that had refused to surface earlier came to
his eyes. He suppressed his weakness, shocked that he
grieved as much for what he wished had happened as
for his father's death.

He found Dr. Winton in the kitchen. The middle-
aged man looked sleepy, his pale blue eyes red-rimmed.
He'd been awake most of the last two nights, as had
Brant and Luisa. "I'll take care of the death certifi-

cate," he said, "and notify the undertaker. You want me to tell the preacher you'll be in to see him about the funeral?"

"Yes, thank you, Dr. Winton."

"Then I'll be on my way."

Brant walked outside with the doctor and watched the buggy out of sight, then went to the stable. He found Walt in a stall with a sorrel filly they'd recently found in the brush, coaxing the head-shy animal to let him put a halter on. Tall Man leaned against the wall. He looked up at Brant's entrance. "It is finished?" he asked.

"Yes," said Brant. He felt grateful that his cousin had chosen to stay at the Curtis ranch. He was patient with Walt and almost as skillful as the younger man with animals.

Brant knew by now that his cousin's daughter and wife, who had been related to Geronimo, were dead. Tall Man referred to them as "the ones who are not here." Brant hoped Tall Man, without the family tie to keep him with Geronimo, would agree to remain here. His intelligence and skill at organizing made him excellent at any job.

Walt removed the halter from the filly and came out of the stall. "Did you see how I handled her, Brant?"

"Yes, I did," Brant responded. "You have a magic touch as usual. Walt, you must come in the house with me now."

Luisa sat in the kitchen, still crying. Walt instantly responded to her distress. "Luisa, why are you crying?"

She rose and put her arms around him, the small dark woman looked strange comforting the large blond man. "I weep for your father."

Walt patted Luisa's cheek, his ready sympathy aroused by her unhappiness, but his face held no understanding.

"Come, Walt," Brant said gently, and led his brother up to the bedroom.

Walt looked at the pale face with the eyes closed.
"Is Papa still asleep?"

"No, Walt. He's dead."

"That means he won't wake up again." Walt sounded
matter-of-fact.

"Yes." Their father had paid even less attention to
Walt than to Brant as a child. Brant doubted that Walt
would noticed his death much. Rupert had been disappointed in both his sons, not because of anything
they'd done—just for what they were. It saddened
Brant that in two months Tall Man had come to mean
more to Walt than his father.

A sudden early snow fell the morning of Rupert
Curtis' funeral. On the way into Rio Torcido, Margarida
snuggled inside the robes in the surrey and admired
the jeweled frosting on the tall pines. When they
reached the lower elevation of the town, the snow was
already melting, turning the yard around the small
church to mud.

When she followed her parents into the church, she
saw Brant sitting with Walt on the front bench. It
reminded her of that August day during the wedding,
when she'd searched for him in church, and of her
foolish plans to humble him. She was glad the black
veil on her bonnet concealed the blush heating her
skin.

Quickly she looked away and saw Priscilla Welles
watching her. Margarida smiled, hoping they'd get a
chance to speak after the funeral. She hadn't seen
Priscilla since J.J. left.

Samuel Newcomb, the minister, entered in his black
robes, and the service began. As Margarida listened to
the eulogy, she saw that her father's eyes were wet.
He and Rupert Curtis had been early partners and
friends, so maybe he'd known a side of the aloof
Englishman that she hadn't.

Her mother was weeping openly, and as the organ began a mournful hymn, Margarida knew Mama must be imagining that J.J. might be dead. She put her arm around her mother, understanding how unhappy she had been the past weeks.

When the service ended, Jesse took his place as one of the pallbearers. Margarida held her mother's arm, and they followed the somber procession up the slope behind the church and through the picket fence that surrounded the graveyard. A sifting of white snow remained on the earth piled to one side of the open grave. One edge of Margarida's veil pulled loose from her bonnet and caught annoyingly against her eyelashes. She lifted up the veil and tucked it around the brim.

The pallbearers stepped aside, and Margarida found herself directly across from Brant. He was staring down at the coffin, and his face looked strained and tired. He seemed a stranger in his high white collar and black frock coat. Beside him Walt shifted restlessly, as if he were anxious to escape from the confinement of formal clothes.

Margarida felt a rush of sympathy that brought tears to her throat. She hadn't liked Rupert Curtis; he hadn't seemed like a loving father to either Brant or Walt. Still, he was their father, and they probably felt some grief.

Brant looked up, and his eyes met hers. As if he sensed her feelings, the tense line of his jaw softened. At that moment Margarida felt a flow of emotion between them so strong that she was sure Brant must sense it too. Those years of her childhood connected them in some way. Though she might hate him sometimes and he her, she felt certain the bond would always be there.

As Brant received the greetings of the departing mourners, Margarida waited, feeling constrained by the look which had passed between them.

Her father approached the brothers, and Margarida and her mother followed. Papa put out his hand to Brant and said, his voice emotional, "I'll miss Rupert. He was a good friend to me all those years, ever since the early days when we shared our first mining claims."

Brant gripped Papa's hand in return. "Thank you. I hope we can continue to be friends and good neighbors."

"When things settle down, come to see me."

"Yes. I'd like to discuss activities in our valley with you," Brant replied, and Margarida realized he must be talking about the Indians on his land and his hopes that her father would agree to their ranging over Ross land as well.

The pain of this reminder surprised and distressed her. It made her voice formal as she said, "Please accept my sympathy for your loss."

Brant's "Thank you" was equally stiff.

She moved to Walt. "I'm sorry about your father's death."

"Yes, thank you," he said, as if carefully repeating words he'd been told to say. His face relaxed into its normal pleasant expression. "When will we go riding?"

Being careful not to look at Brant, she said, "Soon, Walt. When the weather's warmer." Behind her she heard her mother's polite voice, and she escaped down the hill.

Though Brant tried not to watch Margarida leave, he couldn't keep his gaze from her. He should be thinking about his father, but she'd intruded. Even in her black mourning dress, she still had that appealing vitality. Would he ever get to the time when he didn't feel excitement arcing between them, like lightning between storm clouds? From the look they'd exchanged earlier, she felt it too.

"Brant," Walt said impatiently, "when will we go home?"

Brant turned his attention to his brother. "We have to go to the preacher's house for a while, and maybe stay the night in town. Be patient a little longer," he said, and thought if he could take that same advice himself, surely one day Margarida would seem less attractive to him.

When Margarida reached the church, Priscilla was standing in front; Mrs. Welles was nearby, talking to the schoolteacher. "Hello, Priscilla. How are you?" Margarida put her arm around Priscilla and gave her a hug.

"All right," Priscilla said, but her voice didn't match her words. Margarida looked more closely and saw that Priscilla looked thinner, and tiny lines around her eyes and mouth gave her the unhappy expression Margarida remembered from earlier times.

"I haven't been able to come into Rio Torcido for a long time because my mother hasn't been well," Margarida said. "I'm sorry. I've missed seeing you."

Priscilla's eyes showed a little more animation. "Yes, I missed you."

Her mother walked over to them. "Margarida, how nice to see you, even though this is a sad occasion."

"It's pleasant to see you also, Mrs. Welles."

"Priscilla," Mrs. Welles said nervously, "your father will be here soon and will expect us to be over at the parsonage. We mustn't keep him waiting." Priscilla's face lost its color. Mrs. Welles nodded to Margarida and started across the road.

Wanting to sound cheerful, Margarida said, "Do you still see Lee Hansen?"

Priscilla flushed and looked at Margarida almost defiantly. "Yes. He's very much in love with me."

Uncertain how to respond to Priscilla's tone, Margarida said, "That's wonderful." She waited, wondering if something would be said about an engagement. Priscilla's strained face kept her from asking more about Lee.

"Does Enoch Springer call on you?" Priscilla asked.

"Yes, he's come out to our ranch several times."

From over her shoulder Margarida heard Nat Welles's harsh voice. "Why are you dawdling here, Priscilla?" His manner softened only a little as he said to Margarida, "Sorry, but my family knows I can't wait around for them."

Margarida kissed Priscilla. "I will come to see you," she said, sympathy for Priscilla welling up at the reminder of Nat Welles's unpleasant ways. Priscilla nodded, then hurried after her father.

As Margarida waited for her parents, she watched people crossing the road to the parsonage. Sadness filled her—for Brant and Walt's loss of their father, and for her loss of them and of J.J. She let her tears finally fall. Then resolutely she planned the activities that would fill her days at home.

Late March had brought the first warm days of spring when Brant came to the Ross ranch one Sunday afternoon. From the patio Margarida heard her mother greet him in the living room, and then his tall form appeared in the doorway. She knew he'd come to talk to her father before, but she hadn't seen him for the three months since the funeral.

As Brant looked at her, Margarida felt especially pleased that she'd chosen to wear one of her favorite dresses—a peach-colored muslin with a high ruffled collar that brought out the warm glow of her skin. The skirt fell softly from the tight waist in lines which made her look particularly graceful.

Enoch Springer and Fernando Reyes had both arrived earlier, and they sat in the patio. They'd taken to riding back and forth to Rio Torcido together, neither one apparently wanting to risk his rival's arriving at the Ross ranch ahead of him. She thought Brant hesitated momentarily when he saw the two men, but then he walked smoothly to where she was sitting. Enoch and Fernando rose.

Brant bowed politely. "Good afternoon, Margarida."

To her chagrin, she could feel her heart beating faster. Beside Brant's chiseled features, the other men's faces looked young and uncertain. "Hello, Brant. You know Enoch Springer, I believe. And this is Fernando Reyes."

"Yes. Nice to see you, Enoch, and you, Mr. Reyes."

The men shook hands, and Margarida noticed that while Brant seemed completely at ease, both Enoch and Fernando looked like boys with a plate of cookies who see another, larger boy arrive. A laugh rose as far as her throat; she caught Brant's eyes and saw a similar amusement there.

Nettled that he didn't look at the two men with some of the antagonism they displayed to each other, she smiled seductively at Enoch. "Enoch was just telling us about a trip he plans to Socorro. I'll miss him."

Enoch's face flushed and he grinned with pleasure; Fernando scowled. Brant only said comfortably, "I'm leaving for Santa Fe Tuesday. I plan to take the narrow-gauge line from Silver City to Deming, then the train north."

"I'm not going until May," Enoch said, "and I can't afford the train. I'll ride to Socorro."

"You're smart," Brant said, "Camping out is more comfortable than the train. I can't take the extra time. Please excuse me, Margarida. I must talk to your father."

Brant stayed in Jesse's office for some time. Enoch told of a cattle drive when the cook had deserted, and he'd cooked until one of the cowboys threatened to shoot him. Fernando talked loudly of bullfights in Madrid, and upset a patio chair trying to demonstrate the bullfighter's stance. Margarida found her attention wandering, and when they said they must leave, she didn't urge them to stay.

She waved good-bye to them from beside the corral and started back to the house. Brant and her father came out on the veranda. "I hate to be gone," Brant said, "but I can't straighten out the inheritance without going to Santa Fe. I appreciate your agreeing to drop over to the ranch occasionally. Probably no need—Juan Martínez is a capable foreman, and my cousin can help him with any problem that comes up. I'll be back before the spring roundup."

"Glad to look in while you're gone, Brant," Jesse responded. "You taking Walt with you?"

Brant paused, one foot resting on the bottom step. "No. He's happy here with my cousin to look after him, and I want to get my business done in Santa Fe as soon as possible. It will go faster without him."

He tipped his hat to Jesse, then turned and started toward the stable. Margarida had her breathing firmly under control this time. "I hope you have a pleasant journey, Brant." She was proud of how coolly polite she sounded.

He stopped, and despite her composure, she felt again that pull between them, the invisible tie she hadn't been able to destroy. He looked at her, his dark eyes velvet black with a moment's sadness. Then he smiled, and she wondered if she had conjured up that flicker of expression. "Thank you, Margarida. Have you heard anything from J.J.?"

"No." In an almost nostalgic need for the reassurance he'd provided when she was a child, she confided, "Mining in California sounds dangerous. I worry about J.J."

He smiled again, but this time with an amused indulgence that irritated her. "That's because you're a woman. J.J.'s off on an adventure. It's something men have to do. No need to worry."

Her irritation turned to anger. "I don't worry because I'm a woman. I envy J.J. the chance to go off like that."

"Danger is part of a man's life, not a woman's," he retorted, and she wanted to hit him.

"Plenty of women do dangerous things. I've heard that Apache women go on raids with men."

His eyes lost their amusement. "You're not Indian, Margarida."

"Fortunately!" She stomped around him to the house.

Brant felt his face flushing as he walked to the stable. What a stupid fool he'd sounded like, he fumed. Dammit, why had he said those things about women? He wasn't sure he believed even part of what he'd spouted.

As he found Chid and swung into the saddle, he recognized why he'd deliberately goaded Margarida. The sight of her, so beautiful, basking in the cowlike admiration of Springer and Reyes, had infuriated him. With a string of silent curses he put Chid into a lope.

Inside the *sala* Margarida, still angry at Brant, poured herself a glass of sherry, ignoring her father's frown.

"Why does Brant have to go to Santa Fe?" she asked her father, wishing she weren't curious, but still wanting to know. "Doesn't the ranch belong to him now?"

"Rupert originally bought his land from a large grant held by the English crown," explained her father. "It makes transfer of title a little complicated. And Rupert actually left the land to Walt, with Brant as his guardian and heir."

"Why did Mr. Curtis do that?"

"I don't know. Maybe because of Brant's Indian blood. Rupert might have thought the land could be taken away from Brant because of that."

Brant without his land! The startling thought banished Margarida's anger. She couldn't imagine Brant without the Curtis land. "Do you think Brant could lose the ranch?"

"No. Not likely. But he's smart to go to Santa Fe and get it all settled."

Her fear subsiding, Margarida sat beside her father

on the leather couch. At times she'd wanted something terrible to happen to Brant, like being thrown off his horse in front of a bunch of cowboys, or his getting so ugly no girl would look at him. She couldn't imagine either thing really occurring, but she'd enjoyed her fantasies. Still, she didn't wish for something so terrible as the loss of his ranch. She could never dislike him that much.

The letter from J.J. arrived two weeks later. A warm April morning had turned into a chilly afternoon when Carlos returned from Rio Torcido with supplies. A trader from California had given the letter to him, with a request to pass it on to Margarida. Carlos handed it to her in the stable, where she was doctoring a lame mare that had mesquite thorns in her hock. Margarida hid the envelope in the pocket of her old skirt until she finished, and then ran to her room to tear it open.

J.J.'s handwriting scrawled across the page, as if he had hurried with the writing.

Dear Margarida,

I got here without any trouble, but there's not as much gold left as I hoped. I had a wonderful piece of luck, though. I met a man at Monoville who's prospected the Mono Diggings for years. His name's Michael Quinn, and he knew Papa from a long time ago. He told me the real money now is in silver. He knows a perfect spot to prospect, and he's going to take me with him. It's someplace in the Utah Territory, along the San Juan River. When I find out where I'll be, I'll write again.

Your loving brother,
Jesse

Along one side of the page was crowded another sentence: "I hope everyone is fine at home."

Margarida sat with the letter in her hand, trying to decide what to do. Finally she concluded that J.J. hadn't said not to show it to her parents, and it would be cruel to keep it from them. It wouldn't tell them just where he was, and it would reassure Mama that J.J. was alive and well.

Without bothering to change her work-stained skirt, she hurried to the dining room, where she knew her parents would be waiting. "Mama, Papa. A letter from J.J. He's fine."

Elena gasped and snatched the page from Margarida. She read it, her face first flushing and then going pale. "But he's not coming home," she wailed.

"Please give me the letter," Papa said impatiently, and took it from his wife's limp hand. He read partway, and then gave a groan. His face looked almost as white as his hair, and he sat down suddenly in a chair.

Margarida rushed to his side. "Papa. What's wrong?"

He dropped his head into his hands. Terrified that he might be having a heart attack, Margarida tried to unfasten his collar. He looked up and pushed her hand away, his face still drained of color. "I'm all right."

His hands trembled, and Margarida didn't believe him. "Then why are you so upset?"

He shuddered, then seemed to gain control of himself. Some of the color returned to his skin. "Mike Quinn—the man J.J. met—is an old enemy of mine. Years ago I killed his brother in a fight, and wounded Quinn. He never believed that it was a fair fight, and he swore he'd get even. I used to watch out for him, but he never came here, and I forgot about him. He must have run into J.J. and figured out he was my son."

Margarida's fear returned. "When he left, J.J. said he was going to go by his real name of Jesse."

Elena stood before her husband, all of her hysteria gone, only cold determination left. "Then you're going to find J.J., no matter how long it takes. You can go to Monoville. Someone there will know about it. Or you can go to Utah. But you have to find him."

Margarida had never before heard her mother speak to her father that way. For a moment he sagged, looking old and crumpled. Then he straightened his shoulders. "Yes, Elena. I'll have to go. Margarida, Frank Vincent hasn't worked out to be much of a foreman, but he can manage. I'd planned to look for someone different before the spring roundup, but Frank will have to do for now. If you've learned anything by watching, you may have to help out. When Brant's back from Santa Fe, ask him for advice."

He turned to Elena, his movements vigorous again. "Tell Rosa to pack for me. She'll know the clothes I'll need for a trip like this. I'll take Carlos with me. In spite of his bad eyes, he's the smartest man we have. You'll have to make do with Pedro for any special errands."

After her mother and father left the dining room, Margarida stayed, struggling with her fear—and with the memory of her mother's accusation that she should have prevented J.J.'s leaving. Though she told herself the guilt she felt was unwarranted, she couldn't banish the tight feeling around her heart. But Papa would find J.J.—he must!

The next morning Margarida watched with her mother until Papa and Carlos had disappeared from sight. Elena, still with the calm of the night before, said, "You might see if you can help Mr. Vincent. I'll manage the house." She walked firmly inside, leaving Margarida to follow, bewildered by the transformation in her mother.

Margarida didn't understand, but she was grateful when her mother's resolution persisted. It was as if her husband's doing what she'd wanted—going to find her son—had restored her equilibrium. Margarida was particularly glad her mother took over the household, because Margarida's knowledge of the ranch was far more limited than she'd thought. She did know enough to see that Frank Vincent didn't do a good job as foreman—the carelessness of the ranch hands was evidence.

One day a week later she came back just before noon from inspecting the meadow where they would gather the horses for the summer drive. In the dining room behind the cookhouse she found Frank Vincent eating his meal. Stopping in front of him, she slammed her hand down on the table hard enough to make the utensils clatter. "Mr. Vincent—I want to see you in the office."

Without waiting to see what he did, she turned and stamped out and into the house. When Vincent arrived, she didn't give him time to speak. "Why haven't you started the pens for the *remudas*?"

He frowned. "No need yet. Drive's not till July."

"Right after the spring roundup, we have to confine each stallion with the mares he'll lead on the drive."

"Just a minute—I don't need you to tell me what—"

"Yes, you do. Get started on it."

His face almost matched the red bandanna around his neck. He glared at her before he gave a surly "I was planning to do it anyway," and left.

Margarida sat abruptly in her father's chair, uncertain whether she felt more pleasure or relief. Pleasure won. She *did* know enough about some of Papa's jobs.

By eleven that night, her pleasure had vanished under worry about Papa and J.J. and uncertainty over the ranch. She turned restlessly in bed. One victory over a disgruntled Frank Vincent didn't mean she'd won control. Brant hadn't returned from Santa Fe or she might have subdued her pride enough to ask for his counsel.

Lobo had been asleep on the end of her bed when

he suddenly raised his head and gave a low growl. He jumped down and padded to the door, where he whined to be let out.

Margarida listened, but she heard only the dog's breathing. "What is it, Lobo?" He whined again, and she put on her robe and opened the door. He shot across the patio to the kitchen entrance. In the light from a waxing moon, she could see the patio was empty. She hurried after Lobo and let him into the kitchen, where he dashed to the door to the outer yard and whined again.

When she opened that door, he bounded around to the front of the house. She hesitated, wondering if she should rouse someone else, then decided Lobo would be protection against almost anything and followed him. As she reached the front, she saw Lobo sitting beside the veranda steps, thumping his tail in the dust.

A tall shadow detached itself from the veranda. "Señorita Ross?" Even in the darkness she recognized the man's height and accent.

"Tall Man—what are you doing here?"

"I would like to see your father."

"Papa isn't home."

"I heard that he had gone away. I hoped it wasn't true. Is there someone else here to help with something very difficult?"

Fear squeezed her chest so that she was afraid she wouldn't be able to speak. She gulped for air before she could ask, "Is it Brant? Has something happened to him?"

"No. It's Walt."

She caught his arm, digging her fingers into the hard muscle. "Tell me! What's wrong?"

"Tonight some men came from Rio Torcido. I was away at the camp in the mountains. Walt stayed at home with Señora Luisa. These men came and took Walt away. The *señora* said they claimed he . . . I'm sorry. I must say it. They said he had raped a girl in town. They took him to jail."

Rape! Horror thrust a knife through Margarida's stomach and paralyzed her voice. She wanted to rage in protest, but she could only listen as Tall Man continued. "Juan tried to stop them, but they had many guns. They threatened to shoot anyone who bothered them. The other men were afraid to do anything."

Shock loosened its grip, and instantly she decided. "I'll get Pedro, and we'll go to town." She thought swiftly. The Ross hands were all Mexican *vaqueros*, except for the foreman, whom she didn't like or trust. The men in Rio Torcido wouldn't listen to ordinary *vaqueros;* animosity toward Mexicans still simmered under the surface. She would have to persuade them to release Walt, and she had a better chance if she went without the Ross hired men. "There's really no one else I can take. You'll go with me, won't you?"

"Yes, of course. But I cannot go into the town with you." His voice, which had been even, almost unemotional-sounding, became bitter. "The help of one Apache in a town is worse than no help."

As she ran back to her room, what Tall Man had said hit her again. Walt—accused of rape! She pictured him, bewildered and frightened, not understanding what was going on, and she felt as if her heart were bleeding. In spite of Brant's warnings about Walt's possible lack of control, she couldn't believe he had raped anyone. Even if he had, it didn't make any difference about helping him.

Hastily she pulled on pants so she could ride astride, and over them a skirt to look respectable when she arrived in town. Snatching up a ribbon, she tied her hair back and pulled on a soft old hat.

On her way out, she ran to her father's office and scribbled a note telling her mother an emergency to do with the Curtis ranch had come up and she was going into town. Fortunately Pedro had a small house all to himself, so she could rouse him without waking everyone else.

As she started to leave the room, she stopped and went back to her father's desk. In a drawer she found the Colt .44-40 revolver he'd used to teach her how to shoot and checked that it was loaded. She took a Winchester carbine from the wall rack and gathered up ammunition for it and for the revolver. She didn't know what she would have to do, but whatever it was, she would be prepared to do it.

9

ON the way to town Margarida wanted to ride as fast as Halcon would go. But though the half-moon provided some light, the darkness required caution. Tall Man rode ahead of her and Pedro, and he set a faster pace than she would have dared by herself. She had to be content with that.

Where the trail crossed a meadow, she was able to pull abreast of Tall Man. On seeing her, he slowed his horse to a walk. "Do you wish to speak?" he asked.

"Yes. Who were the men who took Walt?"

"Señora Luisa did not know them. One of the *vaqueros* told me two names. Bodmer and Henderson. There were eight or nine men. The *vaquero* did not see all their faces."

Margarida's already knotted stomach squeezed even tighter. Bodmer and Henderson—two of the men Brant said murdered the half-breed Indian. Hoarsely she asked, "What girl did they say Walt had . . . attacked?"

"They would not tell Señora Luisa."

"Did . . . did they hurt Walt?"

Even in the half-light, Margarida could see the lines of Tall Man's face harden into an ominous blankness. "Men like that are not gentle."

The meadow narrowed into another tree-covered ravine, and Margarida dropped behind Tall Man again. She must keep her feelings under control, so it was better not to ask more questions until she could see Walt.

Never before had she ridden the fourteen miles to town at night. Nor was she used to the pace for that long a time without rest. But rage at Walt's accusers, as intense as her fear for him, strengthened her muscles and kept fatigue away. Only once did she allow herself to think about Brant, to recognize how desperately she wished he were here. Then she shut that knowledge away—he wasn't here, and she would have to do the best she could without him.

When they reached the last descent into town, Tall Man reined in. "I do not go into Rio Torcido with you. I will be nearby where I can see you but not be seen."

"I'll go to the jail and talk to Walt. I'll make Sheriff Jones understand that Walt wouldn't have done what they claim. If I promise I'll bring him back to town, surely they'll let him go home with me."

Tall Man's voice chilled her. "I know white men's jails. They will not let you take Walt home. You must find the good men who live in Rio Torcido. Men who will stop the others from what the white man call Judge Lynch."

Hanging! Without trial! A wave of terror swept over Margarida, but she pushed it back. She couldn't let fear paralyze her now. "No—I can't believe that would happen."

"It can."

Though Margarida still didn't want to accept Tall Man's words, she couldn't risk being wrong. "Then I must get to Walt right away." She turned to Pedro. "Go to the minister's house. Tell him I'm at the jail, and he must come. Get Henry Franklin too, and ask him to find anyone else he thinks would help."

"Two men—not many," Tall Man said somberly.

"Enoch Springer lives just after the first ford south of town. Tall Man, you could get him. You ride the fastest, and he'd believe you and come." When she saw Tall Man's hesitation, she added, "I'll be at the jail with Walt. No one would do anything while I'm there."

He turned and disappeared into the night.

Pedro spoke worriedly. "Señorita Margarida, I cannot let you go to the jail alone. After we get there, then I will go for Señor Franklin and Señor Newcomb."

Protesting would take too much time. She spurred Halcon toward the jail. Houses and stores were dark, but she saw lights in the saloons and horses tethered outside.

When Margarida reached the brick courthouse, she slid from her horse and took the revolver from her saddlebags. She pushed it into her waistband, feeling the cold steel even through her clothes. The heavy jacket she'd worn over her pants and skirt concealed its shape.

Pedro reined in just behind her at the jail and dismounted. "Pedro," she ordered, "go on now."

"No, Señorita," he said, leading Halcon and his horse to the hitching rail. "I will go when you are inside."

Seeing that arguing was again useless, she took the carbine from its leather boot beside her saddle and handed it to Pedro. "Here. Take this. And hurry."

She gathered her skirt and ran around the courthouse to the back, where light shone through the window beside the entrance to the jail. She tried the door and felt its resistance, then pounded on it with both fists.

A face peered out of the window, and she heard a voice say, "It's a woman."

A bolt screeched faintly, and the door swung open. The bean-pole figure of the sheriff, Mickett Jones, blocked the entrance. "Who is it? What do you want?"

She glanced over one shoulder and saw Pedro's retreating shadow. Turning back to the door, she pushed past the sheriff, provoking him to a "Wait now . . ." and then a startled "Miss Ross!"

Hike Jones, Mickett's younger brother, stood beside a battered desk. A deputy's badge on his worn denim vest looked almost too heavy for his narrow chest. Two Duplex oil lamps on the wall illuminated the jail office. Behind Hike Jones a stout wooden door reinforced with steel straps shut off the entrance to a corridor. Through the barred window in the door she could see a lantern hanging from the ceiling in the middle of the passage and the bars of the cells on each side.

"Miss Ross, what are you doing here?"

She swung back to face the sheriff. "You have Walt Curtis in jail here?"

He scowled. "Yes, that's right."

Her knees felt as if they might give way. She'd held in a fear too terrible to face—that the men hadn't brought Walt to jail, but had murdered him. Stiffening her untrustworthy legs, she announced, "I want to see Walt."

Mickett Jones's scowl deepened, contorting his thin face. "I can't let you do that, Miss Ross. Walt Curtis is a dangerous prisoner, charged with . . . a heinous crime."

Fury erasing the last of her trembling, she stepped forward and planted her finger on the sheriff's chest. "He's not been charged with anything. He's been accused, but that's all."

The sheriff stepped backward. "He didn't deny it."

She grabbed the edge of his vest, glaring up into his flushed face. "You know very well he wouldn't understand what he was accused of. He doesn't even know what rape is."

"Miss Ross! You mustn't say—"

"It's all right to accuse an innocent man of rape, but not for a woman to use that word?"

He pulled away from her, sputtering. "Now, just a minute—"

"If Brant Curtis or my father were here, you wouldn't

have Walt in jail. They're not, and I'm going to see Walt, and *you're going to let me.*"

He retreated a step. "I can't let Walt Curtis out here."

"Then let me talk to him in the cell," she insisted.

Mickett Jones looked at her as if she were a crazy woman, and Margarida knew she'd won. In a surly voice he said, "I'll have to lock you in the cell too."

"Fine."

He turned to his openmouthed brother. "Hike, you see if you can find Bodmer. I think Miss Ross better hear what he has to say."

Margarida felt her fear returning at the thought of Carl Bodmer. Had he accused Walt of raping his daughter?

Hike took a sheepskin jacket from a peg on the wall and left. Mickett bolted the door after him and picked up a lantern from the desk, then chose a key from a ring on his belt. As he fitted it into the lock on the windowed door, Margarida asked, "What girl is Walt accused of attacking?"

Mickett wouldn't look at her. "That's none of your business to ask." His voice became nasty. "Let Walt Curtis tell you, if he knows enough so he can."

Though she resented the slur at Walt, Margarida said nothing more. Obviously she'd pushed the sheriff as far as she could right now. He opened the door and preceded her down the passage, then stopped at the far cell.

Walt was sitting on a narrow bunk against one wall. A small barred window high overhead let in bleached moonlight. At the sound of the sheriff's key in the cell door Walt looked up. He stared at Margarida, his eyes wide and his mouth slack, as if he couldn't believe what he was seeing. When she entered, he pushed himself to his feet. "Margarida?" he said, his voice uncertain.

The sheriff put the lantern on the floor, and Margarida

gasped when she saw Walt clearly. One eye was swollen almost shut. A cut on his cheekbone had left dried blood on the side of his face, and his shirt was torn so badly that one sleeve was loose at his shoulder. Raw, red lines showed around both wrists.

She turned fiercely to the sheriff. "I need some water. And a blanket."

Mickett pointed to the corner. "Water in the bucket. One blanket on the bed is all he gets." He slammed the cell door shut and locked it, then stomped down the corridor and locked that door as well.

Margarida put her arms around Walt and held him close. "Oh, Walt" was all she could say over the tears that threatened to choke her. Tenderness and love and fury at Walt's accusers all churned inside her.

Her longing for Brant was so strong that she thought she must have said something aloud, then realized it was Walt speaking. "When will Brant be here?"

"I don't know, Walt. He had to go away on a trip. But he'll be back soon."

"Yes," he said forlornly, "I remember now." He shivered, and tears began to mix with the dried blood making red streaks down his face. "When those men came, Tall Man wasn't home either."

"I know," she soothed him. "I'm here to help you now, Walt. And Tall Man will be here soon." She took the blanket off the bunk and wrapped it around him, then used her handkerchief to bathe his face.

"Brant will be mad. He always told me not to hit people if I could help it. But those men hit me and I got really mad at them. So I hit them."

"Good. Brant will be glad. And so am I. They were wrong to hurt you." She moistened the handkerchief again and held it against his eye. "Lie down, Walt, so this will stay on your eye."

He lay down and held the cloth. "I want to go home. When can we go home?"

"Soon," she said, praying she was right. "Walt, I must ask you some questions."

"Sure, Margarida." He sounded so trusting that tears almost overwhelmed her again.

"Those men who hit you and brought you here. Do you know why?"

"They said I hurt someone. A girl. I told them I knocked Luisa down the other day. It was an accident. I just bumped into her. But they said they didn't mean that."

Margarida almost stopped. To question seemed disloyal, but she had to know. She twisted her hands together, trying to think how to ask. "Walt, you know how stallions mount the mares. And bulls with the cows." She swallowed, then forced out, "Did you ever do that with a woman?"

He looked at her apprehensively. "I don't know what you mean." His expression told her he didn't understand. In some way he realized his own limitations, and Margarida knew at times he must be confused and afraid.

She began again. "Did you ever touch a woman here?" Blushing, she put her hand to her own breast. "Or here?" She touched the front of her skirt at her groin.

His face relaxed with a smile of pleasure. "You mean when I put my cock in her."

His answer shocked Margarida. Had Walt truly raped someone? For a moment the room swung crazily around her.

He continued happily. "At first I thought I was hurting her because she kind of yelled. It scared me, but Brant said it was all right. It meant she liked it."

"*Brant* said?"

"Yes," he went on. "I was glad she did, because I liked her. She sat on my lap, and then she let me get on the bed with her. Brant said I made her happy. She told him he could get on the bed with her, but he said she was just for me. I liked her so much, we gave her some money."

Brant had arranged a prostitute for Walt! Margarida's heart settled back into place and the shaking inside her subsided. "Did . . . did you see her again?"

"Yes. I forget how many times."

Another question still had to be asked. Her voice steady now, she said, "Did you ever lie down on a bed with someone else, when Brant wasn't there?"

He looked at her with a shocked expression. "No. Brant said I shouldn't do that with anyone else. She wouldn't like it if I did."

"Oh, Walt. I love you so much." She held tight to his hand, a great rush of relief and love mingling.

Through the closed door to the sheriff's office, Margarida caught the high tones of a woman's voice. A minute later the passage door opened, and Mickett Jones appeared, followed by Adela. He strode hastily to the door to Walt's cell and unlocked it.

"Adela!" Margarida exclaimed. "Why are you here?"

The sheriff spoke before Adela could answer. "You have to get out of here, Miss Ross. Some men will be headed for the jail any minute now. They plan to take the prisoner and be their own judge and jury."

Margarida's heart began to pump so hard she could hear the beat in her eardrums. "You mean . . . lynching. But you won't let them have Walt. You can't!"

"I sure don't intend to, ma'am, but they can be pretty rough."

"Then you have to let Walt get away," Margarida cried. "I'll take him with me."

"I can't do that," the sheriff said, his voice grim. "I'll protect him."

Adela took Margarida's arm. "I overheard men talking in the Imperial. A bunch of them are drunk, and Carl Bodmer has them all worked up. I came to warn the sheriff. I didn't know you were here. You must go with me."

Margarida pulled away. "No! I won't leave Walt."

"You can't stay here," Adela protested.

From behind Margarida she heard Walt's bewildered voice. "Margarida, when can we go home?"

She turned and made her voice calm. "Soon, Walt."

"Miss Ross," Sheriff Jones said urgently, "we can't wait. You've got to get out now."

"No, I won't leave him."

"I don't have time to argue with you. At least don't stay in the cell." He motioned to Adela. "Come on, now." He stepped back and waited.

Margarida thought rapidly, then went out into the corridor. It might be more useful for Walt if she were in front of the cell. He could still see her, and she could look into the office. Then if something happened to the sheriff, she would know. Perhaps she could persuade the men to stop, or she'd see someone whose reason and humanity she could appeal to.

"Adela, can you get Miguel? Will he help us?"

"Yes, I'll go for him right now."

Adela and Sheriff Jones went through the heavy door into the office, and Margarida heard the key turning in the lock. Then the front door slammed, followed by the screech of the bolt.

"Margarida, are you going away?" Walt's voice sounded frantic. He pushed at the locked cell door, then stood, holding on to the bars, watching her.

She ran back to him and took one of his hands. "No, Walt. I'm going to stay here with you." She reached through the bars and pushed his blond hair away from his eyes. "Go lie down and put that wet cloth over your eye."

He held her hand a moment longer, then obeyed. "I don't like it here," he said mournfully.

She could feel tears rising again, but she stifled them. This was no time for weakness. Later, when Walt was safe—then she could cry. "I'm just going to look through the window into the office. I'm not going away."

Thoughts whirled chaotically through her mind. Where was Pedro? He should have been back with Henry Franklin or Samuel Newcomb. And Enoch and Tall Man. Maybe she should have kept Tall Man here instead of asking him to go for Enoch. Then she realized she'd been here only a few minutes. It just seemed much longer.

The first sound from outside was hushed, almost like the murmur of water. It grew into confused shouting, and finally the hammering of fists against the outer door. Margarida rushed to the door and stood on tiptoe to peer through the barred window into the office.

A strident voice became distinct. "Open up, Mickett."

The sheriff stood in the center of the room. His answer came quickly, "What do you want?"

A roar sounded, and then the single voice emerged again. "You know what we want. That dummy bastard."

Mickett Jones's back stiffened, as if bracing himself. "He's my prisoner, and he stays here. You men better get on home. You can watch your hanging after the judge is through."

Another voice, reedy and slurred, came through the door. "We ain't goin' to wait till that brother of his talks some fool judge into lettin' the bastard go."

Someone shouted, "Open up, Mickett. We're gonna protect our womenfolk. They ain't safe when a animal like him's alive."

A crash thundered through the room, and the door shivered against the bolt and hinges. Another violent crash shook the door, and Sheriff Jones backed up against his desk. Margarida saw he had a gun in his hand.

With a splintering sound the boards of the door gave way at its hinges. It swung inward, hanging askew from the still partly fastened bolt. Men spilled into the room. At the front was Hike Jones.

"Hike!" Mickett said, and Margarida could hear his relief. "You get over to my right," he ordered.

"No, Mickett." Hike stood where the wall of men had pushed him. "They're right. We got to protect our women, and the judge probably won't do it."

"But you—" Mickett Jones didn't get to finish his sentence. In the moment when his attention was on his brother, two of the men fanning out from the door lunged at him. One shot from the sheriff's gun hit the ceiling, and then he went down under the weight of the men who jumped him. Behind them Margarida saw faces she recognized—Carl Bodmer, Willis Henderson, Mr. Thornton, Nat Welles.

Carl Bodmer shouted, "Get the keys, Hike."

Margarida whirled and ran to the hanging lantern. As she was getting it down, she cried, "Walt, blow out the lantern in your cell." His light went out a moment after she blew out the one in the corridor.

Taking her revolver out of her waistband, she faced the door into the office and said over her shoulder, "Walt, get against the far wall of that room and stay there." With both hands she lifted the revolver up in front of her and realized that though her heart still thundered, she wasn't trembling. She would shoot if she must.

The key clanged in the lock on the corridor door, and it swung open. Men's voices whirled around her head. Hike Jones was silhouetted against the light, with Carl Bodmer just behind him.

"Stop!" she shouted.

Their momentum carried them forward another step. She raised the revolver and fired over their heads. Momentarily she jerked back from the recoil, then steadied again and pulled back the hammer.

Voices stopped for a moment; then Carl Bodmer pushed around Hike Jones. "What the hell . . . ?"

Margarida lowered the gun so that it pointed at Bodmer's chest. The last of her fear left her. She felt as calm as if she were aiming at a straw target. "Stop right there," she repeated, "or I'll shoot you."

From behind Bodmer she could hear drunken shouts, but neither Hike Jones nor Bodmer moved. "Shut up back there," Bodmer threw over his shoulder. "Now, Miss Ross, this isn't your business. Put down that gun and move out of the way."

"I'm not going to waste a shot in the air again," she said calmly. "Walt Curtis did not rape anyone, and I'm not going to let you harm him."

From in back of Bodmer someone shouted, "She probably showed him how to go crazy over a woman." Margarida recognized the voice—Nat Welles's.

"I told you. Walt is innocent."

Bodmer snarled, "You don't know. But Nat Welles does. It's his daughter the dummy raped."

Priscilla Welles! Margarida had time only for the startling thought to register before Bodmer barked, "Give me that gun and get out of the way."

He took a step, and Margarida fired. Bodmer screamed, then staggered back against Hike Jones, clutching his right shoulder. Startled voices rose in a jumble of sound. This time she'd been prepared for the recoil and recocked immediately, still holding the revolver in front of her.

"Rush her," someone said.

Over the noise she made her voice carry into the next room. "You do, and I'll kill some of you."

Hike Jones, supporting Bodmer, started to back away, when Margarida heard other shots, coming so fast she couldn't tell how many they were. The fear she'd suppressed began to swell inside her. If the men in front of her were willing to risk death, she couldn't shoot all of them.

But the crowd was melting backward, leaving Hike holding Bodmer. Over the noise she heard a shout she recognized—Enoch. From the darkness behind her another urgent voice ordered, "Get down." It was Tall Man, his command coming through the window. She looked quickly back; in the moonlight she saw the muzzle of a rifle.

Still holding the revolver, she swiveled toward the men in front of her. Hike Jones was helping Bodmer back into the office. Beyond them she saw Sheriff Jones, standing again, and men shoving their way out through the shattered front door. Staying to one side, she moved to the opening, her gun still trained on Hike and Bodmer. Enoch stood, a pistol in his hand, waiting as the room cleared.

"Hike, take Bodmer and get out," ordered the sheriff. "You're a disgrace to our family."

"She shot me," Bodmer moaned.

"And you were going to do a lot worse," Mickett Jones said coldly.

As Hike Jones helped Bodmer out the door, Henry Franklin appeared, followed by Samuel Newcomb. Over their shoulders Margarida could see Pedro's worried face. Suddenly the revolver was too heavy for her to hold; she got as far as the desk before she dropped it.

Enoch stepped forward, but Henry Franklin reached her first. She leaned against his rounded stomach, clinging to him, feeling her legs start to shake. Over her head he spoke angrily to Sheriff Jones. "What's going on here?"

"An attempt at a lynching," the sheriff responded wearily. "I'm sorry, Miss Ross. And I thank the dear Lord you made me let you stay."

"Margarida!" The cry came from the cells.

She straightened her shaking legs and hurried back to Walt. He stood holding the cell bars.

"I'm here, Walt. Everything is all right."

"I thought they were going to hurt you." His agonized voice wrenched her heart.

"No, I wouldn't let them. And now Tall Man is here, and some friends. No one will harm either of us."

Tears ran down his face. "I thought they were going to hurt you," he repeated.

"No, Walt, no. It's all right now. I'm going to ask the sheriff to let me stay with you." She went back to the office. "Sheriff Jones, please let me into Walt's cell. I'll stay here the rest of the night."

"All right, Miss Ross." The sheriff's subdued tone told her she could ask for anything right now.

Tall Man ducked under the door and entered the office. "And Mr. Tall Man will stay here tonight also," she added.

Mickett Jones glanced around, and his shocked eyes settled on Tall Man. "An Indian? I can't have him in the office."

"Yes, you can," she asserted. "He's . . . Brant Curtis' cousin, and he'll help you if you need him." She wondered briefly at herself—that she'd introduced Tall Man as Brant's cousin. She turned to the other men. "Enoch, Mr. Franklin, Mr. Newcomb—thank you all for coming."

They all looked as if they didn't know quite what to say. Enoch finally gave a relaxed grin. "You sure didn't act like you needed us. I guess you kind of put us in the shade." The others exchanged rueful smiles that Margarida returned gratefully.

"But I did need you. I couldn't have lasted much longer. And there's something else. Someone must have the telegraph operator wire Brant at all of the stations along the railroad. Tell him what's happened."

"I'll do that for you," Mr. Franklin offered, "and then I'll have to get back home. Mrs. Franklin can't be left alone too long. I'll take care of Halcon, Margarida, and bring him back in the morning."

He also insisted on escorting her to the privy and back before he left. Margarida knew she should have been embarrassed at the mention of her needs, but too much that was really important had happened that night. And Walt was still in jail.

When she returned, Miguel and Adela had arrived. Adela embraced Margarida, holding her tight. "Margarida," Adela said, "Walt will be safe now. Please come to my house tonight."

"Thank you, Adela, but Walt needs me with him. I'll come to see you in the morning." After another hug, Adela left, still looking doubtful.

The sheriff picked up his keys and went to Walt's cell. Someone had already relit the lanterns. As she followed him, Margarida heard the minister, Enoch, and Miguel discussing with Tall Man how they would arrange to guard the jail for the remainder of the night.

Inside the cell with Walt, holding his hand, she realized that she was touching him as much for her own comfort as his. The weakness she'd feared earlier swept over her, making her tremble and grip his hand even tighter. She closed her eyes, and saw Brant's face. If only magic could bring him here right now.

She should feel strong—she'd protected Walt, even shooting a man for the first time in her life. But she longed for Brant's strength.

"Margarida, I want Brant."

"So do I, Walt. So do I."

10

MARGARIDA awoke the next morning curled up on her side, feeling the hard bunk under her as well as the unaccustomed restraint of her clothing. For a moment she stared at the patterns of sunlight and shadow created by the barred window before she realized where she was. With a rush of remembered fear, she looked around. Walt lay sleeping on the floor, wrapped in a blanket.

Still groggy, she sat up and saw Tall Man, a rifle across his knees, squatting in the corridor. He gave her an austere smile, and she wondered how she could ever have thought he looked like a savage.

As her mind cleared, an image gripped her—of Carl Bodmer screaming and clutching at his shoulder. Her throat burned with nausea that she resisted—it wouldn't do any good to brood about what she'd done. Though she was glad she'd hit him in the shoulder instead of the chest, she would shoot him again if things were the same. She'd intended to kill him.

In last night's turmoil, she'd pushed aside the startling information that the woman Walt was accused of raping was Priscilla Welles. Now Margarida knew she must talk to Priscilla immediately. She remembered Nat Welles's livid face in the mob last night and was sure he'd try to prevent her from seeing his daughter.

Walt stirred and opened his eyes. He stared at the ceiling with a puzzled look; then his face blanched. He wrenched away the blanket and sat up, his frantic gaze searching around him.

Instantly she reached him. "Walt . . . I'm here."

"Margarida." His voice shook. "I thought you were hurt. I thought some men shot you."

"No, no. We're all right." She smoothed his rumpled blond hair back from his face. "You had a bad dream. Some men did come last night, but they didn't shoot me. See, Tall Man is here too. No one is going to hurt us."

"Yes, I see Tall Man," he said, but he didn't sound reassured.

The door to the office swung open. Mickett Jones gave Tall Man an apprehensive glance, then unlocked the cell door. "You'll have to leave now, Miss Ross. Mrs. Ramírez is in the office."

"I'd like to take Walt with me."

"You know I can't let you do that," he said, and Margarida saw from his expression she wouldn't be able to change his mind. "But don't worry. Preacher Newcomb is organizing shifts to help guard the jail."

Margarida felt a sudden pressure of Walt's fingers on her hand and heard his choked voice. "I want to go too."

She said as gently as she could, "You can't go just yet. But I'll be back soon, and then we'll go home."

His voice trembled. "Please don't go away, Margarida. I don't want you to go away."

Tall Man moved to the cell door. "I will be here."

The sheriff frowned and began, "Well, now—"

"After what happened," Margarida interrupted sharply, "you'll let Walt's cousin remain, won't you, Sheriff Jones? I'm sure the people in town would approve of your taking extra precautions."

Mickett still looked unhappy. "All right. But I'll have to lock him in the cell too."

Margarida turned back to Walt. Tears had formed in his eyes, and she had to force herself to smile. "I'll be back as soon as I can. I just want to ask you—do you remember Priscilla Welles?"

He looked puzzled. "I don't know."

"Now, Miss Ross," Mickett protested, "that's enough."

She turned on him. "No! Nothing's enough until Walt's released." Swinging back to Walt, she continued, "Priscilla's tall with brown hair. She lives here in town."

The tears that waited in his eyes crawled down his face. "I'm sorry. I can't remember."

"Don't worry," she soothed him. "Just rest here with Tall Man, and I'll be back soon."

His doleful "All right" tore at her as she left.

In the office she found Enoch and Adela, who embraced Margarida and said, "Please come home with me."

Margarida realized that in spite of the few hours she'd slept, she was still exhausted. "Yes, I'll do that." Maybe, she thought, Adela could help with Nat Welles. She seemed to know a lot about what went on in Rio Torcido.

Enoch looked at her admiringly. "Margarida, you did a brave thing for Walt Curtis last night."

"Thank you, Enoch, for coming to help." Impulsively she hugged him, then retreated, feeling a little shy at the delight in his eyes.

She turned to the sheriff. "About last night. I know you did everything you could when those men got here."

Red color washed over Mickett's face until it showed through his thin hair. "Thank you," he mumbled.

Not letting her voice show how difficult the question was, Margarida asked, "How is Carl Bodmer?"

The sheriff shook his head. "Arm's pretty bad."

Margarida's throat felt bone dry. "He's ... not dying?"

"No, ma'am." At Mickett's answer, her heart beat

again. At least she hadn't killed someone. Despicable as Carl Bodmer was, she was glad.

"I'll see you ladies to your buggy," Enoch offered, and Margarida gratefully took his arm. As they went out, she noticed that during the night someone had reinforced the door with diagonal boards and replaced the hinges.

Pedro was waiting outside. "I have Halcon," he said.

Sheriff Jones came out behind them. "Miss Ross, here's your gun."

Margarida didn't want to touch the revolver. "Pedro, would you take it and meet us at Mrs. Ramírez' house?"

The sheriff handed the gun to Pedro, and Adela led the way to her buggy. Halcon and Pedro's horse were tethered beside it. Pedro mounted and took Halcon's lead rein.

Enoch helped Margarida up and smiled reassuringly. "Don't worry about anything here."

As she felt the buggy's motion, Margarida leaned back and closed her eyes, but her mind couldn't rest. She sat up and saw that they were passing the shops and saloons. The barber was putting out his awning. "Adela, what time is it?"

"About eight-thirty."

"Please, could we stop at Lawyer Haines's office? He should be there by now."

"But, Margarida, shouldn't you rest first? It'll be quiet—Miguel's already gone to his job at the *comancheros'* stables."

"No, not until I've done everything I can for Walt."

Margarida found Thomas Haines at his desk. He was a man her father's age, with sagging lines under his eyes and a slick head that had only a fringe of hair. He moved a stack of papers to clear a chair for her. "I heard about the trouble last night," he said. "I wish someone had rousted me out."

Since he had a reputation for being drunk by nine o'clock every evening, Margarida only said dryly, "There wasn't time to think of everyone. Can you get Walt Curtis out of jail this morning?"

"No, Miss Ross, I can't. He's been accused of a capital crime. I don't condone lynching, but he's got to stay where he is until a trial."

Margarida wanted to grab the lawyer's bow-string tie and twist it until he did what she wanted. Instead she said, "Mr. Haines, *Walt Curtis is innocent.*"

"Now, now. You can't know that for sure, Miss Ross. We'll have to wait and see what the evidence is."

Disappointment tasted bitter in her mouth. She rose and went to the door. "I'll find the evidence."

At the open doorway he caught her arm. "As a friend of your father's," he said in a low voice, "I should advise you, Miss Ross, that your reputation will suffer if you continue to be seen in the company of Mrs. Ramírez." He gave a slight nod toward Adela, waiting in the buggy.

Margarida's temper boiled up, but the scathing answer he deserved didn't seem worth the effort it would take. She shook off his hand and walked swiftly out to the buggy.

"Can he do something?" asked Adela.

"No," Margarida snapped.

When they arrived at the two-room adobe, Adela showed Margarida inside and insisted that she wash and eat.

"No. I can't take the time."

"It will give you the chance to think," Adela replied, putting on a pot to heat water. "Remember, *quien mas corre, menos vuela.*"

"Whoever runs more, flies less," Margarida translated. "I know—the more haste, the less speed. All right. A wash would be wonderful."

By the time Margarida had finished, she had de-

cided on a plan. She went back into the living room/
kitchen where Pedro was finishing a plate of food at
the table. He rose. "Señorita Margarida, I'm going
outside to have a smoke."

Adela filled another plate with hot tortillas and shredded beef mixed with egg, put it in front of Margarida,
and sat beside her. "Margarida, the talk is that Walt
raped Priscilla Welles the night of Rupert Curtis'
funeral."

"That's four months ago," Margarida protested.

"Brant and Walt did stay over in town that night.
They were in the Imperial for a while."

"Adela, would you go to the freight depot and see if
Nat Welles is at work? I'd do it, but I don't want him
to see me. If he's there, I'm going to talk to Priscilla."

Adela gave Margarida a kiss and rose. "I'll go now."

Determined not to be discouraged, Margarida tried
to eat while she waited for Adela to return. After the
first bites, her stomach felt queasy. She covered the
plate and put it in the cooler, then paced the small
living room, sipping on a mug of coffee.

Adela reappeared, out of breath. "Nat Welles just
got to work," she said. "I saw someone from the
Imperial on my way back. He said Dr. Winton had to
amputate Carl Bodmer's right arm. The bone had
shattered."

Margarida felt her stomach lurch upward and knew
if she thought about Carl Bodmer she really would be
sick. But she had to see Priscilla, and that was all that
mattered right now. "I'm going to the Welleses' house.
Thank you, Adela. I'll see you as soon as I can."

"Take Pedro with you," Adela said anxiously.

"Yes," Margarida agreed, already halfway to the
yard to get Halcon.

When Margarida and Pedro arrived at the Welleses'
house, she had him conceal the horses in a clump of
box elder down a nearby slope. "Bring the Winchester," she told him, "and get as close to the house as

you can. If Mr. Welles comes home, I might need you." At his nod, she straightened her rumpled skirt and walked rapidly to the front door.

As she raised her hand to knock, she discovered it was trembling. She waited, struggling to get control of herself. Walt's frightened face haunted her, but it wasn't fear that made her shaky now—it was rage at Priscilla's accusation. She took a long breath, reminding herself she hadn't heard Priscilla's side yet. Her hand was steady when she knocked on the door.

Mrs. Welles' polite smile froze when she saw Margarida. As if unable to prevent the familiar phrases, she said, "Margarida, how nice to see you. Please come in."

"Thank you, Mrs. Welles." Before the woman could recover, Margarida stepped inside and closed the door. "I would like to see Priscilla, please."

Mrs. Welles' face went white. "She . . . she's not feeling well."

If her goal were not so important, Margarida might have sympathized with Mrs. Welles's distress. But not today. "Is Priscilla in her bedroom?"

"Yes—I mean, no. You can't—"

Margarida pushed past Mrs. Welles to Priscilla's room. As she reached it, Priscilla opened the door. Her hair hung around her face in tangled brown strands. Dark smudges shadowed her eyes, and a bruise discolored the side of her jaw. She wore a cotton dress that was faded and wrinkled. "What do you want?" Her voice was shaky but belligerent.

"I must talk to you."

Behind Margarida Mrs. Welles' voice squeaked. "Priscilla, don't say anything."

Margarida gripped Priscilla's shoulder. "You must. Walt's *life* depends on this."

Priscilla wavered, looking from her mother to Margarida. Finally she stepped back into the bedroom, and Margarida followed. Priscilla turned, and for a moment was silhouetted against the window. The thickening around her waistline was obvious.

"You're going to have a child," Margarida gasped.

She could barely hear Priscilla's whispered "Yes."

Mrs. Welles grabbed Margarida. Anger distorted the woman's thin mouth and mottled her cheeks. "You're the one to blame. You're the one who brought him—" She stopped, and her eyes widened, as if she'd just heard what she said.

"It was Lee Hansen," Margarida said. Mrs. Welles didn't answer, her hand clasped tightly over her mouth.

Margarida turned to Priscilla. "Was it Lee Hansen?"

Priscilla stared at Margarida, her only movement her hands twisting together. She swallowed, as if she wanted to speak but couldn't. Finally she whispered, "Yes."

"Priscilla!" Mrs. Welles' wail seemed to loosen her daughter's control. Priscilla began to cry, great rasping sobs that burst out as if they'd lain inside her for months. Mrs. Welles gave a distressed moan and left the room.

Feeling her own rage retreat in the face of the other girl's despair, Margarida put her arms around Priscilla and pulled her to sit on the bed. When her sobs quieted, Margarida asked, "But why did you say Walt raped you?"

"I know he's not right in his head, and I thought no one would do anything to him."

"Why didn't you make Lee admit he's the father? He can't escape his responsibility. He'll have to marry you."

Priscilla's voice dropped so low that Margarida had to strain to hear. "He said he wouldn't. That I couldn't make him. He said . . ." Her next words came mixed with renewed sobs. "He said he knew some men I'd . . . done that with, and it was probably somebody else's baby."

She raised her head and looked into Margarida's

eyes, her voice shaking. "But that's not true. I did do that a few times—but not since I knew him. He threatened he'd get them to say I had. I didn't know what to do."

Margarida felt buffeted by emotions—rage at Lee, fury over Walt's plight, and growing sympathy for Priscilla. "But you still haven't told me why you said Walt raped you."

"Papa found out I was pregnant. I was afraid to say it was Lee. Papa hit me and yelled, and I was trying to make him stop, so I said someone attacked me." Priscilla's handkerchief tore under her twisting fingers, but she didn't seem to notice. "Then Papa said who was it, and maybe it was Walt Curtis, that he would probably do something like that. I said yes, to make Papa stop."

"How did you explain why you waited so long to say anything? What kind of a story did you make up?"

"I told Papa I'd gone to the privy, and Walt followed me back and climbed in my bedroom window. I said I hadn't told because of the disgrace."

She began to sob harder, and Margarida could hardly hear her words. "Then I thought the baby might have blond hair and be big like Lee, and Walt is big and has blond hair. I didn't think it would matter to him. He wouldn't know the difference."

Margarida held Priscilla, waiting for her sobs to lessen. When Priscilla seemed calmer, Margarida said as forcefully as she could, "It *does* matter. A mob almost hanged Walt last night because of what you said."

Priscilla wouldn't look at Margarida. "I know," she whispered. "I'm sorry. It was a terrible thing to do. I was just so scared."

Margarida stood up. "Come on, Priscilla. Pack what clothes you need. I'll take you to my house. You can stay there until we make Lee Hansen understand he has to marry you. But first we have to go to the jail so you can tell the truth about Walt."

"Papa won't let me," Priscilla said fearfully.

"You're eighteen. You can stand up to him. I'll help you, and Brant Curtis will help you, but you can't let Walt suffer when he's innocent."

Priscilla began to cry again, violent sobs. "I'm too scared. Papa will do something terrible to me."

Barely controlling a desire to scream, Margarida pulled Priscilla to her feet. "Do you want to murder Walt? That's what you'll be doing unless you tell the truth."

Through her tears, Priscilla stared at Margarida. After what seemed like forever, she whispered, "All right."

They were in the living room, Margarida carrying Priscilla's valise, when the door burst open. Nat Welles stood in the doorway. His eyes narrowed and his mouth thinned to a threatening line. "What are you doing here, Margarida Ross? And what do you think you're doing, Priscilla?"

Margarida kept one hand clamped on the valise and the other on Priscilla's arm. "We're going to the jail to see that Walt is freed, and then Priscilla is going to stay with me until Lee Hansen marries her."

Nat Welles didn't change expression at Lee's name, and Margarida realized he must have known all along that Lee had gotten Priscilla pregnant. Through her almost paralyzing rage, she heard Priscilla say in a trembling voice, "Yes, that's right."

"No, you aren't." Nat took a step forward, his fists clenched and his eyes menacing. It took all Margarida's courage not to move backward. "We're gonna see that Walt Curtis gets what he deserves," he snarled. "And before he dies, we'll cut off his balls, just like that breed—"

Nat stopped, a shocked look on his face. In the

doorway behind him Margarida saw Pedro, holding the muzzle of the Winchester against Nat Welles' back.

Margarida shuddered, trying to erase the picture Nat's words had created. "Pedro . . . thank God. Come on, Priscilla." She steered them both around Nat Welles. Pedro backed out the door with them, still holding the carbine pointed at the purple-faced man. To the accompaniment of curses from the doorway, Margarida found a horse for Priscilla and retrieved Halcon and Pedro's horse. Nat was still shouting as they rode away, but he made no move to follow them.

"Don't worry," Pedro assured her, "I see a lot of men like Señor Welles." He glanced at Priscilla, then lowered his voice. "Very brave against a girl, but he won't follow a man with a gun."

Within half an hour a white-faced and barely audible Priscilla told Sheriff Jones that she'd been mistaken about Walt Curtis. Under Margarida's determined stare, the obviously curious sheriff accepted Priscilla's word without insisting on any further explanation and freed Walt. Margarida knew from the way Walt clung to her that he was still terrified.

Enoch arranged for a surrey from the livery stable. When she thanked him for all he'd done, he smiled and touched her hand. "Don't worry about Nat Welles. I'll talk to the preacher, and we'll watch that he doesn't trouble you. The rest of the men in the mob last night have sobered up. I think they'll feel ashamed. At any rate they won't like it that Nat stirred them up against an innocent man."

Pedro drove the surrey, and Tall Man rode behind, leading the extra horses. For once, Walt didn't want to ride one of the horses and sat close to Margarida.

The trip home seemed to last forever. Walt gripped Margarida's hand as though she would leave if he let go. Exhaustion blurred Margarida's responses, and soon she felt she was clinging to Walt rather than the other way around. Priscilla sat stiffly and avoided looking at Walt.

It was early afternoon before they reached the fork between the Ross and Curtis roads. When they took the left side, Walt said in an alarmed voice, "Margarida, you promised me we were going home. This is the wrong way!"

"I thought we'd go to my house and stay there until Brant comes back from his trip."

"No. No. I want to go home. You promised." Walt sounded terrified again. He started to climb down from the surrey, pulling Margarida after him. Pedro reined in the horse and put on the brake just before Walt reached the ground, dragging Margarida with him.

"Wait!" She righted herself and looked at him. His desperate face told her she had to take him home.

Tall Man caught up with them. "What is wrong?"

"Walt and I need our horses. We're going to the Curtis ranch." She felt Walt's grip on her arm relax a little. "Pedro, take Miss Welles to our house. Explain to my mother that I'm going with Walt. I'll be home as soon as Brant returns. Priscilla, all you need to say to Mama is that I invited you to come visit me."

Tall Man frowned. "I cannot go with both of you, and I do not like to leave either one."

"I have the Winchester," Pedro said. "I'll take good care of Miss Welles. And I'll set guards around the house."

"Yes, we'll be fine," added Priscilla, and Margarida realized that Priscilla wanted to get away from Walt. She must feel ashamed and guilty about what she'd done.

Walt looked more like his usual cheerful self. "I hope you feel better soon, Miss Welles."

Priscilla's tears burst out again. Pedro snapped the reins, and the surrey moved off.

Walt helped Margarida mount Halcon, and he rode Pedro's horse. Halcon's familiar motion soothed her, and she noticed that the sun was warm and that clusters of blue-purple lupine decorated the south-facing slopes. Spring-green aspen reminded her that life renewed itself.

Her mood darkened again when they passed the curved "Curtis Ranch" sign where Brant had said the murdered Indian was left. The same half-breed, Margarida felt sure, Nat Welles had meant when he'd talked of what they would do to Walt. Was Nat the fifth murderer Brant was looking for? Margarida shuddered. Too much had happened since last night to think about anything else terrible now.

As if he'd noticed her distress, Tall Man moved closer. "There will be guards around the Curtis ranch for as long as needed. No one will get a chance to hurt you or Walt."

Margarida felt grateful for Tall Man's strength, not sure how much of her own she had left. Now she understood Walt's admiration for this man.

In less than an hour they reached the hill above the familiar buildings, Walt racing ahead when the ranch came in sight. Margarida knew his confidence had been severely shaken, and he needed her until Brant returned. Tall Man couldn't take her place for this because he wasn't part of Walt's childhood. Part of the childhood she'd wanted to retreat to and Walt still lived in.

When Margarida and Tall Man reached the ranch house, the *vaqueros* had gathered around Walt, embracing him and pounding him on his back. Luisa hugged him and wept over him, and some of the men also had wet eyes.

"Where is Juan?" Margarida asked Luisa.

"He is in our house. Those men who came shot him in the leg."

Margarida sent Tall Man a reproachful look before she put her arm around Luisa's shoulders. "I'm so sorry. Tall Man didn't tell me. If I'd known, we could have brought the doctor with us."

"We don't want the doctor," Luisa protested. "I take better care of him myself. He is getting along fine, just bad-tempered. Talking to him is like touching a porcupine."

Margarida decided Tall Man probably hadn't told her about Juan's wound because he, too, had greater faith in Luisa than in a doctor.

Though Margarida knew Brant wasn't there, she looked for him in each room of the house and listened for his deep voice and firm footsteps. Unable to stifle the lost feeling his absence produced, she told herself it was because of Walt. When Brant returned, he would take over the responsibility for his brother, and that's why she longed for his return. But she didn't convince herself.

By night Walt's frantic energy had abated into the same exhaustion Margarida felt. Luisa offered to stay in the house to chaperon Walt and Margarida, but Margarida refused. Juan needed his wife's nursing, and Margarida cared nothing about the propriety of being alone all night with Walt. Afraid he would have nightmares, she wanted to be near him.

She was right; several times Walt cried and thrashed himself awake, calling for her and his brother. She held and soothed him, then went back to the bedroom that had been Rupert's. There, in spite of the lantern she left on, she had to wrestle with her own nightmares. In each one she shot Carl Bodmer, sometimes in the shoulder, sometimes in the chest. Then he would reappear, once in a coffin, once with a bloody stump. Toward morning she thought wearily that if everyone were as tormented as she, no one would ever try to kill another person.

As dawn approached, she wondered if she would ever feel safe again. Her longing for Brant too great to suppress, she rose and tiptoed along the hall to his bedroom. She hadn't been in it since she was a small girl and Brant had taken her to see a cast of an ancient footprint that he'd found. As soon as she pushed open the door, she smelled the bay rum which she associated with him, so distinctive because he didn't smoke as most men did.

In the faint light she saw the high bed in the center of the opposite wall. She crossed to it and slipped under the covers.

The sheets smelled fresh from drying in sunshine, and that clean odor also reminded her of Brant. The pillow curved up around her head, and the quilt nestled around her body. She stretched her legs, and the chemise Luisa had lent her rode up around her thighs so that the sheets touched her bare skin like the caress of a hand.

In the shadowy cottonwood tree just outside the window, birds began to call to each other. For the first time since she'd started off for Rio Torcido with Tall Man, she felt protected and safe. She lay, gradually warming, until she slept without dreaming.

When she woke, the sun shone on the bleached boards of the ceiling, and she heard the clatter of pots in the kitchen below. Horrified, she sprang from bed and hastily smoothed the covers. What had possessed her to come into Brant's room like that? Her nightmares had confused her.

After she straightened the bed, she peeked out into the hall, then rushed back to Rupert's room as fast as she could without making any noise. Once inside, she leaned against the closed door, trying to settle her rapid heart.

But her turbulent thoughts kept her pulse racing. What if Luisa had come upstairs and found her? Or if Brant had come home during the night and discovered her in his bed, in only her chemise? She must have been insane from emotion and fatigue. Embarrassment heated her face. Brant would have thought she was throwing herself at him—again. She pulled on her clothes and hurried downstairs, wanting to find Walt and escape her own painful speculations.

As the day progressed, Walt seemed almost like his old cheerful self, except that he wanted Margarida within sight at all times. Luisa had to insist he leave the kitchen so Margarida could have a bath. Later when he bathed, Margarida stayed in the dining room, chattering to him through the door. As long as she was with him, he would go out to see Juan and the horses and talk to the cowboys nearby. He spent a long time grooming Chid and rode him around the corral. But even in her company, he didn't want to get far from the house.

In the early afternoon Pedro arrived with fresh clothes from Elena. He also brought a note asking when Margarida would be home and worrying about the propriety of her staying at the Curtis home. Pedro left with the message that Margarida must wait for Brant's return, and the assurance that Luisa was chaperoning them.

That evening Margarida tried to interest Walt in playing cards. Though he didn't display his usual enthusiasm for three-card monte, he won most of the hands. It always amazed Margarida that Walt seemed to keep track of numbers better than people of normal intelligence. She seldom won any card game against him.

They had just started up the stairs to the bedrooms when Walt stopped suddenly. "Brant!" Walt shouted, and bolted back down the stairs, the lantern in his hand making wildly swinging shadows on the wall. Her breath coming so fast it hurt, Margarida ran after him. Let it be Brant, she prayed.

When she reached the kitchen, Brant was holding Walt in a tight embrace, the black head resting against the blond one. A great surge of emotion burst inside

Margarida, so intense she couldn't tell whether she felt pleasure or pain.

Brant looked across Walt to her. "Tall Man told me what happened," he said, his voice so hoarse it hardly sounded like him. He held out his arm, and she ran to him, to be held fast against both men. Someone shook with sobs, but Margarida wasn't sure who. It could have been any one of them, so close were they together.

Finally she pulled away. Tears ran down Brant's face, startling her. His controlled exterior had never slipped enough for her to see him cry before. She felt tears on her face as well.

Only Walt wasn't crying, and his voice rang out. "You're home, Brant. You're home. Don't go away again."

"No—not now. Not for a long time."

Gently Brant reached across and wiped the tears from her cheek. She did the same for him. "Margarida," he said, his usually restrained voice husky with emotion.

His arm still across Walt's shoulders, he took her hand and pulled her with them to the pine table. "I've been in the saddle since yesterday noon," he said. "I'm thirsty."

Brant's ordinary tone broke the mood, which Margarida guessed he'd intended. The punishing pace of his trip showed in his eyes, red with fatigue, and in his dust-streaked face. Grime covered his jacket and pants. He shrugged off his jacket and dipped himself a large glass of water before he sat down.

Her shaky legs made her reach for a chair. Searching for the same self-control he'd achieved, she asked, "Have you been to Rio Torcido?"

"No, your telegram reached me at Socorro. I bought three horses and a saddle and started across country. Since the shortest way to Rio Torcido is through here, I stopped to find out what I could and get Chid. Tall Man met me and told me what happened."

Walt said fearfully, "Some men came and said I

hurt someone. I hit some of them, but they hit me first. They took me to the jail. And they were going to shoot Margarida. But she shot them."

Brant looked at Margarida, and she could see that his composure was a facade. "She was very brave, and I thank God for her."

She felt her chest constrict and at the same time her heart beat faster. Even under lines of dirt and fatigue, his face was beautiful to her. The warmth in his eyes fired her blood, making it rush through her body.

"I was afraid," Walt said. "I wanted you at home."

Brant's eyes glittered, and the muscles along the side of his face clenched in tiny ripples. "I know, Walt, and I can't tell you how sorry I am I wasn't here. But I will be now, and those men won't hurt you again."

Margarida's fear returned, this time for Brant. What would happen when he confronted the men who'd tried to lynch Walt? No—she wouldn't think of that now.

"Tall Man couldn't tell me why Priscilla Welles lied about Walt," Brant said, "but maybe that can wait until morning. What I can't wait for," he added, his tone back to normal, "is a bath."

An old image returned to Margarida, of Brant standing naked beside a tub in this kitchen. Though it had been more than three years ago, she could still picture him. A blush crept up her neck to her face. She could tell from the crinkles around his eyes that he knew what she was thinking.

She rose quickly. "I'm off to bed. I'll explain about Priscilla in the morning."

Brant got up also. "I'll light the kerosene light, and you can take the lantern."

She picked up the lantern, then remembered they had no chaperon. Except for Walt, they would be alone, sleeping a short distance from each other. It would be intimate in a way that even the line shack hadn't been last summer.

An unwanted excitement made her breath unreliable. "Luisa has to stay in her house with Juan," she said uncomfortably, "so I'm sleeping in your father's room."

A grin curved Brant's mouth. "I could offer to sleep in the barn, but since you're obviously capable of defending yourself from me or anyone else, I plan to stay right here."

Walt, who had momentarily looked alarmed, relaxed. Margarida envied him.

"You go on to bed too, Walt," Brant suggested. "I'll have to heat some water, so I'll be up after a while."

"All right, Brant," said Walt happily, and followed Margarida as she fled up the stairs.

As Brant found clean pants and waited for the water to heat, he thought of the things he and Margarida hadn't said tonight. He hadn't told her of the terror that had gripped him when he read the telegram at the railroad station in Socorro, terror that stayed with him as he pushed himself and his three riding horses to the limit. The wire had said only that Walt was in jail, accused of attacking a girl. It hadn't mentioned the lynch mob, but Brant had imagined what could happen.

He hadn't told her of his sick feeling as he approached home—a torment which left only when Tall Man met him. She hadn't told him what it had been like to face those men—to stand between Walt and death. To risk death herself. He wasn't sure he could endure the pain if she or Walt died.

The lid of the kettle on the stove rattled with escaping steam. He carried the bathtub in from the veranda and drew several buckets of cold water. After adding the boiling water and finding a towel, he stripped off his dirty clothes and stepped into the tub. His tired muscles welcomed its warmth, and after he soaped, he lay back, letting the water soak away his tension.

He looked at the ceiling. Margarida was overhead, in the large bed Walt's mother had brought from England. How often, Brant remembered, he'd disapproved of Margarida's impulsiveness. It was that trait which had saved Walt.

If she'd stopped to think, she would have known that one woman would be helpless to do anything. But she'd seldom stopped to think before. Brant felt the most profound gratitude that she hadn't this time. Otherwise Walt wouldn't be safely asleep above him.

The image of Margarida in the bed upstairs was having an effect on his body. It was all too easy to imagine himself joining her, sliding his hands into that silky brown hair, loose now across the pillow. Stripping off whatever she wore, allowing his hands to do what they always wanted when he was around her. And finally losing himself in her.

Trying to shake off his thoughts, he levered himself out of the tub and picked up a towel. As he rubbed his wet skin, he reminded himself what Jesse Ross's friendship meant to him—a natural hunting area for the young men of his grandmother's band. But right now it was difficult to remember why that was important.

The question he didn't want to ask himself couldn't be avoided. Was his responsibility to his mother's people worth giving up the chance to have Margarida, to love her and to have her love? He didn't know, but duty had always forced him to answer yes. A duty he'd welcomed because it made him feel like one of his Indian relatives. So why did that obligation seem so bleak now?

He heard a cry from upstairs, and then another. It was Walt. Quickly he pulled on his clean pants and ran up the stairs. When he reached Walt's room, he saw Margarida sitting on the edge of Walt's bed, her arms around him. She looked like a silver wraith in the moonlight, with her hair in a dark cloud over her shoulders.

"It was a dream, Walt," she said softly. "It wasn't real."

Brant joined her, holding on to his brother's hand. "Margarida's right. It was a dream. You and Margarida are safe."

Walt calmed quickly, and soon his eyes closed again. "You're here now, Brant," he mumbled, and slept.

Margarida rose and tiptoed to the door, and Brant followed. In the hall he stopped her. "Are you all right?"

He heard a long-drawn breath and a shaky "Yes."

"Have you had bad dreams too?" Again he heard her struggle to breathe. "You have, haven't you?"

Her whispered "Yes" dissolved in a gasp, and then sobs so painful that he felt as if they were twisting his gut. He pulled her close in his arms, tenderly smoothing her hair, knowing that if Carl Bodmer and Nat Welles were here now, nothing could prevent him from killing them.

He barely made out her words. "I . . . keep seeing him. I shoot him each time. Sometimes he's . . . dead and then he isn't."

"Hush, Margarida. Hush, love. It's all over now. They won't hurt you again. I won't let them."

Her sobs quieted, and she began to shiver. He swung her up into his arms, then carried her into his father's room and sat on the bed, still holding her. She clung to him, her face pressed against his chest. He stroked her hair, then rubbed his hands along her arms and shoulders, feeling the warmth of her skin through the thin chemise. She put her arms around him, and he felt her hands against his bare back.

The pants he'd pulled on were an old pair, worn so soft they clung to his body. Now he became intensely aware of how thin they were, and of the growing pressure in his groin. The desire which had built up when he was in the bathtub returned, even stronger.

Margarida's hair smelled like sandalwood soap; silky strands lay across his arm. Where her hands gripped his back, fire spread over his skin. He felt her against his chest, at first the soft rounds of her breasts, then the firm points of her nipples. If he didn't move away from her, he knew he'd lose all control.

She lifted her head, her eyes under their thick lashes as dark as Apache eyes. In the dim light from the lantern he saw her lips trembling. He heard her make a faint sound, part gasp, part moan. And he felt, not just his physical desire, but a longing for her that swept aside everything but his need to hold her, comfort her—and to become part of her. As he captured her lips with his own, he tried to remember why he must not make love to her. But it was too late.

11

MARGARIDA felt Brant's lips touch hers, gently, tenderly, and they drained the remembered terror of her dreams. His arms held her against him, creating a circle of warmth and strength, of safety. But she also felt a new turmoil—of longing to be even closer to him. Rippling excitement began deep inside her and radiated outward.

His mouth moved against hers, opening, tasting, and the excitement reached to the tips of her fingers, making her aware of every muscle and nerve. One of his hands still cradled her head, his thumb gently circling, rubbing the nape of her neck. The other stroked the tender inside of her elbow. More urgently he savored her lips, inviting her to taste the sweetness of his. She felt the rasp of his beard against her face, the quivering in the muscles of his back, his heartbeat in agitated rhythm with her own.

He raised his head and whispered, "Margarida?" and it was a foolish question. Her hands, reaching to bring his mouth back to hers, answered him. Her nipples, pressing almost painfully into his chest, answered him. Her breath, leaving and then returning in a gasp as his hand slipped inside her chemise and found her breast, answered him.

Brant heard that rush of breath and knew a shuddering joy. Her nipple hardened against his palm as if it had always known his touch. This was Margarida, willful and passionate, and nothing else mattered but making her feel the pleasure of this moment and finding his own with her.

Margarida felt the pounding rhythm of his heart that matched the breathless pulsing of her own. Desire trembled over her skin, making her feel as if she would dissolve with joy against him. The muscles of his thighs bunched underneath her legs and his erection thrust against her hip. This was Brant, strong and sure, center of her longings for all the years of waiting for this time.

The barrier of the chemise was intolerable to him. "Margarida," he breathed, "I must look at you." He lifted her from his lap and pulled the chemise over her head, letting his eyes feast on her.

She couldn't stand his trousers between them, and found the opening at his belt and loosened it. As he stood and stripped off his pants, she looked with wonder and delight at his naked body. Below his broad chest, his flat belly and lean hips emphasized the muscled power of his thighs and legs. His penis, springing erect from the black hair at his groin, was part of that masculine beauty. Impatient, she wanted to touch him, to feel his chest and stomach and thighs against hers. Reaching out, she pulled him down to the bed until he lay beside her, their bodies matching in a searing path.

For Brant, to see the perfection of her nude body seemed like the most valuable gift he'd ever received. He rejoiced in her face, made for laughing, her breasts, pale except for the pink centers, her curving waist and hips and mysterious pubic shadow above silken legs. He had to know everything about her, learn each curve, breathe the scent of her skin and hair, let his fingers discover her female secrets.

Despite the force of his desire, he knew he must somehow manage the restraint to go slowly. She was a virgin, and he must let her savor the building of pleasure so that she would be eager and unafraid. "Margarida," he breathed, and kissed her waiting mouth.

"You're beautiful." With his lips he traced the curve of her neck and the slanting collarbone, then lingered on the racing pulse in her throat. "More beautiful than I could imagine." His hand found her breast, lifting its fullness to his mouth.

He discovered the ache of delay was also a special pleasure. Her gasping response as he caressed her breasts and kissed her nipples to tautness intensified his. The fire in his groin built at he slid his hand over the faint roundness of her stomach, stroked the soft warmth of her thighs, found the silky thatch of pubic hair, and then the hidden center.

For Margarida, Brant's touch captured all sensation. She heard nothing, saw nothing, sensed nothing, outside of the world he created around her. She thought fleetingly that she would no longer be a virgin, that nothing would be the same again, and waited for his movements to feel strange or frightening. Instead his mouth seemed made for her breasts, the tugging at her nipples sheer pleasure. His fingers between her thighs, sending fire up inside, promised fulfillment that suddenly was as essential as breathing. She wanted to learn about his body, but her own was sweeping her along, so that she was barely aware of the smooth plane of his chest, the rigid cords in his arms, the pressure of his penis hard against her thigh.

His breath rasped with his words, "Oh, God, Margarida. You're wonderful. I've dreamed of you like this—in my arms. I want you. Do you . . . ?"

Margarida knew nothing in the world was more important than this moment. She gasped, "Yes!"

His touch worked magic, drawing her into a universe where only the gathering tremors in her center existed. Then he was above her, his weight bringing him into that world with her. His hands held her face, his mouth captured hers, and she felt his rigid shaft pressing on the opening that had to be filled or she would die.

He began to push against her, gently, then retreating and pushing again. She could feel herself stretching with each movement. The tension tightened, shivering through her in violent waves. His hands were under her hips, lifting her in an increasing rhythm. She gripped his shoulders, moving with him. "Margarida," he groaned. "I don't want to hurt you, but I can't wait." A final thrust, and he filled her with himself.

She felt a sudden pain that subsided just as quickly, obliterated by the trembling sensation which surrounded his hard shaft within her. He lay, his head beside hers, and she shook with the beat of his heart. Then he raised his head. "Are you all right, love?"

"Yes, but I want . . ."

"I know. I do too." She felt his urgent kisses on her mouth, and her pulsing blood knew she couldn't bear any more or she would explode. She was wrong.

The excitement widened, but he was with her, moving within her, easing back and then thrusting again. At each stroke she felt that she wanted even more of him. The rhythm he created pushed her upward, receding and building again until spasms shook her in a final shattering. She heard his gasps and felt him shudder with the same wrenching release. And he was there to hold her as she fell back into herself, more whole than she had ever been before.

When Brant could breathe again, he wanted to stir, speak, ask if he had hurt her, tell her how great his pleasure had been. More than pleasure—a fulfillment of something in himself he didn't quite understand. He'd lost himself in her, and her response had intensified his enjoyment beyond any he'd known before. But the toll of the last two days was too much. "Margarida, loving you was wonderful," was all he could say, and hope she knew all it meant.

For long moments he held her close, kissing her eyelids, her forehead, the side of her mouth. Strands of hair trailed across her face, and he gently brushed

them aside and captured her lips for a lingering kiss,
and another, and still another. Then he reluctantly
eased out of her and shifted to his side so that they lay
curved together. He rested one hand on her breast
and let oblivion overtake him.

Margarida sensed as much as heard his breathing
soften into sleep. She felt boneless, that if she moved
away from him she wouldn't be able to manage her
arms and legs. And above all she felt serene; the
confusion and uncertainty she'd lived with since she
returned from school had vanished. She loved him and
she'd made love with him—and it felt wonderful. To
her surprise she was able to fumble for the cover
which she'd thrown back to answer Walt's cry an impossible time ago. She pulled the quilt up over them
both and drifted into sleep.

Drowsily Brant stretched. His muscles protested,
telling him how strenuous the ride from Socorro had
been. He turned, felt the warmth beside him, and
opened his eyes.

Margarida's dark curls were tangled around her face,
and her thick eyelashes lay in half-circles against her
cheeks. Her wide mouth tilted slightly upward in a
sensuous curve. One shoulder showed velvet skin above
the edge of the covers. She stirred, gave an unintelligi-
ble murmur, and burrowed into the pillow again.

The incredible pleasure of last night came back to
him, but his mind, cleared of fatigue, brought back
judgment as well—and the judgment was harsh. With
a sick feeling in his gut, he thought about what he'd
done.

Margarida had saved Walt's life. For that, he owed
her more than he could repay. Last night she needed
tenderness and reassurance—and gratitude. Instead,
when she'd been exhausted and distraught, he'd seduced her. Fear and distress had left her defenseless,
and he'd repaid her by taking her virginity. One trait

he'd genuinely admired in his father, and in the Apache, was restraint. He'd lost his.

No honorable Apache man would violate an unmarried girl's chastity. If *shiwóyé* knew how he'd behaved last night, she would condemn him.

His pain drove Brant from the bed. He found his discarded pants and pulled them on, then moved back and stood beside the bed, staring down at her. God, how could he have been so weak?

He'd been exhausted from the long ride and his fears. No—that was no excuse. She'd been willing, had tried to get him to make love to her before, but that didn't relieve his responsibility either. He was older and supposed to be wiser. And, he thought bitterly, he'd been so proud of his self-control. That he'd had more pleasure with Margarida than with any woman he could remember somehow made it worse.

Last night he had put his impulses ahead of his obligation to safeguard Margarida from herself. And he hadn't even thought of her father's anger and the effect on his people. He didn't behave with the decency of an ordinary white man, much less of an Apache. The bitterness and pain of self-condemnation cut through him like the thrust of a knife.

Margarida turned, exposing the top of one breast, and even in his distress, he felt a stirring in his groin. Hastily he turned his back. He and Margarida would have to get married. At least then it wouldn't matter that he hadn't protected her against pregnancy.

Did he love her? Was that why he'd seduced her? The thought startled him. If he did, that didn't excuse him. He sat on the side of the bed, his head between his hands.

Margarida felt the motion of the bed, and it roused her from the last remnant of sleep. She opened her eyes and saw Brant sitting on the bed, his back to her, with his head forward as if it ached. For a moment she lay savoring the picture he made—black hair lying on his neck, well-defined muscles stretched in geometric patterns from broad shoulders to narrow waist, and trousers over lean hips.

At the memory of what lay under the pants, a lightning streak of excitement spread from the juncture of her thighs. What a shame she and Brant hadn't made love sooner. He'd been crazy to resist her when lovemaking brought such delight. His concern about her father's reaction and his Apache relatives couldn't be important enough to deny themselves so much pleasure. She thought again of last night's passion and was sure that happiness must be glowing from her like a brightly burning fire.

She sat up and touched his shoulder. He jumped, then turned, and at the sight of his white face and tormented eyes, anxiety overshadowed her joy. "Brant, what's wrong? Is it Walt? Is he hurt?"

He pulled back from her, and his voice came out stiff and strained. "Margarida, I can only say I'm sorry."

"Sorry about what? I don't understand what you mean."

"It was my fault, and I have no excuse. I'm afraid I lost my self-control last night."

She didn't want to believe what he was saying. "You mean you're sorry we . . . made love last night?"

He went on in his anguished voice, as if he hadn't heard her. "I should have been stronger."

The last of Margarida's joy vanished under the icy weight of understanding. What had been such pleasure for her was a mistake to him. Pain pressed on her like an instrument of torture, opening a wound where her heart should be.

He glanced at her and then quickly looked away, his face flushing. She realized that the covers had fallen to her waist, leaving her breasts bare. She snatched up the sheet and pulled it up to her chin.

His voice sounded ragged. "Of course, under the circumstances, we'll have to marry as soon as possible."

Stunned, she stared at him. He thought he had to rescue her after their regrettable night together. Once she'd thought she wanted to marry him more than anything else in the world. But not like this! She searched for a defense and found it in pride and anger.

"Married?" She let her question drip disdain. "Don't be foolish, Brant. Why would I want to marry you?"

"Because—" he began, and then stopped, his eyes appalled. "Oh, Christ. I've made it worse." He reached for her hand, but she pulled it back. "I'm saying this all wrong. I am sorry, Margarida, for the way things happened last night, and I'm angry with myself. But please don't think it wasn't wonderful to make love to you. It was."

She heard his words, but she knew she couldn't bear the hurt if she didn't cling to her enraged pride. Otherwise, she might dissolve in helpless weeping. Or worse, give in and let him marry her out of remorse.

Deliberately she dropped the sheet, holding herself erect as if showing her breasts to him meant nothing. All the self-control she had went into keeping her voice calm and unemotional. "Well, I enjoyed it too. So there's nothing to be sorry about. I wanted to try out lovemaking, and since I've known you all my life, you were the natural one to begin with. That doesn't mean I want to marry you."

His face hardened into a scowl. "Don't be foolish, Margarida, and don't try to pretend." The lines of his jaw softened as he made an obvious effort to restrain himself. "I've said I'm sorry, and I know I hurt you by the way I said it. Of course we'll get married."

She could tell from the shaky feeling in her stomach that her composure was deserting her. Sliding out of bed, she pulled the quilt with her and wrapped it around her before she faced him. "You arrogant lout! What makes you think you're so desirable that I would marry you? I was curious, and you gave me a competent introduction."

"*Competent introduction!*" Now he looked furious. "And how would you know what was competent?"

With great effort she produced a superior smile. "You don't know everything about me."

"I know you were a virgin." He took a deep breath and lowered his voice. "Margarida, I've said everything badly this morning, but I've already apologized twice."

"I don't want apologies. Just go away, and don't worry—I won't tell my father anything about this. I won't spoil your plans to have your relatives use our land."

"That's not important," Brant snapped, but from the sudden flush on his face and clenching of his jaw muscles, Margarida knew he'd been thinking of the Apache.

She could feel tears coming, and she couldn't bear to cry now in front of him. "Get out."

He started to speak, and then the kitchen door slammed. Luisa had come into the house. "Get out," she hissed, and he turned and left.

Margarida sank onto the bed and pulled the quilt closer around her, fighting back tears. She hated women who cried constantly, and she wasn't going to become one because of *him.* Holding herself rigid, she conquered her tears, but didn't stop the pain. Last night had seemed all she'd ever dreamed making love could be. When she'd awakened, she'd felt wonderful—as if she'd learned secrets that would transform her life. But Brant had destroyed that feeling.

Now he expected to do his duty by marrying her. Never! Let him do his duty to the Apache who were so important to him. She wouldn't be his charity case!

She rose and washed in the cold water from the pitcher, not yet ready to face Luisa in order to have hot water. After she dressed, she brushed her hair.

The pull against her scalp soothed her, and she felt
almost calm as she straightened the bed, refusing to
think about what had happened there. Closing the
door of Rupert's room behind her, she went downstairs to face the day.

When Brant reached his room, he found the door
open and Walt standing in the center. His eyes were
wide and frightened; his hands clutched his tousled
hair. "Brant! I thought you went away again." He
stumbled across to Brant's embrace.

"No. I'm right here." As he held his brother, Brant
groaned to himself. He was doing everything wrong.
Walt didn't ask why Brant wasn't in his room, and he
wouldn't notice that the bed hadn't been slept in. That
was the only fortunate thing so far this morning.

When Walt quieted and was reassured enough to go
back to his room to dress, Brant pulled on his denim
workshirt and thought about Margarida. He realized,
now that it was too late, that he'd been so disgusted
with himself he hadn't thought about her feelings. Last
night he'd been dishonorable. This morning he'd been
an ass. No wonder she was angry with him.

That explained her refusal to marry him, and her
ridiculous claim she'd only wanted to try out sex.
Competent introduction! Her words riled him all over
again.

He stamped his foot into his boot with more force
than necessary. He knew from her response that his
performance had been more than competent, but she
certainly wouldn't know how to judge. Or would she?

The second boot rested on the floor, his foot raised
halfway to the boot top. Slowly he lifted the boot and
pulled it on. Had she been experimenting with someone?

Enoch Springer's face intruded into Brant's thoughts,
along with a vision of Margarida smiling seductively at
Enoch across the Ross patio. He slammed down on
the second boot so hard the floorboards quivered.

He heard a call from the bottom of the stairs—Luisa's voice. "Brant? Something the matter up there?"

"No. Everything's fine," he shouted in response, and descended the stairs in as foul a temper as he could remember.

Margarida's appearance didn't improve his mood. She sat at the kitchen table beside Walt, sipping a cup of coffee. Her dark brown hair made a silken coil around the back of her head, and a soft yellow dress with high collar and flowing skirt emphasized the enticing lines of her breasts and hips. She and Walt were laughing, and she looked as carefree as the butterfly her colorful dress and dark hair and eyes always made him think of.

By saying little, he managed to subdue his ill humor during breakfast. Luisa had made fresh corn tortillas along with the bacon and eggs that had been customary when Rupert was alive. Brant had eaten only beef jerky and dried peaches on the ride from Socorro, and breakfast should have tasted good. It didn't.

Luisa and Margarida were clearing away the dishes when Tall Man came in. Brant knew his cousin had been up all night with two of the *vaqueros*, guarding the house, and should sleep. But Brant's need to talk to Margarida without Walt was compelling.

"Walt," he said, "the three horses I rode from Socorro need to be looked over. Fortunately it wasn't hot yesterday, but even when I shifted mounts, I ran them hard. Would you take a look at them and see how they are?"

"Sure, Brant."

Brant turned to his cousin. "Tall Man, would you give Walt a hand after you've eaten? I need to talk to Margarida."

"I must go home as soon as I can this morning," Margarida objected.

Brant looked at her and saw that she was barely

keeping her facade of serenity. "We haven't talked about Priscilla Welles yet," he reminded her.

Her eyes flashed with quickly disguised anger before she finally said, "Yes, all right."

"I ate with the hands," Tall Man said. "Shall we go to the stable, Walt?"

"You're really going to stay here?" Walt asked Brant.

Brant rested his hand on Walt's shoulder for a moment. "Yes, I'm going to stay. I'll be out soon."

Walt gave a beaming smile. "I'll take care of the horses. And Tall Man can help me."

When the door slammed behind the two men, Brant took Margarida's arm and escorted her down the hall into the parlor, closing the door after them. She jerked her arm away from him and went to sit in a single chair beside the square grand piano, across the room from the sofa and other chairs. He followed her and sat on the piano stool, receiving a glare from her as he did.

Her anger sparked the temper he'd barely subdued during breakfast. "I'm not going to touch you, but I don't want to shout across the room," he snapped.

"You're right that you're not going to touch me," she responded, her tone as irate as his.

He made a half-turn on the stool, staring at the multiple reds and blues of the Persian rug on the floor, cursing himself for another failure of control. When he turned back, he said quietly, "Please tell me about Priscilla Welles."

Margarida relaxed some of her guard at Brant's even tone, and thought back to the scene at the Welleses' house. Ordinarily Priscilla wouldn't want anyone to know about her problems, but she'd forfeited the right to privacy by her accusation of Walt. And regardless of what Priscilla had done, she'd been promised help, which Brant would have to give.

"Priscilla," Margarida began, "is pregnant, by Lee Hansen," and went on to describe what Priscilla had told her. When she reached the part about Nat Welles suggesting that Walt must be the rapist, she saw Brant's face go white and the muscles stand out in cords on his neck. She put her hand over his clenched fist. "Brant, I know how you feel, but you mustn't go after Nat Welles now. Walt needs you here too much."

"You're right," he said, his voice as thin as the edge of a razor-sharp knife. "I won't go see him—yet. Please tell me the rest."

Margarida realized she was holding on to his hand and quickly drew her own back. She looked across the room at an oval picture of Walt's mother while she calmed her breathing, and then continued telling him about getting Walt released. "And so," she ended, "Priscilla is at my house, and I promised to help her. I know she did a terrible thing, but her father is mostly to blame. And she did tell the truth at the end."

"Thanks to you, Margarida. I think I can convince Lee Hansen that he wants to do his duty and marry her." Brant flushed, and Margarida wondered if he'd realized that he'd said almost the same thing to her. He rose and paced the room, coming back to stand before her. When he spoke, his voice was husky. "You know what Walt means to me. I owe you more than I can repay."

She rose also, uncomfortable under his steady look. "I did it because I love Walt." She started to the door. "If you can arrange someone to go with me, I want to go home now. Walt won't need me here now that you're back."

He caught her arm, swinging her around. "We have something else to discuss. Margarida, I want to marry you."

Her churning anger resurfaced, and she jerked her arm away. "Don't try to be so damned noble. You've already told me how grateful you are. That's enough." She turned again to leave.

He stepped in front of her, his jaw clenched, and

said furiously, "No, it isn't enough." He stopped, then continued in a calmer voice, "I don't want to fight with you, Margarida. And God knows I don't want to hurt you. I owe you too much."

She stared at him, and rage gripped her chest so tightly she wasn't sure she could breathe. With both hands she rammed at his chest, staggering him backward before he caught himself. "Owe! Duty! Those are the words you like best. And let's not leave out honor. I'm sure you've never missed a chance to do your honorable duty."

Brant grabbed her shoulders, and she thought he was going to shake her. Then he stiffened, and she could see him get control of his anger. "When I was seventeen and left home, I didn't think about duty. But when I came back, Walt was ignorant, ignored by my father, treated with contempt even by the *vaqueros*. I found out then that duty means something."

"Well, you don't have any duty to me. Walt's happiness repays me for anything I did for him."

He still held her shoulders, his fingers pressing tightly. "Margarida, I love you and I want to marry you."

Her heart rushed up into her throat, but the stiff lines of his face made it drop again just as fast. For years she'd waited for him to say he loved her, but not like this, with eyes that looked so uncomfortable—so reluctant. She'd thought she couldn't be more enraged, but she was wrong.

With one foot she kicked as hard as she could against his booted leg and pushed his surprised hands away from her shoulders. "So now you've decided to love me. How convenient for your conscience. Don't be such a hypocrite. You provided a very pleasant lesson last night. I'm sure I'll be able to use it. But I certainly don't intend to marry you."

Stamping around him, she flung the door open and headed for the stairs. On the bottom step she looked back. He still stood in the parlor doorway, and his face had a closed, hard expression. She made her voice just as distant. "If you'll see that Halcon and an escort are ready, that is *all* I want from you."

When she reached Rupert's bedroom, she closed the door behind her, proud of how firm she had sounded. But as she gathered her belongings, anger drained away, leaving only exhaustion. She welcomed it as protection against misery.

Half an hour later, Brant stood by the corral and watched as Margarida rode away with Tall Man. From a seat on the corral fence, Walt said, "I love Margarida."

At his brother's words, Brant acknowledged to himself he shared that feeling. He loved Margarida, had loved her as a girl, and now as a woman. He loved her beauty and warmth and passion, and even more her audacious spirit.

"I love her too," he said, and cursed himself for having botched saying those words to her. And for not having known the truth until now, when it seemed too late.

12

FROM her seat at the desk in her father's office, Margarida heard quick footsteps in the hall, and then Priscilla's anxious voice. "Margarida, someone's coming. Do you think it's my father?" Priscilla had been at the Ross ranch a week, and she spent much of each day looking and listening for Nat Welles' dreaded arrival.

Margarida rose. "Don't worry," she said, "we won't let your father bully you."

When they reached the veranda, she saw three horses approaching. Her stomach did a flip-flop as she recognized Brant on Chid. She hadn't seen him since she'd left the Curtis ranch after the night she didn't want to remember. The other two men were Walt and Lee Hansen.

"It's not Papa." Priscilla sounded relieved, then flustered. "My dress. It looks terrible. I'll go—"

"No," Margarida interrupted firmly. "You don't need to fuss over Lee. He doesn't deserve it."

Priscilla's distressed face showed Margarida's words were wasted, but by holding Priscilla's hand, Margarida forestalled any retreat. She didn't prevent a moment of regret that her own blouse and skirt were old.

By the time the three riders stabled their horses and were crossing to the house, Margarida felt sure of her composure. When they reached the porch, Walt's eyes lit up with pleasure as he greeted her. Lee wouldn't look directly at them, mumbling his sullen hello to the flowerbeds beside the veranda. Brant's greeting gave away nothing, his eyes distant and his mouth an indecipherable line.

Margarida gestured toward the *sala*. "Please come in." She led the way inside and went to the patio doorway. "María," she called to the maid who was sweeping, "please bring coffee and tea to the *sala*. And tell my mother we have company."

After a hard look from Brant, Lee said, "I would like to speak to Miss Welles privately, please."

Priscilla's face turned white, then red. "Why . . . I suppose . . ." She looked helplessly at Margarida.

Seeing that Priscilla was going to do nothing on her own, Margarida said, "You can use the small dining room off the kitchen. Priscilla, please show Mr. Hansen the way."

Priscilla gave Lee a distressed look and started out the doorway to cross the patio. Lee, with all the enthusiasm of a man going to his own hanging, followed her.

Slowly Margarida faced Walt and Brant and searched for words to conceal her agitation. "I see you talked to Lee" was all she could think of.

"Yes, and his father," Brant replied, and she envied his even tone. Damn him, she thought, why doesn't he at least look uncomfortable?

María brought coffee in a pottery jug and tea in a blue china teapot with gold trim. While Margarida poured tea for Walt and Brant and coffee for herself, she listened to Walt talk about a colt he was training and surreptitiously watched Brant. He was looking at Walt, and the expression on his face had softened. Unwillingly she remembered how his face had looked that night, his eyes glowing, his mouth passionate. The pain she'd denied all week caught her.

During the week since they'd made love, she'd been telling herself she'd find someone else—a man who would love and appreciate her. Virginity wasn't so important as she'd once thought; it was a story fathers and mothers told their daughters to keep them in ignorance. Now that she knew about lovemaking, she'd be ready for . . . well, she couldn't think of anyone, but there would be someone.

"Walt," Brant said, "the wagon should be here with the trunk. Would you mind seeing about it?"

"Sure, Brant." Walt rose and bounded out the door.

Margarida's heartbeat quickened as Brant came over and crouched in front of her, resting his elbows on his bent knees. "I know this isn't the time to discuss . . . everything." The bronze skin of his face became even darker before he continued. "But there is something we didn't talk about that can't wait. You could be expecting a child."

Her skin felt hot enough to be at least as dark as his. She rose and moved away from him, but he stood and caught her arm. She shook it off and faced him defiantly. "That's my private affair."

His voice sliced the air. "Not anymore, Margarida. I must know." His face was alive with expression now—anger in his eyes, determination in his mouth and jaw.

Nights during the past week when she hadn't been able to exhaust herself enough to sleep, she'd worried that she could be pregnant. Her distress eased a little to think Brant had worried too.

She hadn't intended to be so close to him. Now she wanted to touch him, rest her hand on the side of his tense face, tease his mouth into a sensual smile. Quickly she clasped her hands, which could easily betray her, and drew back to the distance she must have to protect herself. "All right. I don't know yet, but I'll tell you when I do."

Brant saw the proud lift of her chin and turned away to pick up his teacup. He hadn't anticipated how difficult it would be to see her. He'd never been in love before. And dammit—he didn't like it. He wanted to kiss her eyes, even flashing dislike at him, run his hands over the velvet skin stretched across those wide cheekbones and down to the sweetly shaped lips. These thoughts made him feel awkward and stupid, like an inexperienced kid.

When he faced her again, he hoped he looked detached. "I haven't seen Nat Welles," he said, and was glad to hear he sounded rational. "I don't want to go into Rio Torcido and leave Walt behind just yet."

She looked thoughtful, then dismayed, as if she'd remembered something she didn't like. "The Indian you told me was murdered," she said, "had he been . . . the way a horse is gelded?" Color flooded her face.

The fury of the day he'd found the tortured Indian came back. "Yes, he'd been castrated. How did you know that?"

At Brant's clipped words, Margarida almost wished she hadn't remembered what Nat Welles said. It would mean more trouble. "That day at Priscilla's house," she explained, "before we went back to the jail for Walt, her father said he and the other men were going to . . . do to Walt what they'd done to an Indian."

Though Margarida knew it wasn't possible, Brant's eyes became even blacker. "The fifth murderer," he said. "Another score to settle with Nat Welles." The quiet menace in his voice was more threatening than if he'd shouted.

"Here's the trunk, Brant." At the sound of Walt's cheerful voice from the doorway, Brant's face changed so rapidly that Margarida thought she might have imagined the fearsome expression it had held.

Walt had a small metal trunk balanced on his shoulder. He carried it into the room and set it down on the floor. "It's something for Priscilla to use," he confided to Margarida. He looked at Brant. "Can I tell Margarida?"

Brant's mouth crinkled into a teasing grin. "Make her guess what it is first."

Walt laughed delightedly. "Yes! Guess, Margarida."

Glad for the diversion, she put her head on one side, prolonging one of Walt's favorite games. "Let's see. A puppy?" He shook his head. "A horseshoe?"

He shook his head again. "You give up?" He didn't let her answer. "It's a dress, my mother's wedding dress. Brant said Priscilla might like to wear it."

"What a generous idea," Margarida said. Just when she knew Brant was the most difficult man alive, he did something thoughtful. Almost resentfully she wished he wouldn't; it would be easier just to dislike him.

Priscilla and Lee returned, both of them looking uncomfortable. "Lee and I," she began nervously, "wish to get married."

She glanced at Lee. He swallowed, then said, "Yes. Right away."

Margarida hugged Priscilla. "I'm sure you'll be very happy," she said, and hoped that was possible.

"Congratulations, Mr. Hansen." Brant's voice had a tinge of sarcasm. Lee nodded glumly, and Margarida wondered if he realized how lucky he was. If that mob had killed Walt, Brant might not have let Lee Hansen live either.

"We have something for you," Walt announced eagerly to Priscilla. She flushed a bright red and looked past Walt's ear. He didn't seem to notice her discomfort and pointed to the trunk. "Go ahead and open it."

Uncertainly Priscilla raised the lid. The dress she lifted out had the voluminous skirt worn in the 1860's, made to go over a crinoline. The bodice and skirt were pale green satin, with flounces of transparent tarlatan muslin over the sleeves and at the hem. Narrow bands of dark green velvet trimmed the neckline and waist. "It was my mother's wedding dress," Walt said proudly.

"It's lovely," Priscilla said hesitantly. "I've never seen anyone wearing anything like it."

Margarida could tell what Priscilla was thinking—

the dress was old-fashioned. Quickly she searched her memory and hoped she'd found the right name. "I've heard that Lady Caroline was tall like you, Priscilla," she said, blithely elevating Walt's mother to nobility. "You'll look elegant in her dress."

Brant had lines of amusement around his mouth. "Yes, I remember how beautiful she was."

For the first time that day, a pleased smile appeared on Priscilla's face, and she looked directly at Walt. "Thank you for letting me borrow it."

Elena came in and greeted the men, then exclaimed over the dress. Priscilla became pretty in her excitement, and even Lee began to look more like a willing groom.

"We'll be here Saturday with Reverend Newcomb to perform the ceremony," Brant said, "if that is satisfactory, Mrs. Ross."

"Of course," Elena responded. "Will the Hansens and Mr. and Mrs. Welles be coming?"

Brant answered, as if it were natural that he rather than Lee should make the arrangements. "I'll be glad to bring Mrs. Welles, but I'm afraid not Mr. Welles."

Priscilla broke the uncomfortable silence, her voice quavery. "No. If Mama came, it might make trouble."

Only Walt still looked happy when the men said their good-byes and left. As Margarida and Priscilla stood on the veranda watching the three men ride away, Priscilla said with unusual determination, "I know Lee doesn't want to marry me, but I don't care. Mama says it doesn't matter why a man marries you, so long as he does the right thing."

Margarida felt pain rush back into the wound made by Brant's regret after they made love, and then his offer to marry her. It wasn't so easy to know what was the right thing. She felt sure it wasn't always duty.

Priscilla returned to the *sala*, and Margarida heard her talking excitedly to Elena about the dress. Slowly Margarida went inside to join them. If she were preg-

nant like Priscilla, maybe she'd have to marry Brant.
But she'd never think the reason they married didn't
matter. It would matter too much.

Saturday was an April day on its best behavior. A
few white strands of clouds enriched the aquamarine
sky. Wind teased the new aspen leaves into a confusion of green and silver. By noon, pine needles sighed
in the sunlight and exhaled their resinous fragrance
into the air.

Margarida fastened the mother-of-pearl buttons on
her apricot silk dress and adjusted the long sleeves and
high collar. The bodice hugged her waist and ended at
her hips in a swath of material which gathered at the
back. The pleated skirt touched the top of her white
kid boots. Her hair, the curls for once conquered in a
bun at her neck, completed her appearance of severe
elegance.

In the past few months she felt as if she'd been on a
seesaw—her feelings constantly changing. At times
she'd been sure she loved Brant, then as certain she
didn't. Just now she knew only one thing—the emotions he aroused in her were too strong and painful.

She must, she concluded, learn to be indifferent to
him. That might be hard, but she'd faced a lynch
mob—she could conquer her feelings. After she was
sure she wasn't pregnant—it had to turn out that way—
she'd concentrate on the ranch. When Papa came back,
she might even go somewhere else, use her education
to get a job teaching school.

"Margarida." She heard her mother's voice, and the
door opened. Elena looked impatient. "I need you.
Priscilla can't seem to get her petticoats right."

Margarida followed her mother around the patio to
the guest bedroom. Half an hour later a nearly tearful
Priscilla was ready, her skirt carefully arranged over
three stiffly starched petticoats. Elena went to greet
the arriving guests, and Margarida stayed with Priscilla.

Lee and Priscilla would visit an uncle in Chicago until the baby arrived, and then return to Rio Torcido. The Hansens had six daughters, but only one son, so Mr. Hansen insisted that Lee come back to the ranch. "What do you think people in Rio Torcido will say about me?" Priscilla asked for the dozenth time.

"They'll talk about you for a while," Margarida responded, "but then they'll forget. You'll be married."

"Yes. I'll like that. All except . . ." Though no one else could hear, Priscilla lowered her voice. "That part isn't any fun, but I guess I'll have to put up with it."

Surprised, Margarida asked, "You mean . . . making babies? But . . . I've heard that it gets . . . really nice."

"Maybe. Men like it, and they do nice things for you and tell you they love you. I like that. But I don't think they mean it," she added resignedly, "or Lee would have wanted to marry me right away."

Margarida's face felt hot and then cold, and she went to the mirror, pretending to rebutton the high collar. She remembered the intense pleasure when Brant had made love to her. How could anyone not like those feelings? If only Adela were here to ask! But even if Priscilla was wrong about the pleasure, her other words were painfully apt. Margarida couldn't forget that afterward Brant had said he loved her. In the mirror her face looked white, and she pinched her cheeks for color.

Lupe knocked on the door, then opened it. "It's time, Señorita Priscilla," she said, and disappeared in a trail of youthful giggles. Margarida followed Priscilla, glad to have her thoughts interrupted.

Bouquets of wild lupine and iris and delicate white poppies filled the *sala*, where Priscilla shyly took Mr. Hansen's arm. He was tall and blond like his son, with bulging muscles from hard ranch work. The unpleasantness surrounding this marriage apparently didn't disturb his stolid calm. Margarida guessed he was willing to overlook Lee's behavior because of the prospect of a grandson.

Lee and the minister stood at the other end of the room. Brant and Walt sat on one side, and Mrs. Hansen with four of the Hansen daughters on the other. While Elena played the traditional Mendelssohn march on the spinet piano, Margarida slipped inside to a chair near the door.

During the brief service, Margarida carefully stared at the ruffles on the back of Priscilla's skirt. Only once did she glance at Brant. He was looking steadily at her, his eyes dark and probing, reminding her of the hawk she'd sometimes called him. She almost put her hand over her stomach to find some answer to the question she knew was in his mind. Instead she watched Lee give Priscilla an awkward kiss, and realized the ceremony was over.

The celebration afterward was brief. Mr. Hansen had brought white wine and whiskey, and Elena had arranged a modest meal. Margarida kept herself busy helping serve from the table in the large dining room. She didn't want to risk being alone with Brant. In spite of her resolutions, she was a long way from indifference to him.

"I need to speak to you, Margarida," she heard him say behind her. She turned, but didn't look above the black embroidery of the lapels of his Mexican-style jacket. "It's less than three weeks to the spring roundup . . . and there's another important question to discuss."

"I'm sorry, but I must take Mrs. Hansen some tea." She picked up a cup before she looked at him. His eyes narrowed slightly, and a muscle tightened along his cheek, but she couldn't decide what emotion he was feeling. Hastily she took the cup and sat down to visit safely with Mrs. Hansen, a large woman with an incongruously frail voice, who seemed bewildered by the afternoon's proceedings.

Priscilla and Lee planned to stay overnight with the

Hansens and then go to Silver City, where they would start their train journey to Chicago. Mr. Hansen had promised Priscilla that they would skirt Rio Torcido and she wouldn't see her father.

When Mr. Hansen looked at his pocket watch and said it was time to go, Margarida took Reverend Newcomb aside. "Can you tell me," she asked, "how Carl Bodmer is?"

An understanding smile warmed the minister's moonlike face. "It's hard for him, losing his right arm, and I guess you feel bad about that. But you mustn't. He brought it on himself." He patted her hand, and she gave him a grateful look before rejoining the others.

When Priscilla came out of the guest bedroom in a blue traveling dress and a new feather-trimmed hat, she gave Margarida a final hug. "Thank you," she whispered tearfully. "I know I'd hate myself if you hadn't made me tell the truth. And I wouldn't be married."

Margarida kissed Priscilla, hoping that her life would be better with the Hansens than it had been with her father.

Brant and Walt waited on the veranda with Margarida and her mother as the Hansens and Reverend Newcomb departed. "I'll pick up the trunk later," Brant told Elena, then turned to Margarida. "I'll be back in a week to talk to you—about anything we need to decide."

Elena watched them leave, then looked at Margarida. "What did he mean?"

"He wants to discuss the roundup," Margarida said, knowing she couldn't ever tell her mother all the truth.

Three days later, Margarida discovered she was not carrying Brant's child. She felt relieved, but another, unexpected emotion surprised her—a feeling of loss.

That night she dreamed she was in a house which was her home, but no one else lived there. All the rooms were empty. When she woke, she lay disturbed over the dream. Perhaps she was ready for marriage if she felt such grief about not being pregnant now. The trouble was that once she'd looked forward to having Brant's babies.

Lobo jumped off her bed and stretched, then padded to the door to be let out. She had too many other things to do to spend time remembering childish fantasies, she scolded herself, and slid out of bed.

As she dressed, she thought about Frank Vincent. The foreman, even with her prodding, had made only confused plans for the roundup. When she talked to him, he said he would see to everything, but he didn't—as if he didn't have to take her seriously.

At midmorning Margarida came back from riding out to the large meadow where the cattle and horses would be corralled and found the foreman having coffee in the bunkhouse kitchen. "Mr. Vincent," she charged, "the fences of the temporary corrals still aren't repaired. Why haven't you taken care of it?"

The white skin on his forehead where his hat shaded his head from the sun turned pink. "I'll get to that."

"When?"

He stood up, flushing to a deep red. "Miss Ross, I've been patient with you, but I'm the foreman. I'll decide what to do unless Mrs. Ross tells me different."

Frustration almost choked Margarida. "All right," she retorted. "We'll go see my mother right now." She turned and stamped out, leaving the foreman to follow.

They found her mother in the small dining room, yawning over coffee. "Mama, Mr. Vincent doesn't believe he needs to listen to me. He says he has to hear from you. He hasn't organized the work teams for the roundup. The *vaqueros* are getting careless and slacking off because he's not doing his job. Will you please tell him to follow my directions?"

"Mrs. Ross, I was hired by your husband," Frank Vincent snapped, "and not by Miss Ross."

Elena gave Margarida an impatient look. "My husband said we should ask Brant Curtis for help." She sounded cross; Elena hated to be bothered when she'd just gotten up. "Let Brant be in charge."

"That's fine with me," the foreman said. "Brant Curtis knows his business. I don't mind taking orders from him."

Her frustration growing to rage, Margarida barely managed not to shout. "Mama, this isn't settled! I don't want to ask Brant."

Elena's eyes lost their sleepy look, and her lips compressed into a thin line. "You may go, Mr. Vincent." When he left, she turned angrily to Margarida. "You can't expect the foreman to listen to you. Asking Brant for help is the only sensible thing to do for the good of the ranch."

Margarida recognized the expression, though she'd seen it only a few times. On the rare occasions when Elena fixed on an action, nothing changed her mind. Two concerns triggered that immovability—J.J.'s welfare and the prosperity of the ranch. When she'd insisted Jesse go after J.J., worry about her son had been more important than the ranch. Margarida's desire to manage without Brant wasn't.

"Send Pedro with a note asking Brant to come over," Elena said, her tone making clear the matter was settled.

Brant and Walt arrived late that afternoon. Lobo greeted them both exuberantly, and Walt stayed out by the corral, petting Lobo and watching Pedro show off his skill with his rawhide lariat. Brant followed Margarida into Jesse's office. "Your note says your mother wants me to be in charge of the roundup," he said.

"Frank Vincent isn't working out very well," Margarida said defensively. "And he won't take my advice."

A black eyebrow went up, and Brant's mouth took on an amused look. "Then you won't be doing the branding?"

Resentfully Margarida glared at him. "All right— the branding upsets me, but I could manage. Don't sound so superior because you think you know my biggest weakness."

His lips softened to a smile which Margarida would have thought wistful on anyone else. "I think," he said, "your biggest weakness is the same as mine, and it isn't getting sick when animals are branded."

Margarida felt excitement burst through her like a newly lit flame. Trying to restrain her feelings, she took the chair at her father's desk, but today it didn't give her a feeling of composure. Brant sat across from her, his long legs crossed at his ankles.

Margarida couldn't help noticing his look of controlled masculinity. He wore a faded cotton shirt and denim pants, work-worn and soft. When he shifted his position, the cloth followed the movement of his muscles. Even more distracting was the way his pants fit his groin closely enough to show a slight contour. Unwillingly she remembered how he'd looked naked, his penis jutting from the thatch of black hair. Desire quivered through her abdomen.

Shocked that she could feel so much passion just by looking at him, she quickly hunted for the list she'd prepared for the roundup.

Brant watched Margarida's hands search through the stack of papers on the desk and felt his whole body tensing. Her print cotton dress with its high neckline and long sleeves should have looked modest, but it followed the curves of her breasts too well. The thick braid of her hair rested over her shoulder and across her right breast. He wanted to pull her close until that braid was caught between them, and have her tell him what he wanted to hear.

But what did he want to hear? Nights short of sleep

hadn't helped him decide. Duty—that idea she'd scorned but which meant so much to him—told him it would be disastrous if she were pregnant. Jesse would be furious and probably unwilling to tolerate Indians in the valley, much less on Ross land. And Brant would have a wife who often seemed no more than an impetuous girl—and one who had been forced to marry him. His pride would despise that.

For the sacrifice of duty and pride, he'd gain Margarida. Impulsive and childish—and also generous in spirit and passionate in lovemaking. God, he almost wished he didn't know that.

He stood up abruptly, and knew his voice would sound harsh and angry. Just now it was the only way he could get the question out at all. "Are you pregnant?"

Margarida's hands stopped. She stared up at him, her eyes as dark as the shadows at the back of a cave. "No."

The single word exploded in his head, the fragments drifting down through his body, draining warmth with them.

Margarida heard the paper under her fingers crackle and looked down. She had crumpled the list she'd been hunting for. Keeping her eyes carefully on the blurred writing, she smoothed the paper until she knew her voice would be steady. "I've written down some of the things," she began.

"Why don't you just let me have your paper? I know your father's routines pretty well. I can ask about any plans that aren't clear." Brant's voice sounded flat, as if he'd erased emotion from it. Tiny lines radiated from the corner of his expressionless eyes. He must feel relieved at my news, she thought.

Silently she rose and gave him the list. Out of her confusion of emotions, resentment surfaced. He couldn't have made his impatience clearer. Well, she'd given him the answer he'd wanted, the same one she'd hoped for, so how he felt didn't matter to her. Or at least it soon wouldn't.

When the roundup began two weeks later, Margarida found the idea of being just an observer too painful to watch the work. Frank Vincent answered her questions readily, as if he could afford to indulge her now. She decided she disliked him intensely.

Brant came to the house every few days, but Margarida persuaded her mother to see him and stayed out of the way. Later she read the notes he left and thought that his script looked the way he behaved—cold and decisive.

Her father had been away a month and a half, and when May slid into June and then July, Margarida's twentieth birthday passed with only her mother to celebrate. Though no word had come from Jesse, Elena seemed unworried. Margarida couldn't so easily dismiss her concern about him and J.J., but she admired her mother's confidence and realized worry wouldn't bring them home sooner. Her mother's accusation that she was to blame for her brother's leaving still lingered in her mind. It wasn't true, but she was glad her mother seemed to have forgotten.

The only really good news was that Nat Welles and his wife had left Rio Torcido. Though Margarida was trying not to care what Brant did, she was relieved he wouldn't be facing Nat Welles.

Summer storms renewed the pastures, and work revived Margarida's spirits. She spent long hours riding and practicing roping. It was the range skill that the *vaqueros* most respected.

Halcon wasn't good for work with cattle, so Margarida adopted a wiry chestnut mare Miguel had trained the previous year. Margarida called her mare Bailarina, because when the horse heard music, whether a harmonica or guitar or even a whistled tune, she lifted her feet as if to dance. Miguel had taught Bailarina to stop rapidly to pull a lasso taut. She could, as the cowboys said, stop on a quarter and give back fifteen cents change.

Enoch made regular visits to the ranch, and under Elena's careless supervision he found opportunities for kisses which mildly excited Margarida. Fernando Reyes called once, but she sent him away, no longer amused by his assumption that someday she would find him as attractive as he obviously found himself. Though she thought she should do something to encourage other men, it was easier to drift with Enoch's comfortable and pleasant attention.

Brant, always sending a note first, came periodically to check on the Ross ranch, and Margarida arranged to be away from the house. Eventually she'd test her plan for indifference to him, but she wasn't ready yet. He must want to avoid her, she decided, or he wouldn't so carefully let them know ahead of time. It should have pleased her that his desires coincided with her own.

The track from town was dry and hot on an early August afternoon when a stranger appeared, riding a tired-looking mule. Margarida had been out on Bailarina and was crossing from the stable to the house when she saw him and waited. Dust covered his bushy beard and rough clothes and obliterated the color of a battered hat. He stopped beside the corral and asked, "This the Ross ranch?"

"Yes. Please stand down if you wish."

The man dismounted. "I got a message for Miz Ross from her husband."

Margarida's feelings shuttled between joy and dread. "Is he all right?"

The man looked down and shifted his weight, scuffing up dust onto his already dirty boots. "Was when he give me the paper," he mumbled.

If she hadn't restrained herself, Margarida would have kissed this rough stranger. "I'm Margarida Ross."

He took off his hat, showing hair as nondescript as its covering. "Please to meet you, ma'am. Name's Ted Breedon."

"Please take your mule to the stable, and one of the hands will look after him for you. Then come on to the house. I'll tell my mother you're here."

"Much obliged, Miss Ross." He replaced his hat and started for the stable.

Margarida ran to the house, taking the veranda steps in an undignified leap. "Mama!" she cried to the empty *sala*, then raced on to the patio. "Mama!"

Elena appeared in the kitchen doorway. "Margarida, why are you so noisy?"

"Someone's here with a message from Papa."

Her mother's face turned white. "And J.J.?"

Margarida was halfway back to the living room. "He didn't say."

In a few minutes, Ted Breedon came hesitantly into the *sala,* a faint trail of dust sifting off the hat in his hand. "Mama, this is Mr. Breedon," Margarida said. "Mr. Breedon, this is Mrs. Ross."

"Pleased to make your acquaintance, ma'am." He fumbled in his vest pocket and pulled out a folded sheet of paper. "I'm a miner, and I been prospectin' near Glory Creek, a little town on the San Juan River in Utah. A man heard I was comin' south to New Mexico to try my luck here. Said he was Jesse Ross and asked me to bring you this."

"Thank you, Mr. Breedon." Elena took the paper and said, "You must be tired and thirsty. Margarida, please see to some refreshment for Mr. Breedon."

Admiring her mother's composure, Margarida got a bottle of whiskey and a glass from the sideboard in the dining room, then hurried back to the *sala.* She poured a half-glass of whiskey for Mr. Breedon before looking impatiently at her mother. "The note says he knows where J.J. is," Elena said in a shaky voice, "and he expected to catch up with J.J. in a few days. Carlos

García got sick when they were in California and had to be left behind there. Carlos might be back home anytime."

"When did Papa write?" asked Margarida.

"About three weeks ago. July twelfth."

Ted Breedon cleared his throat. "It took me a while to get here, Miz Ross."

"Just where is Glory Creek?" Margarida asked.

"On a bend of the San Juan, east of where it joins up with the Colorado."

Elena gave him a sparkling smile. "We're so grateful that you came. Will you stay for supper and overnight?"

The miner put down his glass and rose, shifting his hat uncomfortably from one hand to the other. "I thank you, but I better be gettin' on. I'm on my way to join up with my brother south of Lordsburg, and that's a fair piece to go."

"I'm sorry, Mr. Breedon. We'd like to repay your kindness if we could."

"Oh, Mr. Ross sent me off with a good bottle of whiskey." He stood, staring at his hat and twisting it until Margarida wondered if he would demolish it. Finally he looked up at Elena. "There's a thing else I got to tell you. The same day, after your husband give me this note, he was in a gunfight at the saloon. With some Irish feller who jest come in from upstream. I only seen the end of it, but somebody told me it started over one of 'em accusin' the other of killin' someone. The Irishman got killed, and your husband took a real bad wound."

Margarida's joy turned to horror. Elena screamed, clutching the paper to her chest. "Oh! Oh! He's dead!"

"No, Mama. He didn't say that." Margarida put her arms around her mother, then looked at Ted Breedon. "Do you know anything more? My brother—he's also called Jesse Ross, or maybe J.J.—did you hear anything about him?"

He started backing toward the door. "No, ma'am, I don't know nothin' about him. He coulda been the one the fight was about. Weren't no doctor in Glory Creek, but they took your papa to a squaw outside of town who does nursin'. I waited around a day, but all I heard was he was bad. Then I had to leave." He was in the doorway now. "I'm right sorry to have to tell you this." He escaped outside.

"They're dead." Elena was sobbing hysterically. "I know Jesse and J.J. are both dead."

"I don't believe it, Mama. Papa was still alive when Mr. Breedon left. And he didn't know anything about J.J."

"He said that they fought about J.J. being killed."

"No—he said they fought about *someone* being killed. It could have been about Papa killing Michael Quinn's brother. Remember Papa told us about that." Margarida pulled her mother to a chair and forced her to sit down. With shaking hands she poured her mother a glass of whiskey. "Here, drink this."

Elena thrust Margarida's hand away, sloshing the liquor down her skirt. "I know things like this," she cried. "I tell you they're dead. And it's your fault. If you'd told us when J.J. left, none of this would have happened."

Margarida knew her mother wasn't rational, but the words pierced her like a shard of glass.

Rosa appeared in the patio door, with Lupe and María behind her. Their frightened faces provoked another hysterical burst of sobbing from Elena. She pushed Margarida away and rushed to Rosa, and it was the middle-aged servant who managed to get Elena to her bedroom.

Margarida paced the *sala* for hours, rereading her father's letter. It said only what Elena had reported, that he'd located J.J. and was going after him, so J.J. was alive then. It didn't mention Michael Quinn, but Margarida decided he had to be the Irishman Ted

Breedon had referred to. Even so, she couldn't believe her father and brother were dead. She didn't *feel* their deaths the way her mother did, and somehow she was sure she would.

Elena had swung from unnatural calm to unrestrained hysteria. She'd behaved the same way earlier after J.J. left—almost a collapse at first, and then unworried composure when Jesse went to find J.J.

Margarida tried not to think about her mother's accusation. "I'm not to blame," she said, appealing aloud to the empty room. "I'm not!" But guilt settled inside her knotted stomach, guilt she couldn't escape by telling herself her mother was irrational. About two o'clock exhaustion finally drove her to bed and to sleep.

For the next three days Elena kept to her room, refusing to see anyone but Rosa. Margarida reassured herself that her mother's hysteria would pass and tried to banish her own feelings of guilt. To accept blame for what might have happened to her father and brother was wrong. The agony of worrying about them was suffering enough.

When Margarida woke on the fourth morning and went to the small dining room, she found Elena standing beside the table, drinking coffee. Her eyes were red and swollen, but her white face was composed. She was already dressed in a brown riding habit.

Margarida stopped, startled. Was her mother so convinced of her father's death that she was already going to see their lawyer? "Where are you going, Mama?"

"To make arrangements to save this ranch." Elena's voice trembled, but her expression was determined—fanatic. "We don't have Jesse to look after us. I must do it."

"Mama, I don't believe Papa is dead. Please wait until you're calmer."

"No!" Elena's voice became shrill and cruel. "You

don't care whether we lose this ranch, but I do. I'll decide what's best, and you'll do whatever I say.''

Silently Margarida followed her mother to the doorway, then watched while Elena marched across to the stable, where Pedro waited with two horses. He helped Elena mount and then got on his horse and followed as she rode away.

Margarida pulled her robe closer around her. Though Elena might not be rational, she was determined. Margarida didn't know what her mother planned to do, but fear enveloped her like sleet from a winter blizzard.

13

B RANT took his Winchester from the wall rack and checked his ammunition. The rifle was more awkward to carry in the saddle sling than his Sharps carbine, but it had greater range. He could have asked his young Apache cousins to hunt the mountain lion that had killed so many cattle, but he wanted to go himself. The activity might help diminish the restlessness that had plagued him all summer.

Walt came down the hall, headed outside. "All right if I get the horses ready, Brant? Is Tall Man going with us?"

"Sure, and you could ask him." Brant grinned to himself. Ndè-ze probably would prefer to go to the Apache camp. A widow there was taking a good amount of his time. Her dead husband's family had no other son she must marry, and Brant thought it likely she'd accept Ndè-ze if he asked.

If his cousin were permanently nearby, Brant would be delighted and it would ease his mind. If something happened to him, Walt would have someone else to take care of him.

The question of Walt's welfare brought Margarida painfully to mind. As he did too often, Brant wondered what she was doing and how she was feeling. After she'd made plain she didn't want to marry him, he'd been careful to allow her the choice of seeing him or not; he'd done her enough harm. She'd chosen to avoid him, and he heard she was spending plenty of time with Enoch Springer. At that thought, he gripped the rifle so hard his hand hurt.

He picked up the bag of ammunition and strode through the kitchen to the outside door. Activity—that's what he wanted. To hell with thinking!

As he crossed to the stable, he saw two riders on the trail from the Ross ranch. Astonished, he recognized Elena Ross on her sorrel mare. Pedro rode beside her.

He felt the muscles tense on the back of his neck. Elena hadn't come to the Curtis house in years. Why was she here? Had something happened to Margarida?

"'Here, Walt," he called, and gave the rifle and ammunition to his brother, then forced himself to wait calmly. When Elena and Pedro came close, he saw that her face was white. Perspiration broke out on his own.

He lifted Elena down. "What's wrong, Mrs. Ross? Has something happened to Margarida?"

"No." The muscles in his neck relaxed a fraction. "It's worse," she finished.

Though she seemed composed, he guessed that underneath she was not far from hysteria. "Mrs. Ross, come inside, please. Then you can tell me what's wrong."

By the time he settled her on the sofa in the parlor, she had a little more color in her face. He drew a chair over and sat in front of her. "Tell me what's wrong."

"It's my husband and son." She clasped her hands tightly together. "They're both dead."

Shock hit Brant like a blow to his stomach. "My God! How did it happen?"

She spoke calmly now. "Jesse died in a gunfight with Michael Quinn, the man who killed J.J. It was in Utah. Jesse had traced them there."

Brant understood Elena's earlier distress, but her manner now worried him. Her composure was too complete, almost unnatural. "How did you find out?"

"A miner brought this letter four days ago." She

took a dog-eared paper from her pocket and handed it to him.

Quickly he read through it. "I don't understand. According to this letter, your husband and J.J. are alive."

"The miner said that right after this was written, Jesse and Michael Quinn were in a gunfight. They were both killed."

"What about J.J.?"

"He'd been killed first—or he would have been there and prevented it."

The combination of Elena's strange attitude and the uncertainty of her words about J.J. raised Brant's doubts. "The man who came—the miner. Did he see Jesse die?"

"He saw the fight—and that Jesse had a terrible wound and was going to die."

"Mrs. Ross, reports of gunfights and killings can be wrong. If the man who brought you this letter didn't see Jesse die or J.J. killed, it may not be true."

She reached over and gripped his arm, her nails painful through his shirt. Her voice rose sharply. "Don't try to tell me what I know. You're as bad as Margarida. She keeps saying that Jesse and J.J. aren't dead. She doesn't care."

Brant knew how unfair that was, but he could see that Elena wouldn't listen to any defense of Margarida now. "Is this man who brought the letter still around? I'd like to talk to him, if you don't mind."

Elena let go of Brant's arm. "No. He wouldn't stay. But it doesn't make any difference."

"There's something else I could do," Brant suggested. "Notify the federal authorities. Ask them to look into this report." Brant wasn't sure that anyone would respond to such a request, but he could try. "Or I could locate a private detective to investigate."

"It wouldn't be any use. Jesse is my husband. J.J.'s

my son. Don't you think I'd know if they're dead?"
Her hands trembled and her voice grew shrill.

"Please, Mrs. Ross. I understand how you feel,
but—"

"*I know*! When I was a little girl and my parents
died in a fire, I knew it before anyone told me!"

"All right. Let me have Luisa get you some tea."

He started to rise, but Elena stopped him. To his
surprise, he saw that she appeared calm again, and the
look she gave him was as shrewd and determined as
any he'd ever faced across a cattle-deal or poker table.
"I didn't come here to talk to you about what's
happened. That can't be changed. But I'm not going
to give up everything my husband worked for. I know
that until their deaths are legally established, I'll have
problems about the ranch. It's almost impossible to
find someone to run it efficiently."

"I'll help you in any way I can. What would you
like me to do?"

She waited a moment, still with that assessing look
in her eyes. "I want you to marry Margarida."

Brant thought he hadn't heard her correctly. "What
did you say?"

Incredibly she repeated herself. "I want you and
Margarida to marry. I know you're willing to help us.
But that isn't the same as being family."

Speech deserted him. He stared at her, his thoughts
a confusion of shock and disbelief. My God! Was she
mad? She returned his look steadily, her determination clear.

One question overshadowed the uncertainty of
whether Jesse and J.J. were actually dead, of whether
Elena was sane. "What does Margarida say about
this?"

"I haven't told her. I came to talk to you first."

He wanted to laugh. "You haven't *told* her?"

"No," Elena said in that strange, unruffled way.
"But she'll do what I decide. It's her duty."

He couldn't help it. He did laugh. "You may find out that Margarida doesn't think too highly of duty."

Elena's face stiffened into offended lines. "She'll do what I say. She has to."

No, Brant thought, Margarida doesn't have to. Even if her mother put pressure on her, he wouldn't allow Margarida to be coerced into anything she didn't want to do. He'd already done enough of that himself—in a different way.

"Mrs. Ross. It's natural you're upset. When you've thought more about this, you'll realize that it isn't necessary for Margarida to marry me."

The poker player in Elena was back, and from the glint in her eyes Brant decided she must think she had a winning hand. "The only ties that count are family. My daughter saved your brother's life. Do you feel any obligation because of that?"

That she'd ask such a question angered him. Then he thought of her situation and reminded himself to control his temper. "Of course I feel an obligation, but—"

"You have Apache relatives living on your land who occasionally go over onto our property. Would you like to have the Ross lands for them to use as well as your own?"

In spite of his anger, the lure of what she was suggesting grabbed at him. "You seem to know quite a lot about me."

She smiled, but her serene expression didn't reassure him about her state of mind. "Most people think I'm silly. I know Margarida often does. I pay more attention to what's going on than she thinks. Jesse would never have agreed to my idea. But he was foolish about that. And he and my son are dead now."

Her voice wavered, and for the first time that day, Brant saw the real grief behind Elena's composure. It made him want to comfort her, no matter how bizarre she acted.

"I don't care," she went on, "that you have Indian blood. You're a strong man. You can protect your family. I need a son-in-law. Then the ranch will be safe. It's to your advantage to marry Margarida. You owe her that much."

Brant knew she was right about his debt to Margarida, but something else bothered him about what she'd said. That she needed a son-in-law. Was he only the first man she intended to approach to find a candidate? The thought of Margarida pressured to marry someone else appalled him. "I'll consider it."

"No! I have to know *now* if you're going to say yes." She leaned forward, her eyes glittering, her lips compressed in a white line.

Thoughts and feelings roiled in his mind. Clearly Elena wouldn't accept an equivocal answer, and he couldn't risk her doing something even more drastic. She was disturbed, but still in command of herself—no madwoman to be taken to a doctor. "All right. I'll marry Margarida—but only if she agrees. And I doubt that she will."

Elena stood up. "She will. Now I think I'll go in the kitchen and have a cup of tea with Luisa after all. Then I must get back home to talk to Margarida."

Brant followed her to the kitchen, his apprehension growing with her confidence. What sort of pressure did she intend to put on Margarida? Not any, if he could help it.

He waited while Elena chatted with Luisa and drank her tea, then escorted her outside. "I'd like to go with you, Mrs. Ross, to talk to Margarida." And make damn sure Margarida is really willing, he added to himself.

Elena pulled on her riding gloves and said crisply, "I'll talk to her first, alone. Then you can discuss it with her yourself, if you're worried that I might force her into something she doesn't want."

Surprised at Elena's shrewdness, Brant said reluctantly, "All right. This morning I'll go into Rio Torcido and send a wire to Fort Bayard, to ask about army help in locating your husband. The sheriff or the lawyer may know about private investigators."

"Yes, that's a good idea." As pleasantly as if she'd come for a morning's inconsequential chat, Elena smiled at him and went to the corral, where Pedro helped her mount.

When the two riders were out of sight, Brant found Walt in the stable. "Walt, I'm sorry, but I can't go hunting today after all. I must go to Rio Torcido." He put his hand on his brother's arm and said gently, "If you don't want to go with me, you could stay here with Tall Man."

Walt's eyes grew distressed, and his mouth drooped. Since the night in jail, he hadn't been to town, and neither had Brant. Nor had Brant gone anywhere without Walt. Sometime that had to change.

"I guess I'll stay here."

Brant gave his brother a hug. "Tall Man's here."

"Yes," Walt echoed more happily, "Tall Man's here."

Within a few minutes, Brant was on his way. He wanted to get to town as soon as possible and then to the Ross ranch. Probably no one in Rio Torcido could help; it would take a trip to Silver City or to Fort Bayard. But if he sent some telegrams today, perhaps that would pacify Elena.

If she thought something were being done to check on Jesse and J.J., maybe she'd wait. Give up the crazy idea that Margarida must get married right away.

As Brant urged Chid into a lope, he wasn't sure whether he really wanted Elena to be sane.

After her mother's departure, Margarida dressed in the breeches she often wore for riding around the ranch, but she found she was too worried to leave the house. For once, she thought, Frank Vincent could handle ranch affairs. She tried to help in the kitchen until the cook became exasperated. After that she paced the veranda.

The only thing she could imagine her mother intended to do was to sell the ranch, though that wouldn't "save" it. Also, selling it wouldn't be possible without Papa's permission. Even if anyone else believed Papa was dead, legal settlements took a long time.

About noon she saw her mother and Pedro appear through the trees. As she ran to meet them, it struck her that they hadn't been gone long enough to go to Rio Torcido. Maybe Mama had realized how foolish she was being and turned back.

Her mother's cheerful face buoyed Margarida's hope. "Are you feeling better, Mama?" she asked cautiously.

"Yes, I am." Elena smiled at Margarida as Pedro helped her dismount. She took Margarida's arm, and they walked together to the house. "I have some good news."

"Did you hear from Mr. Breedon?"

"No. I'm sure he's gone, and he couldn't tell us anything more."

In the living room Elena pulled off her gloves and sat on the couch, patting the place beside her. "Margarida, sit down. We must talk."

Margarida felt her stomach ease for the first time since the prospector had brought her father's letter. "Oh, yes, Mama. Mr. Breedon's story about Papa is terribly frightening, but I know we can think of a way to do something. What's your good news?"

Elena took both of Margarida's hands. "We must face facts, Margarida. I know you don't want to accept that your father and brother are dead."

Margarida's hope that her mother would be reasonable faded. "But, Mama, we don't *know* that they're dead."

"All right, it's possible they're alive." From her mother's voice, Margarida knew Elena was only hu-

moring her, and she wanted to scream in frustration.
Instead she clamped her lips shut, resolving she'd just
have to listen and hope time would help. "Even if
they're alive," Elena continued, "we have to go on
and keep the ranch safe. Make sure it's all right."

"Yes, that's true," agreed Margarida. "Maybe we
could get Miguel to come back to be foreman again.
He ran things well before he went to jail."

Elena gave an impatient wave of her hand. "No,
that won't work. Miguel drinks too much. He only did
a good job because your father was here to supervise
him."

"I can see to the ranch. I've learned a lot since Papa
left."

"That's nonsense." Elena's dark eyes gleamed with
intensity. "All the miners who are sure there are lost
gold mines in our canyons will be after our land. A
woman couldn't stop them. Accidents happen—people
get killed. It wouldn't be safe—you couldn't even ride
out by yourself. Eventually the fortune hunters would
run us out. You don't know what it can be like when
men start thinking there's gold around. They only
respect a strong man."

Elena took Margarida's hand. "I know you saved
Walt. You were very brave. But facing a mob isn't the
same as running a big ranch and keeping prospectors
away."

Alarmed by her mother's flushed face, Margarida
decided reasoning wasn't going to work. Best to try
agreeing. "All right. Brant helped us with the roundup.
Maybe he can find a better foreman for us."

"Brant is going to help us. He's agreed to marry
you."

Margarida stared at Elena, convinced she'd lost her
reason completely. "I don't believe you. When did
you talk to Brant?"

"This morning."

Fury propelled Margarida up, her hands clenched,

trembling from the force of her anger. "This is your good news? That he offered to marry me?"

Elena looked almost pleased. "Don't yell, Margarida. It wasn't his suggestion. I asked him to marry you."

"*You asked him to marry me?*"

"Yes, and he agreed."

"Well, I refuse!"

"That's what he said at first. But I persuaded him to change his mind." Elena rose and started toward the door. "I'm very thirsty. I'm going to get something to drink."

Margarida grabbed her mother's arm. "No! How did you get him to agree?"

"I reminded him of what he owes you for saving Walt."

Rage exploded in Margarida's head, so strong that for a moment she couldn't see. She let go of Elena's arm, afraid she would hurt her. "Brant doesn't owe me anything."

Elena marched to the door and slammed it shut, then faced Margarida again. "Stop screaming," she hissed. "Do you want everyone to hear you?"

"I'm not screaming, but I don't care. You had no right to use what I did for Walt to get Brant to agree!"

"I have the right to do anything I need to save this ranch and our life here. And fortunately Brant recognizes his obligation."

Margarida had to sit down again. She felt really ill, as if she might lose her breakfast, except that she hadn't eaten anything. Her stomach hurt, and a headache began behind her eyes. "So Brant is willing to pay his debt," she said bitterly.

She felt her mother's hand on her shoulder and shook it off. "I also explained to him," Elena said more quietly, "that if he married you, his Apache relatives could hunt on our land as well as his."

Margarida's hurt and rage coalesced, taking her to her feet. "Your effort's wasted. I won't marry him."

Elena's responding fury had an insane quality. Her eyes looked feverish, and her skin stretched over the bones of her face as if it would tear. Horrified, Margarida stepped backward, but Elena followed, her voice a hiss. "If you had warned us that J.J. planned to leave, none of this would have happened! He'd be here. Your father would be here. But you went on your own way—as always. Now it's up to you to salvage something. *You'll marry Brant.*"

Margarida put her hands to her temples. "I'll have to think about it. There must be something else we can do. We can wait until we find out more about Papa."

"No, we can't." Elena sounded quieter but just as fanatic. "Brant's the only man around here who's strong enough to take care of us. I know what you're thinking. That you love Enoch Springer. But for years you thought you were in love with Brant. Enoch won't do. You like the way he kisses you. Yes—I've noticed all that. But that's just animal lust—like stallions with the mares."

She smoothed Margarida's hair. Margarida tried not to shrink away, but she trembled beneath her mother's touch. "You should marry someone because there are real interests to hold you together," Elena went on in a gentle tone, as if she and Margarida were just having an intimate talk. "You and Brant will have land—it lasts, but passion doesn't. Men go on discreetly to other women, and women have babies. Children are a woman's real world."

Every quiet word felt as if it were being burned on Margarida's heart. Bitterly she said, "I don't think you've had much pleasure from me."

Seeming not to hear, Elena continued almost tenderly. "Brant can give us protection. And men respect him, so they'll respect us. I'm not going to lose my home too." Her eyes clouded, and her hands trembled. She began to weep. "You've taken away my son. My only son!"

Margarida felt as if she were struggling for her life. "Mama, that's not fair."

"You could have stopped him," Elena cried.

"No. No." Even while Margarida protested, she knew that her resistance was fragile. She remembered her father's story about Mama's childhood, how much she lost then. Desperately Margarida had to ask herself if she could refuse to do something which would ease her mother now.

Elena's weeping became more frenzied. "No one will ever be like J.J., but Brant will make a good son."

A good son. Those words settled over Margarida like a black cloak, bringing guilt and defeat. Numbly she found her handkerchief and wiped away her mother's tears. "All right, Mama. I'll marry Brant."

Brant knew where he'd find Margarida. As he walked Chid up the slope through the pine trees, he saw her sitting on the rock with the dogged pine tree growing from the center. She had her legs drawn up with her arms around them and her chin resting on her knees. In the late-afternoon sun, the tall pines near the rock threw elongated shadows across the small clearing around the boulder, but one beam of light caught the silky surface of her hair.

Lobo raised his head from his place beside Margarida and gave a welcoming bark, then scrambled down to race toward Brant. She looked up, but stayed where she was. As Brant halted Chid below her, he could see the stiff posture of her head and back, and the lines of tension in her face that made her eyes seem larger than usual.

He felt even more keenly the confusion of emotions he'd carried to Rio Torcido and back. "Are you coming down? I'd like to talk to you."

"How did you know where I was?"

"Rosa said you'd ridden in this direction."

"Did you talk to Mama?"

"Yes, briefly. She told me she'd discussed her plan with you."

Margarida drew herself up even straighter. "Then you know I gave in," she said defiantly.

His skin grew warm under his chambray shirt, but he kept his voice cool. "I know you said you'd marry me, but that doesn't mean anything if it's not what you want."

She laughed, but not with amusement. "What difference does it make what I *want* to do? Or you? How willing were you to agree to what my mother asked?"

"Margarida, are you coming down?" She pulled her feet closer as if to anchor herself to the rock. Impatiently he swung down from Chid and tethered him to a tree. Warding off Lobo's attempts to get his attention, Brant climbed up and sat down beside Margarida.

"We're acting like two boxers," he said, "circling, trying to size up each other's strengths and weaknesses. But I don't want to fight. I'm trying to find out how you feel."

The defiance in her face drained away, leaving sadness. He wanted to hold her, comfort her, but things between them were too uncertain until he knew more about her feelings. He could tell her he loved her, but she probably wouldn't believe him any more now than when he'd said it before.

She broke a dried pine needle into tiny pieces. "I'm not sure how I feel. Except guilty about J.J. and Papa."

"Because of what your mother said?"

"Well, she's right. I could have stopped J.J. from leaving."

"He would have left some other time without telling you. You shouldn't blame yourself." His feelings told him he was crazy to be arguing with her. But he didn't want her to marry him because of guilt.

She looked at him, her gaze intent. "Do you know

of any gold mines that are supposed to be in this area? What people call lost mines?"

Surprised at her question, he thought of stories he'd heard. "Yes, a couple. A Frenchman, named Rouget, with an Apache guide, was supposed to have discovered a canyon in this area with a stream full of gold nuggets. That was in the fifties. He went to Socorro for supplies, told a friend, but then disappeared, maybe killed by other Apaches. There was another story about three prospectors who claimed they found gold around here, but started quarreling and killed each other. Why do you want to know?"

"Does anyone ever come now to hunt for the gold?"

"Once in a while miners try to, but we don't let them. My father and yours agreed that the stories probably weren't true, and they didn't want anyone prospecting here. I feel the same way. You didn't tell me why you're interested."

Margarida heard his question, but there didn't seem any point in answering it. She picked up a pebble and rolled it between her fingers; looking at it was easier than facing him. His eyes were too sympathetic—she couldn't stand pity from him. "I'm afraid for Mama. She's been acting so strange. Did she tell you the prospector didn't even know for sure that J.J. was killed or that Papa died?"

"Yes."

"I believe Papa and J.J. are alive, but she's certain they're dead. If I don't marry you, I don't know what she'll do."

"You have to think of what's best for yourself." His voice had a flat quality which meant he was disguising his feelings. His face looked tense, telling her nothing.

She wanted to shake him, force him to show her what he was thinking. Resentfully she wondered how he could be so calm and logical about whether they would get married. "That's what you do?" she challenged. "Think of yourself first, before Walt or your grandmother?"

A tiny muscle twitched beside his mouth, and he looked at her with the beginning of emotion in his eyes, though she couldn't tell what. "Maybe we could stall," he said, "and hope your mother changes her mind. Word might come from your father. I can go to Silver City and try to get an investigation started."

Margarida stood up and angrily brushed the needles off her breeches. "I'm sorry to disappoint you, but Mama insists we must get married right away."

Brant rose also. Against the slanted sunlight, his face was an unrevealing silhouette. "Why are you so sure I'm disappointed? I asked you to marry me last spring."

"And for the same reason—because you thought you should!" She turned and half-slid from the rock. He followed her, taking tiny pebbles rattling down with him.

She started toward the tree where she'd tethered Halcon, but he caught her arm and pulled her around to face him. "No. That's not the reason—or not the most important one." His deep voice sounded even lower, and a white line appeared around his mouth. "I *want* to marry you. Don't you understand, Margarida? I *love* you."

Her heart did the same awful flip-flop as when he'd said those words to her in April. For a moment she wanted to say that she loved him and believed him. But she remembered the pain of the last year—the effort she'd made to be indifferent to him. Did she dare believe him, or would she only be hurt again? It frightened her that he affected her so easily.

She wrenched her arm away. "You seem to remember it only when it suits you."

"My God, Margarida!" He was practically shouting now. "All summer I've stayed away from you, left you alone."

"And that's supposed to show you love me?"

He grabbed her shoulders, and for a moment she thought from his flashing eyes and angry mouth that he was going to shake her. But then he wrapped his arms around her and lifted her against him, bringing her mouth up to his.

She could feel his kiss scorching her from her lips along the length of her body to her dangling feet. Her arms pressed painfully against her sides, imprisoned by his, until she slid them around his back and clung to him.

His lips gentled, inviting her to return the kiss. Tentatively she tasted his mouth, then opened hers to his eager tongue. Finally he lifted his head and let her slide down against him. Through her clothes she could feel the firm plane of his chest rubbing against her breasts and his erection pressing her abdomen. Her feet didn't want to support her when they touched the ground, but it didn't matter because his arms still held her.

Her face rested against his chest, and his heartbeat sounded as if he'd been running. "Margarida, I understand why you can't believe me, but I do love you. I didn't know it for a long time. Last summer you said you loved me. I thought you were just playing then, but things have changed. I hope you'll feel that way again."

She raised her head so that she could look up into his face. "Oh, Brant. The trouble is what you just said."

"I don't understand."

"Things have changed. You didn't want me to be in love with you then. Your plans were more important."

"Margarida, *you* are important. *This* is important."

His hands cupped her buttocks, lifting her again until she rested on her toes, the bulge in his trousers fitting against the juncture of her thighs, intensifying the shivering feeling that had begun with his kiss. His lips explored her face, kissing her eyes, the side of her mouth, searching in her hair for the top of her earlobe, before his mouth returned to capture hers.

When the kiss ended, he said huskily, "You make me want you until I can hardly think about anything else." His hands moved from her hips to the waistband of her breeches and pulled her blouse loose. He found her breast and caressed it through the thin camisole, adding sparks to join with those from her thighs. She leaned into his hand, remembering the delicious sensations of their night together, feeling her body willing him to go on.

Brant looked at her, savoring the pleasure of seeing her desire—her eyes languorous, her mouth soft and passionate, her breasts rising and falling with her quickened breathing. He released her breast, but he still held her close. "At least you have to believe we have passion together. And I believe we'll have love."

Her face changed, as if she'd remembered something that troubled her. She pulled away from him, her eyes looking sad and distant again. "How long would passion last?"

Perplexed, Brant studied her. "I'm not sure what you mean."

"Mama says passion doesn't last. Men go out chasing women, and women get wrapped up in babies."

His anger flared at all women who told their daughters stupid stories, and at Elena in particular. "Good God, Margarida. Are you going to start believing every foolish thing your mother tells you? We can't guarantee the future, but I can't imagine not feeling passionate about you."

He hoped she'd come back to his arms. Instead, tucking in her blouse, she walked to her horse and untied the reins from a pine branch.

He followed and lifted her onto Halcon, loving the feel of her waist, letting his hands slide along her softly curved thigh. She flushed and backed her horse away. "Regardless of love and passion, you'll have lands for your Apache relatives. We can't forget that."

His pleasure diminished. "That doesn't mean I don't love you," he said.

"But," she persisted, "it is important."

He didn't understand why she had to bring up the Apache again. Irritation made his voice sharper than he intended. "Yes, of course it is. You know that."

She gave a sad smile, and he cursed himself for apparently saying the wrong thing again. But how the hell could he tell what was the wrong thing with her?

Halcon started off. "Wait until I get Chid," he said, "so I can see you home."

To his surprise, color flared in her face. "I don't need an escort," she snapped. "I've been riding alone in these mountains all my life, and I'm perfectly safe. At least now that you'll be here to protect us, that won't change." She slapped her reins.

He watched as she put Halcon into a gallop down the hill, with Lobo racing behind. The sound agitated Chid, and Brant had to keep a firm hand when he mounted. "Dammit," he shouted, "calm down," and knew he was shouting at himself. Margarida could arouse him in more than sexual ways.

As soon as he'd ridden Chid out of the trees, Brant dismounted and stripped off his shirt and changed his boots for moccasins. If ever he needed to run off his frustrations, it was today.

The next day was a hot Sunday, and Margarida wakened in a rebellious frame of mind. She'd spent hours getting to sleep the night before, trying to sort out the confusion in her head. Did Brant really love her? Did she really love him? That she had to answer the second question "Yes" made uncertainty about the first harder to face.

Yesterday she'd wanted to ask him whether he would be so sure he loved her if it weren't for the Ross land.

But she hadn't been able to. She had her pride, maybe too much, and she couldn't ask. What if he hesitated about answering, or looked uncertain? A year ago she'd have been ecstatic to know she and Brant would be married, but this morning she didn't even want to think about it.

She spent the first few hours going through her clothing, ruthlessly throwing away dresses that she decided looked too girlish. "But Señorita Margarida," Lupe protested, holding up a flowered blue cotton which had barely been worn, "this is beautiful."

"Then you take it," Margarida snapped.

With a roll of her dark eyes, Lupe took the dress and quietly slipped away, leaving Margarida to finish the demolition of her wardrobe in churlish silence.

At midmorning Margarida decided to make *posole* and got some relief from pounding the dried chilies and chopping the garlic and onions.

About noon Elena came into the breakfast room, looking cheerful and alert. "Oh, Margarida, I'm glad I found you here. We'd better think about your wedding and be sending invitations to people."

Margarida looked hard at Elena. "The one person I want invited is Adela Ramírez." The distressed look on her mother's face pleased Margarida immensely.

"But, Margarida, she works in a saloon. I don't think having her here would be suitable."

Margarida went to the door and turned back to say, "If she isn't here, I won't get married."

She left to her mother's huffy "Well, all right."

After that she settled herself in the patio, deciding she wouldn't inflict her bad temper on anyone else. Although she was wearing one of her coolest dresses, a pale green batiste with loose sleeves and a wide V neck, the breezes coming through the open kitchen doors still felt warm. She had just succeeded in reading two pages of *A Lady's Life in the Rocky Mountains* when she heard the sound of Brant's voice. He and her mother came from the living room, and she thought resentfully that they both looked much too cheerful.

Brant wore black pants and a white shirt of such sheer cotton that she could see the golden tinge of his skin through it. His black hair and eyes made him dramatic even in the simple clothing.

Walt wasn't with him and, she realized, hadn't been yesterday. "Where is Walt?"

"He went fishing with Tall Man. He doesn't need me around all the time any longer."

"Brant and I were talking," Elena said, "and we thought it best for you to be married soon. I think next Saturday."

"Next Saturday!" Margarida felt as if a whirlwind had picked her up and were carrying her along. "Well, if that's what you and Brant have decided, of course that's what we'll do." She pointedly opened her book again.

"Oh, dear," Elena sighed, and then Margarida heard the receding click of her mother's shoes. When Margarida finally looked up from the page she hadn't read, Brant was lounging in one of the chairs, watching her as amiably as if she'd greeted him with delight.

"I thought of another story about a lost gold mine," he said. "It's not supposed to be in our area, but since you seemed interested, I thought you'd like to hear it." He launched into a long, detailed account of six prospectors who had disappeared near Fort Apache in Arizona.

For the next half-hour, with only an occasional "Yes" or "How strange" from Margarida, he continued to talk in the same good-natured way while she grew more perplexed. She thought of explaining to him she really didn't care about every lost mine in the territories, but she became curious as to how long he would continue. He didn't stop until Lupe came to interrupt.

"Excuse me, Señorita Margarida. Señor Springer is here."

Brant looked at her and grinned, and she knew why he'd come visiting today. Though she'd forgotten it was Sunday, Brant hadn't. He'd expected Enoch to call.

As Enoch entered, Brant rose and extended his hand to the other man. "Enoch, a pleasure to see you."

Margarida knew Enoch's expressions well enough to see his disappointment that she wasn't alone, but he smiled and said politely, "And you, Brant."

His smile to her was much warmer. "You're looking beautiful, as usual, Margarida. I've been hoping we could go on another picnic." His voice took on an intimate tone. "Like the last one."

Brant moved over beside her and casually rested his hand on her shoulder. "I'm certainly fortunate to be getting such a beautiful bride." His finger gave a tiny stroke along her skin above the edge of her dress.

Enoch's face lost its color. "Your bride?"

"Well, not quite. Next Saturday. We hope you'll join us here that afternoon to help us celebrate."

Enoch looked at Margarida, his face stiff and hurt. "I didn't know, Margarida, that you were planning to marry."

She felt her irritation expand to anger at Brant's treatment of Enoch. "We decided rather suddenly." She wanted to say more—that she was sorry to hurt him—but she feared it would offend his pride.

His mouth looked as if he had to force it into a smile. "I hope you'll be very happy."

After a brief uncomfortable visit, he announced he must leave, and Margarida accompanied him to the veranda, with Brant close behind. When Enoch was gone, Margarida turned on Brant. "That was cruel. I would have told him."

"It wouldn't have been any easier on him," Brant returned, "and he was trying hard enough to make me think you were his territory. All that business about a picnic." Brant gave her a kiss before she realized what he intended. "I'm going now too."

Her mouth still tingling from the touch of his, she watched him ride away, and suddenly realized that her irritation and anger had disappeared. The sky seemed beautiful, the clouds boiling overhead the most glorious she'd ever seen. For the first time in days she felt like laughing. Brant, who never wasted time, had spent his afternoon waiting to warn off another man.

She felt as if a great burden had melted away. For a year she'd struggled not to love Brant—and lost the struggle. She thought of a proverb Adela had told her a long time ago. *Contra amor y fortuna no hay defensa alguna.* There is no defense against love and fate. Maybe she and Brant were fated to be together. He said she was his love. She knew he was hers.

The optimism she'd been afraid she'd lost this past year returned. Maybe Brant didn't love her as much as she wanted, but he'd been jealous of Enoch Springer. And she'd be Brant's wife, with time to make sure he really did love her. Why had she been so upset and afraid?

She did a pirouette, making her skirt flare around her. Marrying him didn't seem so risky as she'd been imagining. In fact, it might suit her very well.

14

"**O**UCH!" Margarida jumped, almost knocking over a basket of thread on the table in her bedroom. "Rosa, you stuck me with your needle."

"Margarida! You must stay still." Rosa's exasperated voice indicated that the hours she'd spent sewing this week had exhausted her supply of patience. "You're the way you were when you were a little girl—all wild and jumpy," she grumbled. "You act like you've forgotten your wedding's at eleven this morning. If I don't finish, I'll be standing up behind you with my needle and thread."

"I'm sorry, Rosa. I won't move," Margarida promised. Her wedding was in less than an hour! She supposed she should feel nervous, but really she felt like dancing. Nothing seemed able to spoil her good mood this week.

When she thought she couldn't remain still a moment longer, Rosa finished. "Oh, thank you, Rosa, for putting up with me." Margarida put her arms around Rosa's comfortable waist and kissed the soft cheek before Rosa left.

Adela appeared in the doorway, looking more plump than usual in a tight blue dress, her dangling gold earrings and dancing eyes spoiling her otherwise staid appearance. Margarida laughed as she pulled Adela into the room. "I was afraid you weren't coming. Look at my dress. Yellow—my favorite color." The silk bodice hugged her breasts and waist. Folded lace formed short sleeves, and tiers of lace swirled around the silk skirt as she moved. More ruffles edged the scooped neckline.

"It's beautiful," Adela said.

"And let me show you my camisole and pantalets." Margarida held up her skirt to show the thin washing-silk undergarments in a startling plum color. She'd purchased them in New York a year ago but had never worn them.

"Margarida, how shocking," Adela teased. "Does your mama know you have underwear that isn't white?"

"No, but now I decide for myself." Margarida thought of the night ahead, when Brant would see the sheer garments. She felt little feet running around in her stomach. "It's getting late. Adela, will you help me with my hair?"

As Margarida sat in front of Adela, she wondered if Brant felt as happy as she did. Would he think she was beautiful today? The feet in her stomach skittered faster.

"There—your hair's finished. Look in the mirror."

When Margarida saw her reflection, her stomach felt better. A soft flush gave her face extra color, and her dark brown hair gleamed with copper highlights. Adela had piled it high on the back of Margarida's head and arranged the curls into a single fall.

I *am* pretty today, Margarida thought happily. Surely Brant would think so, and maybe he always would, in spite of what her mother had said. "Adela, do men get tired of their wives after a while and look for other women?"

"Good heavens, Margarida, why are you worried?"

"Mama said that's the way men are."

"Huh! You should know better than to believe her. Some men do, but some are faithful all their lives. I think Brant's that kind of man."

Margarida gave Adela a joyous hug. "I'm so glad you're here today. You haven't told me a proverb yet about marriage. Your grandmother must have taught you one."

Adela laughed. "Of course. *La vida de los casados los ángeles la desean.* That means, 'Angels envy the life of married people.' "

"I like that proverb."

Elena came in, and Adela winked at Margarida and left. "Brant brought this," Elena said, and handed Margarida a small box that contained a choker with four strands of creamy pearls.

"Oh, they're beautiful!" The necklace felt cool against her skin. Pearls—her first present from Brant of the sort a man gives to a woman he loves.

Elena arranged an ivory lace mantilla over Margarida's hair and gave her a lacquered white fan with a single yellow rose attached. "You look lovely," she said tearfully, as if this were a wedding which followed traditional courtship rituals, including a sentimental mother.

Margarida crossed to the *sala* door, where Henry Franklin stood, and for a moment her footsteps slowed. She felt grateful that her father's good friend was her escort, but she wished sadly Papa were here. Then she thought of Brant, and the excitement she'd felt ever since his visit last Sunday revived her spirits.

Brant, waiting inside at the other end of the flower-decorated room, had to keep himself from pulling at his collar. Luisa had given him one that belonged to some other man—a collar this tight couldn't be his.

He looked around the room. Elena must have sent every *vaquero* on the ranch to deliver invitations, he thought grumpily. He was glad Enoch Springer was here to witness Margarida's married state, but not all these other people. He should have come in the middle of the night and kidnapped her. Taken her to the preacher's house and had the whole business over with by now. Then he thought of the surprise he had for Margarida and decided it was worth enduring this.

When Elena began to play the piano, Margarida appeared, and he needed a sudden gulp of air. God, she's beautiful, he thought. The lace mantilla framed her face, except for one errant wisp of hair. As she walked toward him, he saw her eyes, a little wide, as if she might be scared. Her mouth curved into a smile so inviting that if he weren't careful, his trousers would feel as tight as his collar.

Then she reached him, and he took her hand. He didn't know if he was supposed to wait to touch her until the preacher finished, but he didn't care. She'd be his now, and to hell with everything else.

When Margarida felt Brant's firm grasp, she imagined for a moment she was in the fairy story about the man who touched something magic and couldn't let go. As she looked up into Brant's face and saw the welcome there, she knew she didn't want ever to let go.

Brant's eyes, intense yet lighthearted, seemed to understand her thoughts. The gentle twist of his mouth asked her to share his amusement at this outward show of feelings which only the two of them understood.

Almost from a distance she heard Reverend Newcomb begin, "Dearly beloved, we . . ." After that his words seemed to reach her only in snatches: ". . . join this man and this woman . . . honor and cherish . . ." She heard Brant's deep tones, and someone with her voice said, "I do." Then the service must have ended, because Reverend Newcomb was beaming, and Brant's hands held her face while their kiss became their real wedding pledge.

When they turned to face the room, Margarida was startled to see all the people. Had they been here through the ceremony? They must have been, because they crowded around, offering embraces and congratulations. Walt gave her a hug which almost crushed the flower on her fan. "Brant says Margarida's my sister now," he proudly told the others around them.

The dry-goods merchant offered congratulations to Brant and good wishes to her. Then he said to Elena, "'Too bad Mr. Ross isn't here. Do you have any news of him?"

Margarida had been dreading that question. But Elena just smiled serenely and said, "He's in Utah, and we expect him and J.J. home anytime."

Questions whirled through Margarida's stunned mind. Had her mother's insistence that her father was dead been only a way of persuading her to marry Brant? As she heard her mother repeat the same response to the next guest, she realized from the unnatural pitch of Elena's voice that what she was saying now was the pretense. Her mother still believed Jesse and J.J. dead, but she wasn't ready to admit that to outsiders. Margarida's anxiety about her mother's state of mind revived, but she pushed the worry aside. It was her wedding day—she'd forget other cares for now.

She felt the pressure of Brant's fingers on her elbow and looked up at him. He must have heard her mother also, because his eyes questioned her. She shook her head slightly and saw that he understood.

Enoch stopped in front of Brant. "Please accept my congratulations," he said, but he didn't offer his hand.

Brant's "Thank you" was just as formal.

"And I hope you'll be very happy," Enoch said to Margarida. He didn't ask to kiss the bride.

Before the last guests had given congratulations, the mariachis began to play in the patio. The lilting rhythms revived Margarida's longing to dance. Brant took her hand, and she looked up into eyes alive with teasing pleasure. "Will you dance with me, Mrs. Curtis?"

Mrs. Curtis! She was Mrs. Curtis now. Oh, yes, she thought, I'll do anything. She said only, "Yes."

Then they were whirling around the patio, and Margarida was glad her dress didn't have a train. She loved the movement, the feeling that she was flying off into the air and then swinging back to Brant's strong arms. The madness of it exhilarated her and matched her mood, and when they finished, she was breathless and trembling.

For a moment they held the last posture of the dance, and the attraction between them felt so strong that Margarida thought her heartbeat must be louder than the music. Then others claimed dances, and Brant went on to partner first her mother and then the other matrons.

A little later Walt asked Margarida to dance. His unrestrained exuberance made her skirts flare and her curls threaten to come loose. When he wanted to dance again, she happily agreed. She decided Walt had never looked handsomer and that dancing had never been more fun. The champagne tasted far better than any she'd tried when she was visiting school friends in the East. And her husband—Brant was her husband now!—her husband was easily the most exciting and masculine-looking man she'd ever seen.

"Margarida." Brant's voice was in her ear. "I think you're getting drunk."

She laughed at him. She was drunk, but not with wine. "I didn't thank you for the pearls. They're beautiful."

"Then they match you." He smiled at her, and she thought she might float off over the patio walls.

"We're supposed to do something about a wedding cake," he told her.

"Aren't we going to eat?"

Brant laughed. "Your mother tried to get you to eat, but you wouldn't. Don't you remember?"

Vaguely she did remember. "After this," he whispered, "change your clothes, and then we can leave." His mouth curved in a sensual smile, and she knew he was thinking of the same thing she was—the lovemaking ahead.

The invitation in his eyes made her heart race and sent her hurrying through the ritual of cutting the cake and then to her bedroom. There Adela and Rosa helped her out of the yellow dress and into a rust-colored jacket and skirt. It was lightweight for the August weather and suitable for riding. She put the pearls away regretfully, and then thought of the years ahead when she'd wear them many times.

"Where will you go now? On a trip?" Adela asked.

"We'll stay at the Curtis ranch tonight." At the thought of the night, the disturbance in Margarida's stomach returned, making it hard to continue. "Then we're going to Silver City for a week. After that we'll live at the Curtis ranch, because of Walt."

Adela frowned. "Then your mother will be here alone?"

Margarida smiled at Rosa. "Not alone—Rosa will be here to help her. And Mama doesn't want to live with me. She's had twenty years of that."

"I'll tell you good-bye now. Be happy, Margarida." Adela hugged her and left.

Rosa started to pick up the small valise which held Margarida's toilet articles. Her trunk had been sent to the Curtis house the previous day. "Wait, Rosa. Please leave the valise. I'll bring it."

When Rosa had gone, Margarida quickly opened the doors of her tall wardrobe. At the back she found the pale blue muslin gown she'd worn to the line shack over a year ago. One of the maids had laundered it then and hung it in Margarida's wardrobe. She'd pushed it to the back, but she'd never returned it to her mother's trunk.

Now she unfastened the leather straps which closed the top of her bag; the gown just fit along one side. She wasn't sure why, but she wanted to take it with her.

Brant was waiting on the veranda, where the guests were lined up. He pulled her through the shower of rice and shouts and across to the corral, where Walt had Chid and Halcon and his own horse ready. She was a little surprised that Brant hadn't brought the buggy, but she didn't mind because she preferred to ride horseback, even sidesaddle.

After he tied her valise behind the saddle, he put his hands around her waist. Suddenly he kissed her, a short but urgent kiss. "I love you," he said, and lifted her into the saddle.

He and Walt swung up onto their horses. She waved to the guests on the veranda and to the *vaqueros*, who were celebrating also. With Walt on one side and Brant on the other, she started in the direction of the Curtis ranch.

From the height of the sun, she decided it must be about three o'clock. Just four hours since she and Brant were married. Feeling almost shy, she looked at him, and found that his eyes were on her breasts. He glanced up and caught her gaze, and his face colored until he resembled the "redskin" of newspaper stories.

Walt kept up an animated chatter, and Margarida felt relieved that she barely needed to respond. Her unfamiliar shyness made her feel awkward, so she looked everywhere but at Brant. She noticed how the wind made the pine needles shiver and the aspen leaves turn their backs to show their silver underside. On a slope above the trail, a gray squirrel investigated a pine cone for seeds.

Where the trees widened into a meadow she was surprised to see Tall Man sitting on his horse and holding the lead rein of a string of four horses. Margarida gasped at how magnificent they looked.

They were all mares, one a golden palomino, another a dun with stripes above her knees and hocks. The third was a bright chestnut with a blaze, and the fourth a buckskin with a black mane and tail. "They're beautiful," she exclaimed, and turned to Brant. "Are they your horses?"

He was grinning, and Walt looked ready to explode with excitement. A laugh struggled to escape from

Tall Man. "No," said Brant, "they belong to your father."

"My father? I've never seen them before."

"Let me tell her," Walt burst out, "please, Brant. I kept the secret, just the way you wanted. And I won't tell the other secret."

Brant's laughter rang out. "All right."

"They're a present for your father, because you and Brant got married. But you have to keep them for him till he gets home."

"There's a stallion that goes with them," Brant added, "but he's at home, waiting for you to meet him later."

Margarida felt her heart surge with love for Brant and gratitude that he wouldn't admit her father was dead. "I know Papa will love them," she said softly.

"Brant told me the reason he has to give them to your father," Walt went on excitedly. "When an Apache man wants to marry a woman, he takes horses to her father's lodge. He ties them up outside. If her father likes the man, he puts the horses with his herd. Then the man knows he gets to marry the woman. Did I tell it right, Brant?"

"Yes, just right."

Margarida felt a faint disquiet. "But I'm not Apache. I don't know what an Apache woman is supposed to do."

Brant gave her another of the looks that made her breath leave her lungs and her blood race madly around her body. "You know everything you need to know."

"That is right, my sister," Tall Man said, and a teasing grin lit his face. "You must not let my brother frighten you." His smile softened. "I welcome you as my sister now. May you and my brother wake each morning together to greet the blessing of the sun."

"Thank you, Tall Man," said Margarida, moved that this fierce yet gentle man considered her his relative now.

"Come," Tall Man said to Walt. "We must get these mares back to their pen."

"All right," Walt responded. "Good-bye, Margarida. Good-bye, Brant." He fell in beside Tall Man, who started off, leading the mares.

Surprised, Margarida looked at Brant. "Aren't we going to your . . . to the ranch house?"

"And let all the young men around provide us with a shivaree? No. Come on." He guided Chid to the left and started into the trees.

"But where are we going?" Seeing he wasn't going to answer, Margarida nudged Halcon and followed.

Before they had gone far, Margarida knew where their direction could take them and knew why he hadn't brought a buggy. "Brant, are we going to the line shack?"

He just laughed and let Chid lope ahead.

Margarida hadn't been to the line shack since that day last summer when she'd gone there intending to seduce Brant. Now she had what she'd wanted a year ago, but everything was different from what she'd imagined then.

How naive and innocent she'd been, so sure she'd get her own way—not imagining it might not be what she really wanted. If she'd succeeded and they'd married because Brant "had" to marry her, thinking he didn't love her, it would have been a bitter success. Then she hadn't realized how rigorously he followed his conscience. The surprising part was not that he'd resisted her attempt to get him to "compromise" her, but that they'd ever had that one night of lovemaking last spring.

As they approached the shack, she thought that she'd learned a lot about herself in this year too. She had as much pride as Brant, and she wanted love only if it were freely given. She believed him when he said he wanted to marry her because he loved her and not because of her mother's manipulations. A voice in her head interrupted, reminding her that Brant would also achieve one of his most cherished goals—more land for his people. She refused to listen today.

The clearing looked the same, except a little browner because the summer had been dry. The stream still bypassed the rocks with an impudent song, and Indian paintbrush waved spiky orange heads on the slopes above the tiny meadow. But the small cabin looked different.

At first she couldn't decide why. The pine walls were still weathered gray-white except for a few edges where bark remained. Rust gave the stovepipe its usual streaked color. But the shutter over the window was up, and sun gave back a dazzling reflection from a new glass pane.

Brant's face looked the happiest she'd ever seen it. He dismounted and tethered Chid at the rail, then came to stand beside her. His black eyes seemed to glow with mysterious colors, and his hands were eager as he put them around her waist. She leaned on his shoulders as he lifted her down, then held her close.

"Margarida . . . Mrs. Curtis . . . my wife." He cupped her face, running his thumbs across her cheekbones, tilting her head until her lips were just below his.

She could feel his breath against her mouth, and then she couldn't wait longer. She pulled his head that last unbearable distance to claim the kiss he promised.

When she could get her breath, she said, "You're too slow, Brant Curtis. You'll have to do better than that."

He slid one hand down her shoulder and lightly touched her breast, creating waves of sensation. "I plan to."

His hands lingered as if reluctant to let her go, then released her. He tethered Halcon to the hitching rail and untied her valise. "Should we unsaddle the horses?" she asked, a little surprised she could say anything.

"I'll do that later. I want you to see inside first." He

looked like a boy who's sneaked into the parlor on Christmas Eve and peeked into the packages. Impatiently he pulled her to the door, where he took out a key and opened a shiny padlock.

"A lock," she exclaimed. "You've never locked any of your line shacks before."

The grin, which seemed permanent, broadened. "Just making sure no one disturbs anything." He swung her up into his arms and carried her through the door.

When he set her on the floor, she understood why he'd safeguarded the cabin. Someone had transformed it from the shabby room of a year ago.

The walls sparkled with fresh yellow paint, and the floorboards had been polished to a glossy brown. Blacking concealed the age of the potbellied stove, and a white damask cloth covered the scars on the small table. A vase held pink shooting stars and speckled orange tiger lilies, which Margarida knew could only be found in the very highest meadows this time of year. The new window even had hinges so that it could be opened.

The narrow bunk was gone; in its place, covered with a crocheted white counterpane, stood the large bed from the room which had been Rupert's—the bed where she and Brant had made love.

"Oh, Brant" was all she could say.

His smile glowed with pleasure. "I wanted us to have different memories of this room."

"How did you manage all this?"

"Hard work—and help."

She put her arms around him, holding on to his back, pressing her face against his chest. "I love it." Boldly she added, "And I loved what we did in the bed," and then couldn't look at him.

He wouldn't let her hide against his shoulder. Surprised, she saw that his eyes were wet. "So did I, and I want you to wake up tomorrow morning happy, not with me acting like a fool."

A moment of discomfort touched her at the memory of that morning. Then he ran his hands down her sides, brushing the outer swell of her breasts and the curve of her hips. "Maybe I wanted to come here today because I had such a struggle to keep from making love to you here before."

Glad to restore a teasing tone, she admonished, "You certainly acted indifferent. I felt like a silly girl. If you suffered, you deserved it."

"But you're going to make up for it now, aren't you?"

She pretended to consider. "Maybe—if you're very nice to me."

He caught her hand and put it against the front of his trousers. "I'm ready right now."

For all her efforts at boldness, she felt her face grow fiery hot, and she pulled her hand back. Last year she had had the brash confidence of ignorance. And when they'd made love after the terrible struggle to save Walt, she'd been swept along by her emotions and the comfort Brant gave her. "But it's daylight," she offered lamely.

"All the better to see you with, my dear," he retorted, but he smiled at her tenderly. "I want to see all of you. Watch your pleasure. Let you see mine. And," he added teasingly, "it's all right. We're married, and we get to do anything we want."

She thought of how he would look without his clothes, and her hand wanted to touch him again, but with no barrier in between. "Anything?"

"Anything." He kissed her, and she waited for the kiss to deepen, but instead he let her go. Surprised, she saw that he looked as flushed as she felt, and he was breathing rapidly. "I think I'd better see to the horses while I still can. Margarida, I don't want to wait until dark to make love to you. I hope you feel the same way."

She didn't quite succeed in looking at him. "Yes."

He kissed her once more quickly and left.

The valise still rested where he'd dropped it by the door. She put it beside the bed and took off her jacket and skirt, then her shoes and stockings. For a moment she regretted that Brant wouldn't see the plum-colored underwear, but he'd see it another time.

The sheer gown was slightly wrinkled, so she shook it out carefully. She pulled off the camisole and pantalets, then put on the gown. With clumsy hands she took the pins from her hair and let the mass of dark waves fall down her back. Her clothes went on a peg on the wall and her underwear on a chair. Feeling a little uncertain, she looked at the bed and finally decided to turn down the covers. Behind her the door opened, and slowly she turned to face her husband.

At the sight of Margarida, her body barely veiled in the pale blue dress, Brant felt as if he'd received a blow that might topple him. But then the blood rushed back into his stomach, filling his loins as well, sending him across the room to take her into his arms.

He looked down into her wide eyes and the thought he'd had constantly this week returned. How could he have been so crazy as to turn her down a year ago? Of course he knew why, and all the same reasons would exist if her father hadn't gone away. But it was hard to remember he'd been strong enough. Thank God now he didn't have to be.

Her diffidence surprised him, but he reminded himself she was still very innocent. He'd go slowly. If he could.

"Does this mean I get to help with the undressing?"

She tried twice before she managed to say, "Yes."

He lifted her and put her on the bed. Guessing she might feel more at ease if he were naked first, he started on his own clothes, trying not to hurry, but even so pulling a button loose from his shirt.

As Margarida watched, a fluttering began in her chest and grew to a pulsing beat that threatened to cut off her breath. Daylight showed her clearly what she'd tried for so many months to forget—the broad sweep of his muscled chest, the trim waist and belly, the grace of his long legs and hard thighs. As he stooped to slide off his pants, she felt a jolt of pleasure at seeing his tight buttocks, and then his erect penis. Nothing concealed his desire when he turned back to the bed.

Brant saw her wide eyes, and his own excitement flared even higher. He sat on the bed beside her, and she put her arms around him. "Hurry," she whispered, "I think I'm ready too."

Undressing her became a ritual of exploring with his mouth everything that his hands uncovered. He unfastened the gown with hands that were not quite steady. As he slid the material up, the beauty of her slender yet firm thighs, the triangle of dark hair decorating her belly, and her quivering breasts assaulted his senses again. She lifted her arms, so softly rounded, to help him remove the gown, and he groaned. "God, Margarida, how can you be so beautiful?"

When the gown was set aside, he had to kiss first the curve of her neck, the faintly damp spot just above her ear, the indentation down her back under the thick fall of her hair. When she turned so that the curls fell across her breasts, that was another reason to cup the soft mounds and caress the nipple to the hard point he loved to taste. With each catch of her breath, his own excitement grew.

He had to share his discoveries. "Your eyes are the most beautiful shape in the world," he decided. Then, "No, it's your breasts . . . You have a dimple in each buttock," he told her. "Your skin tastes a little like the grass I used to chew on when I was a boy." And later, with delight at a new find, "You're saltier behind your knees."

She didn't wait for her turn, but used her hands and fingers to explore his back, his chest, and as she grew bolder, to send shock waves through him by touching his penis. Her exploration produced surprises, too, ones she was a little shy about describing.

Too quickly she learned how to rub and hold his shaft, until he sucked in a sharp breath and pulled her hand away. He distracted her by caressing her thighs and finding her musky center. With his fingers he stroked her until she arched against his hand. Then he slid down between her legs and his mouth took the place of his hand. At her startled "Brant!" he lifted his head.

"I want to love you all ways—this way too," he said.

When he heard her moan, "Yes! Don't stop," the pounding in his loins told him he was no longer capable of anything but going on. As he finally eased into her, he had to exert all his control to keep from spending himself at once in her tight heat. But more than anything else he'd ever done, he wanted to give her pleasure. Almost holding his breath, he waited, barely moving, letting her adjust to him. He concentrated on kissing her, letting her know how he felt. "You're wonderful. This is so good. I love you. I want to hear you say you love me."

Passion darkened her eyes. "Oh, yes, Brant. I love you."

"And you're only mine. Just as I'm yours."

Her voice came in gasps. "Yes. Yes. Always."

Slowly he began to thrust, feeling her rising tension.

Margarida felt her excitement grow with each movement of Brant's swollen shaft, and she thrust against him in return. She was in a whirlwind, drawn into its vortex so completely that only she and Brant together existed—two halves of the same being. Another thrust shattered her, and she cried out, abandoning herself to the need to grip him and hold him deep within her. As waves rippled through her, pulling her into rapture, she heard his gasp and felt his shuddering release.

When their breathing slowed, Margarida felt the same encompassing lassitute she'd experienced when they made love before, as if she never wanted to move again. At the same time, her senses felt intensely alive—the sunlight reflected on the newly yellow walls almost hurt her eyes. The fragrance of the wildflowers filled the room and mingled with the musky odor of their bodies.

"Margarida—my wife," he murmured. "I'll never get enough of you."

When her breath returned, she asked, "Is loving always like this?"

"No, but with us I think it may be. And I don't intend for you to find out with anyone else."

He started to shift to his side, but she managed enough strength to cling to him in protest. "No. I like your weight on top of me. It's like being part of you."

His response was a kiss, but after a moment he rolled to his side, bringing her with him so that they didn't separate. "I'll crush you," he murmured in an explanation that she was almost too sleepy to hear.

When she woke, the sun still slanted in through the window. Brant must have been up, because it was open now, and a breeze had cooled the air. He'd also pulled the sheet over them. He lay on his back, his eyes closed and his breathing even.

She couldn't remember when she'd seen him like this—relaxed, nothing making his eyebrows come together or the lines of his face intent. His shoulders looked broad and dark above the edge of the sheet, and suddenly she was impatient with the covering. She wanted to look at him, see if he really was beautiful. Men weren't supposed to be, but "handsome" didn't seem to describe the lean sweep of his muscles, his flat abdomen and smooth skin.

Carefully she lifted the sheet and pulled it down. His skin was light golden brown. The planes of his chest had only a sprinkling of hair around the brown nipples. Lower down, a line of black hair began just above his waist and widened to the thatch of curls at his groin around his relaxed organ. Even in sleep the muscles of his thighs looked hard, as if he could be ready to move in a moment.

Her gaze turned back upward, fascinated by the difference between his penis now and how it had looked earlier, swollen with desire. Then she noticed, just above the black hair, on the left side of his abdomen, three parallel scars. They were pale; he'd had them a long time.

"Everything still there?"

She jumped at the sound of his voice. He was watching her, lying with his arms crossed behind his head. She waited for the blush, but it didn't come. Being here with him seemed so natural—the most natural thing she'd ever done. "Did we use it all up?" she asked, and her skin heated after all.

"Not with you around." He reached for her hand, pulling her toward him, but she resisted. Lightly she ran her finger over the strange scars. "How did you get these?"

His laugh sounded half-embarrassed. "A child's foolishness."

She moved into his arms and snuggled against him, but her curiosity wasn't satisfied. "I'd like to know."

He tipped her head up and kissed her, his mouth inviting her to forget her questions. For a moment she savored the pleasure, feeling the tremors beginning. Then she pulled back and persisted. "Please tell me."

"It was after I'd spent a summer with my mother's people. I was six years old. After my mother died, my father went to England and left me with the Eliot family in Socorro. I knew *shiwóyé* and her band were in the mountains near Ojo Caliente. I tried to run away so often to find them that Mr. Eliot finally took me up to *shiwóyé*'s camp for the summer. I wanted to stay with them all the time, but at the end of the summer *shiwóyé* sent me back."

"But how did you get the scars?"

"Apache boys are trained to endure pain. In case they go raiding and are wounded, they have to be able to go on silently, without crying out or slowing down the others. Girls also have to learn endurance, but it's more important for boys, who will be warriors."

He stroked her hair, but she felt his thoughts were far away, in the past she'd insisted he recall. "I thought if I learned as many Apache skills as I could, *shiwóyé* might let me stay with her. So all winter I ran races against my horse, swam in the creek, practiced tracking, and made a bow and arrows which I used for hunting. One of the more foolish things I did was to cut myself and then reopen the wound each day, to prove I could endure the pain."

"Oh, Brant!" She couldn't help a shudder.

"You're right. It was silly. I kept it up for a month. No one knew I was doing it, so I thought I'd proved I could be as strong as any Apache boy."

"What did your grandmother say?"

"When I went back the next summer, she told me that I wasn't an Apache and that I couldn't stay with her more than a few months. That I belonged with my father. So I have the scars for nothing."

She shivered, but not because the room had grown cooler. An image came to her so strongly that it was almost as if she had once seen it—the intense boy, still a child, with his black hair and eyes and lean face. And his skin, which wasn't dark enough for an Indian's. That boy—enduring the pain, prolonging it, in order to join a world that was cruel and demanding. And so very strange to her.

Doubt intruded—doubt she didn't want but couldn't ward off. Reluctantly she wondered whether the desire for an Apache way of life still pulled at him so strongly. Would it always attract him? Could it sometime come between them?

"Such a frown. Does it upset you that I have scars?" His voice was teasing, and his hand, which was gently stroking her side, moving around to her breast, also teased her, with a touch she loved.

She leaned closer to him, letting her hands know him, discovering the feel of his skin. Her mind, relinquishing that much younger Brant, reassured her that now he and she were beginning a life together. They would live on the ranch, in the valley that was so familiar and dear to her. It would be the kind of life she'd always known.

Then his touch and kisses grew passionate, and her touch and kisses matched his. Again they started on the enthralling spiral of sensual love that banished the rest of the world, and her doubts with it.

15

It was dark when they got out of bed. Brant stretched, and padded across naked to open the door. Margarida put on the plum-colored camisole and pantalets and reached for her petticoat and dress.

Brant stopped halfway to the door. "Wait, Margarida." He reached out and took her dress away. "I like that underwear." She turned, posing for him.

He ran his hands along her sides, setting off prickles of excitement. "I like it so much that if you hadn't just exhausted me, you'd have to take it off again."

After they put their clothes on, Brant lit the kerosene lantern, then built a fire in the stove and retrieved a jar of lamb stew that he'd submerged in the stream that morning. While the stew heated, Margarida set a bottle of wine from his saddlebags beside the flowers and found real silverware and china on the shelf, instead of the battered tinware usually kept in the shack. With the meat, they had fresh sourdough bread Luisa had baked early that day, and then finished with grapes.

"Oh," Margarida groaned, leaning her elbows on the table. "I was so hungry, and now I'm so full."

"You were always like that—forgetting food to do something interesting. Then eating like a greedy pup."

"Well," she said boldly, "I was certainly doing something interesting," and then blushed because she wasn't quite as bold as she thought.

"Come on." He got up and carried dishes to the

shelf along one wall. "Time to clean up." He took down an enamel basin from its nail on the wall and filled it with water that had been heating on the stove. After he swished some soap in, he handed Margarida a towel. "I'll wash."

"You're very handy at this," she observed.

His hands still in the dishpan, he leaned over and kissed her quickly. "Enjoy it now—the next time may be your turn. You should have come to my house this morning and cooked breakfast for me."

"Why?"

"That's the way an Apache girl tells a man she's willing to marry him."

"By cooking breakfast?"

"A little more than that. The boy and girl have known each other all their lives. When they're old enough, she chooses him as a partner at special dances. He lets her know he's interested. If she thinks she wants him, she goes to his wickiup and stays with him for five nights."

"You mean they make love?"

"Oh. no. They share the wickiup, but they don't make love. That would be a disgrace. The Apache are very strict with their young men and women." He dried his hands and took away the dish she had in her hand. Holding her face up so that he looked into her eyes, he said, "That's one reason I was so upset after we lay together last spring. No decent Apache man would have been so dishonorable."

She didn't like his judging his actions by Apache standards. "But, Brant, I was as willing as you were."

The lantern light emphasized the lines around his mouth and the sad expression in his eyes. "I was to blame, not you. You'd been through a terrible, frightening time. You weren't in a state to know what you wanted. I should have protected you, not seduced you."

She knew she shouldn't ask, but she couldn't stop herself. "Are you still sorry?"

"Not sorry to love you, But, yes, I regret that I behaved as I did that night."

Though she wasn't sure why, she knew that wasn't the answer she'd hoped for. She gave him a teasing push. "Come on, get your job done. And tell me why I should have cooked your breakfast this morning."

The lantern light caught rainbows in the soap bubbles on his hands. "At the end of the last night, if the girl's decided she wants to marry the boy, she cooks breakfast for him. She puts his bedding out to air and catches and saddles his horse. If he eats the food she's cooked and rides the horse, it means he wants to marry her. She goes home, and he offers the bride price to her relatives. Very often it's horses. If the family accepts his gifts, she moves to his house and is his wife."

Margarida watched as he washed the pot. "Then I'm worth five horses?" She kept her voice lighthearted.

He flicked a soap bubble at her. "Maybe only two, but I want to be known as a generous man."

When they lay in bed later, she snuggled against him, delighting in the feel of his skin against hers. She remembered how it looked in the light, not so much darker than hers. One of the questions which circled in her thoughts surfaced through her contentment. "Why do you want so much to be Apache, Brant?"

"I *am* Apache, and I'm proud of that. The Apache are close to nature, and they have strong religious beliefs that they really live by. They're the most honest people I know."

"I can see why you'd admire that, but didn't you say your grandmother told you that you weren't Indian— that you belonged with your father? You're mostly white."

"I'm both. *Shiwóyé* was sending me back to what she thought would be a better life for me. And my father wouldn't have given me up. Sometimes I wasn't sure why. I know he was ashamed I had Indian blood."

Though he spoke in a matter-of-fact tone, Margarida felt pain for what he'd missed. Though she grieved for her father, and the worry about him was never far from her thoughts, she at least knew that he'd loved her and was proud of her. Brant hadn't known that with his father.

He continued, his voice happier. "Did I ever tell you my Apache name?"

"No." She felt intensely curious, yet not sure she wanted to hear the name. It would identify him even more as an Apache. "I never heard Tall Man call you anything but Brant," she said evasively.

"My people don't address others directly by their Indian names. It's not considered polite. My name is Hàcké hàdè-c, which means Angry-He-Looks-About."

"Oh, Brant, I could never pronounce that," she protested, and knew she didn't want to. It sounded too alien, as if she'd be talking to a stranger if she used it.

He laughed, and turned over, pulling her closer. "You won't have to. The Apache language is very difficult to learn. I stumble when I use it."

Her curiosity won out over discomfort. "How did you get that name?"

"When I was little and first went to *shiwóyé*'s camp, I was sure the other children would make fun of me. I was ready to challenge anyone who looked sideways at me. So the name. Usually other names are given later, but my first one stuck. I wonder," he teased, "what your name would be."

"It's the name of a white flower," she suggested, not sure she wanted a name, but pulled along by his gaiety.

"White Flower. Mm. More likely you'd be called She-Who-Gets-Her-Own-Way."

"Huh! You get your way pretty often," she protested. She couldn't avoid the sharp thought that he'd gotten his way about Ross land for his Apache people. Her unasked question followed—would he have married her if it meant giving up the land?

Then he kissed her again, and she forgot about everything except the delight of his caresses and the pleasure of knowing his desire was as great as hers. Later, when their passion built together to shattering fulfillment, she felt so much a part of him it was hard to believe they could ever be separate.

When Brant closed the padlock on the cabin door the next morning, Margarida didn't want to leave. She knew she wouldn't like living in a one-room cabin, but last night had been special, just the two of them, with no thought of the other obligations in their lives.

"Will we leave the things here?" she asked Brant.

"No. It has to be used as a line shack, and be open for anyone who needs it. Tall Man and Juan will come later and dismantle the bed and collect the other things."

What Brant said was reasonable, she knew, but she felt sad that she'd never come back to find it again as it had been last night. She looked back once as they rode away, and thought that at least the new glass window under the shutter would remain. A touch of luxury, and a reminder of their wedding night.

The day was too beautiful and Brant was too beautiful for her sadness to last. She loved the way the sky looked like a crystal-clear lake which had been turned upside down. A glimpse of a red fox trotting across a rock on the other side of a ravine delighted her. So did the way Brant looked at her, a permanent grin on his face.

She thought of living at the Curtis house. It would be strange at first, but Walt would be there too. Thinking of him reminded her of a question. "Do you still . . . take Walt to the woman in Rio Torcido?"

She enjoyed the way Brant's mouth dropped open. "How did you know about that?"

"He told me. When I first found him in the jail, I had to ask him . . . about whether he'd done anything that could be called rape."

His mouth turned up in an amused quirk. "I haven't taken him into Rio Torcido; Juan brings Walt's lady friend out here." More soberly he asked, "Will you object to having her come to our house?"

"No. I think Walt deserves that part of his life. I wish he could have a wife," she said wistfully. "Some woman ought to love him for his sweet disposition. I do."

"Some things can't be changed," Brant reminded her. "You love Walt, but as a child. It's tragic, but it's so."

They reached the last rise and started down to the ranch house. "Will we stay here tonight?" Margarida asked.

"Yes. We'll take the stage for Silver City tomorrow. I've heard of a reliable man there to send to Utah. And we'll go to Fort Bayard and see if the army has done anything to find your father."

His words made Margarida realize how completely she'd shut out everything except Brant for the last week. A shout from below told them Walt had seen them. As they trotted their horses into the yard, he raced to meet them. "Margarida, are you going to live here now?"

"Yes, I am."

He helped her down, his face radiant with pleasure. "I want you to live here always." She embraced him; when J.J. and Papa returned, her family would be complete.

When they reached Silver City, they walked along Main Street to the Southern Hotel, at the corner of Broadway and Hudson Street. It was brick, with wide

pillared galleries. After Brant escorted her to their
room, he went to talk to the sheriff about the man he
hoped to send to Utah. She ordered a bath, and as she
waited for the tub and water to arrive, looked out the
window of their second-story room. The houses beyond
the business area appeared substantial, and spires indicated at least two churches. To the south, small adobe
houses covered a higher hill.

By the time Brant returned, she'd finished her bath.
"I was wondering why you were so long," she said
after he kissed her.

"I checked about the man I want to send to Utah.
His name's George Slack, and the sheriff says he's
reliable and resourceful. I left a message at Slack's
lodging house to come here. He may join us for supper." He sat down and pulled off his boots. "And now
I'm on my way to the bathroom to get off the grime."

"You aren't going to bathe here?"

"Nope." He took a towel from the rack above the
washstand and kissed her again. "Might take too long.
You look very tempting, and I want to get downstairs."

That helped a little, but she was still disappointed as
he left. Seeing Brant naked was one of the great
pleasures of being married.

They had just started their meal in the high-ceilinged
dining room when George Slack joined them. He looked
about forty, tough and wiry, and had a bushy brown
mustache that overshadowed a small goatee. After the
introductions, Brant explained about Jesse, and Slack
agreed to go.

Later, as they climbed the stairs to their room,
Brant said, "I think Slack will do a good job for us."

If he did, Margarida thought, and Papa and J.J.
came home, she couldn't ask for anything else.

The next morning while Brant went off to arrange
supplies for George Slack, Margarida wandered through
the stores near the hotel. One small shop had beauti-

ful Indian jewelry, with several necklaces of hammered-
silver disks, the sort she had seen Tall Man wearing.
She hesitated over one particularly beautiful necklace.
Brant would probably love it, she thought, then knew
she didn't want to give him anything that looked so
Indian. Instead she went to a dry-goods store, where
she bought a white cotton shirt with intricate white
embroidery along the tucked front.

In the late afternoon she returned to the hotel
room, impatient for Brant to finish his business. When
he arrived an hour later, a relaxed grin on his face, his
first words were, "Slack is on his way to Utah."

He hugged her, and she held fast to him. "He'll find
Papa and J.J. I just know he will."

"I think he might—he has a reputation for being an
efficient and thorough man."

She showed Brant the shirt. "I intended to keep it
for a surprise," she confessed, "but I couldn't wait to
see your reaction."

"It's the most handsome shirt I've ever owned," he
assured her. "I have something for you." He produced
a small box from his pocket. Inside was a small gold
chain. "It's an anklet. Very fashionable, the jeweler
claimed."

A kiss seemed the best way to show her pleasure,
and from Brant's lusty response, it was obviously his
pleasure too. He held her, pinned against him, and bit
gently on her earlobe. "Hm! I haven't had much to eat
today," he teased, "and none of it tasted as good as
this." She felt heat race through her as she remembered ways his mouth could give her pleasure. He
nibbled her bottom lip, then the side of her neck,
while his hands cupped her buttocks to pull her more
tightly against him.

When he released her, she couldn't wait to get her
clothes off. Brant's laughing attentions hindered her,
his fingers teasing her nipples through the cloth of her
bodice, his thigh rubbing between her legs until she

abandoned her efforts, writhing against him. When he finally relented, his fingers had become as clumsy as hers, and she had a small revenge by touching his erect shaft while he was still trying to remove his trousers.

They fell on the bed with his legs still entangled in his clothes, and when he kicked free, he pulled her on top of him. "You're feeling so frisky," he charged, "you do the work."

His laughing eyes sent sparks of passion through her as he put his hand between their bodies to stroke between her legs. When she was aching with arousal, he lifted her to bring her onto his penis. Startled, she gasped as she encompassed him, seeing through her own desire the delight and passion in his face. Caressing her breasts, he asked, "Do you like this?"

"Oh, yes. But it feels different. Bigger."

His laughter rippled boyishly. "I've done my part. You do the rest."

But as she began to move, not quite sure, he helped her, until their two rhythms joined, feeding the delicious fire between them. At its final blaze he pulled her down against him, and they shuddered together, so close that their damp skin felt like one.

He held her head close against him. "My wonderful wife."

"Oh, Brant. I do love you," she whispered into his sweaty neck.

Later, when they were dressed again, he asked, "How shall we spend the evening after dinner?"

"There's something I've always wanted to do."

"You mean we haven't yet?"

She ignored his leer. "Gambling. In a regular gambling room. The hotel has one, off the lobby."

His leer turned into astonishment and then an admiring grin. "You certainly can surprise me, Margarida. They may throw us out, but we can try."

Their entrance that evening into the card room caused

some startled looks, but no one objected. Two men
with soft southern drawls invited Brant and Margarida
to join their game of five-card poker. The third man,
whose red hair and brogue suggested he was Irish,
gave a reluctant consent.

Soon a ring of men made an admiring audience
around Margarida. Brant spent so much time sending
scowls in other men's direction that he lost his gambling money fairly soon. Margarida won and enjoyed
herself immensely.

She enjoyed even more what they did when they
returned to the room, including several things they
hadn't tried before.

The next morning they took the stage for the nine-
mile trip northeast to Fort Bayard. At the army post,
they went to the adjutant's office, a whitewashed adobe
building beside the post hospital.

The officer on duty, a tall, thin lieutenant with a
narrow brown mustache, came out to the reception
area and listened politely to Brant's explanation of the
situation about Jesse, but then shook his head. "I'm
sorry, Mr. Curtis, but I'm afraid we can't help you."

Brant pulled a paper from his pocket. "I have here
a reply to a wire I sent you over a week ago. It says
you will cooperate in trying to locate Mr. Ross. This
wire carries the name of your adjutant, Captain
Reynolds."

The lieutenant's face flushed slightly. "Captain Reynolds is not here at the moment."

"Then I suggest you find him." Brant's words were
polite, but Margarida could tell from the tone of his
voice that he didn't intend to accept a refusal.

Apparently the lieutenant could hear the same tone,
because he spoke to the enlisted man who sat at a
desk nearby. "Private, see if you can locate Captain
Reynolds." Turning back to Brant and Margarida, he

said stiffly, "Would you care to come into the office and sit down?"

Captain Reynolds, a large man with a weathered face which the brightest sun couldn't burn, arrived ten minutes later. He greeted Brant with recognition. "Oh, yes, Mr. Curtis. When we received your wire, we telegraphed to both Fort Wingate and Fort Lewis. We don't have installations in the area you described. I'm not sure whether there's been a reply. Lieutenant," he ordered, "have someone check with the telegraph operator."

"If there's no word," Brant suggested in a coldly polite voice, "you could wire again."

Captain Reynolds measured Brant with a look, then said, "Yes, of course."

As they waited, the captain told Brant about conditions in the area, but Margarida's stomach was too knotted for her to listen. She wanted to rush inside and force the telegraph operator to give her the answer she wanted.

When her fingers were aching from keeping them so tightly laced together, the lieutenant returned and gave a paper to Captain Reynolds. "Good news, Mr. Curtis," the captain reported. "Fort Lewis has a patrol going west in the San Juan River area. They wire that they'll look for information about Mr. Ross and his son."

Brant shook the captain's hand. "Thank you. My wife and I and Mrs. Ross are grateful for your help."

Margarida, her heart swelling with hope, gave the officer her most exuberant smile. "Oh, yes, Captain Reynolds. I thank you so much." His sudden color and admiring look added to her feeling of cheer.

Outside, Brant said, "You can't help flirting, can you?" She could see he wasn't teasing.

After the tension of the wait in the adjutant's office, she felt her temper flaring. "I wasn't flirting, only thanking him."

"It's the same thing," he snapped. Then his face relaxed a little. "Sorry, Margarida. I'm afraid I lost my patience in there. If we hurry, we can just make the stage back to Silver City."

When they reached the stage, they found three cattlemen already seated. When the men saw Margarida, they moved to the back-facing seat, leaving the bench opposite free. Brant thanked them and helped Margarida inside.

He felt uncomfortable at his sharp words to her earlier—especially since he realized he'd spoken that way because he'd been jealous. He hated to admit it, and he couldn't apologize to her in front of others.

The cattlemen's conversation centered about problems with rustlers. Brant barely listened, glad that Curtis and Ross cattle ranged an area so inaccessible that thieves seldom bothered them.

"The army," declared a burly white-haired man, "should give us protection from rustlers and outlaws."

"Yes," grumbled another, who sounded as if he'd spent the morning with a bottle. "They need to earn their pay."

The third rancher, a small man, apparently less upset than his neighbors, said, "Well, at least the army took care of those Apache. Did you hear that Geronimo and the last of his bunch of hostiles surrendered to General Miles three days ago—September third? One of the officers just told me. General Crook almost had Geronimo talked in last spring, but then that degenerate and some others bolted."

Brant could feel every muscle tighten and his heart begin to beat faster.

"Crook!" the bellicose man said. "He wanted to be too easy on them. Insisted he'd made promises to the hostiles that Sheridan in Washington wouldn't keep. Miles knew better than to coddle them."

"Maybe now," added the drunk, "decent people

like us can live in peace. Those red fiends shoulda been crushed to death a long time ago."

Only the pressure of Margarida's hand on his arm and the knowledge he might endanger her kept Brant from grabbing the other man's throat. Struggling with his rage, he managed to restrain himself enough to say only, "Perhaps if Apache land hadn't been stolen from the rightful owners, and if Indians hadn't been betrayed and slaughtered, we might all live in peace together."

Apparently his voice carried enough of the physical violence he would like to do them that the two sober men retreated into silence. Only the intoxicated man said belligerently, "Say, you sound like one of those Apache lovers. We don't have much use for them around here."

"I *am* Apache."

This time, even through his liquor haze, the man obviously understood his danger. His face turned white, and he shrank back into his seat.

It took a long time for Brant's heartbeat to return to normal. From Margarida's rapid breathing and strained face he knew she was upset. He shouldn't have said anything when she was with him, but it had been impossible to hold back his words. At least he hadn't attacked the men. He forced himself to watch the juniper-dotted hills. Their companions all finished the trip in silence.

When they arrived in Silver City, the three cattle-men climbed hastily out of the coach. Margarida's face still looked pale, but she said nothing as Brant helped her down. They started across the road, passing the two sober travelers. He heard the white-haired man ask, "What's a good place to get whiskey here?"

Brant slowed his steps, listening for the answer.

The small rancher said, "The bar in the Tremont House, at Main and Yankie, has about the best whis-key in town. I'm planning to go there myself tonight. Maybe you'd like to join me."

The white-haired man nodded. "Thanks, I'll do that."

Margarida heard the conversation and felt her apprehension grow. She'd spent the coach ride wondering whether Brant was going to attack the cattlemen or if one of them was going to pull a gun, and remembering the Indian murdered on Curtis land. Now she could tell from the quivering muscles in Brant's arm and the cords standing out along his neck that only by great effort was he holding himself in. She didn't know whether she was more alarmed for him or angry at him.

Her silence lasted until they reached their room. "Brant, why were you so concerned to hear where those men are going? What do you intend to do?"

At first she thought he wasn't going to answer. His mouth tensed, and his jaw looked bone hard. "Have another talk with them tonight."

The uncertainty of the stage ride had left her temper ready to ignite. "That's stupid!"

His anger flared into as fierce a flame as hers. "I can't ignore what they said."

At the fury in his voice, she felt almost frightened, but she stiffened her back and glared at him. "And you can't fight every man who talks that way about Indians. That would be most of the men in the territory."

"You want me to betray my people?" His eyes sliced her with their black rage. "That's what I do when I ignore men like that."

Fiercely she spat back at him, "I don't want you to betray anyone, but how can it help the Apache for you to get into a brawl in a saloon?"

He stared at her, and she could see reason begin to conquer his feelings. The lines around his eyes softened, and color came back to his skin. He said, his voice tempered, "Yes, I know. But all my life I've heard things like that. If my father hadn't been rich and related to English nobility, it would have been worse."

The anger and fear in her chest began to ease. "I understand how you feel. But please don't go hunt for those men. Stay here."

For a moment she thought he'd refuse. Then his face lost the last of its rigidity. "All right."

Later that night as she lay beside him, Margarida thought that she didn't know how Brant felt. She could guess—after hearing his voice and seeing his face when he told the travelers in the coach he was Indian. But the part of him that adhered so fixedly to his Apache heritage seemed alien to her.

She was glad they were going home in the morning. Brant's anger frightened her. She missed her valley, and the secure feelings she had there. In that spot Brant seemed more the man she'd always known—and knew now as her loving husband. That was the man she wanted to live with, not the Indian who needed to defend his people.

16

"MARGARIDA, I want to go to *shiwóyé*'s camp so you can meet her."

Margarida's stomach did a little flip. They had just left the livery stable in Rio Torcido, where they'd retrieved Chid and Halcon after arriving on the stage from Silver City. "You want to go there first?"

"No—we have to talk to Elena and take care of things at home." Margarida's stomach settled down again. "But I want to take you to meet *shiwóyé* as soon as we can get away," he continued.

"Yes," Margarida agreed, but hoped the opportunity to visit the Apache camp wouldn't come too soon. When she did go, she would be an outsider. The prospect recalled the pain of this past year when Brant had rejected her because of the land for his people.

They started along the main street. On the left, a man was walking along the boardwalk. His empty right sleeve was pinned to the shoulder of his jacket, and he walked with a slight lurch, as if not quite sure of his balance. She recognized Carl Bodmer.

Dread reached inside Margarida, twisting until she couldn't breathe. She reined in Halcon and started to turn.

"What's the matter?" Brant asked.

"It's Carl Bodmer. I don't want to see him."

He blocked her way. "Margarida, would you shoot him again if you were in the same situation?"

"Yes."

"Then we won't turn around. You did the right thing, and you have to live with the consequences."

Strengthened by his stern, yet sympathetic expression, she started forward again. As she passed Carl Bodmer, he glanced up. His face blanched, then turned a dull red, and his eyes looked murderous. She could feel them on her back as she rode up the street. When she turned off onto a road going north, she had to stop and remove her gloves to wipe the perspiration from her hands.

Brant smiled at her, encouraging her to produce a shaky smile of her own. "When I shot Carl Bodmer, I didn't think about what would happen to him—only about Walt and me."

"Sometimes you don't have much choice about what you do." She started ahead, but Brant called, "Wait. Before we leave town, I'd like to stop at the Ramírez place." He turned to the right, and she followed.

Still caught up in her feelings about Carl Bodmer, Margarida was outside Adela's house before she wondered why Brant wanted to stop there. By then Adela was coming out to greet them, her black eyes excited.

"Margarida! Brant. How happy I am to see you. Did you have a good trip to Silver City?"

She hugged Adela. "I won some money gambling, almost as much as Brant lost." As they walked inside, Brant told Adela of their efforts to locate Jesse.

To Margarida's surprise, Miguel was home. He and Brant exchanged friendly greetings, and Adela soon provided steaming cups of her mixture of coffee, chocolate, and cinnamon.

Brant said to Miguel, "I heard that you weren't working for the *comancheros* any longer. Would you consider coming back as foreman for the Ross ranch?"

Margarida barely suppressed a gasp. He didn't know how Mama felt about Miguel; she'd refuse to have him as foreman, which would humiliate Miguel and probably upset Brant.

Before she could think of a way to interrupt, Miguel gave a broad smile. "I would like that very much."

"Then we're agreed." Brant and Miguel shook hands. "Frank Vincent will need a couple of months' notice, but I think it would work out best to pay him off and let him go now, before the fall roundup."

"We can move out anytime," Miguel responded.

"It will be grand to live out there again," Adela said, her eyes sparkling.

"Yes." Margarida hesitated, but added with enthusiasm, "I'd love having you closer."

She concealed her dismay until they were on the road home. "Brant, Mama won't agree to having Miguel back."

Brant's expression didn't change. "I think she will."

"I suggested it before, and she absolutely refused."

"I guess we'll see" was all the response he gave.

Exasperated by his assurance, Margarida imagined her mother's expression when she heard of Brant's plans. Then he won't look so unruffled, Margarida thought.

At the Ross ranch, Elena greeted them warmly. Her mood was apparently still the contented one that had prevailed since Margarida agreed to marry Brant. Lobo forgot his manners completely and jumped on Margarida, almost knocking her over until Brant called him to heel.

While Brant described everything that had been arranged in Silver City, she waited impatiently for him to tell her mother about Miguel. Finally he said, "And I asked Miguel Ramírez to come back to be foreman here."

Elena smiled pleasantly. "What a good idea, Brant."

Brant flicked Margarida a grin which verged on arrogance. When she recovered from her astonishment, she wondered whether it was possible to love someone and at the same time want to inflict on him some sort of temporary but quite painful wound.

It was too late for riding on that night, so after supper they went to her old bedroom, with Lobo, despite his drooping tail, firmly excluded. Margarida waited until Brant closed the door to say, "You didn't have to be so pleased about Miguel. How did you know Mama would agree?"

He gave her a self-satisfied grin and started unbuttoning his shirt. "It's just my extraordinary charm."

Pushing him back on the bed, she discovered when she rolled against him that she wasn't as annoyed at him as she thought. But she continued to pummel him until he caught her arms and kissed her.

Being back in her mother's house reminded Margarida of what her mother had said about marriage. Men did "stray." Maybe it was because their wives were busy with children. When they undressed and were in bed, she said, "Brant, I'm not sure I want to have children right away."

"All right. We can probably avoid having children, if we're careful."

Afterward, when Margarida's breathing melted into sleep, Brant thought of her request. It might already be too late; she might be pregnant now. A thrill ran through him, and he laid his hand tenderly on her belly. Still, he knew it would be better to wait. But as he settled down to sleep, he had a feeling of wistful regret.

During the next weeks, Margarida found that learning new responsibilities required more self-discipline than she'd expected. Adjusting to the ways of a different household, even sharing a room with someone else, at times frayed her temper. She tried moving Lobo to the Curtis house, but he got into three fights with other dogs the first day. Her father's and J.J.'s safety lay at the edge of her thoughts, but being busy kept her from worrying about when George Slack might return.

Two things always delighted her. One was Walt's company. He seemed to have recovered from the terror of the previous spring and was almost always happy. His "friend" still came to visit at the ranch. Margarida expected someone who wore lipstick and scanty clothing, but she was wrong. Bertha, whose last name Margarida never learned, looked like an ordinary housewife. She was a little overweight, with brown hair and a shy smile.

The other thing that never disappointed Margarida was making love with Brant. Sometimes they would look at each other across the supper table and know they couldn't wait any longer. Brant would make some excuse no one believed, and they would hurry upstairs and struggle with buttonholes that wouldn't release their buttons and snaps that froze together. Once Margarida tripped on her petticoat and fell to the floor. Brant started to help her up, changed his mind, and they made love on the carpet, with her clothing tangled around her legs.

Other times they made love slowly, savoring each other, prolonging the tension, until one of them would choose a caress that drove the other beyond longer delay. Twice they found reasons to go back to their room after breakfast, and Margarida felt as if she were stealing some special favor from the gods which one day might have to be returned. Some nights they didn't make love at all, and at those times just sleeping beside Brant seemed satisfying too.

One warm morning in early October Brant found Margarida sitting on a stool at the kitchen table, chopping onions and red peppers. His work, overseeing their ranch and settling Miguel into the Ross ranch, had finally eased up. He paused for a moment to admire the color in her damp cheeks and the hair that had escaped from her braid and clung to the side of her neck. "This would be a good day to visit *shiwóyé,*" he said, leaning down to taste a salty spot behind her ear.

She glanced up, then down at the vegetables spread out on the chopping board in front of her. "I can't go today. Luisa's teaching me to make corn relish. You should be happy about that, since you love it so much."

Disappointed, he said, "All right, but let's go tomorrow."

"I promised Mama I'd be over to see her tomorrow. Really, Brant," she said, continuing to chop, "I need more time to plan."

Annoyance surfaced along with his disappointment. "Then you've changed," he said, more sharply than he'd intended. "You always used to love doing things on the spur of the moment."

Red color crept up the back of her neck. "Yes, but I have more responsibilities now."

As Margarida heard him leave the kitchen, she knew she hadn't told him the whole truth. She was curious about the Apache champ, but afraid too. Margarida, she scolded herself silently, don't be a coward.

She gave a red pepper a particularly hard whack. The camp meant a great deal to Brant, and that was what bothered her. She couldn't banish the feeling it had a hold over him which drew him away from her. But that attraction also made it important for her to go with him.

At supper three nights later Brant asked, "Would it be all right with you, Margarida, to visit *shiwóyé* tomorrow?"

Margarida's smile didn't come quite as easily as she wished, but she hoped Brant couldn't tell. "Of course." His look of pleasure rewarded her.

"Can I go with you?" Walt asked. "It's fun there."

"I'd like that," Margarida interjected quickly. If Walt went, she wouldn't be the only outsider.

"Fine. We'll leave early in the morning."

New Mexico displayed its most extravagant fall finery the next day. The last few nights had been chilly, and the aspen leaves suddenly announced their coming departure by putting on yellow and gold dress, with a few wayward trees insisting on orange. Margarida thought if she were high enough, she could see all the way to Mexico City.

Brant seemed no older than Walt, laughing at everything Margarida said, teasing his brother, and challenging them both to race their horses across a stretch of meadow. His rowdy spirits set hers off. Her reluctance to visit his grandmother seemed foolish and the day an adventure.

They climbed higher into the mountains, following a creek to a place where rocky canyon walls narrowed, leaving barely room for the trail beside the stream. Past this opening, the canyon widened, and Margarida saw dwellings scattered along the stream.

"How many people live here?"

"Thirty-seven, unless there have been more babies since I was here last."

Vines and grass covered the conical-shaped wickiups; smoke drifted up from the tops where the supporting poles met. Each dwelling had one east-facing door. Among them were several ramadas, square structures of poles with brush on three sides and the top. Women were going in and out of the wickiups, but Margarida didn't see any men.

A tumble of children greeted them. She counted seven small boys and girls, who shouted words she couldn't understand. Brant swung down and handed his reins to Walt, then squatted to welcome the assault of wiggling arms and legs. Finally he rose with one small boy perched on his shoulder. Brant's obvious pleasure in the children surprised Margarida. She wondered why he'd agreed so quickly that they not have a child yet. These children were Apache. Could that make a difference?

Walt dismounted and helped Margarida down. A

circle of women ringed them now, laughing and calling out words which sounded welcoming. Walt responded with a cheerful hello.

Some of them returned the greeting in accented English. Margarida smiled and tried a tentative "Good morning."

To her the women looked confusingly alike. All had straight black hair, parted in the middle and falling back over their shoulders. They wore loose cotton blouses over gathered calico skirts, similar to clothing she'd seen in stores in Rio Torcido. Their beaded necklaces and bracelets and high moccasins with turned-up toes were what she'd expected. Two women carried infants in cradle boards.

As the women gathered around Brant, chattering to him, he put down the boy and took Margarida's hand. He said something in Apache which she concluded meant she was his wife, because they smiled and made what sounded like exclamations. "*Shiwóyé* is inside," he said to her, "and asks us to join her."

Despite her resolutions, Margarida felt apprehension sweep back over her. What if she said or did the wrong thing? If his grandmother didn't like her, how would he feel? "What about Walt?" she said, wanting an ally.

"He's busy." Brant pointed to one side. Walt had tethered the horses and was squatting on his heels, surrounded by children. He was laughing, and matching their torrent of Apache with English, as if he expected them to understand. "Walt's a favorite with everyone. The Apache respect any kind of difference in someone. To them it means the gods have given that person special powers. They think his skill with horses proves his power."

She tried to ignore the increasing tension in her stomach as they walked toward one of the wickiups. "Please tell me again what your grandmother's name is."

"Ha-na-sba ekaiye. It means She-Returns-From-War-With-Her-Children. But call her Grandmother. Apaches don't use names directly."

At first the wickiup seemed dark inside. When Margarida's eyes adjusted, she saw a seated figure, and then heard Brant say something in Apache. *Shiwóyé* responded in Spanish. "Welcome, my granddaughter."

"Thank you," Margarida said in Spanish. She settled herself on the hide floor and tried to relax. At least, she thought, they could exchange a few words.

"My Spanish I forget much of," *shiwóyé* explained.

"Yes," Margarida responded. "It was so long ago."

Shiwóyé's eyes looked as if she could see inside Margarida's head. Margarida wondered nervously what they could talk about. But *shiwóyé* said, "Please excuse me, I must tell my grandson some news." She turned to Brant, crouched beside her, and started speaking in Apache.

Relieved just to be silent, Margarida studied the wrinkled face. It was hard to think that this small woman was related to the tall, lean man. But their eyes looked alike, for they had the same intelligence and pride. Margarida could see the toughness which had enabled *shiwóyé* to survive captivity in Mexico. She thought of stories about the cruelty of the Apache. Had *shiwóyé* ever crushed a captive's head with a stone or lit a fire to burn someone to death? Margarida had to repress a shudder.

The old woman turned her penetrating black eyes back to Margarida. "You have been far away, to school," she said. "I would like to hear about that." Margarida almost gave a nervous laugh at the contrast between her thoughts and this mild question. As she described her three years in Connecticut, she began to feel even more awkward. How foolish that sheltered life must sound to this stern woman.

They ate some cakes, which tasted strange, and Margarida had trouble swallowing. Finally Brant rose, and she felt as if a test she wasn't sure she'd passed were over.

"I thank you for coming," *shiwóyé* said to Margarida. "I hope we will have other times to speak more."

"Yes," said Margarida, "I would like to see you again." She couldn't use the word for "grandmother."

When they were outside, she breathed more freely. "Come," Brant said, "we'll go to the game field. You can't get close—women aren't allowed at a hoop-and-pole game—but you can see from a distance."

"Hoop-and-pole, what's that?"

"The men's favorite game. That's where they are now. The object is to throw a pole so that the hoop, which is rolling, will fall in a certain way on the pole."

He left her on a rise where some women were standing, and went on to a large area where men were congregated. Occasionally a woman smiled at her, obviously attempting to be friendly, but she felt like an outsider. Down below, two players rolled a hoop along what looked like furrows and then threw long poles at the hoop. From the cheers and groans at the end of each throw, and the exchanges of various goods, Margarida guessed the men were gambling.

Walt's blond head stood out, but Brant's black hair blended in with the others. For a moment she had a feeling almost of panic—that he would stay here and she wouldn't find him again. Firmly she told herself she was being ridiculous. Walt played and won. When Brant took a turn and lost, she felt glad. She was a little ashamed, but she didn't want him to be good at Apache skills.

At last the players finished and started toward the wickiups. When Brant joined her, he introduced her to the men. They looked even more unfamiliar than the women. Their long hair was loose, held off their faces by headbands. They wore jackets and vests over their shirts, and breechclouts over leggings. The leggings were tucked into moccasins which came almost up to their knees.

Brant identified various people and described their relationship to him, but soon she lost track of who they all were. He seemed to claim some connection to almost everyone there. One explanation startled her. "That man over there," she asked, "with braids and the two young women? Did you say those are both his wives?"

"Yes. They're sisters."

She wanted to ask more, but an older man claimed Brant's attention. Margarida saw Walt ahead, next to the horses, and went to join him. He was tussling with a small boy, so she stood next to Halcon and watched Brant.

He finished talking and started toward her, when a woman came out of a small wickiup. She was a very pretty woman, slender, with even features and glowing skin. Margarida didn't remember meeting her earlier.

Brant stopped and spoke to the woman. Even not understanding their speech, Margarida thought that the woman acted as if she and Brant had some sort of special intimacy.

Anger sent warm blood to her skin. She wanted to rush down and slap the pretty face until the smile disappeared. Horrified at her feelings, she turned quickly and stroked Halcon's neck with a trembling hand. Jealous! She was jealous! Her emotion humiliated her, and she took deep breaths, struggling to calm herself.

"Are we going now, Brant?" Walt's voice behind her warned her, and she tood another breath before she turned.

"Yes, if you're ready, Margarida." Brant looked and sounded just as usual, and angrily she told herself she was a fool to be upset.

But as they mounted and started back along the trail, she couldn't help asking, "Was that another cousin you were just talking to?" She punished herself for the folly of jealousy by adding, "The very pretty one."

"No. She's a widow. Her husband died a year or so ago. I'm glad you got along with *shiwóyé*."

Margarida thought that he'd changed the subject too suddenly, but she didn't want to talk about the widow anyway. "I hope your grandmother will like me," she said. "The camp is different from any place I've ever been, and all the relatives confused me."

"You'll sort them out," Brant assured her, but she wasn't sure she wanted to.

They reached the narrow canyon mouth and were out in more familiar terrain. Some of her tension began to subside. "Your cousin with the two wives. Does that happen often—that a man has two wives?"

"Not often, but it's not unusual when the family needs support and the man can afford it." Brant looked at her, and she could tell from the quirk at the corner of his mouth that he was going to tease her. "It's also handy when there's a child. Apache men are expected to stay away from their wives until the child is weaned. That's usually about three years. To have children more often is a disgrace. So a second wife can be very nice. Maybe it's a good thing you don't have a sister."

She could easily ignore that kind of teasing—it wasn't an imaginary sister that had made her so furious earlier. "So most Apache men have to do without for a long time?"

He grinned. "*Shiwóyé* says that's why they're such fierce warriors."

"And the single men too? Do they have . . . someone like Walt's lady friend?"

"You *are* curious today. Chastity is very important to the Apache, but they're lenient about sex for women who are divorced or are widows. The single men can go to them for favors, and . . ." His voice trailed off, as if he'd just realized what he'd said.

The word "widow" left Margarida without any desire to hear more. But after a pause, Brant went on doggedly. "The man may help the woman out with economic support in return. But it's not like prostitution."

She thought she'd managed the visit without showing too many difficult feelings, but she could hardly contain the revolt that rose within her now. "It doesn't sound too different," she declared, and looked straight at him.

His skin reddened, and he said as stiffly as she, "It is. Very different."

As they glared at each other, Margarida realized how foolish she was being. This camp and all the people in it were important in Brant's life. She didn't want a rift between them because of something that happened before they were married. She already had too much trouble with her feelings about his desire to be Apache.

With great effort, she softened her voice. "Of course. Apache ways just seem so new and strange to me." As the muscles of his face relaxed, she even managed a smile. "Maybe I could learn to speak Apache."

"You don't need to. It's a difficult language."

"I could try it." Then, she thought, no pretty widows could talk to him in a language she didn't understand.

The fall roundup began two weeks later. Midmorning of the second day Margarida took Bailarina and started out for the branding corrals. As she approached, Brant intercepted her.

"You'd better ride a different direction today," he told her. "It's not customary for women to be at the branding and castrating."

She felt her temper rise. "Papa didn't object."

"I do—the *vaqueros* don't like it."

"They've never said so," she argued.

"Of course they didn't, when the boss allowed it. But they don't want you there."

Her temper zoomed. "I just may go anyway."

"You don't even really like to watch." His face stiffened into angry lines. "Running both ranches is my responsibility now. The men accept my decisions and trust me to be fair, and I respect their wishes. So I don't want you at the branding, or chasing up and down the hills."

"I didn't marry you to have a keeper," she snapped.

"Then be reasonable," he returned just as hotly.

She glared at him before turning and riding off to chase up and down the hills. If Brant Curtis thought she'd meekly do anything he said, she stormed to herself, he'd have a lifetime of surprises. When she'd exhausted her anger, she grudgingly admitted that what he'd said was true, but she hadn't expected him to side with the cowboys.

When he came in at the end of the day, he said stiffly, "I'm sorry, Margarida, about the branding, but I have to do what I think is right. I hope you understand."

"Yes," she had to acknowledge, "I do," but she still felt some of the resentment of the morning. She wished he didn't care so much about doing the right thing.

In November, Carlos García, still pale from his illness, returned from California, but he knew only that Margarida's father had gone on alone to Utah.

A week later George Slack came to the Curtis ranch to report he hadn't located Jesse Ross. "I'm sorry Mr. Curtis, Mrs. Curtis. I couldn't find any trace of either Jesse Ross or your brother."

Margarida, seated across from Slack in the parlor, began to tremble. "No! That can't be true."

Brant took her hand. "Wait, let's hear what he says."

He kept her hand in his while they listened. Slack

described the efforts he'd made, his searches in the area, and the people he'd talked to. "But did you see *everybody* in town?" she probed.

"Yes, ma'am, I did. Nobody in Glory Creek or around the area would admit to knowing about Mr. Ross or the Irishman. I found the Indian woman you told me about, the one who lives outside the town and does some nursing. She wouldn't tell me a thing. I asked among the other Utes. Nothing."

The tremor in Margarida's chest grew worse. "Do you think the Indian nurse knew something and wouldn't say?"

"That's possible, ma'am, but if she did, I couldn't find out. I'm really sorry I didn't help you."

Margarida had to grip Brant's hand to keep from screaming. It couldn't be so. It just couldn't! She'd been so sure the man would find Papa and J.J..

"You've told us something," Brant said. "That the Indian woman wouldn't talk about it. It could mean she didn't want to be blamed for his death. Or there might be some other reason."

George Slack rose, and so did Brant. Margarida forced herself to stand also. Papa would be ashamed if she broke down in front of strangers.

"Well, Mr. Curtis," Mr. Slack said, obviously hating to report failure, "the army had already been there, asking around. Sometimes men get pretty suspicious of soldiers. Could be that no one wanted to answer any more questions. That's slim hope, but it's a chance."

Margarida forced herself to offer him a meal and overnight hospitality, but she was relieved when he refused. She'd have to go and talk to her mother, and that seemed all she'd be able to manage.

When Brant returned from seeing Slack off, he took her in his arms, and she let her tears escape. When she was calmer, she looked at him, trying to read his face.

"I still can't *feel* that Papa and J.J. are dead. Am I silly? Do you think there's still hope?"

"Not much, but some. I don't think another trip up there now would do any good. Maybe we'll hear something."

His words comforted her, but she hated feeling so helpless. "Brant, I should have gone to look for Papa."

"Be reasonable, Margarida. How could we leave your mother, and the ranches, with everyone who depends on us here? Slack did everything we could have done."

She knew his reasoning made sense. It was foolish to think she could have succeeded where the army and an experienced man had failed, but she wished she'd tried.

17

THREE days later Margarida and Brant went to the Apache camp again. The group had moved to a cluster of stone buildings in a lower, sheltered valley. Brant explained that when they could follow their old patterns, the Apache had gone to the warmer deserts for the winter.

Brant left Margarida with his grandmother while he went to talk to one of the men. The midday sun was warm enough that Margarida and *shiwóyé* sat outside, *shiwóyé* scraping a deer hide, and Margarida awkwardly helping.

As they worked on the hide, Margarida thought of the stories she'd heard about the cruelty of the Apache. She remembered also Brant's self-inflicted wounds to learn how to endure pain. "I've heard," she began cautiously, "that the Apache are very fierce warriors."

Shiwóyé's glance suggested she understood Margarida's thoughts. "We must be," *shiwóyé* said, "but many times it has been the whites who have practiced the kind of treachery they blame on us. Our great chief, Mangas Coloradas, tried honorable dealings with the Americans. In return he was whipped. Later he was tricked into capture and killed. The Apache respect the lives of those who surrender."

Three women came out of a wickiup and started walking toward where Margarida and *shiwóyé* sat. One was the pretty widow. Margarida's resolution not to be jealous faded, and she found it difficult to listen as *shiwóyé* went on to tell a story about the Chiricahua chief Cochise.

When the women had passed by, Margarida said, trying to sound casual, "What are those women's names?"

"The one in the middle," *shiwóyé* said with a twist of her mouth that reminded Margarida of Brant when he wanted to laugh, "is Na-hilwol dahale. That means She-Runs-Fast."

Margarida didn't listen to the names of the others. The widow would have to run very fast, she fumed to herself, if she ever touched Brant again.

Brant returned soon afterward. As they left, he called a greeting to a short woman whom Margarida hadn't seen before. The woman turned her head, and Margarida had to exert all her self-control not to shudder. The woman had puckered scars where once her nose had been.

After they were away from the camp, Brant said, "I'm sorry. I should have warned you about Short-Maiden. I forgot how strange she'd look to you."

"What happened to her?"

"Her husband cut her nose off because she was unfaithful."

"Cut her nose off! But that's grotesque!"

His face darkened. "Adultery is a crime among my people, as it is among yours. This is a way we punish it and make sure the woman doesn't do it again. It seems grotesque to you because it's not one of your customs."

Hurt that he'd separated "his" people from "hers," she said belligerently, "And what about the man who lies with a woman who's not his wife. What happens to him?"

"Usually not as much because he's the hunter and warrior. His wife's relatives have the right to kill him or make him pay them. If the woman is married, her husband might cut off her nose and the tip of her lover's penis."

"That seems so brutal."

"You know how your mother feels about having a son. It's even more important for an Apache family, since it's up to the son-in-law to take care of his wife's parents."

Margarida couldn't believe she'd ever get used to Apache customs, or that her family's ways were similar. At least, she thought with grim humor, Brant wouldn't chase any Apache wives, no matter how pretty. He'd hate the penalty. She just wished it applied to sleeping with widows!

To prove to herself she trusted Brant, the next time he suggested going to the camp, Margarida made an excuse to stay behind. Suffering is good for the soul, she reminded herself as she waited for his return during an afternoon that lasted a year. When she finally saw him riding through the trees, she decided her soul had improved so much she wouldn't need to test it again.

On a Sunday in December Margarida and Brant went into Rio Torcido to church. To her relief, she didn't see Carl Bodmer, but she was pleased to see Priscilla and Lee.

When the service ended, Brant stopped outside to speak to another rancher, and Margarida went to talk to the Hansens and see the new baby.

"Look at my boy!" Priscilla said proudly. "Isn't he wonderful?"

"He's beautiful," Margarida agreed. Priscilla beamed, and chattered on, apparently absorbed in her infant. Lee acted bored and soon moved off.

When they were alone, Priscilla whispered, "You were right. Everybody's polite to me since we got back."

Priscilla had to go change the baby, and Brant was

still talking, so Margarida wandered through a thick stand of pines and oaks behind the church. A man came around the side of the building and stopped where brush made a curved screen. It was Lee Hansen. Not wanting to talk to him, Margarida stayed where she was. In a moment, a woman in a cloak joined him. He put his arm around her, pulling her farther into the brush so that they were out of sight. Margarida heard a giggle.

Priscilla and Lee's baby was barely three months old, Margarida thought angrily, and Lee was chasing after another woman. He wasn't even discreet.

As Margarida walked toward the front of the church, she began to sing "The Lord is watching all we do . . ." loudly enough to interrupt them, she hoped. Her mother would have pointed out that Lee's actions confirmed what she'd said about marriage. Margarida decided it proved that Brant was nothing like Lee, and went to find her husband.

Before she and Brant left town, they collected their mail, including several weeks of Silver City newspapers. When they reached home, she sorted the mail while he spread the papers out on the dining-room table. One letter in a blue envelope came from Charlotte, her best friend at the school in Connecticut. Margarida read the gossip about teas and flirtations and realized that once such things had sounded exciting to her. She was dismayed to think she'd shared those values.

How far away her school years seemed now, Margarida thought, and how much she'd changed. Palmer, Charlotte's brother, had appeared so worldly to her then; she'd felt so daring, letting him kiss her and brush her breast. How silly she'd acted. At the memory, she glanced almost guiltily at Brant, as if he would know her thoughts.

The sight of his face made her forget everything else. He was staring at the newspaper, his skin pale and his eyes glittering. His lips were compressed in a white line.

"Brant! What's happened?"

"The Chiricahua and Warm Springs Apache from the San Carlos reservation have been sent to Florida." He jerked to his feet, throwing down the paper. "When Geronimo surrendered, the army promised he'd be reunited with his family. But the women and children are being separated from the men. They're being sent to forts—really prisons—in Florida, areas the army knows are unhealthy. And the scouts . . ." Brant's voice was hoarse with bitterness, "the ones who helped track Geronimo down in Mexico—they're also being sent to Florida. They worked as scouts because they were afraid of what would happen to all of them because of Geronimo's resistance. This is how they're rewarded."

He slumped down at the table, his head in his hands. "My God. To have to live like that." When he raised his head, Margarida saw tears in his eyes. "Victorio and Nana and Geronimo raided and killed. But they were fighting back in the way they'd always known. Only a few whites ever tried to understand them. And now all of them—whether they tried to keep peace or not—are prisoners. They'll never see their homes again."

She went around to him, wanting to ease the anguish she saw in his face. "Not all of them. Some of them are here."

He put his arms around her waist, his head against her breast. His voice was muffled. "Yes, thank God for that. And they'll stay. For as long as I can help them, they'll stay." She held tightly to him, hating his pain, vowing to share his concern more wholeheartedly.

During the winter, trying to live up to her vow, Margarida visited the camp whenever Brant suggested it, but she still felt like an outsider. Brant didn't seem to notice her discomfort, and she couldn't banish a shred of resentment that he didn't appreciate how difficult the visits were for her. The sight of the widow still roused tormenting pangs of jealousy.

Reluctantly she recognized why the thought of the Apache widow made her stomach clench into a bitter knot. Her feeling came from that unanswered question about Brant's and her marriage—would he have married her if it meant giving up the land for the camp? Did she mean as much to him as his desire to be Apache? She didn't dare ask him, because it would be childish—and she feared the answer.

As often as she could, she went into Rio Torcido to see Priscilla, and to the Ross ranch. It was a relief to be with people she understood and who cared about her. On a day in late March she returned from a morning with her mother and Adela to find that Brant had gone alone to the Apache camp. Though the visit would have been a strain, perversely she wished he hadn't gone without her.

In the early afternoon Enoch Springer arrived. His smile delighted her, lightening her unhappy mood. "Enoch, it's been months since I've seen you. Please come inside."

He tied up his horse, a handsome bay mare. "I've sold my ranch. Going to move on west, maybe to California."

"You're leaving!" she said, disappointed. She'd always liked him, though she knew those weren't the feelings he wanted. "I'm sorry to hear that."

"I've been restless, and I got a good price for my land, so I decided to go. But I didn't want to leave without saying good-bye to you . . . and your husband."

"Brant's not here now," she said as they went into the house. "He'll be sorry he didn't get to say good-bye." She thought Brant would probably be happy Enoch was leaving.

Over coffee, she heard about the sale of his ranch to

a man from Tennessee. "I'll be around for another couple of weeks, and then I'll be off," Enoch finished, and rose to leave.

She stood up and held out her hand to him. "I'll never forget how you helped me when Walt was in jail. And the fun we had together. You've been a good friend."

He took her hand and held it, his eyes sad. "I wish . . ." he began, then stopped, a flush coloring his face. "I'll always be your friend."

She remembered the night at the jail—her terrible fears, and her relief at the sound of his voice, letting her know help had come. Impulsively she leaned across and kissed him.

His lips felt startled for a moment; then he pulled her close and returned her kiss.

Embarrassed, she pushed away, feeling her face grow hot. "I'm sorry, I shouldn't have. But—"

"Don't!" He spoke sharply; then his smile returned painfully, as if forced out. "It's the best good-bye I've ever had. I'm only sorry it's for that reason."

She followed him outside and watched him mount. Just before he rode out of sight, he turned and waved.

Brant and Walt didn't return until after suppertime. "I was late because of a problem with one of the young men," Brant explained.

Luisa had stayed in the kitchen to warm up food for the two men. Margarida, feeling her jealousy simmering, excused herself and went to their bedroom. Brant followed her up a little later and began to undress.

Trying to sound normal, Margarida said, "Enoch was here this afternoon."

He dropped his boots in the corner with a thud. "Luisa mentioned he was here. I'm glad you finally decided to tell me."

She stopped with her petticoat in her hand. "If you'd been home, you'd have seen him."

He faced her, his mouth thinning, his eyes angry.

"Maybe you were glad I wasn't. It gave you a chance to flirt with him."

"Flirt with him!" She flung her petticoat over a chair and stood, her hands on her hips. "I suppose you don't even want me to smile politely."

"You've never been able to smile at a man without turning it into an invitation."

"That's not fair! The only reason today I—" She stopped, realizing what her temper was leading to.

"You what?"

"I remembered how he'd helped me about Walt, and I kissed him," she finished defiantly.

He walked over until he was right in front of her. She could see the tiny lines around his mouth and the rapid rise of his bare chest from his angry breathing. "That's why you took him in the parlor, to be alone, so you could kiss him?"

Though she shouldn't, she felt defensive, and her discomfort added to her anger. "I knew he was leaving and I'd never see him again."

"Too bad it was a farewell. I'm sure you both enjoyed it." Brant knew that he wasn't being completely fair, but ever since Luisa had mentioned that Enoch had called, his temper had been rising. He'd never forgotten the way Enoch had acted as if he and Margarida had a special tie. "Maybe that's the way you and Enoch Springer behave in polite society, but it's not what I expect of my wife."

Her face flooded with color, and the skin of her shoulders and breasts above the top of her camisole as well. Her eyes narrowed, glaring at him. "It's too bad I'm not an Apache wife. Then you could threaten to cut off my nose. That would ruin any of those invitations I scatter around."

"Maybe I should have an Apache wife. She'd know what modesty is." Even as he said it, Brant knew he didn't mean it; he was letting his anger speak. "I shouldn't have said that. But I won't stand for another man touching you."

His apology didn't obliterate the wound of his earlier words. "But it's all right for you to touch Apache widows."

He glared at her, and his mouth thinned. "That was before we were married. And arrangements like that are completely different from letting Enoch Springer chase you."

Rage and pain twisted so inside her that she hardly knew how she felt. It had been obvious he'd been involved with the widow, but at least he hadn't admitted it before. And now he accused her of flirting! "I only kissed him good-bye. I never slept with him."

"We got married just in time."

As if he heard the ugliness in his voice, his eyes looked shocked, and his anger faded. He stepped closer. She put her hand against his chest, warding him off, and felt the rapid beat of his heart. His voice was softer as he said, "I shouldn't have said that either. I don't want to quarrel with you, Margarida. I'm sorry if I was unfair about Enoch. You know by now how jealous I am."

Since she didn't want to quarrel either, she didn't resist when he pulled her close and kissed the top of her hair. The pain of his words about an Apache wife weren't gone, but as he covered her face with fierce kisses and rubbed his palms over the tips of her breasts, desire became stronger than anger. He pulled off the rest of her clothes, and she finished his undressing, sliding his pants down, releasing his rigid penis, opening herself to his touch.

When he carried her to bed, she was ready to receive him, as if their anger had been transmuted into passion that couldn't wait. His eyes looked like black fire, and his breath came in shallow bursts—his desire like a fever consuming him. His thrusts inside her, rapid and deep, responded to her urgency, and she shook with a frenzy of spasms as he also found his release.

It took a long time for Margarida to fall asleep, and she could tell from Brant's breathing that he lay awake for much of that time also. Their quarrel had ended in passion, but she couldn't forget the words. In anger, she thought, sometimes the truth is spoken.

Two days later, Margarida and Brant were in the dining room after the noon dinner. Her wounds from the quarrel with Brant hadn't healed, but she was trying to forget them. Tall Man came into the room, his face grim. "I'm going east to Socorro," he announced.

"Why?" Brant asked.

"A Mescalero brother has been to our camp. He tells us that Jaspers, the scalp hunter who killed five of our relatives, is living in Socorro. Our cousins He-Is-Given-Tests and Crouched-And-Ready go with me to kill Jaspers. We dance tonight, and tomorrow we leave."

"You'll be going into a town where Indians are always suspected, and with two impulsive and untried young men," Brant protested. "You're taking a great risk."

"I have waited thirteen years to find him. I will not miss this chance."

"Then I'll go with you," Brant said. "I must make arrangements here and at the Ross ranch, but I will do that and join you at the camp."

"Very well," Tall Man replied, and left before Margarida recovered from her shock enough to speak.

"Brant! You can't mean this! To get revenge for something that happened thirteen years ago! Do you even know this man Jaspers?"

He'd never looked more alien to her, his face rigid, his eyes impenetrable. "I know that he killed my relatives and the Mexican government paid him two hundred pesos apiece for their scalps." He turned and strode along the hall.

She followed him, still not believing he wouldn't listen. "This is insane. You should persuade Tall Man not to go—not agree to go with him."

He turned, his hand on the door. "I can't do that. Now I must talk to Juan and then see Miguel."

Still stunned, Margarida watched as he crossed the yard and disappeared into the stable. In a few minutes he came out with Chid and rode away.

During the afternoon, Margarida swung from rage to fear and back again. When he returned, she waited until he went upstairs to pack. While he laid out buckskins she'd never seen before, she began, as calmly as she could, with thoughts she'd been marshaling. "What if hunting Jaspers brings the authorities down on the camp here? And what about Walt? He's more a relative to you than any Apache."

"I don't intend for something to happen to me, but I know you'll take care of Walt."

"Why not go to the sheriff in Socorro?"

Even before Brant answered, Margarida knew what he'd say. What surprised her was how bitter he sounded. "What Jaspers did was legal in Mexico and ignored here. The law won't do anything to him."

Anger began to overcome the calm she was trying to maintain. "You didn't kill the men you know murdered that innocent half-breed Indian last year."

"He wasn't related to me, and I didn't feel I should run the risk, with Walt and other things to think of."

"You have even more responsibilities now. What did Mama say when you told her you'd be away?"

He took out a shirt and began to fold it into a pack. "She didn't say much."

"Did you tell her why you're going?"

"No. I didn't think she'd understand."

"Well, I don't either." The muscles in Brant's jaw tensed, but he didn't answer. Margarida's throat burned with tears that she fiercely denied. "If Mama did know,

I suppose she'd start picking out another husband for me."

For a moment Brant's hands stilled on his pack; then he jerked a strap tight so forcefully that the pack fell to the floor. He picked it up and said quietly, "Margarida, this is something I must do, for Tall Man, but for myself also. No Apache lets murder of his own kin go unrepaid."

"That's it!" All the uncertainty of Brant's reasons for their marriage and her feeling that she could never share the most important part of his life coalesced into deep hurt and anger. "What you really want is to be an Apache, and this is your chance to prove it!"

She could see Brant struggle for control. He put down the pack. "I love you, and I don't want to leave you, but I must go. Will you come to the stable with me to say good-bye?"

"Now? I thought you were leaving in the morning."

"The dances are tonight. I must be there for them."

"What dances?"

"First the war dances for all the men, and the speeches and songs about being strong and brave in battle." He hesitated, then added, "The social dances last the rest of the night."

She thought she'd already felt all the shock and pain the day could bring, but she was wrong. His last night before he went away, perhaps to be killed, and he would be at the Apache camp, not at home with her. "Oh, yes. I remember what you told me about the social dances. That's when girls and boys dance together. I guess that means men and women too. And widows and married men."

"Margarida! Stop." He took her head between his hands and tilted her face up, forcing her to look into his eyes. "Margarida—please listen to me. I *will* come back. I love you. I want to live my life with you."

"You want something else more!"

In his face she saw lines of the same agonizing pain

she was feeling. "Margarida, I don't want to leave this way, with such anger between us."

"But you're going anyhow."

He kissed her, but she wouldn't let herself feel anything. His arms, holding her close, seemed impersonal. Though she recognized the scent of his hair, the texture of his skin, the bony line of his jaw against her cheek, it was the embrace of a stranger.

18

THAT night Margarida lay awake, alternately furious at Brant for going and sad and hurt. She pictured him in the arms of the widow—a woman who understood his feelings about the Apache—and berated herself for letting him leave still angry. She wouldn't allow herself to think he might not come back from Socorro. Though she wasn't sure she could forgive him, that didn't keep her from loving him.

During the day she tried to keep herself so busy she couldn't worry, but she had to struggle to ward off her fears. The trip, she knew, would take at least three days if he and the others rode all night. If they rested at all, they would be gone four or five days.

One of the mornings she visited her mother and was amazed at Elena's apparent contentment and pleasure in Adela's company; it was almost as if Adela were mothering Mama. She tried Lobo again at the Curtis ranch and enlisted Walt's help in disciplining the dog to get along in his new territory. She spent hours on Bailarina practicing roping.

The morning of the fifth day Margarida had just finished dressing when Luisa called up the stairs, "Pedro is here, from the Ross ranch."

Pedro was waiting in the kitchen. "A man has come," he said excitedly, "with maybe news of Señor Jesse." Margarida's heart began to beat with wild anticipation.

On the ride to the Ross ranch, Pedro told Margarida that the man, Hugh Baird, had arrived very early that morning. "An old man, very strange. He talked to Señora Adela first. After that, she sent me to get you. She wanted him to wait until you were there to talk to your mother."

"Did he see my father?"

"Señora Adela said only that he had some news."

When they arrived, Adela ran out to meet Margarida. Her black eyes were snapping with excitement. "From what he told me, this man, Hugh Baird, is a drifter who wanders around doing different kinds of work. He came here because he thinks he knows something about your father. But he'll tell you when he talks to you. Your mother's just getting up. Mr. Baird is in the *sala*."

Margarida hurried to her mother's bedroom, where Elena looked at her with sleepy surprise. "What are you doing here at this hour?"

"Come, Mama. A man's here who may have news of Papa." A frightened look came to Elena's face, but she let Margarida hurry her into clothes and across to the *sala*.

Hugh Baird was small and wiry, with white hair and a soft twang to his voice. "I been all kinds of things, prospector, soldier, trapper, mountain man." He pointed to three jagged scars below his left eye. "Got these from a bear. Well, wandering around like I do, I like to visit a spell with people when I get the chance. Met a man down in Lordsburg. Name of Ted Breedon. Sometime along in January it was. Right pleasant feller."

"Yes, but what about my father?" Margarida asked impatiently.

He gave her a look that said he didn't intend to be hurried. "We got to talking, Ted Breedon and me. Found out we'd both been in Glory Creek. He told me about a man as had a tragedy up there. Reminded me of someone I seen when I was there round about Christmas. Let's see—that must be three months ago now. This Breedon feller thought you folks might like to know about it, so I come here to talk to you. I like to see the country anyhow."

"Mr. Baird," Margarida couldn't help urging, "please tell us anything you know. We've been very worried."

"Well, now. This man I seen was white-haired, about my age. He was living outside town with the Ute. Not quite right in his head. I reckon that's why the Indians took care of him. Indians got great respect for someone not quite right. Think it makes him have special power."

Margarida clenched her hands but knew better than to interrupt again.

"This man come into town once in a while with some of the Indians. He kept asking people all around if they knew somebody called J.J. Asked me, but when I wanted to know who this J.J. was, he couldn't say. Just asked me again. Weren't sure of his own name, but just kept asking. I seen him one other time, and it was the same thing."

Margarida jumped to her feet, feeling as if she might fly apart with excitement. "It's Papa! It must be. Did you see him again?"

"No, ma'am. I don't stay long in one place."

She could have kissed him, tobacco-stained whiskers and all. "Oh, Mr. Baird, we thank you more than I can say." She turned to her mother. "Mama, I know it's Papa! If he was there last Christmas, and with Indians taking care of him, he's probably there now."

"I don't know," Elena said uncertainly. "He sounds sick."

Margarida decided instantly. "I'm going to Glory Creek and get Papa. Once he's home, I'm sure he'll be all right."

"Oh, dear. I just don't know." Elena looked at Adela. "What do you think, Adela?"

Adela took Elena's hand and patted it. "I think Margarida and Brant will do whatever is best."

Elena smiled. "Yes. Of course. Brant will see to it." She turned to Mr. Baird, her manner calm and gracious. "We do thank you, Mr. Baird, for bringing us this very good news. Won't you stay with us until you're rested?"

Margarida waited only long enough to pull Adela aside. "Mama worries me. I hate to ask you to be responsible for her, but I must go for Papa. Can you look after her?"

Adela gave her a loving hug. "Of course. I get along fine with your mother now, and I remember how you've stood by me. But will Brant agree to let you go?"

The question jolted Margarida for a moment. "I don't know. But I'm going. Even if he won't go with me."

"Margarida," Adela protested, "you can't go alone."

"I'll think of something," Margarida promised, then went to say good-bye to her mother. She found Hugh Baird with Elena, who was listening to a story of a bear hunt and smiling as if he were an old friend.

When Margarida reached home, she went first to Brant's desk, where a large map of all the western territories hung on the wall. She'd often looked at the point where the Colorado and San Juan rivers joined, just north of the border between the Arizona and Utah territories. No railroads went near that area; to go by horseback would be a hard trip, but direct. She sat down and began to make a list of supplies and animals they would need.

They! Her thoughts and her fingers stopped on that word. What if Brant weren't willing to go to Glory Creek? Because of Walt and the ranches—and, of course, the Apache at the camp. All the reasons that he shouldn't have gone to Socorro, she thought resentfully.

The pain of their bitter quarrel before Brant left swept over her again. Jumping to her feet, she paced around the room. He'd gone off—well, she wouldn't even wait for him to get back. She'd go tomorrow!

No—she couldn't just go off and leave everything, no matter how angry she felt at Brant. Once, not so long ago, she might have gone, but she'd learned more restraint. Even though he'd left, he knew she'd be here to look after things, so she'd wait until he came back.

The problems of responsibilities here could be solved, she assured herself, and she *had* to go. Whether she were to blame for J.J.'s leaving and Jesse following him didn't matter now. If her father's wounds had affected his reasoning, she would have the best chance of helping him. That meant going herself, not sending a stranger, no matter how reliable and conscientious.

An old jacket of Brant's hung on a peg beside the door. She took it down and held it against her face. The odor brought his image to her so strongly that tears welled up into her eyes. When he'd left to go to Socorro, she'd been hurt and bitterly angry, but even so she loved him and wanted him home safely.

Resolutely she put the jacket back and returned to making her list. If he wouldn't help her go to Glory Creek, she would go anyway—find someone else to go with her. To worry ahead of time was foolish. She'd hope he would understand this was something she must do.

Brant waited until Jaspers left the Socorro saloon and followed him along the night-dark street. It was hard to believe this old man whose steps wavered was the scalp hunter Tall Man had hated and looked for so long. Brant had checked carefully to make sure it was the same man. Watching the uncertain pace of the man ahead of him, Brant didn't feel the anger he wanted, which would spur him to stalk the man and kill him unaware.

When Jaspers turned into the dilapidated adobe

where he lived alone, Tall Man, with Crouched-and-Ready and He-Is-Given-Tests, appeared out of the shadows. They carried bows and arrows. "Two of us should stand guard," Brant said, in a voice so soft it wouldn't carry beyond them. "I will go in with you."

"No, my brother." Tall Man's voice proclaimed his determination. "I have waited too long to avenge my fathers. You are faster and better with a gun than the rest of us. You must guard in front, and Crouched-and-Ready at the back." Without waiting for assent, Tall Man slipped into the darkness, with the two young men following. Brant turned to watch down the road, and a strange feeling came to him, one he hadn't expected. A feeling of relief.

In less than five minutes, Tall Man and the others were back. "It is done."

The sun was just coming up when Brant pulled up Chid and turned in the saddle to look back at Socorro. On the plain below, the buildings clustered beside the Rio Grande were just catching the first morning light. He faced forward and started Chid up the slope.

In front of him Tall Man and the two younger men rode silently. He knew the exultation they felt, and it made his own discomfort greater.

Why hadn't he wanted to kill Jaspers? Because that was the reason for his relief when Tall Man insisted on being the one to execute the scalp hunter. The man certainly deserved to die. Brant had killed before, but then he'd been confronting men who'd tried to kill him first.

To take revenge was the Apache way, and Brant respected the reasons. But he hadn't wanted to do it, and he felt ashamed—that he wasn't worthy of his Apache blood. He pushed Chid harder, wanting to put his doubts behind.

The second night after leaving Socorro, Brant walked Chid down the slope to the house. Tall Man had looked amused at Brant's refusal to camp overnight on the trail again, but they were too close to home. Just before dusk they'd stopped and bathed in a stream, which refreshed him. Even without that he would have pushed on—he couldn't wait longer to get back to Margarida.

His anger on the afternoon he'd departed hadn't lasted; he'd even thought of going home after the dances at the camp, but there hadn't been time. Would her bitterness be gone now? Christ, he hoped so.

The house was dark. The dogs greeted him silently, and no one stirred as he dismounted and took care of his horse. Just inside the kitchen door, he took off his boots and silently ascended the stairs. Easing open the door to the bedroom, he heard the soft sound of Margarida's breathing and smelled the special fragrance of her hair and skin. A rush of desire swept him, and he was ready for her before he discarded his clothes and slid under the covers beside her.

At first Margarida thought he was part of a dream—that her longing for him had conjured him out of the darkness. Then, his arms around her, his warm skin against her breasts as he held her close, and most of all his hungry mouth told her he was no fantasy created by her need. Her heart filled with relief and gratitude—he was alive! Joy pushed away bitterness and anger. "Brant, you're home. You're safe."

If she had doubts left that he was real, they vanished with the sound of his voice. "I couldn't wait to get back to you. To love you."

He proved his words by running his fingers over her face and hair as if to convince himself she was real. Then he found special places she loved for him to kiss—the top of her shoulder, the ridge of her collarbone, the outside corners of her eyes. Her love for him was renewed in his touch, in the sound of his voice repeating her name, in his words as he told her all the things he'd missed doing with her. She had to make sure she remembered the way the bone curved up at the back of his jaw, the muscle of his thigh which seemed so hard it must be bone too, the tiny indentation at the base of his penis. And then the feel of him in her mouth, soft and hard at the same time.

When her sensations swirled in a widening circle, she had to have him at the center. He obliged with his fingers and his mouth and at last his erect shaft, slowly filling her until the circle included them both and then exploded.

They lay, still together, replete with each other. "So much to tell you," he murmured. "But not now."

"No. You're here and safe. That's enough."

It wasn't enough, but she warded off thought. She would steal serenity tonight; tomorrow would come too soon.

The next morning Brant woke to the sound of the bedroom door flying open and Walt's voice. "Margarida, Chid's in the stable! That means . . . Brant! You're home." Brant sat up and was engulfed in Walt's embrace.

Walt pulled back, his face dismayed. "I'm supposed to knock on the door before I come in. I forgot."

Margarida sat up, holding the covers around her, the dark brown tangle of her hair falling over her face and bare shoulders. She looked soft and half-asleep still, and Brant wanted to push her back down and feel her underneath him. Instead he told Walt, "It's all right. Remember next time."

"Did you get to see the man you wanted to talk to in Socorro?" Walt asked.

"Yes." As he got out of bed, he listened to Walt's excited recounting of a fishing expedition and wondered what Margarida would say when they were alone. Last night passion had bridged the gap between them, and he hoped it had healed her anger. He still wasn't sure whether he would tell Margarida he hadn't actually killed Jaspers. It would be hard to admit his difficult feelings.

When he was dressed, he leaned over Margarida and kissed her. Resting his hands beside her on the bed, he said, "I have a lot to tell you when we're alone."

"Let's not wait too long," she said, and her face had a guarded look he remembered from years past. Then it had meant she had some action in mind that her parents would prevent if they could. He wondered what it meant now.

No chance came for them to talk until Brant had greeted Luisa and Juan and admired what Walt had accomplished with Lobo. Finally he walked with her into the woods, where they were alone. Still unsure just what to tell her about Jaspers, he waited until they found a fallen log to sit on.

"What happened in Socorro?" she said. She still had the closed expression he'd noticed earlier.

"No, you first. I think you have something you've been waiting to tell me."

"I didn't want Walt to hear before we could discuss it." Her eyes looked large, and her mouth had the curve which always suggested to him that she had a secret. A hope that he'd decided he wouldn't yet allow himself burst into his thoughts. Was she going to tell him she was pregnant?

"Papa is alive."

His momentary disappointment changed to a different kind of hope. "How do you know? Have you heard from him?"

"No, but a man came who saw Papa in Glory Creek."

As she told him Hugh Baird's story, his excitement grew. "Yes," he said when she finished, "it must be Jesse. We'll have to send someone for him right away."

In her eagerness she grabbed his hands. "No. That won't work. Something's affected his mind, and the Indians are taking care of him. He might not trust strangers. But if he remembers J.J., he'd know me. I'm the one to go."

"Margarida, it's a long way, and in country that can be dangerous. If your father talked to this man Baird, someone else could find him, now that we know he's there."

She let go of his hands and stood, her face determined. "No, Brant. I know I can do it, and I have to. I'll have a better chance than anyone else."

He rose also. "Please, let's be sensible. We'd have to be away for weeks. There's Walt to think of, besides both the ranches."

Her mouth thinned. "You went to Socorro when you weren't sure you'd ever return. You said then you *had* to go. Well, now *I* have to do this."

Under her gingham blouse, her breasts rose and fell with her agitated breathing. A breeze lifted a curl of hair that her braid hadn't caught. He wanted to take her in his arms and shelter her, but he knew at this moment it would offend her pride. "Then we'll work it out to go now," he said quietly, and her face softened.

As their lips met and her breasts pressed against him, he felt the stirring in his loins. Momentarily he considered persuading her to find a smooth place among the leaves to lie down. Reluctantly he abandoned that idea.

"Were you planning to ride off by yourself if I didn't agree?" he asked.

She said, "I'm not that foolish." She didn't look at him, but pink color crept up her face.

His curiosity awakened, he persisted. "What did you expect to do?"

She slowed, then stopped and faced him. "I wasn't sure, but I was going to find someone."

Hurt that she would consider turning to someone else cut through him. With great effort he managed to keep his voice at a reasonable level. "Too bad you don't have a husband who automatically does anything you ask. Your mother should have persuaded Enoch Springer to marry you."

The color in her face darkened to dull red. "At least I know he cared about me."

Brant could feel the blood pounding against his eardrums. Not shouting became harder. "I'm sure you're right. He always liked those friendly kisses you gave him."

Margarida apparently didn't feel the same restraint. "They weren't as friendly as the dances I'm sure you shared with She-Runs-Fast before you went off to murder someone."

"Dances! That's all they were. Just dances." Brant turned and stalked ahead. His rage was partly at himself for having brought up Enoch's name, but also at her.

When she caught up with him, he had his emotions under more control. "I'll ask Tall Man if he'll bring his bride and live here while we're away. Juan will take Tall Man's advice if problems come up. Miguel is very competent. They can take care of things. Walt's my biggest worry."

"Could he go with us?" From Margarida's voice, he knew that the storms weren't all over, but for the present she'd calmed down too.

"Let's talk to him about it."

Just before they reached the yard, she said, "I'm sorry. I didn't mean to talk just about Papa. You still haven't told me about your . . . trip to Socorro."

Brant didn't look at her. All he said was, "Jaspers is dead." It was all he felt like telling her now.

That evening when only the three of them were in the house, they talked to Walt. Brant explained that if Walt wanted to stay home, Tall Man would live in the house.

"We'd go very far away?" Walt asked.

"Yes," Margarida answered, suddenly realizing how much she was asking of Brant.

"Will Bertha still come to visit me if I stay home?"

Brant gave a relaxed grin, the first Margarida had seen since their talk in the trees that morning. "Yes, Bertha will still visit."

Finally Walt said, "I think I'll stay here. But I don't want you to be away very long."

"Not any longer than we can help," Margarida promised as she hugged him.

By the end of the first day on the trail Margarida realized she wasn't as used to riding as she'd been eight months ago when she and Brant married. Household responsibilities had kept her inside too much. Though they traveled only six hours that day, when they stopped, she barely managed to get off Halcon.

"I'll make camp tonight," Brant offered. Though her pride wanted to refuse, her complaining muscles agreed. While she forced herself to move, he took care of Halcon and Chid, the two extra riding horses, and the three burros that carried their gear. If the amused look she saw in his eyes had bloomed into laughter, she thought that, tired and sore as she was, she would have picked up one of the iron skillets and heaved it at him. Even before dark she crawled into the bedroll and was asleep instantly. When Brant, already dressed, waked her the next morning, the only reason she knew he'd slept beside her was the space left in the bedding.

The next day was a little better. Brant made camp again, but Margarida managed to help with the cooking and stay awake until he joined her in the bedroll. After that her muscles toughened quickly and each day they rode longer, finally starting out soon after sunup and riding until sunset, with an hour's rest in the middle of the day. Brant estimated that it would take them two weeks to reach Glory Creek, even traveling as directly as possible.

Leaving from home and being alone restored some ease between them. Margarida could pretend her uncertainties and hurts were gone. She loved sharing a bedroll, even when she did no more than settle close to Brant's warmth. Maybe Mama has things backward, she thought one night after they'd made love. It might be passion that lasts, not love.

Their route took them north and west, through mountains that could have been in western New Mexico or eastern Arizona. In the late April warmth signs of spring came out everywhere—a wild turkey-hen setting on a nest, mountain ferns spreading their feathery fronds, blue and crimson and yellow flowers. At times she and Brant picked their way across wastes of black volcanic rock, and then along streams and up slopes of juniper into canyons where pines grew taller and views grander. If they came across a good patch of wild rye, they stopped to rest the horses and let the burros forage on their favorite grass.

Although during the first days they saw no other travelers, Brant chose campsites which were sheltered and built fires in pockets that wouldn't readily be seen. "This is wild country," he explained, "and I don't care to be surprised by people I don't know."

"But everything looks so peaceful," Margarida commented, surprised. "We haven't met any prospectors, and aren't the Indians on reservations now?"

"Most are, but the ones who aren't might be renegades who fled the reservation because of troubles there."

On the sixth day about noon they saw figures on horseback crossing a distant ridge, and Brant insisted he and Margarida wait in a nearby aspen grove for two hours to be sure to avoid crossing paths with the other travelers. Margarida couldn't quite believe there'd be danger, but she didn't say so.

The afternoon of the eighth day they made a stop in a meadow with good rye grass at the base of some cliffs. While Brant examined a strap which seemed to be chafing one of the burros, Margarida filled the canteens from a small stream. She noticed a clump of particularly vivid lupine partway up a cliff. Putting down the canteens, she climbed up to stretch her legs and to look at the flowers.

Just below the lupine she found a faint trail. It led behind a boulder into an opening in the cliff, almost like a door, which was undetectable from below. She edged along it and came out at one end of a high canyon. From below, no one could tell that the canyon existed.

Retracing her steps, she emerged in front of the boulder and called down to Brant. "There's a secret entrance to a canyon up here. Look. Watch me disappear." He turned and looked up. She ducked around the boulder, waited a moment, then went back out. "Here I am—"

Brant was scrambling up the slope toward her. "Margarida!" His voice was low but penetrating. "Indian above you. Come down. Now!"

For a moment she hesitated, startled, but the urgency in his voice and the speed with which he was climbing toward her sent her down toward him. He reached her, grabbed her hand, whirled, and started back down the slope almost in one motion. Her feet slid on small rocks, sending them rattling down beside her as she struggled to keep up without falling.

She heard a whirring sound, like the hum of bees. Brant turned and crouched, shoving her in front of him so that he was between her and the cliff above. He had his pistol in his other hand. The whir came again, and this time she saw arrows falling around them. Brant shot twice toward the top of the cliff, then pushed her on. "Run! Get on Halcon. Ride for the trees to the right."

As she scrambled down and raced for Halcon, she heard another shot behind her. She snatched the reins loose from a willow bush and mounted, urging Halcon forward even before she dragged herself all the way into the saddle. When she could twist around, she looked back. Brant was on Chid, racing behind her.

At the clump of pines, she started to slow down, but Brant shouted, "Up the slope. Along the trees." A row of trees climbed to what she could now see was a cave partway up another cliff. Halcon hesitated, and for once she wished she wore spurs. She kicked him with the heels of her boots, and he lunged upward.

A gnarled pine stuck out of the cliff to one side of the cave. When she reached it, she slid off Halcon and pulled him as much as possible behind the pine, tightening the reins over a limb to keep him there. When she finished, Brant was beside her. He looped Chid's reins the same way, then snatched his carbine from its scabbard and a sack of ammunition and pushed her across into the cave. It went back about four feet and was high enough at the front for a person to stand up. A ledge of rock formed a low barrier at the opening. They dropped down behind that.

When Margarida's heart slowed so that she could breathe again, she peered cautiously over the ledge. She saw no one, but the burros and extra horses were gone from the grassy patch where they'd been grazing. Brant made a soft sound, and she looked at him. He lay on his left side, working at the shaft of an arrow which protruded from his right leg, just above the knee.

Horrified, she gasped, "Oh, my God," and felt a wave of weakness. Snapping herself to alertness, she said, "What can I do?"

"I have to get the arrow out. Help me twist."

She was sure she couldn't even while she did. His face went dead white, and he gave a groan, but the arrow pulled free. Blood spurted from the jagged wound.

"My bandanna. Make a tourniquet."

With hands she wouldn't let tremble, she unfastened his bandanna from his neck and tied it around his thigh. "Tighter," he ordered. "Put a stick through it and twist."

Among the rocks on the floor of the cave she found a stick. She thrust it through the knot of the bandanna and twisted, holding it until the flow of blood eased. He held on to one end of the cloth. "Take the stick out and jerk," he told her. He jerked at the same time, and the knot tightened.

Brant lay back, his breath rasping, his face pale. Perspiration glistened on his forehead. He picked up the carbine and propped himself up enough to see over the ledge.

Blood had soaked his pant leg. Margarida pulled out her shirt and tore a strip off the bottom. With his knife she cut away his pant leg and made a pad with part of the strip. The rest she used to bind the pad over the wound.

The whirring noise came again. Brant got off two quick shots before the arrows stopped. To one side Chid and Halcon neighed and thrashed. "They've been hit!" she cried.

"No. They're all right. They look too valuable . . . for . . . Indians to kill."

"Who attacked us? Where did they come from?"

"I saw Indian . . . on top of the cliff." He paused, breathing heavily, then went on. "Probably from the canyon . . . you saw."

"But couldn't we call to them, tell them you're Indian?"

"No. Sounds like . . . kind of place . . . hide renegades. Which means . . . dangerous."

His disjointed voice sent terror through her. He lay back, no longer looking out, his face even paler. His breath sounded shallow now. Around the bandage, his thigh and knee were already beginning to swell. Quickly she untied the bandanna.

"Brant. Your leg. It looks—"

"The arrowhead . . . poisoned." He made a rasping sound which was a grotesque laugh. "Someone didn't make poison . . . good enough . . . or I'd be . . . dead now."

"Don't talk. Just rest." She tried to remember what she'd heard about wounds from poisoned arrows. Fatal—they were almost always fatal. No—no! She wouldn't even think that. But he was obviously already very ill. He needed to stay warm—their jackets were tied behind their saddles. Water. He needed water. Then, with despair that squeezed her heart, she remembered. They didn't have water. She hadn't replaced the canteens in the saddlebags!

Frantically she thought of what else there might be. The flask of whiskey. She could pour it on the wound, but he shouldn't drink it. He was almost unconscious now. In her saddlebags were some wild strawberries she'd gathered that morning. She started to get up. Brant reached out a surprisingly strong hand. "No! Stay down!"

As if the words had exhausted him, he closed his eyes. The black lashes against his cheeks made his skin look ghost white. More arrows hit above her and fell down into the cave. She shuddered at the sight of the metal tips as if they were snakes, pushing them aside with her booted foot.

Brant lay now without moving; only his ragged breath told her he hadn't succumbed to the poison. The sun sank toward the horizon. After dark, she reasoned, she could get the berries and flask. The attackers couldn't see her then. Or would they just be waiting to rush the cave? She laid Brant's revolvers and carbine beside her and waited.

Light lingered endlessly. By the time it was dark, no

more arrows had hit the cave for some time. When she could barely see, she cautiously· rose to a kneeling position and waited, her heart pounding so hard she couldn't hear anything else. Brant didn't move. Crawling, she maneuvered an inch at a time across the space to the horses.

Halcon snorted once before she could reach him to quiet him, and Chid stepped nervously, his hooves striking the rocks like timpani. She froze, her back muscles tensed, waiting illogically for the arrow to strike her. When she heard nothing, she untied the jackets, then opened her saddlebags and fished out the strawberries she'd stored in a square tin. Chid backed off when she moved to him, then quieted, and she got out the flask. Both horses must be thirsty, but she couldn't do anything about that.

When she reached Brant again, he was stirring. "Where . . . ?" he said hoarsely, and couldn't finish.

"Right here," she soothed him. She crushed the strawberries between her fingers and forced the pulp between his lips. By the time he wouldn't open his mouth any longer, most of the strawberries were gone. Ignoring her own dry mouth, she closed the tin on the rest of the berries. Praying he would forgive her for the pain, she poured some of the whiskey over the bandage. He jerked, but didn't cry out. Though his skin felt hot, he shivered. She tucked his coat around him and put on her jacket.

The night held only sounds she could identify. The snuffling of the horses. A coyote barking in the distance. An evening breeze soughing through the pines. Nothing told her where their attackers were. They could have left, she thought, without real hope.

Carefully she touched Brant's leg. It felt hot enough to burn her, and she could tell it was more swollen. She arranged the guns where she could reach them instantly and forced herself to lie beside him. Stars, indifferent to human suffering, glittered as engagingly as they had when she and Brant had lain together in the bedroll.

She thought of her bitter anger over his going to Socorro—and her resentment of his desire to be Apache. Her fear he'd leave her sometime because that desire meant more to him than she did. How unimportant that seemed now, when he might die. As she listened to his uneven breathing, she had to fight off despair. No, she told herself fiercely, she wouldn't give in to her fear. She'd wait until daylight and hope whoever attacked them had gone. But she knew she'd never been more terrified of what morning would bring.

19

A sound jerked Margarida awake. For a moment she could hardly believe she'd fallen asleep. She didn't feel Brant next to her and sat up, terrified.

In the gray light of dawn she could just see him, lying on his side a little away from her. Holding her own breath, she listened for his. Her terror diminished— he was alive. He'd rolled so that his weight rested on his wound; it must have been a groan from him that woke her. He turned back, then was still again.

Her mouth felt so dry she could hardly swallow, but she ignored it, listening for noises. Increasing calls of birds and the soft rise and fall of a morning breeze sounded peaceful. Soon she'd know whether the Indians who'd attacked them were still there.

Her mind whirled in a pool of emptiness. No! she told herself. Think. Make a plan. She mustn't give in to panic. Brant couldn't help. It was up to her.

Taking deep breaths, she willed herself to composure. She wasn't sure whether this valley was in New Mexico or the Arizona territory, but these Indians might be Apache. She concentrated on remembering the last visit with Brant's grandmother, when the old woman had talked about Apache ways. If these Indians weren't Apache, that information might not be right. But it was all she had.

Shiwóyé had said that the Apache didn't always kill whites—that they respected the lives of people who surrendered. Margarida remembered that Cochise, the

Chiricahua chief, had gone to a fort under a white flag. The officer in charge tried to imprison Cochise and did kill his two brothers. *Shiwóyé* had said the Apache would never behave so dishonorably.

The story also showed that the Apache used and recognized a white flag. If she surrendered to these Indians, maybe they wouldn't kill her and Brant. She would carry a white flag and try to talk to them. Would she be able to? A few Indians understood English, and more knew Spanish, but what if these didn't? Oh, God. If only she'd learned Apache.

Perhaps the Indians below would spare Brant if they knew he had Apache blood, she thought, and for the first time was grateful for his heritage. These men might be from a group who hated the Apache, but most Indians probably hated whites even more.

Brant stirred again and she touched his forehead. It burned with fever. His leg and knee looked swollen, and she realized she should have removed the boot. Now she wasn't sure she could. The bandage showed dark red where the blood had seeped through. Water— he must have water, and the horses needed it too. Her own thirst nagged at her. How much worse his must be.

Brant's eyelids flickered and then opened. She found the rest of the strawberries and touched his lips with a crushed berry. He moved, but didn't open his mouth.

She spoke softly. "Brant. Can you understand me?"

His lips opened a fraction and he whispered, "Yes."

"You must try to eat this."

"Can't."

She held the berry, juice beginning to run down her fingers, and wanted to weep. Sternly she caught herself. "You must try."

Finally his lips parted, and she let the juice trickle into his mouth. When he closed his lips, he didn't open them again.

She looked at his still face and knew that whatever

chance there would be with the Indians, she had to take it. Brant had mentioned renegades. She shuddered, but their situation was too desperate to waver at the risk.

"Brant!" His face quivered, and he opened his eyes. "What words tell another Apache that you're Apache too?"

His lips moved, but no sound came out. He tried again, and managed a hoarse "*Chihinne.*"

"*Chihinne*?"

"Yes."

The light was growing stronger. Outside Chid and Halcon stirred restlessly on their tethers at the pine tree. Cautiously Margarida looked over the barrier.

Something moved in the trees beyond the meadow where they'd stopped to let the burros graze. In the increasing light, she made out the figures of five men. From what she could tell at this distance, they were dressed like the Apache in *shiwóyé*'s camp. She didn't know if all Indians wore similar clothes, but the familiarity heartened her.

She would need something white. The only things she had were her camisole and drawers. Half-hysterically she thought that it was good she wasn't wearing the plum-colored underwear. She took off her jacket and shirt, then the camisole. The air felt cold on her bare breasts before she put the shirt and jacket back on.

When she looked again, one man was in the meadow, looking up toward the cave. Apparently he felt confident he was out of rifle range, or else thought she and Brant were both dead. *Now*, her reason told her. Now is the time to try, before they start shooting arrows at us.

Brant stirred restlessly, his eyes still closed. What if the Indians shot her as soon as she left the cave, before they saw the white cloth? She'd die, and never see Brant or her family again. Never have his children.

Never grow old. Her resolution retreated. Better to stay here. Wait. Maybe the Indians would leave.

She knew she must conquer her fears. Brant would probably die without more care than she could give him here. If nothing else, the attackers would never go away without Chid and Halcon. Either horse might be able to outrun the Indians if Brant could ride, but she didn't think he could. And the Indians would be on them before they could get down the slope below. She looked out again. The Indian in the meadow had gone back to the others.

The cliff faced east, and a narrow cloud above the horizon was changing from rose to gold. The sun would rise in a few minutes, and sunlight would strike the cliff. Then the white camisole would show up best. Then she must go out. She shuddered, and sweat came out on her palms.

As she waited, a childhood memory returned. She must have been seven years old; she and Walt and J.J. had been following Brant. They came to a deep pool at the bottom of a waterfall. Brant climbed to the top of a boulder and jumped into the pool, a drop that seemed enormous to her then. As usual she wanted to do whatever he did. She went up onto the rock and looked down at water terrifyingly far away. Then she'd shut her mind to thought and jumped. That was what she had to do now—go without thinking.

The sun appeared. She picked up the camisole. Should she put it on the end of the rifle? No—better not to be armed. She thought of getting on Halcon and riding down. But that might look as if she were trying to escape.

She leaned down and kissed Brant's burning cheek and his eyes opened. Gently she pressed another kiss on his cracked lips. He caught her wrist. "What?"

"I'm going down below."

"No." His weakened grip couldn't hold her, and she pulled her hand away.

"I have to." Before she could think, she crawled over the rock ledge. Holding the camisole high in the first rays of sunlight, she started down the slope.

Her feet slid on the pebble-strewn slope. Keeping her arm above her head made her awkward, and she almost lost her balance. She had to watch her feet, so she couldn't look at the Indians below. It was easier not to look.

At every step, she heard imagined whirs and felt imagined arrows piercing her. Perspiration formed on her face and body under the jacket. She slipped again, and in righting herself, dropped the camisole. Panic almost overtook her as she scrambled to pick it up again. Doggedly she thrust it up into the air and continued on.

When the slope leveled off, she dared to look up. Across the meadow the five men stood at the edge of the trees, three with bows and arrows and two holding spears.

The meadow looked miles wide. Her legs began to tremble, and she thought if she tried to walk she would fall down. The men waited, unmoving. God, she thought despairingly, why don't they just shoot their arrows? Anything would be better than having to cross that space!

One of her booted feet took a step forward, and then the other. She watched herself start across the meadow and marveled that anyone so filled with terror could move at all. Her arm ached from holding the camisole over her head. She felt like a crude figure children draw, only her legs somehow moving, everything else frozen in rigid position.

Unbelievably the five figures in front of her grew larger. When the Indians were as far away as across the corral at home, her legs wouldn't move any longer. Her elbow bent, letting down her flag of surrender. She'd done all she could to reach them. It was up to them now.

Her heart raced so fast that she thought it would choke off her breath. But she stiffened her neck defiantly, determined not to cringe. Steeling herself to control her tremors, she stared steadily at the Indians.

They wore buckskin shirts and breechclouts, with cloth leggings. All had headbands around long black hair. Their faces looked menacing, and they held their weapons ready. Round pieces of stiff hide, like shields she'd seen at *shiwóyé*'s camp, lay on the ground beside them. One man had a white stripe painted across his face just below his eyes. The man in the center said something that sounded like the Apache she'd heard at the camp at home.

She tried once to speak and couldn't make her voice work. Desperately she tried again. "Do you know English?"

Again the man in the center said something she didn't understand. *"Habla español?"* she asked. He responded, but not in Spanish.

She spread her hands in a gesture she hoped would tell her meaning and said, "Surrender." The man with the painted stripe raised his lance. Terror rippled through her. The center man barked a command, and the other one put his weapon back down. She breathed again.

The man in the center appeared to be the leader, so she decided to appeal to him. She pointed up toward the cave and said, *"Chihinne."*

The leader looked surprised. Her stomach drew into a tight ball, but she pointed at the cave again and repeated, *"Chihinne."*

A tall man with angry eyes started speaking rapidly. The leader put a hand on the other man's arm and said only one word, but the taller man subsided. The leader walked over in front of Margarida and stood staring, as if trying to make up his mind about her.

She pointed again to the cliff and added a word that she'd learned meant "my husband." *"Shika'. Shika' chihinne."* She thought probably she was using the word for "Apache" that only an Apache would use for himself, but she hoped they would understand her meaning. How could she let them know Brant was wounded and wouldn't shoot at them? She said again, *"Shika',"* and touched her leg, then moaned and held her forehead and closed her eyes for a moment.

Apparently either the gesture or her tone of voice meant something because the leader stepped back, and the men began speaking among themselves. The painted man still watched her, his lance in his hand.

As the Indians continued talking, she began to see details. To subdue her dread she silently assigned them names. The man who'd spoken first was definitely the leader, she decided, because the others deferred to him when he spoke. Leader appeared to be the oldest, sixty or more. Strong lines marked his weathered skin, making grooves on each side of his broad nose, running past a sad mouth. He was medium height with heavy shoulders and thick chest and body. A large star-shaped disk hung from his necklace.

The man next to him looked about Brant's age. He stood a head taller than Leader, with a lean, bony face and straight nose and jaw. His eyes, when he glanced at her, were fierce, as if he would be an unrelenting enemy. The name of Violent One fit him.

The Indian with the painted stripe was young, barely old enough to be a man—a Painted Boy. The fourth and fifth men were older, in between the age of the leader and the others. One, a small man, had a sleepy expression around his eyes and a drooping mouth; she called him Sleepy Eyes. The last was slender and almost as tall as Violent One, but his eyes lacked the same intensity. His face was handsome, and he smiled several times. Because that made him look less fierce, she thought of him as Smiling Man.

Violent One began to shout, pulling out a knife and making threatening gestures toward Margarida. A

barked word from Leader silenced him, but his angry
eyes raised all the terror she'd managed to restrain.
Deliberately she stared back at him, stiffening her face
to conceal her fear. Finally he looked away.

Leader said something more, and the men picked
up their shields. He motioned for her to walk in front
of them, circling to the left, around the edge of the
meadow. This time as she started out, she didn't dread
an immediate arrow. Now her frantic thoughts were
with Brant. Would he be conscious? What was he
thinking? At least if they killed her, he still had the
guns.

Her shirt clung to her, damp with perspiration. She
could feel the sweat under her breasts and armpits, in
the edge of her hair, and trickling down her neck
below her braid. Without the camisole the shirt felt
rough against her nipples. As they neared a stand of
pines, they reached the tiny stream, and suddenly her
thirst was unbearable. She stopped and turned, pointing to the stream. Remembering what she thought was
the word for water, she said, "Tú."

Violent One scowled, but Leader nodded. She knelt
at the stream and scooped water up into her hand.
Nothing had ever felt better on her tongue. She drank
only a little, then splashed some water on her face
before drinking more. She wished she had a container,
to take water to Brant. Realizing her camisole would
absorb some, she dipped it quickly into the stream,
then balled it up so as not to lose too much water. She
stood up and started on.

When they reached the pine trees, she realized this
must be where the men had been the previous day
when they'd shot arrows into the cave. An area of
open grass stretched between this stand of trees and
the pines which grew up the slope below the cave.
Here Leader stopped.

Careful to make no motion that would look suspicious, she waited while they talked. Violent One stepped

close to her, and she had to keep her muscles rigid not to move away from him. He seemed to be arguing with the others. Not until Leader said something in a sharp tone did he walk away, and Sleepy Eyes took the place next to her. The four other men spread out among the trees.

Sleepy Eyes pulled a long knife from his belt. Margarida barely choked off a scream. He put his hand on her shoulder and pushed her so that she had her back to him. For a moment of horror she waited for the knife thrust between her shoulders. But he gave her a shove, and she realized she was to walk toward the cave.

She stumbled forward, struggling to pull air into her lungs. When she could breathe again, worry about Brant gave her new energy and sent her hurrying up the slope. Sleepy Eyes was almost completely sheltered by his shield as they approached the cave. Halcon neighed when she passed him, but she didn't stop until she climbed over the rocky ledge.

Brant had pulled himself back so that he was propped up against the cave wall, a revolver on his lap. She dropped down beside him and set the gun aside. "It's all right. They're Apache, and they know you're Apache too," she told him, and didn't know whether anything she said was true.

She could see by his glazed eyes that only his will was keeping him conscious. With her wet camisole she first wiped his lips, then squeezed the cloth so that the water ran into his mouth. The first bit ran out again, but after that he swallowed. He whispered, "Are you . . . ?"

"I'm all right." She could feel tears starting down her face. Furtively she wiped them away. No tears! she told herself fiercely. From what she'd learned, the Apache admired courage and endurance. If that would win their regard, she would be the bravest, most uncomplaining woman they had ever seen.

Sleepy Eyes picked up the guns and the sack of ammunition. He pointed to Brant's cartridge belt. Margarida unfastened it and gave it to the Indian. After that he went to the mouth of the cave and waved. Soon she heard the sound of the men's voices and their feet on the slope. A shadow fell on her; it was Leader, with Violent One behind him.

Leader knelt and looked at Brant, glancing at his leg but studying his face. She pointed to Brant and said, *"Chihinne."* Leader's face had a look she thought was doubt.

She pointed to Brant again. *"Shiwóyé chihinne."*

Brant's eyelids drooped, but he opened them again. Drops of sweat appeared on his forehead, but he stared steadily at Leader.

The burly Indian examined Brant's leg. He pulled at the bandage, and Brant's face paled even more. Margarida clenched her jaw shut to keep from screaming at the Indian to stop. She felt as if Brant's suffering were part of her, but if he could endure his pain, she must also. Leader looked around, then carefully picked up the twisted arrow that had struck Brant's leg. Margarida saw an expression she might have called awe on a less formidable face.

Violent One stooped down beside them. Leader showed the other man the arrow and pointed to Brant's leg, talking as he did so. Violent One scowled and let out a torrent of angry words. Leader listened, then said something in a stern voice, as if announcing a decision. The other man spat what sounded like a curse, but he left the cave.

Margarida sank back, holding to Brant's hand. He pulled at her, and she leaned close to hear his low voice. "Apache. Not . . . kill us . . . now." The frozen knot in her center dissolved a little. Regardless of the dangers they faced, they were still alive. And maybe one of their captors would know how to help Brant.

A short time later Painted Boy and Smiling One

appeared and collected the arrows scattered on the floor of the cave, handling them carefully. When they finished, Leader motioned to Brant to get up.

"But he can't walk," Margarida protested.

"No!" Brant's hoarse whisper silenced her. He pushed himself up and rolled over, getting his good leg under him. His face whitened at the motion, and she saw the muscles of his jaw clench, but he made no sound. Holding to the cave wall, he dragged himself erect.

She moved to his side. For a moment she thought he would push her away, but then he put one hand on her shoulder. As he took a step forward, she felt the force of the weight he rested on her and also the shudder that went through him. She stiffened her own muscles, trying not to think of his pain, waiting between each tortured step.

At the edge of the cave he let himself down on the ledge and swung his leg over. In the sunlight his skin looked so white that she could see the blood pulsing in the veins at his temples. Perspiration ran down the sides of his face, but he still made no sound.

When Margarida followed, she saw that Halcon was gone. Sleepy Eyes was attempting to untie Chid. The horse was rearing the length of his tether and striking out with his hooves. "No," Margarida cried, and scrambled across to Chid, afraid the Indian might become impatient and hurt or kill the horse. "Chid. Easy. Easy." At her voice he calmed a little. Approaching cautiously, she spoke again, and he subsided and let her stroke his quivering neck. Finally he quieted enough that she could untie the rein from the pine tree. She offered it to the Indian, but he gestured her ahead of him.

Instead, she led Chid to where Brant still rested on the ledge. "You should ride." He shook his head, but he gripped the edge of the saddle and pulled himself to his feet, then grasped Chid's mane. Leader started down the slope. Holding to his horse, Brant followed.

Margarida stayed close beside him, and the four other Indians walked behind them.

Margarida didn't want to watch each time Brant had to put his weight on his right leg, but she couldn't look away. At the bottom where she thought he would try to mount, he continued across the meadow, Chid moving in rhythm to his master's irregular steps. Leader crossed the area where she'd confronted the Apaches and continued into the aspens beyond. Finally he turned and gave a command.

Brant stopped, leaning against Chid, then slowly let himself down to the ground. As if he couldn't deny his weakness any longer, he lay back. She sank down beside him. Chid stood quietly, his reins dangling to the ground.

Painted Boy stayed close beside them with his lance at hand. The others went a short distance away and squatted down, talking. If Brant hadn't seemed at the end of his strength, she would have asked him what their captors were saying. Instead she watched them.

The Indians' voices grew more strident. Obviously they were arguing. Her fear flooded back. She remembered stories of torture and mutilation, and slow, agonizing deaths. She wrenched her attention away from the Indians and concentrated on looking around.

Not far away among the aspens she saw the burros and horses from the Curtis ranch. Halcon was tethered with them. Clothing, supplies, and the open packs lay scattered around on the ground. She saw the canteens, the ones she'd filled yesterday and then so carelessly left out of the saddlebags. A wave of guilt swept her, but she pushed it away. With water they might have stayed in the cave a little longer, but it wouldn't have saved them. And regret couldn't help them now.

The stream curved around the edge of the aspen grove. She looked at Painted Boy and gestured toward the water. *"Tú?"* she asked. He called to the arguing men. Leader nodded, and Smiling Man came and motioned for her to go to the stream. As she stood, her knees felt shaky, as if she had hiked for days instead of crossing a meadow and back.

With Smiling Man following, she circled the still-arguing Indians and got the canteens. After refilling them with fresh water, she went back to Brant. His eyes opened when she knelt beside him, and he drank small sips of the water before he lay back. She doubted he heard much of what was going on, but he was still alive; his body was fighting the poison. She clung to that thought.

Leader raised his voice, speaking sharply, and the men stood up. Violent One stalked off, carrying the carbine. Leader motioned to Sleepy Eyes, who came over to Margarida. He said something to her which sounded like a command and pointed to the place where the packs and gear lay on the ground. She looked at him, trying to understand what he wanted. His eyes lost their sleepy look as he grabbed her arm and pulled her to her feet, then over to the gear. Picking up a pack, he shoved it at her and repeated his orders. Hoping she wasn't showing how frightened she felt, she started collecting the scattered supplies and putting them in the pack.

She'd never loaded the packs before, only helped Brant with them, and fitting the gear in was even more difficult with her shaky hands. Some of the supplies were missing, and she recognized a charred edge of cloth in the ashes of a fire. Violent One came and stood over her, making her blood chill and her fingers fumble even more. After what seemed an hour he hissed, *"Isda',"* and stomped away. Frantically she stuffed clothing and food and utensils in together, not caring what happened as long as Violent One would only leave her alone. When the packs were finally ready, she was trembling so much she had to crouch for several minutes beside the last pack before she stood up.

The men were waiting, looking at her. Why? she wondered. They couldn't expect her to put the packs on the burros. She couldn't even lift them! Anger, wonderful anger filled her, pushing back fear. Without stopping to think, she crossed her arms and stood glaring at the Apaches. For a moment they stared back, then Smiling Man earned his name. With a shrug, he picked up one of the packs and put it on a burro. Surprisingly, Leader did the same, and then Sleepy Eyes loaded one as well. She felt a brief moment of triumph.

When the burros were ready, Smiling Man fastened them in a string with the horses, including Halcon. While he was doing that, Sleepy Eyes obliterated the signs of activity, scattering the fire and covering the burned dirt with other earth, smoothing away tracks.

Under a tree Margarida found a stout branch which Brant might use as a crutch and took it back to where he lay. When she gave him more water, he pointed to Chid. She turned to Painted Boy, touching Chid and saying, *"Tú."* Painted Boy made a sound which seemed like assent, so she led Chid to the small stream and let him drink. This time no one followed her, though Violent One watched her.

When she returned, Leader was standing beside Brant, who was sitting up. She offered Brant the stick, but he shook his head and used the horse to pull himself erect. Even holding Chid's mane, Brant swayed. His face hadn't regained any color, and his eyes looked dull and sunken. She wanted to help him, but Leader motioned her ahead, toward the cliff she'd climbed the previous day.

The string of animals, led by Sleepy Eyes, had already started for the cliff. She followed, carrying the stick, straining to hear the sounds behind her, trying not to look back to see if Brant could manage. But she knew that he would collapse before he would seem to need her help.

They paused while Smiling Man and Painted Boy went back and smoothed over the tracks across the meadow. Then they started up the cliff. The clump of blue lupine which had attracted her yesterday still splashed its color in the sunlight. When they reached the boulder, Sleepy Eyes led the line of animals to the right. Smiling Man, at the end of the string, took Chid's reins. Brant took the stick from Margarida, braced himself against the boulder, and let go of the horse. Immediately Chid began to protest, backing and rearing, threatening to send Smiling Man tumbling.

Margarida shouted, "Wait," and, dodging his hooves, grabbed for Chid's reins. Smiling Man jumped out of the way. Sleepy Eyes halted the string of animals going to the right and looked back.

Leader stood, as if deciding, then said something to Sleepy Eyes, who started the string up again, with Smiling Man walking at the end. Leader motioned to Margarida to take Chid and follow the other animals. She stood paralyzed, dread threatening to overwhelm her. She couldn't go with the horses and be separated from Brant!

Violent One's eyes fixed on her, and she thought she saw in his face the hope she would make the wrong motion. She didn't doubt what he'd do then. Clutching at rational thought, she decided they must all be going to the same place, but the trail past the boulder was too narrow for the horses. She dragged her courage back up from deep inside her and took Chid's reins.

Leader went ahead of Brant and disappeared around the boulder. Brant, leaning partly on the branch and partly against the rock, went next. Painted Boy followed. Violent One made a threatening gesture at Margarida, and she turned and led Chid after the other horses.

They zigzagged up the steep and rocky face of the cliff. Half of the time Margarida's legs shook, and she barely kept a grip on Chid's reins. She understood why no one rode the horses up this way; an animal couldn't have managed with the weight of a rider. At places it took the three men to force the burros upward.

The descent on the other side was little better; most of the time Margarida was sliding, trying to find a hold for her feet. By the time they reached the bottom, Chid had led her as much as she had led him. She could barely stagger when they rejoined the others, too exhausted to feel afraid.

Brant was sitting, leaning against a rock, his eyes closed. When she reached him, she couldn't breathe herself until she saw the rise and fall of his chest.

They were in a deep, narrow valley with a stream running through the center. It looked as if the valley stretched northward for a long distance.

At a command from Leader, Brant opened his eyes and used the stick and the rock to drag himself to his feet. Leader and Sleepy Eyes mounted two of the extra horses, and Violent One took Halcon. When Margarida saw him on her horse, she had to strangle a protest. Smiling Man and Painted Boy rode double on the third extra horse. No one was willing to try Chid.

That meant she and Brant would ride Chid or walk. By now Brant's face was set in lines of pain, but Margarida guessed no one else would know how much he was suffering. She reached out to help him, but he ignored her. He put his left foot in the stirrup and swung his right leg over without a change of expression to show what must have been agony. He even held his hand to her and helped pull her up. But when she was behind him, she felt him sag against her and could hardly bear to think of what his efforts were costing. She leaned into him, helping him to stay upright.

As they started off through the hidden valley, its high walls and rock-jagged rim loomed menacingly above them. In the varying tension of Brant's body,

Margarida guessed that he was going in and out of consciousness. Fiercely she held to him. Last night she'd lain awake, terrified of what the morning would bring. Now she still didn't know what lay ahead, and at this moment she didn't want to know. But she would do everything to survive.

20

BORN-TWICE stood in front of her wickiup, her calico skirt blowing in the afternoon breeze. Under tousled brown hair, her gray eyes looked worried. A frown creased her face, emphasizing lines which showed her thirty-nine years. She hoped the commotion at the other end of the camp meant the men were returning.

Yesterday the guard at the south gate to the hidden canyon had signaled with his mirror that someone had found the entrance. It frightened her. Before he left, Red-Rope had told her not to worry, but her husband didn't worry about anything. She couldn't be like him—she remembered her childhood too well. Though she'd never want to be white again, she couldn't forget how her world had changed overnight—her father killed, her mother captured, and she adopted by an Apache family.

She was glad Old-Man-He-Knows-A-Lot had gone to see what happened, as well as He-Starts-Fights. The younger man was their most skillful warrior, but he didn't stop to think before he acted. She felt sorry his first wife and children had died, but now he loved killing too much. That's why Old-Man-He-Knows-A-Lot didn't want He-Starts-Fights to be their next leader. Even Red-Rope didn't like him.

As long as Old-Man-He-Knows-A-Lot was chief, she felt safe. He'd led them to this refuge when they had to flee the San Carlos reservation after the murders. Because of his caution and good judgment, they'd been here almost two years. If either of the chief's sons had lived, one of them would probably have been chosen to lead the band when their father died. But the next chief might be He-Starts-Fights—and the band might end up back at San Carlos with their men imprisoned, or living hunted lives in Mexico.

Other women and children ran past her to meet the warriors. No use hurrying, she thought; Red-Rope would be last as usual. Then she saw the horses, and her steps quickened too. The horses from the last raid had been poor ones, and too few for both eating and riding. How she loved horse meat! She hoped Red-Rope had claimed one.

When she saw her husband, she knew she'd be disappointed. He was riding double with He-Stirs-Up-Earth. Red-Rope would likely let the young man have the horse, because he knew how much He-Stirs-Up-Earth wanted one. Her husband was too easygoing. Since they had no children, he had a soft spot for a young man who listened to him.

The horses stopped. Old-Man-He-Knows-A-Lot dismounted and was showing guns to the warriors who had stayed in camp. Born-Twice was glad about the weapons—the band needed guns, and especially bullets, which had run out. Then she saw the two captives on the black stallion.

She almost went back to her wickiup. Most whites were evil and should die, but she liked it better when captives were killed away from camp. Though her first mother had been made a slave and not put to death, Born-Twice thought of her whenever she saw prisoners. She couldn't join in the killing with the other women, and she felt ashamed.

The man captive looked sick, she thought, or maybe he was very frightened. Born-Twice had to catch her breath when she saw the woman. She looked like Born-Twice's early memories of her first mother—dark hair in a long braid, golden skin. It gave Born-Twice a shivery feeling.

"Old woman," Red-Rope said at her elbow, "what do you think of these horses?"

"I think you will give ours to He-Stirs-Up-Earth."

"He claimed it from me. What could I do?" He tried to look sorrowful, but the smile he usually wore came back.

She turned away; it was hopeless to argue with him, and she was more interested in the captives. The woman was standing by the horse, and the man was dismounting. Born-Twice could tell from the way he moved that he was hurt. The bloody bandage on his swollen right leg surprised her. The medicine man had made a special poison for the arrows. If the man had been hit by an arrow, he should be dead now. Maybe he had injured himself some other way. The woman was helping him stand.

Born-Twice moved closer to the captives, hoping she might hear them talking. She could still understand English, though it was hard for her to speak now. At first she'd talked to her white mother, and later when the band had lived at the San Carlos reservation, she'd listened to the American soldiers. It had been useful that someone in the group understood what the soldiers were saying, especially when they didn't realize she did.

Two of the warriors took away all the horses except for the black stallion. He-Starts-Fights was arguing with Old-Man-He-Knows-A-Lot. Born-Twice could tell he didn't like the chief's answers, but he gave up and came back to the captives. "We will put them in the center wickiup," he said, his voice still angry.

The captive man spoke. "I must . . . care . . . my horse." Though his voice sounded slurred, to Born-Twice's astonishment, he had used Apache. Few whites learned the language, unless like her they'd been captured.

He-Starts-Fights looked as if he wanted to hit the man, and Born-Twice wondered why he didn't. "It is not your horse," he said angrily.

"Name . . . *ch'üdn binant'a'*," the captive said, and Born-Twice sucked in her breath. Who would name a horse "devil"? It would be bad luck. Didn't this man care?

The woman captive said in English to the man, "Are you talking about Chid? What's the matter?"

He-Starts-Fights pushed the woman back. He bound the man's hands in front of him and then jerked, making the man fall. The woman started forward, but the man said, "No!" and struggled to his feet. Born-Twice thought his swollen leg must hurt very much, but he didn't cry out.

When He-Starts-Fights started to pull the captive away, the horse reared and gave a piercing scream. He-Stirs-Up-Earth caught the reins, but the stallion was too strong. Red-Rope chuckled and went to help the young man. The stallion was dragging both of them off their feet when the woman ran forward and spoke to the horse. The horse quieted, and stood trembling. The two men let go of the reins, leaving him to the woman.

"Let the slave take care of the horse," He-Starts-Fights said.

"Wife . . . not . . . slave," the man said, and Born-Twice was amazed at his defiance when he could hardly stand.

He-Starts-Fights scowled, but he turned to Red-Rope and said, "Take her to care for the horse, and bring her back."

"It is not for you to give me orders," Red-Rope retorted, his usually pleasant voice angry.

"You are right." Old-Man-He-Knows-A-Lot had come up.

"I will do it," Red-Rope said more calmly, "but not because he tells me."

Born-Twice saw fear in the woman's eyes, but she didn't cry or scream. That was different from the way Born-Twice's mother had acted, and she felt a mixture of unwilling admiration and sympathy for this woman.

Margarida, waiting beside Chid, strained to hear every word, as if by listening to each syllable she would somehow be able to understand. She'd heard Violent One say that word again, *isda'*, when he'd looked at her. He'd used it with such hatred and contempt that her skin had gone cold with fear. Then Brant had used the same word, along with one she thought meant "wife."

Now Violent One was leading Brant away. With his hands bound, Brant had to put his weight on his right leg to walk, and she had to marshal all her restraint not to run to him.

Smiling Man motioned for her to follow him with Chid. As they walked in front of the row of wickiups, women and children watched her, chattering and laughing. She should be terrified, but she felt so exhausted that nothing seemed real. If she wouldn't be separated from Brant, and Violent One would leave them alone—that was all she cared now.

Smiling Man had her take Chid to a small stream to drink and then tether him to a tree near a brush corral where she saw Halcon, along with the other horses. Deliberately she turned her back so she couldn't see him. No use thinking about what might happen to him.

Her hands shook so that she could hardly manage to unsaddle Chid. Smiling Man watched her struggles, then helped her lift off the saddle. She said, "Thank you," and wondered at herself. But somehow that gesture made him more human and less frightening. He pointed for her to go back.

When they stopped in front of one of the wickiups, he motioned her inside. At first she could see only Painted Boy crouched just inside the entrance, obviously a guard. Then she saw Brant on a robe on the ground, his hands still bound, his eyes closed. Her knees gave way, and she sank down beside him, turning her face away from her captors so they couldn't see her tears. At least she and Brant would be together. She felt she could bear anything except being apart from him.

He moved restlessly, and she looked fearfully at his right leg. In the light she couldn't be sure, but she thought it was more swollen than earlier. The boot must come off. She wiped away her tears and turned to Painted Boy. He didn't have a knife, as far as she could see, but she pointed to Brant's boot and pantomimed cutting it.

Painted Boy called to someone outside, and a man she hadn't seen before entered. He took a knife from inside his moccasin and forced it under the top of Brant's boot. At the first touch of the knife, Brant jerked awake. All color drained from his face as the man started to saw at the boot. Watching Brant, Margarida felt such pain tear her that she had to hold one hand over her mouth to keep from screaming. Partway through, he fainted, and relief loosened the knot in her chest. After sawing through the leather to the sole, the man with the knife stepped back.

Margarida stared at the boot and knew she must do the rest. Gathering her courage, she gripped the opened boot and pulled. Brant groaned—the first sound of pain he'd made since their capture—and she continued only because she had to. When she finished, her clothes were sweat-dampened again, but the boot was off. She sat down beside him and folded over into a ball to keep from being sick.

When she could straighten up, she pantomimed for the man to slit the trouser leg. After he did that, even in the limited light of the wickiup she could see the red streaks which radiated outward from the wound. Trying not to think about what that meant, she took her camisole from her jacket pocket and wiped Brant's face, then looked at the bloody bandage. Only a few bright stains showed beside the brown ones. Should she do something else? She found a gourd and a basket of water in it and managed to rouse Brant enough to give him water. After she drank herself, she lay down beside him. Nothing seemed as important as resting, and within minutes she felt herself drifting into sleep.

Outside the wickiup Born-Twice hesitated, not wanting to go in. The woman who reminded her of her mother gave her strange feelings, but Red-Rope had insisted. "You are to help with the captives," he'd told her when he returned to their wickiup from the council, "and listen to what they say. We need to know more about this man who looks white and lives when he should have died. His woman says he is Apache, and he speaks the language of the Warm Springs people. He wears the clothing of the whites, but he carries moccasins and breechclout with him."

"Does the medicine man know why this man lives?"

"He says the man may have Enemies-Against-Power for poisons. And for other things too."

Born-Twice finished stirring the stew in the cooking tin she'd carried from the reservation at San Carlos. "Am I to take them food?"

Red-Rope sniffed appreciatively at the smell of the venison. "Yes, but don't let them see you understand what they say."

"What will happen to them?"

"He-Starts-Fights wants to kill them now, but Old-Man-He-Knows-A-Lot says to wait. We need warriors. If this man has great powers, he could help us. He might teach one of us his sacred words." Red-Rope sat on the hide spread out on the floor. "Is the meat ready? I am hungry."

Born-Twice moved the meat in front of her husband and sat beside him. "How could we trust such a man?"

Red-Rope said confidently, "Old-Man-He-Knows-A-Lot will have a way."

So she'd brought food to the wickiup where the captives were. Now she upbraided herself for her silly notions about the captive woman and went inside. "I will help with the woman," she told He-Stirs-Up-Earth.

The woman lay beside the man, asleep. Born-Twice looked at her curiously. Now she wasn't sure if the woman looked like her white mother; it had been too many years. Well, she would listen to their talk—if the man lived to say anything at all. He looked very sick now. She could make a prickly-pear poultice for his wound, but that might interfere with testing the man's powers. The arrow had struck him yesterday. He must have powers or he would have died soon afterward. She'd wait until tomorrow, and if he lived that long, she would ask the medicine man about a poultice. If she helped him, maybe he would teach Red-Rope his sacred words.

Margarida slept through the night, and the next day the world narrowed to the wickiup. Except for trips outside to relieve herself and once to wash, everything centered around Brant. Helping him with his needs terrified her, because it showed how sick he was. It was as if the effort of getting here had taken all his strength, and the poison still might overcome him. Painted Boy removed the rawhide thong from Brant's wrists; obviously it wasn't needed.

Brant drifted in and out of consciousness, and his leg remained so swollen that Margarida thought the skin might burst. When he seemed aware of her, she didn't try to talk to him, other than to reassure him she was all right. Knowing she must replenish her strength, she ate some strange flat cakes and something that tasted like squash. Though Brant drank water, he couldn't eat.

Violent Man and Leader and another old, very small

man came several times to look at Brant and talk among themselves. Each time, Margarida felt as if her blood and lungs stopped functioning until the men left. Violent Man showered hatred on her with every look, and though the other men frightened her, they seemed safe compared to him.

Leader and the others visited early the following morning. After they left, the woman who brought them food and supervised Margarida's trips outside removed Brant's bandage and put a poultice on the wound. Then she rebandaged it with leaves, fastening them in place with long fibers. When she finished, Margarida touched the woman's arm and said, "*Aheeyey*," which she hoped sounded like what she remembered meant "thank you."

"*Ahíyi'ee*," corrected the woman, then looked startled, as if she'd surprised herself by responding.

With her attention on Brant, Margarida had only vaguely noticed that the woman didn't look quite like other Apaches. When she had to go outside again, Margarida scrutinized the woman with her. She looked to be about forty and was short and chunky. Her hair was brown and her eyes gray. Except for her clothing, she could be white, Margarida thought, or partly so. If she were, would that make her sympathetic to them? But she didn't act any different from the guard squatting at the entrance.

By midafternoon Brant's leg looked a little less swollen and the red streaks less pronounced. Surely, Margarida thought excitedly, that meant he was getting better. As she knelt beside him, she felt a touch on her arm. He had wakened and was looking at her. "Are . . . you. . . ?" It was all he could say, but they were the most beautiful words she'd ever heard.

She touched the side of his face. For the first time since the poison had started to work, his skin felt only warm. She picked up his hand and held it against her lips, leaving part of her soul in her kiss. "I'm fine," she said, and for that moment it was true. His eyes closed again, but his hand didn't let hers go. Their clasped hands rested in her lap, where her silent tears fell on them.

Just after dark a guard came whom Margarida hadn't seen before. She'd become accustomed to the guards they had. This new man frightened her, reminding her they were at the mercy of many people she didn't understand or know what to expect from. Brant told her that the Apache had true democracy; they accepted leadership only when they agreed. Leader seemed to command enough respect that she and Brant were alive because he wished it, for reasons she couldn't guess. If it had been up to Violent One, she was sure they'd be dead.

Soon after the new guard arrived, she heard singing. Firelight reflected off the tree trunks across from the wickiup. When the singing stopped, four drumbeats sounded. The fear which she'd been stifling flooded back, making her pulse seem louder than the drums. A different voice sang, followed by four drumbeats, and more songs and drumming. One song went on for a long time, and when it stopped, she heard shouting.

Brant whispered, "Getting ready . . . raid."

She felt for his hand, and his strengthened grip calmed her, but she still waited, muscles rigid, for someone to come—drag them out. No! She stopped herself. If she let fear paralyze her at every unfamiliar sound, she might as well rush outside and die now.

But when a figure appeared at the wickiup, carrying a blazing pine splinter, she couldn't prevent the leap of terror. It was Painted Boy, the stripe on his face renewed, and additional patches decorating the sides of his face and chin. When he approached, she waited, breath suspended. He leaned down and touched Brant's wounded leg, then straightened up and left. Trembling, she recalled her determination to control her fear; to keep that resolution, she would have to be stronger than this.

For the five days the warriors were away, Born-Twice spent most of her time with the captives. The man improved, and though he was very weak, the guard decided he must be bound again. He began to eat, and before she caught herself, Born-Twice felt a kind of pride in his progress. She renewed the prickly-pear poultices, and the swelling in his leg diminished.

She listened for the captives to say something important to report to the others, but she was disappointed. Once the woman said, "I didn't put the canteens back," and started to cry, the first tears Born-Twice had seen.

Born-Twice paid careful attention, but the man only said, in a comforting tone, "It wouldn't have mattered."

Another time he said, "We must plan," and Born-Twice moved a little closer so she would be sure to hear.

But the woman stopped him. "First you must get well." Born-Twice thought the woman was being sensible. The man was getting better, but he was still weak.

At other times the woman mostly talked about people with white men's names, and the man responded, telling her not to worry. Though Born-Twice had seen how frightened the woman was, especially around He-Starts-Fights, she never mentioned her fear. When Born-Twice took the captive to the women's bathing place, she saw how beautiful the woman's body was and wondered if the woman had any children.

Late on the sixth day the raiding party returned. When she saw the *remuda* of horses, delight sent Born-Twice hurrying to find Red-Rope. So many horses! They packed the corral and some had to be hobbled nearby. She saw mules as well, so she knew tonight there would be a feast.

Her husband looked tired but elated. "It was the best raid since we've been here," he told her when they were in their wickiup. "With the new guns we stopped a supply train going to a mine. We captured more guns and much ammunition. He-Stirs-Up-Earth found the horses," Red-Rope said proudly. "He was the one who slipped through and opened the gates to let them out. He says he has power from the captive man."

"And no one followed you?"

"Old-Man-He-Knows-A-Lot took us through such a rocky place that no whites could follow. We lost only one mule with a broken leg."

That meant they had fresh mule meat to eat. Her mouth watered. "Is there a fat horse to kill tonight?"

"Ha, old woman. Always thinking about your stomach. Yes, feasting and dances. In two days the council will decide about the man who has power against poison. He-Starts-Fights still wants to kill him, but Old-Man-He-Knows-A-Lot hasn't agreed. I think he has a plan."

Brant could see from Margarida's expression that the raiders' return the previous day and the night's singing had raised all her fears again. He remembered only snatches of what had happened after he and Margarida reached the cave the day they were attacked—mostly agonizing pain and the need not to show it. Though that pain might be nothing compared to the torture these Apaches could inflict, now he felt a kind of relief. Waiting, testing his strength each day, silently cursing his own weakness while acting calm to reassure her, seeemed almost worse than facing what would come.

She'd surrendered with the hope they'd be spared because he was part Apache. But his heritage wouldn't necessarily protect them from Apaches of a different band from his, and some Apaches hated mixed-breeds almost as much as whites. Also, these Indians were renegades—hiding in the canyon she'd stumbled upon. Though he wasn't sure why he and Margarida hadn't been killed, he remembered enough of conversations from the first two days to guess it had something to do with his surviving the poisoned arrow. He'd tried to talk to the guard, but the man wouldn't respond.

Brant heard people approaching and pulled himself into a sitting position before men crowded into the entrance of the wickiup. The tall man Margarida called Violent One said contemptuously, "He lives, but he is weak."

Though he hadn't stood without help before, Brant knew he must now. He had to use his bound hands and his good leg to lever himself, but he made it to his feet. The pain from the wounded leg sent nauseating thrusts up into his stomach. Margarida moved close behind him, but he wouldn't lean on her unless he had to. He stared at the angry Apache, glad he was taller and didn't have to look up. "Not so weak."

Their chief put a hand on Violent One's arm. "It will be settled next day at council."

Leader and Violent One left. Brant let himself lean on Margarida, then lowered himself to the ground. "What did they say?" Margarida said.

Should he tell her? Yes, she must face it too. "Tomorrow they'll have a council and decide about us." He was glad she didn't ask what those decisions might be.

"Is there any way we can escape?"

He lay back, exhausted. "I don't know." Margarida hadn't mentioned escape before, probably because he'd been so weak. It had been on his mind constantly, but he knew they could do nothing except try to stay alive and hope for an opportunity later.

When the celebration began after dark, the guard checked that the bonds on Brant's hands were tight, then crouched at the entrance where he could look out and still watch them. Margarida sat silently in the darkness. This could be their last night together, Brant thought, and the pain of that seemed as great as the pain from the poisoned arrow. He lay back and held up his bound hands. "Come, Margarida, lie beside me, in my arms."

Though she'd been near him at night, she had been careful not to be close enough to jostle him. Now she crept into the circle of his arms and lay there, her head on his chest. The rhythms of the chanting came to them, a reminder of danger. "What will happen to us?" she whispered.

"I don't know, but since they didn't kill us right away, there's a good chance they have something else in mind. Whatever it is, Margarida, we'll have to do what they ask until we have a chance to escape." He wondered how much more he should say and decided he must go on. "You may be kept as a slave. If that happens, don't give up hope. Do what you must to stay alive. The woman who's been here might help you. I think she has some sympathy for you."

"What about you?"

"Adult male captives aren't made slaves." He didn't need to say more than that.

She shuddered, and he could feel her tears dampen his shirt. "It's not fair. We haven't had even a year together, or any babies."

He couldn't touch her with his hands, but he brushed at her head with his lips. She tilted up her face, and he put all his longing for her into his kiss. "I wish we could make love, but we'll have to remember other times."

She kissed him again, then lay quietly as the singing and drumming went on. Finally she slid out from his arms, but stayed close beside him.

In the morning he stood up again, and tried putting his weight on his right leg. The pain jarred upward, searing him until he felt it even behind his eyes, but he could endure it. The stronger he looked now, the better.

"Brant," Margarida said, her voice alarmed, "shouldn't you stay off your leg?"

He realized his face must have showed the pain. He'd have to do better than that. "No. If they take us to the council, I must walk.'"

All that day they waited. Margarida said once, "This must be a special torture—to know they're deciding, but not know what." He could only kiss her—poor reassurance.

It was nearly night when the young warrior Margarida called Painted Boy came. Before they left the wickiup, the man bound Margarida's hands as well. The woman guard followed behind him with Margarida.

As they went along the row of wickiups, Brant had to prepare himself every time he put his weight on his wounded leg. The camp was larger than he remembered from his fragmentary images of their arrival, and each step became an endurance test he wasn't sure he could continue. He was glad he'd practiced keeping his face expressionless. At last they reached a clump of trees where the warriors were sitting. Doggedly he remained on his feet until the chief motioned, and then let himself down. The woman guard had Margarida sit a short distance away.

There were eleven men in the circle. Around the edge more women and children watched; the band had evidently lost most of their warriors. The women spoke softly to each other, but they didn't laugh and jeer as Brant expected.

The leader stared hard at Brant, and despite his efforts at control, Brant could feel his heart racing. At last the chief said, "Your woman says you are *chihinne*, but you look *ndaa*."

"My father was *ndaa*, but my mother half *chihinne*, and my *shiwóyé* is of the band of Red Sleeves." Brant hoped the name of Mangas Coloradas, the famous

chief, would impress these people. "When I was a boy
I studied Apache ways. I learned much from my
brother, Ndè-ze." He decided he must take a chance
on telling them his name. The Apache did this only in
extreme circumstances, but maybe it would help that
his name was Angry-He-Looks-About. "Among my
people I am called Hàcké hàdè-c."

"Is your heart *ndaa*, or is it *chihinne*?"

Brant could answer truthfully, "I have always wished
to be *chihinne*."

"That means nothing," Violent One said angrily.
"He has a white woman and the possessions of a white
man."

Until Violent One spoke, Margarida had been able
to keep her fear subdued. Leader seemed stern, but
his voice hadn't been threatening. Violent One's hate-
filled eyes and distorted mouth told her he wanted
their death. The terror of the first day rushed over
her; her muscles went rigid as she waited for someone
to seize her and Brant, fasten them to a stake—she
didn't know what. Then Leader directed stern words
at Violent One, and Margarida trembled with relief.
Not yet. They weren't to die this moment.

Other men spoke, some calmly, a few making threatening gestures toward Brant. Finally Leader addressed
Brant again, a long speech, which ended with some
kind of question. At the end, Brant looked stunned,
as if whatever the chief said had surprised him completely. He stared straight ahead, not looking at her.
Finally he answered in what sounded like agreement.

Thoughts whirled madly through Margarida's mind.
Brant had agreed to something—but she couldn't guess
what. To help these Apaches get guns? Brant wouldn't
ordinarily do anything like that, but their situation was
desperate.

Violent One jumped to his feet, shouting. He came
over in front of Margarida and spewed forth words,
including the one she feared the most, *"isda."*

Brant got to his feet, faster than she could have believed, and shouted, *"Dah!"* She knew that word meant "no." He turned toward Leader and spoke sharply, in a defiant way that brought back her terror in great waves. She wanted to shout at him to stop. Now they *would* be killed.

Leader stood up as well. Behind him murmurs rose from the watching women. He made what sounded like a short speech. When he finished, Smiling Man, who was sitting in the circle, said *"Ha'aa,"* and all the other men except Violent One nodded and repeated the word. Violent One gave Brant and Margarida looks of even blacker hatred than before and stalked from the circle. The women on the edge hastily moved aside to let him through.

Painted Boy unbound Brant's hands, then unfastened Margarida's wrists. She moved to Brant's side, not understanding but at that moment not caring. She could see from his pallor the effort he was making to stand, and she wanted to help him. But his expression warned her, and she walked beside him back to the wickiup, trying not to think of his pain. Once inside, he sank down to the ground and lay back, breathing heavily.

"Brant, are you all right?"

"Yes, just give me a minute."

She got water for him. He drank it, then lay back again as color returned to his face.

Her questions jumped out. "What happened? What were they saying? What does *isda* mean?"

"Isda' means 'slave.' The man you call Violent One— his name is He-Starts-Fights—wanted to claim you as a slave."

"But you said no, and they listened to you. Why? What did Leader say to you?"

He sat up and took her hand. "The chief persuaded the others to spare our lives if I'll stay with them and be one of their warriors. I agreed."

"Stay with them?"

"Because I didn't die from the poison, they think I have some special power. The young warrior who touched my leg before they went on the raid had good luck, and they think that's why the raid was so successful."

Relief made her feel dizzy. They weren't to die! She leaned against him. "Oh, Brant."

Brant lay down and pulled her close. "Margarida, I want to make love to you."

"But . . . your leg."

"I'll be careful, but I must." He sounded urgent. It was dark now, and the guard was still there, but it hardly mattered. "Pull down the hide covering the opening. The guard won't come inside."

She did as he asked and went back to him, still hesitant. Tenderly he won her away from doubt—smoothing her hair, caressing her neck, trying out tentative kisses on her eyes and cheeks until he captured her mouth. She helped him remove her shift and his clothing. For long moments he held her, letting her remember how lean and muscular his body was, helping her blot out everything but this moment.

Then he reacquainted her with all the ways he could touch her that stirred her desire, lifting her breasts so his mouth could find the nipples, exploring the gently curved surface of her abdomen. Between kisses he whispered to her, "Margarida, if only I had words to tell you how much I love you. You have such warmth and passion—more than I dreamed any woman could have. I love to touch your breasts, your thighs—all of you is beautiful. And when I'm inside, you feel so good I can hardly stand it."

Fiercely she shut away the outside world, remembering only that he was her husband and her lover, the man she'd worshiped as a child, yearned for as a girl, and from whom she'd learned the secrets of passion as a woman.

Tenderly he caressed her, his wife who was everything he'd ever desired in a woman, wanting to protect her from all hurt, and knowing with anguish that he couldn't. But for now he would make her forget the dangers around them, and hope in passion to push away all but the knowledge of how completely he loved her.

When he eased inside her, he began with long, slow movements to pull her with him up a height greater than the mountain walls that surrounded the valley. In accelerating motion they approached the top, then waited, hovering in unbearable pleasure, until they hurtled over into space and floated down together.

Gently he held her, kissing her mouth and eyes. "My love," he whispered, and settled her close within his arms.

"My love," she murmured, and knew terror had only retreated, but for now she was content. She had been so frightened, but only the safety of his arms mattered as she fell into sleep.

She woke to the uneasy memory of something Brant had said that didn't make sense to her. He was already awake, sitting up, his back to her. She touched him and he turned; his face was as gray as the dawn light. A feeling of dread replaced the relief she'd felt last night. "Brant, even if you agreed to stay here, why would these Indians think we'll really stay? Not escape as soon as we can?"

"I'm sure they'll watch me carefully. And keep close guard on you while I do whatever they ask. You'll be hostage for my actions. And . . ." He stopped, as if he didn't want to go on.

She knew there was something he didn't want to tell her. "And what?"

"I'm to take the chief's daughter as a wife."

She stared at him, at his face, thinner and more hawklike than ever, his cheekbones standing out, emphasizing his Indian blood. She wanted the comfort of disbelief, but instead she felt shock and betrayal. "You knew—last night when we made love—you knew and you didn't tell me!"

"Margarida!" He seized her shoulders. "You must understand. The chief sets this as a condition. So that I'm connected to his family."

Loss and anger, so great she could barely speak, came out as hysterical bursts of words. "Yes," she choked out, "Leader's just like . . . my mother. You look like a . . . prize son. Got you . . . me. Now . . . another wife."

"For Christ's sake, Margarida!" He shook her, then held her against him. "Stop it. I had to agree."

As she leaned against him, gasps that were half-sobs still twisted through her. She had been terrified they would die. Now another threat intensified her terror. A threat that had haunted her so long—the fear of losing Brant to a life she couldn't share.

21

MARGARIDA was alone in the new wickiup. Four days had passed since the council meeting—since Brant had agreed to marry the chief's daughter. Four days of his explaining why he had no choice—and she saying she understood.

Her mind did understand. They were prisoners; their lives depended on the chief's acceptance. But she couldn't convince her heart. It reminded her that to be an Apache was what Brant had always wanted. She felt betrayed, all her fears since her marriage confirmed. He hadn't tried to touch her intimately again, and she was glad. The memory of the last time was bitter.

Earlier he'd gone to the men's section of the stream to bathe and put on his Indian clothes—to be ready for the feasting which would begin at dark to celebrate his taking the new wife. The fading light told her that would be soon.

Most of her extra clothing had been destroyed when the burros' packs had been lightened, and she should be grateful to Born-Twice for giving her the skirt and blouse and moccasins. But the loose clothing she wore felt strange.

How astonishing that Born-Twice spoke English. The day after the council meeting Brant had shouted, "Look out for the snake!" and Born-Twice screamed. There was no snake; he'd used the fear the Apache had of snakes to confirm what he'd suspected, that she knew English. Born-Twice would say only she'd been captured as a child. Margarida was glad someone in the camp besides Brant spoke English.

Yesterday she'd helped Born-Twice build this wickiup. Margarida had clumsily worked at putting up the poles and covering them with hides and then brush. Her first lesson in an Apache woman's tasks had at least tired her enough that she slept last night, here with Brant.

The question of where he would sleep tonight revolved in her head until it drove out all other thoughts. Though she hadn't seen the chief's daughter, Margarida knew her name—Na-a izba, She-Goes-To-War. The name made Margarida shiver. She hoped the chief's daughter was old and ugly with a mean temper. Now she wished she had her old clothes back, dirty as they'd become. She didn't want to look like that other woman—like one of Brant's "wives."

He limped through the doorway; just outside, the Apache guardian squatted. Brant's leg was healing slowly, and his face had regained its color. He wore a buckskin shirt with breechclout, leggings, and moccasins; a red headband around his wet hair made his face look more Indian. An image seared Margarida, of Brant in a wickiup, embracing a woman who looked like the pretty widow She-Runs-Fast.

The thought burned so fiercely that the words she'd resisted the last four days flared out. "Do you have to sleep with the chief's daughter?"

"Yes. Or they won't consider it a marriage."

The pain shouldn't have surprised her. She'd known what his answer would be. She told herself she could accept it and that otherwise they might die. That didn't help.

"Margarida—"

"You've explained," she interrupted, not wanting words that couldn't alleviate her wretchedness. Through her childhood, she'd never lied. Now she did. "I understand."

"Margarida, I love you. I don't want to do this." He touched her arm, a tentative stroke, but she jerked away.

Not quite able to leave the wound alone, she said, "What about the customs—cooking breakfast for the man? And the bride gift?"

"The chief's daughter has been married before, so it's not the same. I told Old-Man-He-Knows-A-Lot that the horses he'd already confiscated from us were the gift."

This time she was wise enough not to ask whether that included Halcon.

Born-Twice came to take Margarida to the bonfire. When they reached the large cleared area, Margarida sat, her heart thudding, her hands clasped in her lap, trying not to show her emotions as she looked for the bride. The women glanced curiously at her as they moved about with pots and trays of food. No one wore any special dress.

The men gathered apart from the women, and soon she saw Brant with Smiling Man—no, Margarida corrected herself, Red-Rope. Brant had told her some of the names, and she remembered Red-Rope because he was Born-Twice's husband. She couldn't forget Violent One's name—He-Starts-Fights.

The voices of the women rose in excited greetings to a tall woman dressed in a decorated buckskin dress fringed along the sides and around the bottom. A necklace of small polished bones hung to her waist. The cold fist squeezing Margarida's chest told her this was the bride.

She-Goes-To-War was sturdy like her father and appeared to be a little older than Brant. Her face was handsome, almost beautiful. She had even features, a sensual mouth, and large eyes. Margarida reminded herself this woman probably had no more choice than

Brant. Maybe she didn't want to marry him. The thought didn't ease Margarida's pain. Jealousy, deep and bitter, impaled her.

She-Goes-To-War looked at Margarida, and her eyes took on a hatred that matched He-Starts-Fights'. Margarida felt a resurgence of the terror that was never altogether gone.

The women set pots of food in the center of the circle of men. Born-Twice pulled at Margarida's arm. "Come." They joined a group of women around one of the other pots, and Born-Twice eagerly helped herself. Margarida's stomach would have refused even familiar food now, and she knew if she tried to taste this, she would be ill. Taking a flat round of acorn-flour bread, she pretended to eat.

When Born-Twice had eaten generously, she offered Margarida a drink from a pottery jug. *"Tulpai,"* Born-Twice said. "Makes you feel good. Made from cornmeal. We soon make *tiswin* when we get mescal." Born-Twice sounded amiable, and Margarida found a fragment of comfort, almost as if Born-Twice were a friend. Margarida took a sip. It tasted pleasantly mild, not like the whiskey she'd sneaked tastes of. She returned the jug, but Born-Twice laughed and pushed the jug back. "More. Drink more."

Several swallows later, it began to taste better. Born-Twice wasn't the only one who seemed affected by the drink. The laughter and talk grew more boisterous.

Soon the food was taken away and men began to chant, joined by a drummer and someone playing a wooden flute. Three girls crossed the open space and tapped men on the shoulders, and the men rose and faced the girls. Without touching, they began to dance in a circle, in forward and backward motions. The swaying fringe on the men's shirts matched the swirling of the girls' skirts.

The bride walked across and tapped on Brant's shoulder. He rose and joined her in the circle of dancers, managing the movements awkwardly because of his damaged leg. The pain in Margarida's chest flowed out into her blood until it filled her. Though she wanted to run back to the wickiup, her pride made her hold her head even higher. She stared at the dancers, but she wouldn't let her eyes tell her mind what they saw. Instead she looked into the past, pretending she saw her home, Lobo, Walt—superimposing images she loved on this scene she hated.

The dancing went on, and she retreated farther, blotting out the present. When the dancers and singers paused and Brant sat down, her neck and shoulders ached. Surely, she thought, she'd watched enough. She turned to Born-Twice. "I'd like to go back to the wickiup."

Born-Twice looked almost sympathetic. She rose.

As they threaded their way through the women, who were still sharing jugs of *tulpai*, no one noticed them until they passed She-Goes-To-War. She gave Margarida the same threatening glare as before. Only when they reached the wickiup did Margarida's terror recede.

Born-Twice lit a pine splinter and then produced a tall, narrow water basket. She drank so eagerly that when she passed it along, Margarida wasn't surprised it held *tulpai*. She took a gulp before returning it.

"What are you called?" Born-Twice asked.

Margarida remembered when she'd joked with Brant about an Apache name for her. She-Who-Gets-What-She-Wants wasn't right now. "My name means White Flower," she said sadly.

Born-Twice took another long drink, then said, "Red-Rope had other wife one time. No children from that wife too. She died. Red-Rope didn't like to have two wives." She gave a satisfied smile. "Not take more."

To Margarida's surprise, Born-Twice patted Margarida's hand. "Not worry. You learn to be good second wife."

"*Second wife!*" Margarida's anguished feelings boiled up like a kettle bouncing its lid off. "I'm Brant's *first* wife. His *real* wife."

Undisturbed, Born-Twice drank again. "Not Apache. So not first wife," she said calmly.

Margarida's anger drained away. Miserably she knew it was no use to rage at Born-Twice. Though Margarida's head already ached, she took up the *tulpai* and drank again. Somehow she had to get through the night.

Brant reflected gloomily that he'd never questioned his virility before now. He'd managed one stint of dancing, and his leg ached damnably, but he couldn't let that show. She-Goes-To-War didn't seem any more eager to continue than he. He didn't even dare drink much *tulpai*, though it might make the rest of the night more pleasant. Even without being drunk he might have trouble performing later.

When Margarida left the fire, he'd had to discipline his muscles not to go after her. Even if his guards let him, it wouldn't do any good. He'd said everything before, told her he loved her, and he hadn't diminished the hurt he saw in her face. He'd have to give her time to accept this situation. But God, how he hated her frozen look. Silently he went through all the curses he knew.

Old-Man-He-Knows-A-Lot motioned to Brant to sit beside him, and Brant moved over. "Tell me more of your grandmother," the chief said, and Brant relaxed a little.

"*Shiwóyé*'s clan is the High-Up-The-Mountain-People." He described the broken treaties which had robbed them of their homelands, their attempts to live at San Carlos, and their settling in his valley. "When Chihuahua and his Chiricahuas came back through New Mexico two years ago," he concluded, "my people were safe from the whites. And they remain on that land now."

Old-Man-He-Knows-A-Lot looked thoughtful. "Then you did well," he said. At the approval in the chief's voice, Brant felt a rush of pleasure. He hoped the chief might recognize his obligations to the Apache at home, but Brant knew that the well-being of his own group came first with Old-Man-He-Knows-A-Lot. For now it was enough that the chief had prevailed over He-Starts-Fights and saved his and Margarida's lives.

He studied Old-Man-He-Knows-A-Lot's lined face. Brant's impressions told him this was a man whose nature was basically peace-loving—very different from He-Starts-Fights. From what Brant had learned, a drunken soldier at San Carlos had murdered one of the chief's sons; Old-Man-He-Knows-A-Lot and his other son had killed the soldier. By that deed—vengeance to them but murder as far as the whites were concerned—they had become renegades, and the group fled. In the pursuit by the army, many of the warriors had been killed, including the second son, before they shook off the soldiers and scouts and came to this hidden valley.

Old-Man-He-Knows-A-Lot looked past Brant and smiled, his face softening. She-Goes-To-War stood before them, and Brant rose. He knew what would happen. After this dance, she would take him to her wickiup.

The dance didn't last long enough, and too soon they arrived at the round brush-covered shelter. Brant reminded himself that She-Goes-To-War was attractive, and of how many women he'd had before Margarida. Everything should go all right. His reasoning didn't get rid of the uneasy feeling in his gut as he took off his clothes.

She-Goes-To-War had hung the hide over the entrance, and he could barely see from light seeping around the edges. She had her back to him, undressing under a blanket. He'd forgotten how careful the Apache were to conceal their bodies from the opposite sex, even keeping babies covered. He almost groaned. He needed something to get him aroused.

She lay down and he slipped under the blanket with her. The first thing he noticed was her scent. She was clean; the Apache were careful about that. But it wasn't Margarida's special scent. He knew he should say something tender, loving—something that would relax this woman. He couldn't.

An image of Margarida came to him—leaning over him, her lips curved in the sensual laugh that hid in the corners of her mouth, her hair falling over breasts that invited his touch. With the image came desire and the rush of blood to his groin that he needed. He touched She-Goes-To-War and found her breast. Too pointed, but he ignored that, remembering Margarida's breasts, building his fantasy, letting it carry him along. He spoke to Margarida, saying how much he loved her, knowing he'd used English and this wasn't Margarida, but by then the image had worked.

Judging from her response, She-Goes-To-War had been pleased. He'd taken so long to get started that she'd think him a good lover. Maybe not. Apache men tried to satisfy their wives, and perhaps her first husband had delighted her. He didn't care.

Now her breathing sounded as if she were asleep. Her unfamiliar scent still bothered him, and he couldn't stay beside her. He sat up and slid out from the blankets, then pulled on his leggings and breechclout. His hand was on the hide door cover before he stopped himself.

A guard would be outside Margarida's wickiup, and another, maybe He-Starts-Fights, watching this one as well. He couldn't go to her; he must appear to be satisfied with She-Goes-To-War. And Margarida probably didn't want to see him; she'd said she understood, but not whether she'd ever let him love her again.

Searching for the calm he must maintain, he lay down on the hide floor away from She-Goes-To-War.

Tonight he may have pleased her, and made himself and Margarida miserable. But he had little choice. He'd have to manage until he could make an opportunity to escape with Margarida.

She-Goes-To-War probably wouldn't care about his leaving. She'd only done what her father demanded. Her father . . . The thought of how Old-Man-He-Knows-A-Lot might react gave Brant a strange feeling, as if escaping would betray the chief. He reminded himself his loyalty belonged to Margarida, and to Walt, and to many others. Not to this man and his people.

Margarida walked along the trail behind Born-Twice, heading north, to the opposite end of the valley from the secret entrance she'd so disastrously stumbled into. Along with most of the women of the band and three of the men, Margarida would help harvest mescal. Fortunately the mescal was just beyond the north end of their hidden valley, only a two-day walk. Even so, they had no campfires at night, to avoid the remote possibility of being seen by someone scaling the mountain ridges.

They had left early the previous morning, and Margarida was glad she'd missed what she bitterly thought of as Brant's "duty call." It had been ten days since the wedding feast when he'd taken She-Goes-To-War as a wife. Each morning he'd come to see Margarida and spent a dreadful half-hour with her. Born-Twice was always there too, so they couldn't talk freely. Margarida didn't want to anyway.

She knew that though he could visit her, he must act satisfied with She-Goes-To-War and not spend much time with his "second" wife. But the only way Margarida managed was to bury her feelings so deeply she could act indifferent.

They exchanged wooden phrases about how his leg was and how she was getting along. Then they had nothing left to say. She saw lines of strain in his face and the tight muscles of his jaw, but that seemed insignificant compared to the misery she felt. It was a relief when he left and she could stay busy learning to use a bone needle and sinew fibers to make another skirt and blouse for herself.

Now she saw that Born-Twice was getting ahead and hurried to catch up. The black glances of She-Goes-To-War, who was behind her, frightened Margarida, and she feared having someone at her back who so obviously hated her.

The trail north of the valley entrance was treacherous, with one stretch barely wide enough for a burro to inch along. In the area beyond, the mescal flourished. Because it was May, blossoms were just appearing. The women set to work immediately, cutting away the long, thorny leaves at the base of each plant to leave a bulbous mass just above the ground. They loaded the cut heads onto the burros.

That night several small campfires were lit in the bottom of a fairly deep arroyo. Margarida sat, almost too exhausted to eat, and watched the others. Then anger at herself put her on her feet. It was cowardice to sit and whine, no matter how terrible her hurts. She went to the pot of meat and took a handful. It looked and tasted strange, but she choked it down and took more. She would eat and sleep tonight and do whatever else she had to.

After two nights at the desert camp, they started back. When they reached the narrow defile, the men unloaded the packs from the burros. By stringing poles through the packs, two men carried them across that section of the trail, returning and leading the animals.

The procedure increased Margarida's nervousness, since she, like the other women, had a burden basket of mescal heads. She watched Born-Twice go confidently ahead of her and followed, feeling clumsy with the pull of the head strap and the unaccustomed weight of the basket. When she reached the middle, her foot slipped on a loose pebble, and she swayed, her heart racing. As she wavered, she felt a jolt, and lost her balance.

Her feet slid over the edge of the sharp drop, and she let out a single scream. Wildly she grabbed at the rock face, snatching for a hold. The strap for the basket caught against a rock, stopping her fall, letting her grab a tiny pine which grew in a crack. From above, hands reached down, pulling at the straps, then under her armpits, dragging her up to the ledge.

For a moment she lay facedown, gasping. Someone lifted her to her feet. It was Born-Twice, with another woman. Margarida wanted to stop there, not take another step, but she gathered her trembling muscles and followed Born-Twice to the place where the trail widened again.

For the rest of the day Born-Twice, her stern face frowning even more than usual, stayed close beside Margarida. Half-hysterically Margarida wondered whether Born-Twice believed she'd tried to escape at the place where she'd fallen. She must have banged her basket against something when she slipped, but she wasn't so crazy as to get off the trail on purpose. When they stopped, Born-Twice, muttering something in a grumbling tone, put poultices on Margarida's hands where she'd bloodied them when she fell.

Margarida ventured a question. "What is this?"

"*Hosh nteeli.*" Born-Twice pointed to a prickly pear.

Though her voice had been unfriendly, her touch had been gentle, and Margarida took a little comfort from that.

By the end of the fifth day after the women left to gather mescal, Brant could hardly keep his mind on anything but watching for Margarida to return. It had been a relief to have She-Goes-To-War gone, but he'd been on edge with worry about Margarida. There was no way to avoid the risk of her going off, but he felt almost as tense as the first days in the camp. That tension was dangerous because his skills at the men's activities were being tested.

Except for running, which he still couldn't manage, he'd done well enough at the other things, even with a bow. They hadn't tried him with the guns, but he didn't worry that he couldn't outshoot any of them. Most Apaches were superb with bow and arrow but not as good as he with guns. When he'd been challenged on tracking, he'd followed He-Starts-Fights, which had brought Old-Man-He-Knows-A-Lot's approval but made the younger man even angrier. By intense concentration he'd won a game of hoop-and-pole against He-Stirs-Up-Earth and then another against Red-Rope. Perhaps fortunately, he'd lost to He-Starts-Fights.

Just before sunset the women arrived. At first he didn't see Margarida, and the effort of not rushing forward tightened his muscles so much he could feel the pain all along his spine. His relief when he saw her lasted until he noticed the wrappings around her hands; then anxiety swamped him all over again.

He greeted She-Goes-To-War, hardly knowing what he said, then walked over to Margarida. She was struggling to put down a heavy basket. Only supreme control kept him from helping her. "What happened to your hands?"

She didn't look at him. "Nothing much."

"Something did." He could hear his own sharpness.

Finally she looked up, and the misery in her eyes was almost more than he could stand. Then the uncaring facade she'd shown ever since he'd been with She-Goes-To-War closed off the glimpse into her feelings. "I slipped on the trail." She turned and went to join Born-Twice.

That night jugs of *tulpai* went around the fire in anticipation that a supply of *tiswin* from fermented mescal would soon be available as a replacement. Brant sat with the other men, not interested in the *tulpai*, but not wanting to go to She-Goes-To-War's wickiup. Finally the other men started leaving, and he rose and walked into the trees, as if needing to relieve himself. Red-Rope followed him—his guard for tonight, Brant thought. But after they were well into the trees, Red-Rope dropped back a few paces.

"Hàcké hàdè-c." His name, coming softly out of the dark, startled him. Born-Twice stepped from the shadows and motioned to him to follow her. Astonishment gave way to fear—something had happened to Margarida or Born-Twice wouldn't have spoken to him and called him by name.

He was breathing as hard as if he'd run ten miles when Born-Twice stopped in a thick grove of aspens. She spoke in a low voice. "Yesterday, She-Goes-To-War tried to kill your white woman. She pushed White-Flower from a high place."

Perspiration beaded at his hairline, but he felt cold. "Do you know why?"

"I only guess. She-Goes-To-War does not want you to have this other wife. She thinks without your white woman, you will be more sure to stay."

"She is wrong. Her father understands this. He would not let her harm Margarida."

Born-Twice's voice had a note of irony. "Will you tell her father he must control his only daughter?"

No, he couldn't, Brant knew. Again the risk Born-Twice was running and the candor of her speech amazed him. "Why do you tell me this?"

She finally said, "White-Flower is brave. And I do not like She-Goes-To-War's actions. She thinks she is being loyal to her father, keeping you here for him, but what she did is not honorable."

Brant said, more to himself than to Born-Twice, "Why didn't Margarida tell me?"

"She thought she slipped. I did not say because I could not speak against She-Goes-To-War. It is for you to protect your white woman."

Yes. It was up to him. He'd thought his acceptance

of She-Goes-To-War protected Margarida as well as
him, but now she was in more danger because she was
his wife. Yet if she weren't, she could be a slave. He
and she both were too carefully watched to escape yet.
Desperately he tried to think what he could do.

"I go now," Born-Twice said.

"Wait." Born-Twice had come to him, breaking the
rules, so she must have some feeling for Margarida.
And, he realized now, she must have persuaded Red-
Rope to let her do this. He made a decision—one that
he already knew he would hardly be able to stand. "I
have something to ask you."

Margarida turned restlessly on the robe which was
her bed. Her hands hurt, though not as much as her
heart. Brant looked more Apache each day, and the
concern for her she'd seen in his face didn't disguise
that. Now he'd be with She-Goes-To-War. The image
of them together was a nightmare Margarida couldn't
escape by waking up. She'd thought she didn't hate
the other woman, but she did. Tonight she hated her
more than she'd ever hated anyone, unless it was
Brant. Yes, she hated him more.

The piece of hide that covered the door stirred, and
she sat up, frightened.

"Margarida." Brant's voice lit a flare of joy that
turned to bitterness as he came and crouched beside
her.

"What are you doing here? Did your wife and her
father let you out of your cage?"

"You are my wife." She heard emotion in his voice,
but she wasn't sure what the feeling was.

"She-Goes-To-War must be having her monthly
time," she spat. Knowing she was only wounding herself, she still couldn't stop. "You always did want it
every night."

"I want *you* every night."

The misery in his voice was clear now. But her own
suffering was too great; it might tear her apart if she

let down her barriers. "No! No!" Dimly she realized her shouts could be heard by anyone, but she didn't care. "You think you can be Indian one night with her and then white the next night with me. Well, I won't do that. You have your Apache wife, your Apache father. Just what you always wanted. *Leave me alone!*"

She began to beat at him, hurting her hands, welcoming the rage that was a shadow of what she felt inside. His arms enfolded her, but he made no effort to stop the blows she showered on him.

"Oh, God, Margarida." His wounded voice matched her heart. "I don't want to be apart from you, I love you. I want to love you now."

"*No!* Go back to *her!*" Twisting, she thrust her elbows at him, fighting him, until she jerked free.

Brant thought: I can't do it. Before he'd come here, it had seemed the only thing. Now he knew his plan was insane—more agony than he could stand. Her scent reminded him that when they made love, her wonderful spasms made his own pleasure greater than anything else he'd known. He couldn't surrender that to someone else.

Even while he told himself this, he knew nothing had changed since he'd talked to Born-Twice. He'd always scorned cowards—now he would gladly be one. But he must be resolute, not give in to Margarida's storms or his. He braced himself to tell her.

"Margarida. We must talk."

Margarida watched him, afraid to hope, wanting to hear him say they would escape. "Why?"

"I thought when I agreed to . . . take the chief's daughter, that would keep you safe. But it hasn't."

She thought of the fierce eyes of She-Goes-To-War. "What do you mean?"

"Born-Twice told me that you didn't slip on the trail. She-Goes-To-War pushed you."

Margarida shuddered with remembered terror. "She's like He-Starts-Fights."

"He hates us because he hates almost everyone. She-Goes-To-War loves her father. She tried to kill you because she thinks I will be more content here without you."

He stopped. She heard the pace of his breathing increase and felt her own heart racing. His voice was hoarse. "Born-Twice admires you. She'll be your friend."

Margarida felt cold, as she had the day he'd told her he was to marry She-Goes-To-War. "There's something else you're not saying," she charged.

His voice retreated to guarded impassivity. "For you to be safe, you'll have to seem separate from me. I've arranged for Red-Rope to take care of you."

Her hands throbbed and her head began to pound. "What do you mean?"

He hesitated, and she hit out at him, not caring about the pain in her hands. "Tell me! What do you mean?"

"You'll live with Red-Rope and Born-Twice."

"I know that flat sound to your voice—you're not saying everything. Am I supposed to be their *slave*?"

"No!" He caught her elbows, holding her still, and finished more quietly, "You'll be Red-Rope's wife."

She shrank back, not understanding at first—refusing to understand. "But I'm *your* wife."

His voice went on inexorably. "Tonight I'll have to take the rest of my things from this wickiup."

"To the Apache that means you're divorcing me."

"Margarida, I must. To protect you!"

"Let's leave. Now."

"You know we can't. We're still too closely watched."

Chaotic thoughts darted about inside her head like frantic birds trying to escape a cage. Brant, who flared with jealousy when she so much as smiled at another man, had arranged for her to be someone else's wife. For her own safety, he said. But it would also leave him with his Apache wife and his Apache father and his chance to live in the Apache way. With his wife who'd tried to kill her!

Grief too devastating to bear turned into rage greater than she'd ever imagined. It all meant nothing—Brant's words of love. A sop to his conscience. She remembered the way he'd gone off to kill the scalp hunter—leaving her so he could act like an Apache.

She jerked to her feet, wrapping the robe around her like a shield. "Go back to her—to your murderous wife. I'm sure your new Apache father will approve, and that's what counts, isn't it?"

Brant rose, his voice careful, concealing his emotions. "I understand how you feel—"

"No," she shouted, not caring who might hear. "You don't."

His voice lost its control, rising to a strained pitch. "Christ, Margarida. Do you think I want anyone else to touch you? But I can't keep you safe while you're my wife."

She had to struggle to breathe, then let her bitterness overflow. "What you haven't explained are the arrangements. Surely there was some trading. Red-Rope must have given you something for a wife like me, even if I am white."

He sounded emotionless again. "It has to look as if he wanted you and I was willing. He's giving me two horses."

She'd asked, but his answer seared her. "You gave more than that to get me. And more for your new wife. You didn't make a very good bargain this time."

He held out his hand as if to touch her face, but she whirled, turning her back to him. She heard him pick up his saddlebags. He stopped then, but she didn't turn around. After a few moments, she heard him leave.

22

RED-ROPE waited in Born-Twice's wickiup for her to return from taking part of his possessions to the white woman's wickiup. He was astonished that Born-Twice had agreed. In fact, her behavior in the whole matter perplexed him. First persuading him to let her speak to Angry-He-Looks-About four days ago, then urging him to accept the man's offer of his divorced wife. The arrangement itself was peculiar; it shouldn't have been the woman's former husband who saw to her affairs.

Born-Twice had used another argument to convince Red-Rope to marry the woman. She pointed out that it would infuriate He-Starts-Fights, who still wanted to kill the man, use the woman, and eventually kill her also. Red-Rope detested He-Starts-Fights' violence and arrogance, and savored a chance to thwart him.

Also, Red-Rope still had the secret hope he might have a child. For that, he'd given two fine mares he'd acquired on the last raid, the one that had been so lucky because of Angry-He-Looks-About's power against poison.

Born-Twice had said the woman's name was White-Flower. Because she was foreign, there hadn't been any feasting for taking her as a wife. Now it was time to go to her wickiup when Born-Twice returned.

Red-Rope felt a pleasant sense of anticipation. It had been a long time since he'd slept with anyone but Born-Twice, and he was curious about the new wife.

She wasn't pretty like Born-Twice—too pale and thin—but he thought her breasts would be good to touch. Maybe she'd be tight, and he could teach her to move just the way he liked. Most of all, he might have a daughter. A man needed daughters, so they would marry men to provide for him when he was old.

Born-Twice came in. "Did you take care of my things?" he asked gruffly, not wanting his excitement to show.

"They are there," she said quietly, "but you should know something. I have told her you will stay during the night but you will not be a husband with her."

"What!" Red-Rope seldom got angry, and almost never with Born-Twice, but now he was furious. "Old woman, you don't decide such things!"

Born-Twice looked at him calmly and spoke in an adamant tone. "She is too unhappy now. I promised her." Her voice softened and wavered. "I remember my first mother, and I want this woman to get used to our ways."

His wife's reference to her white mother shocked him so much that he didn't sound as fierce as he intended. Also, he didn't want anyone else to hear. "I didn't make any promises. I will do what I wish."

He gave her a tongue-lashing for her insolence, but she didn't answer back. When he stalked out of the wickiup, he thought angrily that she knew he wouldn't break her promise. No one else in the camp would know it; Born-Twice had better see that White-Flower said nothing. It would humiliate him to have the others laugh, especially He-Starts-Fights.

As he neared White-Flower's wickiup, he began to feel better. In fact, he had to admit to himself, he felt relieved. Though he'd never tell her so, he'd been a bit offended that Born-Twice had been eager for him to take another wife. Now he realized she only intended to take care of White-Flower, not to share him with her. He remembered the quarrels when he'd had two wives before—never peaceful. Everyone had heard about White-Flower shouting at Angry-He-Looks-About before he divorced her. She might not be a comfortable woman. And in his soul Red-Rope knew he'd never have a child; no woman had borne a baby of his, even before Born-Twice or his other wife.

When he entered the wickiup, White-Flower was waiting, her eyes scared-looking, but defiant too. Making his voice stern but too low to be heard outside, he said, "I do not choose to lie with you tonight." Though she wouldn't understand the words, she would hear his anger.

He settled himself in his robes. Tomorrow, he thought, he'd tell Born-Twice she must teach White-Flower to speak Apache. He wouldn't have a wife who couldn't understand him. And he would sleep in this wickiup for seven nights, to punish Born-Twice. Well, maybe four nights. He already felt a little lonely for her.

Margarida listened to Red-Rope's snoring and felt her heart finally settle down. In spite of Born-Twice's promise, Margarida had been afraid Red-Rope might not agree. When he came in, he was angry—or trying to sound that way. Underneath, he seemed good-natured, maybe even kind.

She felt as if tonight she could finally sleep. The three nights since Brant had told her she was to go to Red-Rope, she'd vacillated between trying to understand how Brant might feel, and jealous rage. The most constant feeling had been overpowering, furious resentment—that he would hand her over to someone else, as if he owned her.

For now she had no choice; she would have to stay with Born-Twice and Red-Rope. At least Born-Twice, by persuading Red-Rope to leave her alone, was making that bearable. Sometime, Margarida thought, she would have a chance to escape. She'd wait and plan, lull them into leaving her unwatched. Then she'd manage to get somewhere to find help, look for her father, and leave Brant behind to live his Apache life.

Brant thought that if Red-Rope arrived at the hoop-and-pole field again this morning with a smug look, he wouldn't be able to keep his hands from Red-Rope's throat. It had been four days since Red-Rope had started sleeping in Margarida's wickiup, and Brant had to swallow more anger each morning.

Earlier, hoping to exhaust his fury, Brant had tried to run with He-Stirs-Up-Earth and an older warrior—his guards for the morning. He hadn't been able to. Though his leg felt stronger, it was healing more slowly than it should, perhaps from the effect of the poison, or maybe because he'd used it too much. He'd steeled himself not to think about anything outside of this valley, grateful that he'd left Tall Man in charge at home. But escape was on his mind constantly. His leg ached now, warning him he'd have to be more fit, a conclusion that didn't help his temper.

He tried to quell his unhappiness by reminding himself of the reasons why he'd chosen Red-Rope for Margarida. Most important, he was Born-Twice's husband, and he also seemed easygoing, with a cheerful temperament. Until the last few mornings, Brant hadn't realized that Red-Rope was also quite handsome, tall and muscular, with even features. He had to be forty-five or more, but he looked younger, and vigorous.

It didn't help that Old-Man-He-Knows-A-Lot had congratulated Brant on divorcing Margarida. "One wife is better," the chief had counseled Brant. "Red-Rope has an easy way with women, but most of us are happier with one."

Patience, Brant told himself, would give time for his leg to heal, to elude Apache watchfulness, and take Margarida away.

When Red-Rope arrived, one of the men called, "So, you can't get up early anymore."

Another gave a ribald laugh. "The one with the new white wife gets up early, but not for hoop-and-pole."

Red-Rope accepted the joking with a satisfied smile, and patience seemed to Brant a worthless virtue. Then He-Starts-Fights appeared also, a reminder that only the chief's influence had prevented the vengeful warrior from enslaving Margarida and killing Brant. That thought kept Brant looking amiable, but maintaining a pleasant exterior took so much effort that he lost two hoop-and-pole games. He had to give up the necklaces he'd won gambling before.

The hours seemed long without a glimpse of Margarida. Since she wasn't his wife, he couldn't speak to her unless Red-Rope was there. He reminded himself of his plan—to seem uninterested in her so that he'd be less well guarded.

As usual, the evening meal was shared with Old-Man-He-Knows-A-Lot, the most pleasant time of the day. Brant liked to listen to stories of the chief's father, who had led large raids into Mexico and against the Navaho and Yavapai. Now Old-Man-He-Knows-A-Lot—probably as able as his father—hid in a small valley with only a remnant of his people. Brant encouraged the chief to keep on talking, putting off going to She-Goes-To-War's wickiup as long as possible.

When he left Old-Man-He-Knows-A-Lot, his mood worsened until it was darker than the interior of the wickiup when he entered. She-Goes-To-War startled him by saying, "I must tell you something."

She-Goes-To-War seldom talked to Brant. At first he'd tried to ask her about herself, but she barely responded, so he'd given up. "What is it?"

"I am going to have a baby."

Shocked, he stared at her. In all the turmoil, he hadn't considered that he might have impregnated this woman. Except for the first night, he'd been careful, withdrawing in time. And though he respected her feelings for her father, since her attack on Margarida he hadn't been able to lie with her at all. He'd claimed his leg bothered him.

His insides churned with questions. Could he leave behind a child of his blood? Try to take She-Goes-To-War with him? Wait until the child was born and take it? Impossible—all of these thing were impossible!

Then thought eased emotion. He'd married She-Goes-To-War less than three weeks ago. Would she know so soon if she'd conceived by him? "How do you know this?"

"I had another baby before, who died. I know." Her voice sounded defensive.

Her answer let his pulse slow down again. If it were his child, it would surely be too soon to know. She was a widow, permitted sexual freedom. For her to be so positive meant he almost certainly wasn't the father.

"Old-Man-He-Knows-A-Lot will be very happy," he responded. "And I will respect you and sleep alone."

"Yes," she agreed. "That is best."

Thankfully he watched as she arranged the bedding so that he had a separate place. The irony of his situation struck him—he was glad to be released from his duties to She-Goes-To-War. But Christ, how the idea of Margarida with Red-Rope hurt.

Margarida carefully pulled the long mescal leaf out of the earth-covered pit where the mescal heads were cooking. The July sun beat down on her, and she wiped perspiration from her face. She picked up a water jug and walked with Born-Twice toward the stream. It was two months since the mescal heads had been gathered in May. It seemed like years.

Then she'd been Brant's wife. Now Red-Rope was her husband. Her twenty-first birthday had passed, but she wasn't sure which day it had been. Two months ago she'd vowed to be strong, to learn, and to take care of herself. She had become stronger, and she'd learned—to cure hides, make moccasins, use a pointed stick to plant corn, build a dam to irrigate the fields—things she'd never dreamed of doing before. But now she had another problem.

Born-Twice walked with an easy rhythm, and Margarida felt grateful when she thought of how different these two months would have been without her. Born-Twice rarely smiled, but she concealed much kindness under her somber expression. As Margarida understood most of what was said and could speak halting sentences, some of the other women had come to treat her kindly, and she could relax with them. Though He-Starts-Fights obviously still hated her, She-Goes-To-War was indifferent now; Brant had been right about that.

She and Born-Twice filled the jugs from the stream and carried them to the ramada, where Born-Twice sat down to rest before going for firewood. In the warm weather, Margarida liked the brush shelter, open to the breeze on one side. She put down her jug and sat in the shade.

"I wish to ask you something," Born-Twice said.

Margarida wondered at the formality. "What is it?"

"Since you have been Red-Rope's wife, you have not . . ." Born-Twice paused, as if searching for a word. "In Apache, we say *ch'ínách'ilwo'*. The woman's time."

Margarida felt the blood drain from her face. Born-Twice knew what Margarida had hoped to conceal. "And sore here?" Born-Twice indicated Margarida's breasts.

"Yes."

A smile banished Born-Twice's phlegmatic expression. Her eyes sparkled, and she clasped her hands together. "I knew I was right! Very soon after you became Red-Rope's wife, I told him I suspected you might be pregnant. We have waited to be sure. Red-Rope will be so happy!"

"But Red-Rope's not—"

"Stop!" Born-Twice's eyes turned fierce, her face

determined. "You are Red-Rope's wife. Your child is his child. All will know that."

"But would he want a child that's . . . ?" Born-Twice knew that Red-Rope hadn't lain with Margarida, but Margarida hesitated to say it. "A child that's mine?" she finished.

"With our people, all children are wanted." Born-Twice's eyes softened, and tears glistened in the corners. "We have waited many years to have a child."

It hadn't occurred to Margarida that Red-Rope would claim a child he knew couldn't be his. She'd thought he might return her to Brant, and then she'd be in danger from She-Goes-To-War.

Escape seemed farther away than ever. Brant and she hardly ever spoke. She told herself it was to lull the suspicions of the Apache, who still never left her completely alone. But when she saw him with Old-Man-He-Knows-A-Lot, she noticed the way they talked and laughed and the admiration on Brant's face. Then doubt tormented her.

Did Brant really want to leave? In two months there might have been opportunities she didn't know about. Maybe without even realizing it, he'd hesitated because being here satisfied a longing he'd had for years.

After the first days of bitterness toward him for giving her to Red-Rope, she'd realized her plan of escaping without Brant was foolish. But she didn't know whether she could forgive him, even now. When she and Brant married, she'd hated the idea that he felt an obligation because of what she'd done for Walt. It would be much worse if he went with her because of a child. Still, it was his right to know, and she needed his protection.

She didn't want to disappoint Born-Twice about the child, but she had to make it clear now. "Brant—"

Again Born-Twice interrupted. "Angry-He-Looks-About is going to have a child too. She-Goes-To-War is pregnant."

How silly Born-Twice looked, saying something so foolish; this was no time for joking. Even as Margarida clung to the thought, the recognition of what she'd heard was rising like a flood. She struggled against it—Brant would have managed to speak to her somehow to tell her something so terrible. Then Born-Twice's revelation submerged her, and she was drowning, the excuses for Brant which had helped her through these two awful months washed away. He would have two children—one Apache and one hers.

No—she snatched at denial like a log floating in the flood. He could have his Apache child and his Apache wife, but this child would be hers. Hers alone! Let him think Red-Rope was the father of her child.

Born-Twice put her hand on Margarida's, a startling gesture for the older woman. "You will say this is Red-Rope's child." Her voice was unsteady, and she looked anxious, waiting for Margarida's response.

"Yes," Margarida promised. "I hope Red-Rope is happy." It would be a brief happiness, she thought, but she wouldn't spoil it today. She owed Born-Twice a great deal.

Later that afternoon Born-Twice and Margarida went to gather firewood along with other women. Though she could hardly stand it, she looked at She-Goes-To-War. There was no obvious sign of pregnancy. For a moment Margarida let herself hope what Born-Twice had told her was wrong, but that hope didn't last. She-Goes-To-War's tall figure wouldn't look much different for a long time. Bitterness and deep rage made a bloody wound in Margarida's heart. Don't think about it, she told herself. It was the only way to endure.

At mealtime that evening Born-Twice said to Red-Rope, "White-Flower is going to have a child."

Red-Rope had been reaching for bread. His hand hovered in midair as if it didn't know what to do. Then it snatched Born-Twice's hand. "A child! We will have a child at last, old woman." He burst into a joyous laugh. If the Apache kissed, Margarida thought, he would have kissed her. "I am very pleased, White-Flower," he added unnecessarily.

A look of love passed between Born-Twice and Red-Rope before he let go of Born-Twice's hand. As if disconcerted by his own emotion, he stood up. "I must sharpen my spear. Old woman, look after my bow and arrows. And see that White-Flower does not touch them now," he said gruffly.

"I know what to do, old man," Born-Twice retorted in her familiar grumbling voice, and Red-Rope went out with a jaunty step.

Margarida wished she hadn't seen how happy Born-Twice and Red-Rope were about her child. It meant their later loss would be greater. She couldn't help that, but knowing how they felt added to her distress.

The next evening He-Stirs-Up-Earth visited Red-Rope, as he often did. Red-Rope liked to act as mentor to the younger man. Because of his frequent visits, Margarida knew He-Stirs-Up-Earth better than the other men in camp, and she enjoyed his gossip. The painted warrior, who had held his spear on her months ago, had faded into a boastful, not-too-confident young man.

He said to Red-Rope, "I am glad the council decided to go on a raid. We are running out of meat, and hunting here has been poor lately."

"You are restless," Red-Rope responded, "but I agree with Old-Man-He-Knows-A-Lot. We should stay here and kill more of the horses we have, and use bows and arrows when the ammunition is gone."

"I think He-Starts-Fights was right," the young man argued. "We should go now. And two of the boys are ready to begin their four raids. They will never get a chance to become warriors if we hide here like women."

Red-Rope laughed. "I think you are ready for a raid."

He-Stirs-Up-Earth grinned and left.

Born-Twice said to her husband, "So there will be a raid?"

"Yes. Tomorrow we will use the sweat lodge, and at night we will have the dances." Red-Rope glanced at Margarida. "Angry-He-Looks-About will go this time."

Brant—going on a raid! Margarida had felt such anguish when she heard She-Goes-To-War was pregnant that she had told herself she would never care what he did again. But dread filled her at the thought of him in danger. And what of the people the raiders might kill—maybe ranchers like her father and brother?

Later she asked Born-Twice, "What happens on a raid?"

"Red-Rope says Old-Man-He-Knows-A-Lot tries to be careful they steal horses secretly, without being seen. If they kill no one, there is less reason for pursuit, and we are safer. He-Starts-Fights likes to kill, but Old-Man-He-Knows-A-Lot doesn't."

"Will the others follow Old-Man-He-Knows-A-Lot?"

"On a raid, one man is the leader, and everyone does what he says." Margarida prayed that would be so.

When the ceremonies began, she saw Brant sitting beside Old-Man-He-Knows-A-Lot, as he always did. Resolutely she watched the dances instead of Brant. Born-Twice had explained what would happen, and Margarida could understand many of the words now. Old-Man-He-Knows-A-Lot, dressed in elaborately beaded high moccasins and breechclout, danced first. "My heart stirs within me as the sun moves overhead," he sang. "That is the way the sorrows of my people make me feel."

The other raiders except Brant each chanted a song. As they danced, they pretended to throw their lances and draw their bows and arrows. He-Starts-Fights danced last, and he pantomimed with his weapons so fiercely that Margarida's old fear of him revived.

After that, all the men who had sung picked up a cowhide and danced four times around the fire with it. Two old women then faced the men, exhorting them to be brave. When that was over, the other women chose partners for dancing. Unlike the previous dance Margarida had seen, the married women joined in. Born-Twice explained, "They can dance all night, with any man, and even if they are talking with another man, it is all right."

A rush of longing for Brant made Margarida feel almost ill. Foolish, stupid, she scolded herself. If she dared approach him, what would she say: Is your wife pregnant? And he would say: Of course.

In response to invitations, Brant danced twice, moving clumsily. Margarida felt alarmed; his leg should have healed by now. How would he get along on the raid? When he crouched down at the end of a dance, she watched him, her heart pulling her one way, her unhappiness and feeling of betrayal another. He looked at her, and she felt invisible cords between them.

She started to rise and saw He-Starts-Fights watching her with such malevolent hatred that her legs trembled. What had she been about to do? Give He-Starts-Fights an excuse to foment distrust of Brant on the raid?

As if she only wanted to stretch her legs, she stood for a moment, then sat down again. If she and Brant could have talked, she wasn't sure what she would have said. Could he tell her anything that could ease her pain? And what of She-Goes-To-War and her child? She didn't know.

At dawn Margarida watched as the men, their faces painted, chanted their final songs. Each sang something different, one of being attacked by a bear and fearing for his life. Another of killing a Navaho man who had climbed into a pinyon tree to escape his spear. The medicine man, who wore a skullcap with long streamers of eagle plumes, sang last. "Death is everywhere. Death comes to everyone. But this is not your time. This time you will return." The drums sounded, and as they left, Brant, a single red stripe across his face, went with them.

Come back, she thought, come back without killing anyone. She might never be his wife again. She wasn't sure what she would tell him about the child. But she didn't want him to be a murderer, and she didn't want him to die.

Brant rode in the center of the file of six men and two novice boys. They were still watching and testing him, he knew. So far he'd been so carefully watched that escape had been impossible. But if he won their confidence now, they might guard him less carefully. If he failed in any way, Margarida would pay, even though she was Red-Rope's wife.

That fear kept his senses at their keenest and prevented him from dwelling on prospects ahead. Stealing horses, he could justify; the horses were on land that had been stolen from the Apache. But he'd never killed someone who wasn't attacking him. Would he kill an innocent person so that he could return to Margarida? He hoped to God he'd be alert and lucky enough he wouldn't find out.

He was on Chid, since no one else could manage him, but he was careful to keep his horse reined back so as not to show his speed. Old-Man-He-Knows-A-Lot's intervention had saved Chid from being killed—another reason for Brant to be grateful to the chief.

They went south, careful to scout ahead and avoid regular routes. About noon on the fourth day, they found an empty stone corral at the edge of a ranch, with fresh signs of many horses. Two posts had bars on each side which could be used to close the entrance. No one was about the corral or the ranch house. The men dismounted on a rocky hillside, con-

cealed among some boulders, debating whether to wait
for night to see what would happen.

Brant saw a dust cloud below. "Horses coming."

As they watched, the horses trotted into the corral
by themselves, with no one driving them. The men
looked at each other and back at the horses. "Someone here has horse power," Red-Rope said.

There was a general sound of agreement. Because
everyone avoided looking at Brant, he hoped they
thought he had power. "I will go and close the gate,"
he offered.

"I will go with you," He-Starts-Fights said quickly.

Brant eased Chid down the slope, then into a lope
across to the corral, careful to let He-Starts-Fights
keep up with him. Together they put up the bars of
the corral and returned to the hillside.

During the afternoon, Brant, his stomach in knots,
waited for the people to come back that he might have
to decide about killing. No one appeared. As soon as
the sun set, Old-Man-He-Knows-A-Lot said, "We will
get the horses now. We will not wait until night."
Praying their luck would hold, Brant rode with the
others down to the corral. "Go ahead and rope the
ones you want," directed Old-Man-He-Knows-A-Lot.
Soon each man had five or more horses.

Brant decided that Old-Man-He-Knows-A-Lot would
make a good foreman for a roundup. When the men
were ready to leave, the chief put He-Starts-Fights and
another man in the lead, then a man on each side of
the herd, and had the others, including Brant, behind.
"We will travel steadily for two days and nights," the
chief announced.

They drove the horses slowly for the first few miles,
then speeded up. When they were four or five miles
along, they heard hoofbeats and saw riders following
them. "The pass," Old-Man-He-Knows-a-Lot shouted,
and pointed east where the hills met in a narrow
canyon. They turned the herd that direction.

As they reached the defile, Brant heard the crack of rifle fire, then the buzz of bullets ricocheting off the rocks. He pulled Chid up at the first rocks large enough for shelter and readied his bow and arrow. Sweat ran in streams down his back and into the tops of his pants. These men were attacking him, but they were only protecting what belonged to them.

The pursuers appeared to be *vaqueros*, two of them skillful riders who could hang down on the opposite sides of their horses. Around Brant the Apaches were shooting revolvers and a carbine as well as bows and arrows. Brant loosed an arrow at the horse of the closest *vaquero*, hitting the animal in the neck, just below the mane. The horse started to buck, throwing the *vaquero* off and impeding the other riders. Another man saw the downed rider and grabbed him up. As if deciding the horses weren't worth the fight, the *vaqueros* retreated.

He-Starts-Fights kicked at his horse to go in pursuit, but Old-Man-He-Knows-A-Lot shouted, "No! We take the horses and go," and He-Starts-Fights halted. In moments the chief had the Apaches moving the herd swiftly through the canyon and up into the mountains. Brant felt shaky with relief.

They rode for the next two days and nights without stopping or eating. The dried venison and nuts which they'd carried with them from camp had been exhausted before they found the herd. On the third day, since they were nearing their camp, they stopped and butchered one of the horses for food, broiling strips over a small fire.

Old-Man-He-Knows-A-Lot crouched down where Brant sat, relaxed against a log, and said, "You did well, my son."

Something melted in Brant—a frozen shard of long-held desire for words such as those. He said, "I am glad you are pleased," and knew he would always remember this moment.

One of the horses, a white mare which Red-Rope had chosen, had a small silver bell around its neck. Red-Rope removed the bell and rubbed it, making it glow in the sunlight. "You can wear that yourself," one of the men said. "Then your women will know where you are."

Red-Rope laughed. "I will save it for my child. I will tell my son or daughter the bell is from the first raid I went on after I found out a child would be born."

Brant's exhilaration vanished. He kept his relaxed pose, but he felt as rigid as the wood behind him.

"Are you saying one of your women is going to give you a child?" asked Old-Man-He-Knows-A-Lot.

Red-Rope smiled, pride sparkling in his eyes. "It is White-Flower who cannot handle my weapons now. She is going to have my child."

For a moment Brant couldn't move. Red-Rope's words pierced him with the agony of another poisoned arrow. The joking which followed added more wounds that sent him to Chid, where he fumbled with a strap he'd already adjusted.

When his insides unclenched enough for thought, he told himself Margarida could be pregnant from the one time they'd made love since their capture. Rationally he knew that Red-Rope was the more likely father, but his hope let him get his pain under control. By the time they left, he'd curbed any sign of his turbulent feelings.

As he rode, he reminded himself he had no right to the rage that he felt. He'd done what he'd thought best at the time. If the choice seemed now more than he could stand, that couldn't be helped. No one was to blame, unless he was for starting out to Utah with Margarida in the first place. It would be unfair to burden her with his feelings, so above all he had to control his jealousy. She might not even know whether he or Red-Rope had fathered her child. At the thought

such frustrated fury swept him that he communicated
it to Chid, who danced nervously.

After he calmed the horse and himself, he began to
plan. Leg healed properly or not, watched or not, he
had to get her away. He thought of She-Goes-To-War
and the child she carried. Any responsibility to her, he
would have to consider later. His first duty was to
Margarida.

Tonight the women would have *tulpai* or *tiswin* to
celebrate the return of the raiders. With the drinking
he might not be so carefully watched. He'd surely
have a chance to talk to Margarida—calmly, with understanding. It would be difficult, but he owed her that
restraint.

When someone shouted that one of the raiders was
back, Margarida ran with the other women to hear the
news. In her fear and excitement, she lost all sense of
the messenger's words. She pulled roughly at Born-
Twice's arm. "What did he say?" she demanded.

"All men are safe." Relief weakened Margarida's
legs, and she held on to Born-Twice as much to brace
herself as to hear the rest. "They will be here by three
hours, bringing many horses. It is good we boiled the
corn for *tulpai*."

Margarida caught a glimpse of Brant when the men
arrived and was startled to see him on Chid. It was like
two pictures which had been torn in half and the
wrong parts put back together. Chid was her real life,
of ranches and Rio Torcido. Brant, with his Indian
garb and painted face, was this life. With a chill that
extinguished her happiness, she wondered if the pieces
would ever fit properly together again.

Red-Rope's return and Born-Twice's pleasure lightened Margarida's mood. Startled, she realized that she
had developed affection for both of them. Born-Twice
was her constant companion and teacher, but Margarida
hadn't expected to feel so much warmth at seeing

Red-Rope's smile again. She wasn't sure she liked having any attachment to them. It almost made her part of that mismatched picture.

When she saw Brant at the bonfire that night, he looked completely Apache. Like the others, he wore only a breechclout. A white band spotted with black was painted over his right shoulder and under his left arm. A similar band with red paint on white went over his left shoulder and under his right arm. He sat near Old-Man-He-Knows-A-Lot, and though Margarida couldn't hear what they said, she thought the chief spoke approvingly to Brant. Not far away, He-Starts-Fights cast looks of brooding anger at the two men.

The chief was the first to sing of the exploits during the raid. He sang of the trip, successfully avoiding enemies, of the discovery of the corral and the return of the unguarded horses, as if a power had sent them to be taken. His chant told of the accomplishments of different men and finished with, "And my son who came to us in the time when the leaves are full-grown secured the horses. When our enemies sought to kill us, his arrow went true. He is a warrior with much power."

In Brant's face Margarida saw the flush of pride and pleasure, and her heart felt squeezed into a tiny rock. It was what Brant had always missed—a father who praised him. Now this Apache father had given him public affection.

The *tulpai* and *tiswin* circulated freely, and no one paid much attention to her. As she'd done at the wedding dances, she retreated into herself, until Brant sang a short phrase praising the leadership of Old-Man-He-Knows-A-Lot and the bravery of the other men. Then the sight of two women shocked her into full awareness.

In her time in the camp Margarida had never seen even baby girls unclothed before their brothers. These two were naked except for necklaces and small pieces of buckskin like tiny aprons that fit over their pubic areas. They were *bizan*, one a widow and the other divorced.

Born-Twice leaned over and whispered, "All men are their husbands."

First the two women danced before the chief until he promised them each a horse. Then they danced for He-Starts-Fights, and he also promised them horses. After that they disappeared into the darkness. Two of the men rose and followed the *bizan*.

The girls began choosing partners. Margarida looked across at Brant, still beside Old-Man-He-Knows-A-Lot, then asked Born-Twice, "Will the married women dance?"

"No. Only the girls. Tonight some of the men will go with the *bizan*." She gave a slightly tipsy but smug laugh. "I think Red-Rope won't."

Born-Twice's words were a lighted match to Margarida's despair, exploding it into seething resentment. Brant had disposed of her as if she were his property, while he kept the freedom to do as he wished. In the fire of her anger, the constraints on his actions were meaningless. One of the men who'd followed the *bizan* returned. When he sat down, Brant rose and walked in the direction the two women had gone. She saw that he limped, but she didn't care.

As she stared blindly at the fire, Margarida felt that any tender feelings she had left for Brant were as consumed as the wood in the hot flames. Finally, indifferent to anyone's disapproval, she left the celebration and started for her wickiup. It was a kind of prison, but at least there she wouldn't have to watch as Brant enjoyed his male Apache glory. She entered, angrily jerking down the entrance cover, wanting to shut out sight and sound.

She heard a soft noise, and a hand on her mouth stopped a scream. "Margarida, don't be frightened." The barely audible voice was Brant's.

Joy flared momentarily, but her bitterness swamped it. She jerked away; only the habit of caution kept her voice low also, but she let it carry her fury. "You were very quick with your woman."

"I didn't go with the *bizan*. I just wanted others to think I had. We don't have time for arguments. I must know how you are."

"I'm fine. Born-Twice is teaching me everything I need to be a good Apache wife, and Red-Rope is a strong man—and a wonderful lover. Of course I'm fine."

His breathing quickened, but his soft voice stayed calm and steady. "Red-Rope says you're with child."

In a few wild moments of hope while she'd waited for the raiders to return, she'd pictured him coming to her, pouring out his love for her, explaining why he hadn't been able to speak to her before. He would deny that She-Goes-To-War was pregnant and swear he hated everyone here—rail at Red-Rope for even touching her. Now his flat voice mocked that hope, and wounded words rose to her mouth. "Pregnancy does happen when there's plenty of opportunity. After all, you didn't take long to get She-Goes-To-War pregnant."

"I'm almost sure it's not my child."

That "almost" finished the destruction his controlled manner had begun. "Then you won't have any regrets when we escape." She heard his hesitation more clearly than words and rushed on, using speech to strike out, inflict the suffering she felt. "If she were having your child, I'd understand why you might not want to leave. It bothers me to desert Red-Rope. He's so happy I'm pregnant."

His sucked-in breath and his voice, even though barely over a whisper, told her of the success of her attack. "We'll leave as soon as any chance comes. Be ready."

He stepped to the entrance and cautiously peered out, then slipped outside.

She stood, shaking with fury. She was ready to go now. Let him wait for an opportunity—but she'd find her own. If he stayed behind, he could be happy with his new father and with his wife and Apache child. Now she'd do the other thing she'd vowed in May— take care of herself.

23

MARGARIDA lay awake most of the night, tormented by her thoughts. If she attempted to get away and failed, she might bring dreadful retribution on herself and on Brant—all the things she'd imagined when she and Brant were first captured. But she couldn't stay, living in fear, for months or years. If she waited very long, her pregnancy would keep her here until the baby was born, and then escape might be even more difficult.

Despite what Brant had said last night, she wasn't sure he wanted to leave. She'd assumed the other Apaches watched him too closely for him to approach her—yet he'd come last night. Each time she saw him with Old-Man-He-Knows-A-Lot, Brant's affection and respect for the chief showed more clearly. Brant carried scars across his belly from the wounds he'd inflicted on himself long ago. That boy who had so desperately sought acceptance as an Apache still lived inside the man.

If she escaped alone, would that jeopardize Brant's life? Some of the Apaches might be suspicious of him, but the chief would surely protect him as he'd done before. Once she was gone, she thought angrily, Brant could stay here for as long as he wanted—until She-Goes-To-War's child was born. The child who would share Old-Man-He-Knows-A-Lot's blood and Brant's.

Her bitter thoughts decided her—she would go. Born-Twice had told her they would use more of the *tulpai* for a second feast. If the Indians were drinking, they'd be less concerned about her. Not long after dark a waning moon would rise, giving her some light; that would be her chance.

When morning came, she dressed and went to Born-Twice's wickiup, planning what she would need—a horse, a saddle, and food. Getting the food was easy. Born-Twice had already given Margarida a deerskin food bag to carry on a thong tied around her waist. Every person in camp carried one, with an emergency supply of dried meat, seeds, and mesquite-bean meal. The Apache, even the smallest children, kept the bags with them at all times, in case the valley should be penetrated and they had to flee. While Born-Twice was busy with the *tulpai*, Margarida added as much food as she could to her bag, and took a pouch made from a cow's stomach to use for carrying water. She hid the pouch with her breeches and a rolled blanket in her wickiup.

When Red-Rope returned from playing hoop-and-pole that afternoon, she asked him to show her his new horses from the raid. How she wished she could take Halcon, she thought, as they walked toward the corral. He-Starts-Fights had claimed her horse, and she hadn't seen Halcon for a long time.

"These are my new horses." Red-Rope pointed out a group of four mares and a gray gelding.

"They are handsome animals," Margarida responded. The gray looked sturdy, as if he could travel all day. She knew He-Stirs-Up-Earth had her saddle; she'd seen him carrying it to his wife's wickiup. In a few unwatched minutes she could get the saddle and a bridle, then hide them near the corral. She'd need one of Red-Rope's rawhide lariats. If no one guarded the corral tonight, the noise from the celebration would cover sounds she'd make.

As she turned to leave with Red-Rope, she saw Halcon at the far side of the corral. His bones stood out, and his head hung down dispiritedly. Unhealed welts marred his flanks. Grief and rage boiled up, and she thought that if He-Starts-Fights were here, she might attack him before she could stop herself.

Red-Rope gave her a sympathetic glance. "Some men are savages, like the whites," he remarked.

When they reached Born-Twice's wickiup, he motioned Margarida inside, then opened a leather bag and took out a silver bell. "This," he said, rubbing the bell with his fingers, "was on that fine roan mare. I want you to put it away safely. I will give it to my first child."

Margarida took the bell, still warm from Red-Rope's hand, and a quiver of sorrow for him passed through her. "Yes," was all she could say.

By evening, Margarida could appear normal only by numbing her mind, refusing to agonize over her plans. She would have liked to wear her breeches under her skirt, but since the proper way for an Apache woman to sit was with her legs straight out in front of her, the breeches would show.

Walking with Born-Twice to the bonfire, Margarida kept her steps measured, but her heart was already racing. She sat, as she usually did, at the back edge of the women's side of the fire. Red-Rope had taken the can of *tulpai* with him to share with the other men, but more *tulpai* as well as *tiswin* passed among the women. Tonight the men wore their regular clothing, without paint, and the two *bizan* had on their calico tops and skirts.

Brant sat next to Old-Man-He-Knows-A-Lot, never glancing her way. The two men talked and laughed together; once the chief put his hand on Brant's arm in an affectionate gesture. Yes, Margarida reassured herself, the chief would see that Brant didn't pay for whatever she did.

Margarida only pretended to drink from the containers going around. She felt as if a web of rawhide

were anchored in her stomach, with narrow strips
stretched to every nerve and muscle in her body. The
intoxicant might calm her, but she couldn't risk any
blurring of her senses.

As the drinking continued, singing began, followed
by dancing. Finally the moon appeared over the horizon. A quarrel broke out between two of the women,
and others tried to soothe them. Now, Margarida's
nerves screamed—she must go now, while the women
were occupied.

She stood up and slipped back into the shadows,
then looked across the fire. Brant was laughing, as if
he and Old-Man-He-Knows-A-Lot had just shared a
good joke. For a moment she felt so weighted with
grief that it anchored her moccasins to the ground.
Then she wrenched herself away into the darkness.

Once she started, Margarida didn't give herself time
to think. No one seemed to notice her, and the wickiup of He-Stirs-Up-Earth's wife was deserted. She found
the saddle and bridle and hid them in bushes near the
corral. At her wickiup, she tugged her breeches over
her sweat-damp legs, leaving on her skirt in case anyone saw her. Last, she plumped up her bedding to look
like a person sleeping.

As she picked up the lariat and her water bag and
blanket, she bumped something that made a heart-
stopping noise. It was the bell Red-Rope had given
her that afternoon. Without stopping to understand
why, she found a scrap of cloth and stuffed it inside
the bell to silence the clapper, then put the bell into
her food bag.

Outside, she saw no one and heard only the singing
and drumming from the direction of the bonfire. She
skirted the wickiups, praying no one would be on
guard at the corral. When she approached, she kept to
the grassy area near the brush fence so as not to make
noise. But she saw a figure—someone stood near the

entrance. Strangling with disappointment, she slumped down next to the fence.

The young guard was scuffing his feet and muttering to himself. She listened, frantically trying to think of a way to divert his attention. A new sound startled her.

"You have a poor job tonight." It was the voice of He-Starts-Fights. She had to choke off a scream.

"The girl who meets me on the water trail would be choosing me for dancing tonight, I know," grumbled the guard.

"It will be all right for you to come to dance for a little while," He-Starts-Fights suggested.

Hardly believing her luck, Margarida held her breath, listening to the guard's agreement and the sounds of the two men moving off. When she heard nothing more, she still waited, then finally put down her blanket and water pouch and cautiously crept to where she could see the entrance. No one was there!

In the pale silver light she quickly located the gray gelding. Getting the rope over his head proved difficult. He backed nervously, snorting, raising her terror with each sound. Oh, God, she thought, she'd spent years watching Walt handle nervous horses. Why couldn't she manage this one?

The gray backed off again, jostling the roan mare that had worn the bell. Margarida looked at the mare, standing docilely, and swiftly put a loop of rope around the roan's neck. It seemed as if Red-Rope had given her this horse. She led the mare out of the corral, picked up her bundle, and went to the trees where she'd hidden the saddle.

The mare hardly moved as Margarida saddled and mounted. She started the horse forward, then thought of Halcon and stopped—leaving him seemed too much to bear. A surge of drumming reached her from the bonfire. A child lived inside her, a child she must think of now as well as herself. The guard, and perhaps He-Starts-Fights, might return. She nudged the roan into a faster pace.

She kept to the trees, glad she'd studied the camp areas so thoroughly. She was sure she'd recognize the way around the hidden entrance. If she couldn't manage it in the moonlight, she would at dawn. No one would know she was gone until then anyway. By the time they followed her trail, she would be out and away from this valley.

The insanity of her actions surged up from the recess in her mind where she'd pushed it. How would she manage alone? How long would it take to find help? Resolutely she shook off her fear, reviving her confidence that she had the strength she needed. These Apache had taught her a lot.

They hadn't taught her how to cure her heart of the pain of loving Brant. That pain would become worse if she stayed here. She urged the horse onward.

Brant had noticed when Margarida left the bonfire, and was glad she'd gone back to her wickiup. If drinking dulled the Apaches' senses enough for an escape tonight, she'd be waiting. He knew where his guns and some ammunition were stored. In his mind was a map of how to get the guns, horses, and Margarida. With good luck, saddles too.

If only his conversation with Margarida last night had been different. Then he'd have waited longer, until He-Starts-Fights was away. Brant thought that would happen soon; the warrior was impatient, chafing under Old-Man-He-Knows-A-Lot's restrictions. It might give him time to decide more about She-Goes-To-War's child. But everything had gone wrong when he'd talked to Margarida.

He tried to look interested in the dancing; instead his mind revolved on her face—disdainful, angry, and softening with pleasure when she spoke of Red-Rope. It made his gut churn to remember. He'd kept his resolution to stay calm, not show her how he felt. After her angry first words, he hadn't told her he loved her—or how much he hated being apart from her. But, Christ, how could he—after she said what a great lover Red-Rope was?

Old-Man-He-Knows-A-Lot laughed, and Brant realized he'd missed a story and should be laughing too. A smile came easily as he watched the chief's face. It looked relaxed, and a glance in Brant's direction held shared pleasure and affection. Brant's love for this man welled up in response.

Margarida's words last night about having no regrets had made him realize how much the chief meant to him. In a few months, under bizarre circumstances, Old-Man-He-Knows-A-Lot had given him love his own father never expressed. From the beginning, Brant had felt a tie with this Apache warrior. His leaving would seem like desertion—betrayal. It made the grief he already felt more bitter.

"A wise man shares his powers, for the benefit of all." The chief was talking, and looking at him. Brant paid attention. "It is good to wait for a special sign that a young man is the right one to learn the sacred words."

"'If a man has no powers," He-Starts-Fights interrupted, "he might wait a long time, pretending he knows words when he knows none." He rose to his feet, his eyes flashing, his mouth curved in a triumphant look which took Brant to his feet also.

"This man has no powers," He-Starts-Fights shouted. The sounds of drums and singing wavered discordantly. "He only pretends to be one of us. Last night he went to see his white woman. Tonight he sent her to steal a horse and ride to the south entrance. He intends to follow. He betrays us."

Margarida gone! The words crashed in Brant's brain. "Wait!" Old-Man-He-Knows-A-Lot's command broke the silence the songs and drums had left. "How do you know this?"

"I have not believed from the beginning. I have waited and watched. Last night I saw him enter the white woman's wickiup. I heard them speaking in the white language. Tonight I watched the woman, and to make sure, took away the guard at the corral. She is on her way now, but the guards at the entrances will stop her."

Brant's shock turned into readiness. Every muscle in his body gathered for action. Surrounded by the other men, he must make no wrong move. He had no weapon. Time—he must create time to get away—to get to Margarida.

In his voice he released the effort his muscles were straining to make. "I deny your words. I did not send the woman. This is a trap you have set."

He-Starts-Fights' chest rose and fell violently as he screamed his madness. "You have betrayed us. For that you die." In a blur of motion he whipped a knife from the folded top of his moccasin and lunged at Brant.

In the second that movement took, Old-Man-He-Knows-A-Lot leapt forward, his arm upraised to grasp the hand with the knife. He-Starts-Fights twisted. The two men collided. The knife descended into Old-Man-He-Knows-A-Lot's chest.

Silence surrounded the frozen moment. The distorted face of He-Starts-Fights. The shocked surprise of Old-Man-He-Knows-A-Lot's mouth. The horror in Brant's mind. A woman's scream rose into a shriek; time started again.

Old-Man-He-Knows-A-Lot staggered backward, then slumped to the ground. Brant caught him as he fell, easing him down, and saw the knife, impaled in the buckskin over the heart, blood oozing around it. Old-Man-He-Knows-A-Lot's eyes stared into Brant's, recognizing him for an instant. Then they saw nothing.

Through horror and rage, Brant knew one thing. He-Starts-Fights must die. Whirling, he seized a knife from the moccasin top of the man next to him and propelled himself at He-Starts-Fights. He-Starts-Fights flashed out his hand, catching Brant's wrist. They reeled, their bodies locked together.

Resisting the crushing pain of the fingers around his wrist, Brant gripped the knife. He drove his other elbow into the warrior's ribs and levered a blow upward against the jaw. Pain jarred through his arm, but the blow loosened He-Starts-Fights' hold on the hand with the knife.

With a wrench, Brant pulled free and slashed at the sweat-gleaming throat. He-Starts-Fights dodged back, his eyes glaring with insane rage. The Apache lunged forward, and Brant crouched to meet him.

Twisting, Brant thrust upward, under the buckskin-covered arm, and felt the shock of flesh resisting and then accepting his knife. He pulled it free and slashed again at the now vulnerable throat. He-Starts-Fights gave a moan that turned to a gurgle. He staggered back and fell.

Heaving himself erect, Brant took in the scene—the horrified men around their chief, the terrified women. He'd have only minutes before shock wore off—before He-Starts-Fights' kinsmen acted. What they'd drunk might delay them a little longer. The map in his mind dissolved to just one route—Chid, and down the valley to catch Margarida.

He ran, past the wickiup of Old-Man-He-Knows-A-Lot's wife, then swerved and stopped. Just inside the wickiup lay the chief's favorite bow and quiver of arrows. Brant slung them over his back, seized a rope and a bridle, was outside again, and raced on to the corral.

At the entrance, he gasped for enough breath to whistle. From the shadowy mass of horses Chid trotted to him. In moments Brant had the bridle on, levered himself up, and kicked Chid into a gallop, following the edge of the stream and praying that Chid would keep his footing.

Brant's injured leg protested, but he'd made it away. No point in being quiet—they knew which way he was headed. Speed would help him leave them behind and catch Margarida.

Had He-Starts-Fights lied? No—he'd be discredited unless what he said was true. He'd plotted this, watching for just such an opportunity, letting Margarida get away. And she'd gone. The painful thought wasn't complete, and Brant forced his mind to continue. She'd gone without him.

Margarida heard the hoofbeats behind her and clutched the reins, thinking frantically. She'd counted on not being missed so soon. Should she try to outrun the horse behind her—or hide? The Apaches would be sure to find her. She leaned forward and urged the mare onward.

"Margarida." The cry came across to her, slowing her as she realized who it was. Brant had come after her! He'd looked for her and guessed which way she'd taken and come after her. The thought sang again. Brant had come for her. They were leaving—together. Now she could tell him about his child. Relief filled her.

In spite of his voice, the first sight of him raised her fears. The man on the black stallion, his hair flying back from the headband, the fringe of his buckskin shirt catching the moonlight, looked completely Indian. "Are you all right?" His voice only partly dispelled the image.

"Yes."

"Keep going, over to the right, to the stream."

Then she realized what he'd said. "But the entrance is ahead."

"We're leaving a trail." His impatience restored his familiarity.

"But how—?"

"For Christ's sake. Don't argue. Don't even talk. I'm ahead of them, but not for long. Just follow me." He put Chid ahead of her, toward the right.

They splashed for some distance down the stream until they came to a sandy bank. Brant turned Chid out across the edge, then back into the stream. She did the same. A short distance farther down, the stream curved close to a slab of shale, then went over a series of tiny falls. Brant dismounted and let Chid drink briefly and drank himself. Again she mimicked him, then got out her water bag and filled it.

Brant watched her, accepting the bitter knowledge that she'd made careful preparations. Deliberately he turned off his thoughts. That would be for later.

He lifted her across, up onto the shale, not letting himself notice how she felt under his hands. Then he took the mare's reins and rode Chid around the falls, leading the other horse. At the bottom he dismounted and led both horses scrambling back up the stream. When he reached the shale, he jumped Chid up onto the rock, making the mare follow, then helped Margarida mount.

He could tell from Margarida's hesitation that she didn't understand what he was doing. It would be better if she knew. Listening for a moment, he heard nothing—though that didn't mean no Indians were near. The Apache could be completely silent.

Carefully he led the horses along a rocky slope up into the trees, choosing each step to leave no trail. When they were in the trees, he went quickly back to erase any evidence of the way they'd come. Returning to Margarida, he lifted her down and leaned close to her ear to speak in his softest voice. "Down below by the stream I was trying to make it look as if we were covering our tracks, but not well enough. Up here I

think we've left no trail. Unless they notice that your
horse wasn't carrying your weight down there, they
should assume we followed the stream to the south
entrance."

Margarida, straining to listen, felt confused. "But
aren't we going there?" she whispered.

"They'll expect that. We'll circle back and go out
the other end of the valley."

"Back toward the camp?" Fear and doubt made her
palms sweaty.

"Yes. Around the canyon rim. Now, give me your
skirt."

Margarida gave a startled "What?"

"I can see you have breeches on. I only want the
skirt to muffle the sound of the mare's hooves." His
voice had a sarcastic edge she didn't like, but she did
as he asked. Tearing a strip from the bottom of the
skirt, he bound pieces over the hooves of the roan
mare.

"What about Chid?" she asked when he finished.

"He has rawhide shoes now that won't make as
much noise on the rocks. Come on. I want to be north
of the camp before daylight. We mustn't talk anymore."

As she rode after him, angling gradually upward,
she thought of things she wanted to know. How had
he found out she had gone, and how did he get away?

They made slow progress as Brant chose the route
which would leave the least evidence behind. Finally
they neared the top of the east ridge just about opposite the camp. Here Brant led the horses even more
carefully; the fading moon, low in the west, provided
little help. Margarida had an insane desire to go farther down, where they could see the camp, know what
was happening there. From that direction she heard
distant sounds, like moans or wails. They drifted eerily
on the wind, ghost voices, sending shivers across her
skin.

She stopped, listening. What did that mean? Ahead of her Brant halted also. Then he went on.

Through the night they continued, keeping just below the top of the ridge, halting once for Brant to replace the now shredded cloth on the mare's hooves. Dawn light marked the eastern horizon when Brant stopped under the overhang of a bluff. A large thicket of tangled aspen, high enough to conceal the horses, sheltered the front.

Margarida slid down, almost too weary to care about anything but rest—and her questions. "Is it safe to talk now?" she whispered.

"Yes." He sounded as weary as she.

"How long will we stay here?"

"We'll hole up during the day, rest the horses, and travel at night. The Apache don't like to fight in darkness unless they're attacked."

"Why not?"

"They believe if they're killed at night, they have to walk in darkness through the Place of the Dead."

His words reminded her of the scary moans and wails that had come from the camp. "What were the sounds we heard when we were closest to the camp?"

He waited, silent. When he finally answered, his voice sounded thick, as if he were having difficulty getting out the words. "The women are mourning the death of Old-Man-He-Knows-A-Lot."

"His *death*? What happened?"

"He-Starts-Fights killed him, partly an accident. Partly because of me." He stopped, and Margarida knew what she heard in his voice—tears. "I killed He-Starts-Fights, and came after you."

Her other questions crumbled at his words. The assumption she'd made when he appeared—that he'd come because of her—seemed like a statue with an unsteady base. It had barely balanced, and now it toppled, shattering around her. Struggling to keep some tatters of composure, she turned to her horse.

"Leave the saddle on the mare," Brant said, and Margarida's temper flared, feeding on the imagined answers to the questions she hadn't yet asked.

"You've given me enough orders for one night," she hissed. "You don't have to tell me how to breathe! I can take care of myself."

"Is that what you were going to do?" His low voice rasped with anger. "Is that why you left without me?"

"Yes!"

"You wouldn't have gone far. It was a trap. He-Starts-Fights set it up. He saw me go to your wickiup last night, then watched you today. He deliberately took the guard away from the corral to let you get a horse. But the scout at the hidden entrance was ready to stop you."

It was worse than she thought. "Then you didn't know I'd gone?"

"Not until He-Starts-Fights accused me of sending you and of betraying them."

If she could have stopped then, asked nothing more, she would have. But she had to face the rest. "And what happened? How did Old-Man-He-Knows-A-Lot die?"

The gray light matched his face, his expression the closed one she hated because it pushed her away. "He-Starts-Fights attacked me with a knife. Old-Man-He-Knows-A-Lot stopped him—and took the blow himself. It killed him." He clenched his hands, and his body was rigid. She knew he was struggling to find words to go on, but she had none to offer. Her own were strangled in her throat.

When his words came out, they were hoarse with grief. "I took a knife from the man next to me and killed He-Starts-Fights. Then I came after you."

Bitter grief and guilt seared her. She wanted to reach out to him, but she was afraid. She'd started a terrible chain by leaving as she did. "I'm sorry about Old-Man-He-Knows-A-Lot."

In the growing light he looked exhausted. "We can't talk more now. We must sleep. We'll have to take turns staying awake, to listen and make sure the horses are quiet. You rest first."

After she wrapped the blanket around her, she lay down at the base of the bluff. Brant took the bow and quiver from his back and put it down beside him, then leaned against the sandy wall. She studied his face. The lines around his mouth looked deep, as if pain had etched them there forever. Her wounded thought had to come out. "If I hadn't left tonight, things might have been different."

"He-Starts-Fights would have found some way to strike at us eventually."

"But Old-Man-He-Knows-A-Lot would be alive now. Today you could still be with him."

"Margarida, I love you. My place is with you." Those strained words that sounded forced didn't help.

"You loved Old-Man-He-Knows-A-Lot. You would have loved an Apache son."

Without hope, she waited for his denial. Instead she saw his tears and turned away to hide her own.

24

WHEN Margarida felt a touch on her arm, she opened her eyes to early-afternoon sunlight filtered through aspen branches. Groggily she sat up, sleep still heavy in her muscles. She started to speak, but Brant motioned her to silence. Of course, she thought, this might be the most dangerous time. By now the Apaches would know the guard to the south hadn't seen them and might be searching this way.

Brant's face looked pale, the skin drawn by fatigue— or grief. Using a curved conch from his necklace, he dipped water for her from the pouch. She took the sip gratefully, knowing they must keep most of the water for the horses. He offered her his food bag, but she shook her head and took some dried meat from hers. She would have preferred the nuts, but the horses could eat the nuts or meal if they didn't find grazing soon.

Brant, watching Margarida, felt the silence between them like a wall. That silence existed, not just because of the danger of being discovered, but because of all that had happened. Speaking was essential—and impossible just now. Even if they didn't have to fear being heard, these weren't the circumstances for the difficult words they needed. And he was still too angry that she had left camp without him.

Her face was thinner and her eyes sad; the crinkles at the corners of her mouth looked faint, as if she seldom laughed anymore. Impulsively he reached out to touch her face. She jerked back, and her dark eyes caught fire. Any words she'd use to him now, he decided, he probably didn't want to hear. In a perverse way, her antagonism reassured him. She still had the courage and spirit he loved, though whether she still loved him, he didn't know.

He lay down on the blanket, and discovered it carried her special scent—and memories of times they'd made love. In spite of his need for sleep, he lay awake for a time, watching the changing shadows overhead, grieving for the loss of Old-Man-He-Knows-A-Lot, and perhaps of Margarida.

At first while Brant slept, Margarida sat absolutely still, waiting for each new sound or movement. When an hour passed with no disturbance, she relaxed a little. Her hair was a tangled mass, which she parted and braided as best she could, fastening the end with a twist of grass. She watched the sky and listened to trills of birds and the rustle of wind through the aspens. Squirrels chattered in the pines below the bluff. Farther down the slope the trees thinned along the stream, and she saw a hawk circling in graceful alternation of soar and glide.

The hawk must have seen a rabbit or snake below, she guessed, because it went into a sharp dive—only to interrupt its flight in midair and turn steeply upward again. At the break in the expected pattern, she tensed with alarm. A flock of blackbirds rose from the trees, and her fear grew. Something had disturbed the birds—something more than a coyote.

When she touched Brant's shoulder, he was instantly awake, sitting up, a question in his eyes. She pointed to the meadow; with one motion he was up and beside the horses, pressing Chid's nostrils. Quickly she joined him and did the same for the mare. As they waited, she heard a voice and the whinny of a horse. Margarida felt the slight quiver in the mare that meant she would have answered if she could.

She strained to listen for more sounds. Once brush crackled on the slope below them, and she feared even to breathe. Every rustle after that turned into an Apache, but no one appeared. What seemed like hours later, she heard another whinny farther up the valley. Surely, Margarida thought, the Apaches didn't guess she and Brant were in the area or they would have stayed and searched. That meant Brant had been successful in disguising their trail when they'd turned back northward. After there had been no more human noises for some time, Brant released Chid's nostrils and stroked the horse's nose. Margarida had to flex her cramped hands before she could pat the mare.

He gestured toward the blanket with another silent question, but she shook her head. She couldn't possibly sleep now. He lay down again and in moments was asleep. Startled, she watched him; it made sense to rest when they could, but it took control she didn't have. Though she knew it was unreasonable, she resented his steady breathing.

Late in the day she heard voices again and was with the mare before Brant reached Chid. This time the voices were louder and passage was in the other direction, back toward the camp. Her hopes rose that the Indians didn't expect them at this end of the valley.

Nevertheless, when they left the bluff after dark, they used all the precautions of the previous night. Margarida was glad they had to be silent. If they'd spoken, her resentment at Brant's restraint might have come out, and she felt ashamed of it. She should be grateful, not unhappy, for his strength and composure.

Soon the demands of traveling in the dark made her forget everything else. Twice they stopped for Brant to rewrap the mare's hooves, and once they found a tiny spring where the horses could drink and she could refill the water pouch. Otherwise they traveled steadily, leading the horses when the terrain was too rough for riding.

Just before dawn they reached the place where the valley ended. Beyond was the canyon through which Margarida had traveled with the women to gather mescal. The guard, and perhaps others, would be here. Choosing each step to stay on ground covered with duff, Brant finally stopped in a thick stand of pines. He tethered Chid to a tree, and Margarida did the same with the mare. After she spread the blanket nearby, she lay down, expecting him to sit where he could see down the slope.

Instead he checked the arrows in the quiver and tested the string of the bow. When he finished, he stood looking at her. In the half-light, she couldn't see his expression, but some uncertainty in his stance made her heart beat faster. Then he gestured for her to stay where she was and started down the slope.

In a moment she was on her feet, following him. He motioned her back, but she only paused, waiting. It was clear he intended to confront the guard or guards, and she was going with him. He stepped close and cupped his hands around her ear to breathe more than say, "Stay here."

The touch of his hands and his head so close to hers startled her with a flare of excitement. Ignoring it, she shook her head. For a moment longer he looked at her, his eyes uncommunicative shadows. Then he brushed a tangled strand of hair back from her forehead before he turned and went on. She followed, still feeling the brush of his fingers against her face.

When they reached the bottom of the slope, he stopped. To their right, treeless boulders flanked the narrow opening out of the valley. Only a clump of willows broke the flat meadow in front of them. To get to the point where the guard would be, they had to cross the area of high grass. Again Brant motioned for her to stay, and again she shook her head. He lay down on his stomach and pushed into the grass, not looking back at her, as if resigned that she would decide to follow or not, regardless of what he did.

For a moment she hesitated, then imitated him. In the camp she'd seen the boys practicing creep-and-freeze—inching forward, then waiting, then forward again. She could do that too.

It was harder than she expected. The sharp edges of the grass scratched her hands and face, and she scraped over small stones and twigs. Each clumsy movement she was sure betrayed her. Hardest of all was keeping her head down, not looking. At every sound, her back prickled with imagined discovery. By the time she reached the willows, she could only rest, dragging big gulps of air into her lungs.

When she lifted her head, she saw that light enveloped the meadow, and sunlight touched the tops of the trees along the east ridge. A horse was tethered near the bottom of a boulder; Margarida's hope leapt that one horse meant only one man. Something moved on top of the rocks at the canyon entrance. It was an Indian, his back to them, looking out to the north. A rifle leaned against the rock beside him. He shifted, and she recognized He-Stirs-Up-Earth.

A confusion of feelings filled her. She had grown to like He-Stirs-Up-Earth during his visits to Red-Rope. Now he was the enemy who blocked the way out of the valley.

Brant strung his bow and crouched just behind the front screen of the willows. He took an arrow from the quiver, fitted it to the bow, and pulled back on the string. A cold hand seemed to be holding Margarida by the throat, cutting off her breathing, bottling her anguish inside. She put her hand over her mouth as he lifted the bow and sighted along the arrow. He-Stirs-Up-Earth stood in clear view, the sunlight striking his black hair and red headband.

She turned her face away, trembling, waiting for the whing of the bowstring, but it didn't come. She looked at Brant. He still stared up at He-Stirs-Up-Earth, but he'd lowered his bow. Perspiration ringed his mouth, and his face was full of pain. He started to raise the bow again, then looked at Margarida. She didn't need words to know he shared her anguish.

There must be a way besides killing He-Stirs-Up-Earth. She thought she saw that way. Using Brant's phrase, she said, "Stay here out of sight." Moving too quickly for him to stop her, she stood up and stepped out into the meadow, waving and calling, "*Shû!*"

At her hello, He-Stirs-Up-Earth grabbed his rifle and leveled it at her, almost sending her back into the willows. Bracing herself, again she shouted, "*Shû.*" The rifle wavered, and she could breathe. He-Stirs-Up-Earth started down, holding the gun.

She moved two paces forward and waited, her blood pulsing against her ears as he crossed the grass and stopped in front of her. At the fierce expression on his young face, her Apache deserted her. She could think only of "*Noshkaah:*" Please, I beg you.

His Apache words came at her in a torrent. She heard "Death" and Old-Man-He-Knows-A-Lot's name, but terror swallowed the meaning of the others. Only his anger was clear. She backed away, trying to remember her plan—yes, it was to circle so that his back would be to the willows.

Her fear made her stumble, and he raised the rifle to strike her. As she scrambled to one side, Brant leapt from the willows and caught He-Stirs-Up-Earth around the throat. They swayed together, and then were down, with Brant on top, wresting the rifle away.

When he stood, the rifle trained on He-Stirs-Up-Earth, she said shakily, "I thought he wouldn't shoot me."

His chest heaving, Brant gasped, "You were right, but it was an insane thing to do."

After they tied a sullen He-Stirs-Up-Earth to a pine tree, Brant went for their horses. From He-Stirs-Up-

Earth's supplies Margarida took matches and an extra rope. Chid and the mare grazed briefly before Brant put He-Stirs-Up-Earth's saddle onto Chid and then attached a lead rope to the young Indian's horse.

When they were ready to go, Brant spoke to He-Stirs-Up-Earth. "Others will come soon and free you." The Apache wouldn't look up or answer. Margarida wanted to ask about the camp—about what had happened after Brant left—but she knew He-Stirs-Up-Earth wouldn't tell her.

It was barely midmorning when they started through the canyon. When they reached the narrow part of the trail, they led the horses. With every step that she inched along, Margarida remembered She-Goes-To-War's attempt to kill her here. It seemed as if her feet were slipping again. Her clenched hands ached and wanted to hold to the canyon wall. When they reached the end, Margarida's legs still trembled.

A herd of antelope grazed in the place where the mescal grew. Brant pointed to the animals. "That means no one has been here recently. It's safe to go on." When they rode beyond that area, Margarida finally began to feel as if they'd left the camp behind.

The day moved past her, narrowed to numb plodding. Brant guided them across rocky stretches in order to leave no tracks, and over descending slopes out of the mountains. At dusk he stopped and built a campfire. Margarida looked for a place to tether the horses, but he said, "We're not staying here."

Fatigue made her voice cross. "Then why are you building a fire?"

"To make someone think we are here and slow down to find out."

It was several hours into night by the time they stopped in the side canyon of a deep arroyo. Margarida was barely keeping herself erect after the exertions of the previous night and day. "We'll spend the rest of tonight here," Brant told her, "and go on tomorrow."

"Is it safe? Won't they catch up with us?" she mumbled, not sure she had enough strength to care.

"I think they won't pursue us this far out of the valley," Brant responded. "I'll take the horses back to the spring we passed, to water them and fill the pouch. You're to *stay here*."

Not wanting him to leave but too exhausted to argue, Margarida complained, "Why didn't we camp at the spring?"

"Most travelers stop at springs. I don't want to be surprised by anyone."

She expected to be frightened, listening for every noise, until he returned. But the blanket lured her, and when she roused, morning light was creeping across the sky. Dazed, she looked around. Brant was asleep, leaning against a saddle, the blanket they'd taken from He-Stirs-Up-Earth around his shoulders.

Sleep had cleared her mind, and she looked at him, seeing dusty lines of strain on his face. He grieved over Old-Man-He-Knows-A-Lot, she knew, but he didn't act as if the uncertainties with her bothered him. Of course, they hadn't had time to talk. Even so, she couldn't forget he hadn't seemed upset that she was having a baby—a child he thought Red-Rope had fathered. The prospect of telling him it was his child made her stomach churn again.

She sat up, and at her movement he was awake and up on his knees, grasping the rifle. Startled, she said, "It's all right."

He looked around, blinking, and for the first time since the nightmare of escape had begun, he gave a half-smile. "I'm afraid anyone could have crept up on us," he said ruefully. He rose and picked up the saddle. "We need to get going right away. We'll have to stop in the middle of the day because of the heat."

Vaguely she remembered that yesterday the noon sun had burned down on them and realized this must be about the first of August. The thought was strange—

as if she had lived a whole life since they'd left the ranch at the end of April.

After a few hasty bites of the dried meat she was beginning to detest, Brant helped her into the saddle. He mounted and started off into the sun. "Wait," she called. "We're going the wrong way."

He paused and looked back. "No. Fort Wingate's east of us."

"Fort Wingate?" She urged her mare until she was beside him. "But we're going to Utah, to find Papa!"

He looked at her as if she'd said they were going to the Atlantic to swim to Europe. "Margarida, we're heading to the closest army post, and then we're going home. We've been away for months. Everyone must be worried and probably looking for us. Your father has been where he is for a long time. If he's alive, we'll see about him later."

Until this morning, she hadn't really thought about where they were going. But now it seemed as if everything that had happened would be insanity unless they finished what they'd started out to do. "No. I *won't*. I won't go home until I find Papa."

"Are you suggesting we start off on a trip we should never have made in the first place, with two food bags, a rifle, a little ammunition, and a bow and arrow? And a knife. I forgot the knife. That makes it all right then."

She knew he was tired, that she was tired, that she couldn't think rationally. But his sarcastic voice loosed the hurt and rage she'd stored up for months. "You've been in charge of my life for the last time!" Dimly she knew she was screaming, and that was exactly what she wanted to do. "I'll decide what I do from now on!"

His voice erupted with a savage intensity that penetrated even her rage. "When we get home, all right. For now, you'll do what I say, even if I have to tie you up. You'll go home, and you'll stay there until our child is born."

All she could hear was Brant ordering her life again—as he'd done when he bargained her off to another man. He'd given her away to Red-Rope, so he'd given away their child at the same time. Furiously she struck back. "Don't you say *our* child. It's *my* child. Not yours. Not even Red-Rope's now. If you want a child, go back to She-Goes-To-War."

"I can hardly do that now."

"And it's my fault, of course. Because I found a chance to leave and took it. You'd have waited forever. So cozy with your Apache father and your Apache wife and your Apache child."

He looked at her, muscles tight along his jaw, his chest rising rapidly, but with the control she couldn't stand. "We'll talk about this later."

Rage and bitterness and loss tumbled from her. "It's too bad you left. Now you don't have any of those—a father or a wife. Or a child."

The slashing words lay between them like slivers of glass, melting and fusing into a barrier that grew wider until it pushed them far apart. Slowly, almost wearily, he said, "Any child you have is my child," and turned and rode east toward Fort Wingate.

Her rage drained away, leaving a cavernous hole where her heart should be. She watched him, then put her heels to her mare and followed.

They hardly spoke after that. To Margarida each hour seemed to blur into the next. Sometimes the sun blazed down, and they crawled under mesquite or juniper for shade and waited. When the roan mare stumbled with fatigue, Margarida rode the third horse. At springs they got water, but they camped in arroyos or gullies. The horses found scrubby grass for food, and though they looked more scrawny, they held up. Several times Brant killed rabbits. Then, at midday, he used very dry wood he'd collected along the way for a smokeless fire to cook the meat.

On the evening of the sixth day after leaving the valley, Margarida emptied her food bag and found the bell at the bottom. She unwrapped it and looked at it, remembering Red-Rope's face when he gave it to her. Brant was watching, with the same distant expression he'd had constantly since their quarrel. Wanting to provoke him, she said, "Red-Rope gave this to me, for the child," and then felt ashamed.

"I know," he said, as calmly as if she'd mentioned how hot it had been that day.

She wanted to ask him how he knew, but before she could speak, he said, "We need a story to explain what happened to us."

Startled, Margarida realized she hadn't considered what to tell people. "Yes, but not the truth."

"No. That might bring soldiers down on the valley. Since I have a limp and a scar, we'll say we had an accident. I was hurt and our gear was lost. We had to wait until I was well enough to travel, and some passing Indians helped us."

"All right."

He looked away, then back, as if he'd rather not face her but felt he must. "When we get home, I'll see first how conditions are there. Probably they'll be fine. If they are, as soon as things are settled down, I'll leave for Utah to look for your father. It's been a long time, and Jesse may be dead, but I must look for him myself. It won't be the same as if you went, but if your father can recognize anyone, I think he'd know me. I'll take Tall Man and several *vaqueros* who work for your father, men he'd know, Carlos García for one."

Margarida felt a confusing mixture of gratitude and resentment that lingered from his refusal to go now. "I'm glad," she said.

"I plan to do something else as well." He sounded as if he expected her to argue with him. "After I've found your father, or at least definite information about him, I'm going back to the camp."

"What!" If he'd hit her, it wouldn't have stunned her more. "But how could you? You'd be killed."

"I've thought about this very carefully. If Jesse is well enough, I'll let him wait with Carlos and the others. I'll tell them I want to make a detour to look for the Indians who helped you and me. Tall Man will go with me, and we'll approach the camp over one of the ridges, not let anyone see us until we can tell how things are."

Her mind whirled around the question she feared to ask but had to. "Why?"

The muscles along his jaw tensed. "If I can, I must see She-Goes-To-War. Find out that she and her baby will be safe."

Margarida gripped her hands to keep them from trembling, but that didn't stop her fury. Brant had just shown clearly what was important—a child who was Apache. From deep inside she dredged a calm voice. "You said the baby isn't yours."

"I think it isn't. She-Goes-To-War knew she was pregnant too soon for it to be my child. But I feel a responsibility to her. It's hard to explain, but I did take her as a wife. I need to know whether she suffered because I killed He-Starts-Fights."

What about your responsibility to my child? she wanted to shout. But she'd relieved him of that by letting him think it was Red-Rope's child. "Then why did you leave the camp?"

"You know why."

Her restraint wavered, the bitterness seeping through. "Yes, I'd left, and you had to look for me."

"Margarida, it won't help to go back over that." His voice told her his control was less than it appeared. "My first concern will be your father. If he's alive, I won't jeopardize him. And I'm not going to take any unreasonable risks myself. I know what I'm getting into this time."

"I understand," she said, and remembered when she'd told him that before—when he agreed to take She-Goes-To-War as a wife. Her words were lies both times. She hadn't thought she could feel new resentment and bitterness, but now she did. At least his plan settled whether she should tell him about their child. Brant could go on thinking that Red-Rope was the father. Then Brant could look for his Apache wife without having to worry about a child at home—a child he didn't need. "I hope you'll be able to see how Born-Twice and Red-Rope are getting along."

His mouth tightened again as he said only, "Yes."

She rolled herself in her blanket and lay down silently. Words seemed too dangerous—whatever she said, it would be wrong.

Late on the afternoon of the next day as they came over a rise, a cloud of dust moved toward them from the far horizon. "Those rocks, to the right," ordered Brant, and put Chid into a gallop. She followed, sliding off behind a yellow sandstone formation that jutted up enough to give them cover.

"Keep the horses quiet," he directed, and climbed up the rock until he could see over the top. She tried to work up enough resentment at his tone to divert her from fear, but she was too tired.

He dropped back down beside her, a grin she hadn't seen in months creasing his face. "Cavalry. Must be from Fort Wingate." He lifted her into the saddle and swung up himself.

"Brant, wait. From a distance they'll think you're an Indian. They might shoot you."

He paused long enough to give her an assessing look. "You're no different." He jerked on the lead rein of the extra horse and started around the rocks.

She followed, expecting rifle fire any moment. Instead she heard Brant give a shouted hello and saw him gallop, with upraised arm, toward the line of cavalry. When she reached the column, men were clustered around him. They stared at her, and she realized how strange she must appear.

What surprised her was how she felt. For a panicky moment she wanted to turn and run. These were her people, white people, but they looked alien. She felt that she'd lost some part of herself, so that she no longer belonged with them. Or with anyone.

25

MARGARIDA finished buttoning her too-tight morning dress and decided she must make maternity clothes. She was in the bedroom that had once been Rupert Curtis' and had been hers for the month since she and Brant returned. She explained the separate room by saying her pregnancy made her restless at night; as with their explanation of the summer, everyone believed her.

Brant had stayed home only two weeks before he left for Utah. During that time he'd been away from the house a good deal, seeing to the ranches, and all his spare time he spent at the Apache camp. Since he took Walt with him and came home at night, Margarida hoped he didn't visit the widow, but he never said what he did.

The silence between them had lasted through the confusion at Fort Wingate and the trip home by stage and railroad. Since then it had become worse, like a fast-growing tree, easy to uproot when young, but resistant as its roots spread. When they did see each other, they talked politely of the ranch and of other people—externals that hardly mattered. But of her confusion—the bitterness and anger she felt—she said nothing. If anything bothered Brant, he didn't tell her or show it in his manner.

Now she wandered restlessly to the bedroom window, trying to decide where to ride. Brant hadn't been gone long enough to hear from him, so staying at the ranch was pointless. She hadn't resumed the chores that Luisa had managed completely over the summer. Visits with her mother and Adela and trips to see Priscilla took some of her time, but she didn't relax with them, trying to be careful of what she said. Walt, usually her solace, was with Juan. She decided to get Bailarina and ride—somewhere.

An hour later she sat on her favorite rock. The pine trees had the fragrance she loved and the morning sun warmed her, but these things didn't soothe her unhappy spirit. Where else could she go?

Not to the line shack. She'd gone there once since she'd been home. It had been foolish—a wistful attempt to recall the happiness of her wedding night. The building had looked lonely, the door closed and the window shuttered. She'd noticed something glinting under the window—sunlight reflecting off shards of broken glass. Of the special efforts Brant had made for their wedding, not even the window remained. It was shattered—like their marriage.

Lobo bounded up from a futile chase after a squirrel and gave her a doggy kiss. Absently she rubbed behind his ears. "Lobo, why can't you talk?" she asked him. "I love you, but I need . . . I need . . ."

Slowly, with a sense of shock, Margarida admitted to herself that she missed Born-Twice. She felt lonesome for Born-Twice and the other Apache women—for the pleasure of communal tasks, the friendly joking among them. The way they helped each other. Startled, she realized where she wanted to go—to *shiwóyé*'s camp.

Since they'd been home, Brant hadn't asked her to go with him to the camp, as if he'd reclaimed its Apache life as his alone. She hadn't considered going without being asked; it would be as if she were checking up on him.

But he wasn't here now. She scrambled down and mounted Bailarina. "Lobo," she commanded, "go home." He stopped and looked at her as if he couldn't believe her. She couldn't take him; the camp had too many dogs. "Go home!" With a look of dejection, he trotted into the trees.

As she rode, both her anticipation and her apprehension grew. She wanted to see the women, smell food cooking, hear the men shouting from the hoop-and-pole field. But how would *shiwóyé* receive her? Had Brant told his grandmother what happened over the summer?

The first sight of the wickiups and ramadas brought her a rush of pleasure. When she reached *shiwóyé*'s wickiup, she dismounted, feeling a mixture of shyness and longing. Then Brant's grandmother came out, and her smile lessened Margarida's trepidation.

"Welcome, granddaughter. Come inside."

Shiwóyé spoke in Apache, and relief dissolved Margarida's last fear. Brant must have told his grandmother what had happened. She didn't have to pretend.

Inside she saw that *shiwóyé* had been making moccasins. Without asking, Margarida found another bone needle and strip of sinew and began to sew a soft upper to the rawhide sole. As Margarida sewed, *shiwóyé* prepared food for them and reported what had gone on in the camp. Margarida felt more peaceful than she had in months.

She only half-listened, studying *shiwóyé*'s face. It had the same strength as Old-Man-He-Knows-A-Lot's—a strength learned in a difficult way of life. Then a particular name caught her attention. "She-Runs-Fast has taken a husband?"

"Yes." A smile danced in the old woman's eyes.

Margarida didn't try to hide her own pleasure. "I'm glad," she acknowledged.

They ate stew and dried shreds of mescal. Margarida wondered how food which now tasted delicious had ever seemed strange to her. From the shadows outside, she could tell she must start home, but she hated to leave. Her turmoil of resentment and bitterness and self-doubt seemed too much to contain. Words burst from her. "Everything is so terrible between us, and I don't think it can ever be fixed."

Once loosed, more words tumbled out. "Brant always wanted to be Apache. That's what made it so hard for me. He was so calm—he didn't seem bothered when he sent me to Red-Rope. And now he wants to find out about She-Goes-To-War. I don't understand that. What should I do?"

Shiwóyé's eyes looked sympathetic. "I cannot tell you. No one can make another person different from what he is. You will have to find inside yourself what to do. But I can tell you that it is a man's duty to protect a woman. He must be strong and not burden her with his feelings, no matter how hard it is for him."

She paused, then went on. "My grandson knows well how to conceal his heart. Maybe because it is too tender. And he understands we value children above all else and must guard the welfare of any child."

Margarida felt hope stir within her, like the first fluttering of the child that was hers and Brant's. Could they have a life together again? Had Brant concealed unhappy feelings, even some remaining tenderness for her? She'd never know unless she had the courage to talk to him. She rose. "I must go home. Thank you for the food and listening to me."

"I hope you will come to see me often."

"I would like to."

As she rode home, Margarida's peaceful feelings dissipated. While she listened to *shiwóyé*, it seemed possible to speak to Brant. Though it would be hard to approach him, to breach his closed face, she could do that. What she couldn't stand would be for him to feel obligated to her again. Maybe pretend he loved her for the sake of the child, when his silence and indifference since they'd been home showed he probably didn't.

She would hate that. And would he even believe her now?

The next afternoon Margarida was working alone in the kitchen when someone knocked at the door. She opened it and saw a tall bearded man in dusty clothes and a hat that shaded his eyes. Her heart leapt. Maybe Brant had sent him with word of Papa. No, two weeks wasn't enough time.

"Margarida, don't you know me?"

It was J.J.'s voice! He took off his hat and she recognized his eyes as well. J.J.'s eyes in this stranger's face. Then he pulled her into an exuberant hug, lifting her off her feet, swinging her in a wild arc that matched her feelings of joy.

"Oh, J.J., I knew you were alive. I knew it! How wonderful you look, even with that beard. And you're taller."

"You look good. A little plumper, I see."

"When did you get home? Did Brant find you—no, that couldn't be. Mama must have had a fit when she saw you."

He sat down, stretching out legs that were longer than she remembered. "I haven't been home yet. I came through Rio Torcido and ran into Henry Franklin. He told me you and Brant were married and that Papa's been away a long time. I thought I'd stop and see you and Brant—find out what that's all about before I go home. You know how Mama is—she can get really upset. I can guess how she felt when I left. I'd rather know what I'm facing."

"Yes, you're right. She's been . . . very worried."

"Where's Brant?" J.J. asked. "Around outside?"

"He went to the Utah territory, to find Papa."

"What's Papa doing in Utah?"

Margarida began to feel that nothing made sense. "Papa followed you and Michael Quinn there. Remember, you wrote you were going prospecting with him in Utah?"

"I didn't go. I decided something was wrong with Quinn. I went a little way with him, but then he made me uneasy, and I skipped out. I've been all up and down California since then." He grinned. "I've had plenty of adventures. Not dull, like staying home."

Margarida sat down suddenly at the table. Could it all have been for nothing—Papa's injuries, the troubles she and Brant had—for nothing? The thought almost made her feel sick. "Staying home isn't always dull."

"Why did Papa go after me?"

"Michael Quinn and Papa were old enemies, over a shooting that happened in California a long time ago."

"So that's why Quinn was interested in me. But it's still crazy. Why would Papa think he'd find me?"

"Mama made him go. And he did find Michael Quinn." She went on to tell her brother most of what had happened in the two years he'd been gone, though she didn't include the real story of the past summer. By the time she finished, he looked as stricken as she felt.

He rose and picked up his hat. "I guess I started a hell of a mess. I'll see Mama, and then go to Utah."

"No!" Margarida jumped up and grabbed the edge of his coat. "You won't leave Mama again now! If anyone can find Papa, Brant will do it."

"I guess you're right. You always did think Brant could do anything. At least you finally got him for a husband."

As he kissed her and left, she thought sadly that she didn't really have Brant—not anymore.

Glory Creek looked much as Brant had imagined a small town in the Utah territory. The dry-goods store could have been the one in Rio Torcido, dusty and shadowed. While the owner lamented his lack of business, Brant listened, then asked, "Do you have many Indian customers?"

"They come into town every month or so, the ones who still live around here. Always visit my store. Matter of fact, they ought to be along any day now."

Brant's heart began to pump faster. He'd decided before he arrived in Glory Creek that he would first ask store owners about the Ute Indians. Now was the critical question. "Do they ever have a white man with them?"

The owner looked Brant over. "You're not army? No," he said, answering his own question. "You must be talking about the one who's not quite right in his mind. Yes, he's usually along."

Brant felt almost shaky with relief. Margarida's father was alive! Now, he thought exultantly, if his luck held with the Ute, he could take Jesse home.

An anxious week later, he stood across the street from the store and watched the Indians arrive. He hardly recognized the old man with them. Jesse Ross moved uncertainly, peering at faces of people near him. He had a white beard and wore a shabby shirt and pants. Only his leather hat with a braided red band looked familiar.

One of the Ute women stationed Jesse beside the entrance to the store and said something. Then the Indians went inside.

Apparently the people in the town had seen Jesse many times, because the ones who passed by paid no attention to him. He appeared to ask each one a question, but no one answered. His heart sad with pity, Brant crossed the street.

Jesse looked at Brant without recognition. "Have you seen J.J.?" His voice, though hesitating, was familiar.

"Mr. Ross, I'm not sure where your son is, but I know him. And I know you." The faded eyes looked startled, then perplexed. "I'm Brant Curtis. Do you remember me?"

"Have you seen . . . ?" Jesse voice trailed off uncertainly, as if his thoughts had become tangled.

A Ute man came out, an unfriendly expression on his face. Brant put his hand on Jesse's shoulder and hoped the Indian understood English. "I'm Mr. Ross's son-in-law."

"Yes," Jesse said, his voice shaking. "Brant."

The Ute said to Brant, "Your father?"

"Yes," Brant said. The other Indians came out of the store and gathered around. They looked at Brant warily. One old woman said something to Jesse, who didn't answer, staring at Brant.

Careful to keep his apprehension from showing, Brant spoke to the first Ute. "I know you have all cared for my father well, and I too will care for him. I will take him home to his wife and daughter."

The Ute conferred with the others, then said to Margarida's father, "Do you want to go with this man?"

Jesse looked at the Ute, then at Brant. "Yes," he said in a trembling voice, "I want to go."

Brant felt as if he'd watched a tornado approach and then disappear. He thought of offering the Indians something for all they'd done for Jesse, but he didn't want to insult them. He said, "I thank you for caring for him so long and so well. If I can serve you in some way, I wish to do so."

"We do not want payment for helping an old man," the Ute said, his face proud and dignified.

When Brant took Jesse to the hotel, Jesse didn't recognize anyone at first, but later he called Carlos by name. He was most at ease with Tall Man, and he didn't ask any of them about J.J. Brant spent two more days inquiring about J.J., but as he expected, no one knew anything.

From Glory Creek they traveled east to Fort Lewis, where the post doctor examined Jesse. The doctor found evidence of a head wound and suggested that

Jesse's confusion and loss of memory resulted from that wound and probably a very high fever afterward. Though weak and frail, Jesse seemed to have no other ailments, and the doctor offered no remedies except taking him home.

By the time they left Fort Lewis, Jesse was more alert, making confused references to home that showed some returning memory. When they reached the place Brant and Tall Man would leave the others temporarily, Jesse was clearer in his mind. Brant felt confident they could wait while he went to the hidden valley.

Two days later, Brant and Tall Man reached the north entrance of the valley. Brant crept to the rock where He-Stirs-Up-Earth had been, but no one was there. Brant should have been pleased; they could go on easily. Instead he felt alarmed.

They stopped to rest in a sheltered spot near the ridge, and Brant indicated that he would take the first watch. Tall Man was asleep moments after lying down. Brant watched the sun's indifferent course across the sky and thought about Margarida. Coming here may have further endangered his marriage. If he still had one to endanger.

He'd been more careful than he would ever have guessed possible, to give her time to get over the shocks of the summer. When she laughed with Walt, with the old gaiety, he hoped things were better. But when she looked at him, her laughter died, and he knew he had to wait longer.

After the baby came, he tried to reassure himself, she'd change. Surely she'd love a baby, even of an Apache father. Then he remembered how she'd praised Red-Rope's skills as a lover, and he felt all his old anger.

He thought he couldn't have stood it without *shiwóyé*. She and Tall Man were the only ones who knew what had happened. If he couldn't have seen her, he'd have gone crazy. She listened without judging or offering comments.

Early the next morning he and Tall Man arrived above the camp. They heard no voices; not even a dog barked. There was no smell of smoke from cooking fires. Moving cautiously, Brant reached a place overlooking the camp.

Nothing moved below. The corral was empty, and the landscape as silent and undisturbed as a graveyard. Loss swept over Brant like a chilling wind. Just what he mourned, he wasn't sure.

Two wickiups had been burned; they were those of Old-Man-He-Knows-A-Lot and of He-Starts-Fights, destroyed because they had died. So there probably hadn't been an attack. But what had happened? Then in front of one wickiup he saw a small, bent figure. It was Two-Walking-Together, the oldest woman of the band.

After waiting and seeing no one else, Brant and Tall Man descended to the camp. Two-Walking-Together was startled but not alarmed. After he greeted her, Brant asked, "Why are you here? Where are the others?"

"They went to San Carlos. They decided that without the one who was your father, they would not be safe here. Better to go back to the reservation. But I have no sons or daughters left, and not much time to live. Why should I go to that place?"

Brant could see that she was very ill, coughing and spitting blood. He thought of forcing her to go home with him, so he could get medical care for her, but he didn't have the right to interfere. Before he and Tall Man left, they killed a deer for her and cut more firewood, then left her the jerky and meal they had with them, and their coffee and sugar. Though Brant felt sad to leave her, he admired her determination to finish her life on her own terms.

As he and Tall Man rode north to return to Jesse

and the others, he thought of two women, waiting for children to be born. She-Goes-To-War was carrying the grandchild of Old-Man-He-Knows-A-Lot, a child that might be his. Margarida carried a child he wished were his.

J.J. tossed down his cards in disgust. "Anyone who plays cards with you, Walt, must love to lose."

Walt smiled. "I like to win."

"We could play for money," Margarida suggested, giving her brother a mischievous smile.

"Margarida," her mother chided from across the Ross *sala*, "ladies don't gamble."

"Not so, Mama," J.J. disagreed. "I saw ladies . . . well, women anyway, in California who played for plenty of money."

"J.J., such talk! And don't encourage your sister," Elena scolded, but she smiled happily at J.J.

With J.J. home, nothing could spoil Elena's good humor. Margarida had spent much time recently at the Ross house. It helped curb some of her restlessness, and let her see her brother, whom Elena wanted close by. J.J.'s patience amazed Margarida. Her brother had grown up a lot in two years. She hoped she had also.

"How long has Brant been gone?" Walt asked this question frequently.

"About six weeks," Margarida responded, and thought how much longer it seemed. Walt's question also called up her confused feelings about Brant's trip. Hope for her father. Dread over Brant's desire to revisit the Apache village. And an irrational fear that he would stay there, not return home. It was foolish, but logic didn't banish feelings.

"Let's play another hand," she suggested, not liking her thoughts.

"This time," J.J. said. "I'm going to win."

The front door exploded open and spilled Pedro

inside. "Señora Ross! They're coming, and I . . . I think Señor Jesse!"

Margarida knocked her chair over getting up, and ran out the door. J.J. raced past her toward the corral, where dust obscured the figures. Could one be Papa? Was Brant with them? She saw Chid, and relief lightened her feet.

As she caught up with J.J., he stopped in front of an old man beside Brant. "Papa?" J.J. said hesitantly. Margarida felt the same shock she heard in his voice.

The man who must be Papa stared at J.J., then turned to Brant. "I can't remember who he is. You'll have to help me." He looked back at J.J. "I'm afraid my memory's not very good just now."

It sounded like Papa! Suddenly the sun gave glorious warmth; she felt as if angels were laughing around them.

"Mr. Ross, this is J.J., your son," Brant said gently, "but he doesn't look the way he did when you saw him last. I'm not sure I'd know him."

"It's the beard, Papa." J.J.'s voice held tears.

Margarida stepped around J.J. "Papa, I'm Margarida, and I'm so happy you're home."

"Margarida." Jesse gave a relieved smile. "Yes, I remember." She put her arms around him and hugged him. His body felt frail, and his hug in return was brief, as if he weren't used to having anyone so close.

"Papa," J.J. said, "here's Mama."

"Yes." Jesse's voice wavered. "Elena."

Elena's face showed shock and hesitation, but she said, "Welcome home, Jesse," and kissed his cheek.

Margarida's joy overflowed. Brant had accomplished the miracle she'd believed in so long. Not sure whether he moved or she did, she was in his arms. "Oh, Brant. You found Papa."

He laughed, his exuberance making him young and boyish. "Yes!" His mouth was close—irresistible. Her happiness freed her to pull his head down for her kiss.

His lips held hers, sending a stream of sensation through her that flowed around her heart. It left her trembling and longing for more. So long! her body cried to her. So long since she'd felt that physical magic.

Excited voices brought her back to herself, and to memory. Embarrassed, she drew away. The wall between them was still there. One kiss didn't solve their problems.

Brant's hopes subsided faster than his desire. He'd be foolish, he knew, to mistake Margarida's welcome for more than pleasure in her father's return.

Walt grabbed Brant's arm. "You're home. I'm glad. Is that really Margarida's father? I see Tall Man." He rushed off toward the stable.

Jesse, with Elena and J.J., was walking slowly toward the house, impeded by the *vaqueros* who crowded around, and then by the women collecting on the veranda. Margarida turned to follow, and Brant fell in beside her. "Where did J.J. come from, and when?" he asked. "It was a shock to see him, especially with that blond beard."

"He appeared three weeks ago. He'd never been to Utah at all. Michael Quinn acted strange enough that J.J. left him before they got out of California. Tell me about Papa."

"It was pretty much the way that prospector told you. Your father was with Indians, who'd taken care of him. I convinced them I was his son, and he knew me enough to trust me. We stopped at Fort Lewis. The doctor there guessed your father's still suffering from the effects of the fight with Michael Quinn. He'll need to see Dr. Winton soon. His memory's been returning, but he doesn't remember several months before and after he arrived in Utah."

He wondered if she was thinking about the hidden valley. He'd have to tell that part of the story when others weren't around, but he didn't look forward to it. Margarida would want to know about Red-Rope. The devil of jealousy prodded him at the thought.

"Why do you think Papa got in a fight with Michael Quinn?" Margarida asked.

"We'll probably never know what happened. My guess is that Quinn claimed he'd killed J.J., to taunt your father."

Inside, Margarida joined her father. Brant greeted J.J., who grinned and said, "So you're my brother now. Where are the scars from living with my sister?"

"They just don't show."

The *sala* filled with a confusion of people until Jesse began to look around nervously. Brant took J.J. aside. "Your father isn't strong yet. You might explain that to your mother and to Adela. She's good with Elena. The ranch may be pretty much on your shoulders now."

J.J. shrugged. "I might even like it. Besides, Miguel really manages the work. I can just look important."

When the room emptied and Jesse went to his bedroom, Brant found Margarida. "I imagine you want to stay here overnight," he said, "but Walt and I'd better go on home. I'm sure Juan's already started the roundup. I'd like to speak to you. Can you come outside with me?"

As they went out on the veranda, Margarida thought that for Brant to be away one more night wouldn't make a difference about the roundup. But of course Brant didn't want to stay here, where they'd have to share her old bedroom. Her anger welled up, at him for not wanting to be close to her and at herself for caring that he didn't.

When she saw that no one else was around, she let her resentment out in her voice. "I suppose you were welcomed at the camp?"

"The valley was deserted, except for Two-Walking-Together. Everyone else had gone back to the reservation at San Carlos, including Red-Rope."

Everyone gone! She couldn't imagine the valley empty except for the frail woman. The idea shocked. "How could they leave Two-Walking-Together behind?"

"They didn't *leave* her." His tone disapproved of her question. "They respected her decision to stay there."

Margarida wasn't sure why she didn't feel happier that the Apache, including She-Goes-To-War, were gone. "So you didn't see She-Goes-To-War."

"No. How have you been feeling?"

"Fine. I've been to see *shiwóyé* several times."

He looked surprised. "I'm glad. I think she'll be happy when . . . our baby is born."

His hesitation over "our" hurt her almost as much as his decision to go home tonight. Had he started to say "your"? No, she thought savagely, he was much too noble for that. A tone of indifference was her weapon against him. "She'd be happy about any child, no matter whose."

"You're right." His voice now was as cold as hers.

She turned and went back inside.

Adela was alone in the patio. Margarida gave her a hug. "Thank you, Adela, for helping so much with Mama."

Adela laughed. "I'm used to her now." Her plump face sobered, her eyes concerned. "I worry about you, though. You seem sad. Are you frightened about having a baby?"

"No, but . . . there's something I've wanted to ask you for a long time. At Miguel's trial, I was afraid something bad might happen. But now you and Miguel seem fine."

"I've done crazy things, and he did some too. But he's really a good man, and I love him. So we forgive each other. It's the best way." She laughed, a glint of mischief in her eyes. "Besides, *olvidar la injuria es la mejor venganza.*"

"To forget the injustice is the best revenge,"

Margarida repeated. "Revenge"—an ugly word. Was that what she was doing, she wondered, getting revenge on Brant by not telling him the truth about the baby?

That night as she lay sleepless in bed, she felt the movement inside her, especially strong tonight. It was a reminder that in three and a half more months, a baby would arrive. She had to tell Brant this was his child. No matter what he'd done, it wasn't fair or honorable to go on letting him think Red-Rope was the father.

Telling Brant months ago would have been difficult; it would be even harder now. That was part of the price for letting her anger keep her silent before. She wished she could see into his mind, know his feelings. Then she might not be so afraid. But she loved him too much to deny him a child—and she already knew she would love that child too much to rob it of having Brant as a true father.

During the last weeks, she'd thought back over her hopes for marriage. Having Brant had been her goal—having him all to herself, as a husband, in the familiar way she'd known him. But Brant's longing to be Apache was part of him, and she had to accept that along with everything else about him. At least now she knew some of the reasons he admired the Apache so much. In any case, no matter how much anguish she felt at the prospect of telling him, it was more important to her that he and his child be happy.

Would he forgive her for letting him think it wasn't his child for so long? She didn't know, but she had to tell him anyway. In the past two years she'd done things that took courage—facing the lynch mob, crossing the meadow to surrender to the Indians, escaping from the hidden valley. Compared to doing any of those things, confessing to Brant ought to be easy. But she couldn't fool herself that much. It would be terrible.

26

A last stitch completed the embroidery on the tiny infant dress, and Margarida put it carefully away. Usually the pleasure of working on the small garments lingered with her, but today it faded quickly. She went to the window of the bedroom, looking out, but really seeing only into herself. It was almost a week since Brant had returned, and she hadn't spoken to him yet. Coward! she derided herself. It was something she'd never been before.

Each morning she resolved she would tell Brant that day, but each day her courage failed. She had excuses; someone seemed to be around all the time. One day she'd spent taking her father to see Dr. Winton. What made telling Brant even harder was that he'd been warmer toward her since he'd returned. He acted concerned about her and interested in the layette she was making. That should have made telling him easier, but instead, it became more difficult. Now she risked even more by confessing she'd lied.

If Brant believed her now, he'd know she'd lied before. If he didn't, he'd think she was trying to deceive him this time. Either way, he'd probably despise her. In moments of great cowardice she even thought everything might work out by itself, and she wouldn't have to confess and lose any feeling Brant might still have for her.

No! She wouldn't be that weak! She had to tell him and face the consequences.

As if fate were giving her no chance to escape, she saw Brant cross the yard and come into the house. By the sound of his footsteps, she traced his passage up the stairs and into his bedroom. She realized Luisa had gone to her house for an afternoon nap. Juan had taken Walt with him to look at a sick horse. She and Brant were alone in the house. This was the time.

She went along the hall, then stopped at the bedroom door. The bedroom where they'd made love. Had anything before been this hard? It must have been, but now this seemed worse. She knocked.

Brant opened the door and stepped back to let her in. His face held a serious expression that sent her heart plummeting from her throat down into her abdomen. Quickly—she must speak quickly.

"Brant, there's something I—"

"Margarida, I need to talk—"

Their words collided. She retreated first. "Go ahead. I can tell you later."

"What did Dr. Winton say about your father?"

"About the same as what you told me from the doctor at Fort Lewis. Dr. Winton thinks he'll recover some more, but probably never be the way he used to be."

He smiled sympathetically at her. "I'm sorry. It must be hard for you that he's not as strong as he once was. What did you want to tell me?"

Pleasure at his concern became pain at the thought of destroying it. The words struggled in her mouth.

Alarm replaced his smile. "Margarida, what's the matter? Don't you feel well?"

"No, I'm fine. I think."

"Then what is it?"

His worry felt like a reproach, more bitter because she accused herself. "Brant, there's something I must tell you. I lied about Red-Rope. We . . . he never . . . he was not my husband . . . that way."

Color drained from Brant's face, leaving his eyebrows and eyes black gashes. "The baby . . . ?"

"Is yours."

When he spoke, his voice sounded distraught. "You're going to have *my* child?"

"Yes."

"Why did you let me believe Red-Rope was the father?"

She gripped her hands to stop their trembling, and began. "I think I wanted revenge for what I suffered when you were with She-Goes-To-War. I wanted you to feel the same way. And," she went on, realizing only now more of what she'd felt, "partly, I didn't believe there wasn't some way to escape from the camp sooner than we did, in spite of the guards."

He started to speak, but she hurried on. It had taken too long to get to this point to risk stopping now. "No—don't say anything. Let me finish. I knew your leg was bad, and He-Starts-Fights was so violent and hated us so much that he might do anything. But you always wanted to be Apache. I've always felt left out of a big part of your life because of that. And I could see how much Old-Man-He-Knows-A-Lot began to mean to you. It was a chance for you to live the way you'd always longed to. I felt I was having to give you up because of that. To stay with Red-Rope because of that."

The lines around his mouth were taut with strain. She swallowed and continued. "I was jealous because She-Goes-To-War was pregnant. By the time you said you probably weren't the father, I was so angry I didn't believe anything you told me. And after we got home, everything got worse—until I started going back to see *shiwóyé*. She helped me understand how you might feel. I admire your people now, especially how they feel about children. Then I realized what I'd done. Of course," she finished miserably, "I know that's no excuse. I don't blame you for not loving me now, but you *must* love the child we'll have. It's not the baby's fault."

Now—she was done. Why didn't he say anything? He just stood looking at her with that tight jaw, an expression she couldn't read. She couldn't stand it. Let him say it—whatever it was. "Say something!"

Brant felt her words releasing him from the rigid control he'd kept. Idiotically, the first thing that came out was: "I was waiting for you to finish."

He believed the baby was his, and it seemed too great a gift from the gods. It wasn't hard to know what he wanted to say next. He put his hands on either side of her face. "I love you, Margarida."

She struck his hands away. "Dammit! Don't be so *nice* to me. You don't have to say that. Didn't you hear what I said? I *lied* to you, about this baby not being yours!"

Her anger reassured him even more than agreement would have. She was herself again—squaring up to punishment. He pulled her close, holding her head against his chest. "I heard everything you said. And you were right about some things—things I should have known myself, but didn't. I thought I had no other choices except to do what I did. At first that was true, and I hated the idea of you with Red-Rope. But maybe later I exaggerated how hard it was to escape because I didn't want to get away."

He faced a truth about himself he'd known, but without recognizing how much it had affected him. "My own father was never the father I wanted. After I was around Old-Man-He-Knows-A-Lot, I wanted to be his son." He let himself feel his grief—for what he and his father had never had, and for what he'd lost when Old-Man-He-Knows-A-Lot died.

Tilting her head up, he looked into her eyes. "But you can't accuse me of not loving you—because I always have." Afraid she would move away, he cupped his hands around her face. "What about you? I've done you as much wrong as you've done me—maybe more. Can you love me again?"

Margarida felt as if a tangle of brush that had been choking off the vital stream of her life had just been swept away. "I've always loved you, ever since I was a little girl. I do now. I just hope I'm more grown-up about it."

He held her close, as if she must be part of him. "Margarida, I love you." He kissed her, sending shivers of delight through her. "I love you." He kissed her again, and her heart raced. "God, why did I wait so long? Let so many weeks go by without telling you that? I thought I had to be patient. Or maybe give myself time to know that I wanted your child, no matter who the father was."

"Perhaps I needed the time, to know how wrong I was."

He lifted her hand to his mouth and kissed her fingers, then stroked her face and tilted up her chin. "Do you know what I want now?"

"Yes, but I'm not sure if we can—if it's too close to time for the baby."

His laughter sounded joyous. "You must think I have only one thing on my mind. Well, you're right. I know we have to be careful now, but we can make love. And I want to sleep with you—be close. Share a bed again tonight, and every night of our lives."

He pulled her even more closely against him, and she reveled in the strength of his embrace. He believed her. He loved her.

She looked into his face and saw his sensual mouth curved in a tender smile. His eyes, which for so long had concealed his feelings, shone velvet black with love and passion that his caresses urged her to share. Without him, she knew, she'd been a shell of a woman. Now under his touch she felt herself whole again.

"You've given me a wonderful gift today," Brant said, his voice husky.

"No—I just returned what belonged to you all along."

Epilogue

May sunshine warmed the wickiups in a narrow canyon near Fort Apache in Arizona. Margarida watched Brant walk toward the one where he would find She-Goes-To-War and her baby. Despite all Margarida's resolutions, apprehension made her throat tight. She hugged her three-month-old son closer and reminded herself that they had come here because she'd insisted.

That morning at home two months ago she'd known what she must say. "Brant, let's try to find She-Goes-To-War."

He had looked astonished. "Why?"

"To know that she and her baby are safe, and whether it could be your child." Before she could think how hard it might be for her, she said, "And I think we should ask She-Goes-To-War to bring her baby to New Mexico."

"Do you realize what you're suggesting?"

"Yes, I've thought about it a lot. If the child is yours, it would be right to have it near you."

"She-Goes-To-War probably wouldn't want to leave her relatives, but yes, I'd like to look for her and ask." His face was purposeful and happy. For a moment Margarida felt a pang of the jealousy she knew she'd have to battle. Then Brant kissed her, and his eyes were soft and tender. "Did I tell you today how much I love you?"

"Yes, but I don't mind if you repeat it."

The search had been difficult. They'd almost given up, when a Fort Apache scout told them of the camp. Here this morning they found Red-Rope and a thinner Born-Twice, who directed Brant to She-Goes-To-War's wickiup.

While Brant was inside, Margarida waited for her heart to calm. It didn't, so she asked Born-Twice, "When was She-Goes-To-War's baby born?"

"During the time of cold-even-around-the-fire."

December! Too soon for it to be Brant's child. Margarida felt almost ashamed of her relief.

When Brant emerged from the wickiup, Margarida couldn't tell from his face what had been decided. With sadness and affection, she said good-by to Born-Twice and Red-Rope.

Brant and Margarida rode silently until they were away from the camp. Then he said, "She-goes-To-War wouldn't leave her people." Margarida felt glad for herself, but also sorry that Brant wouldn't see Old-Man-He-Knows-A-Lot's grandchild grow up.

"Let's stop a while and rest the horses," he suggested.

She found a fallen log in the shade of a large pine tree and nursed the baby, enjoying both the feeling and Brant's pleasure in watching. When she finished, Brant said, "Let me take him."

With his son settled on his arm, Brant leaned back against the tree. "There's something I've been mulling over. Maybe we should move, live somewhere new."

Astounded, she looked at him. He was serious. "Away from the ranch?"

"Yes. J.J.'s settled in. He could take over."

"Why?"

"Where we are, men like Carl Bodmer will always think of me and our children as Indian."

His explanation stunned her even more. "But that's what you've always wanted. To be part of the Apache way of living. And what about *shiwóyé* and your people?"

"We couldn't leave as long as they're there. But that may not be much longer. The young men are too confined."

"I thought you wanted our children to grow up knowing about their Apache heritage."

He looked down at his son, sleeping in his arms, then at her. "I do, but maybe it's not good, being mostly one thing and wanting to be another. Years ago when *shiwóyé* sent me back to my father, perhaps she was right. I was already part of the white world. I'm not sure I should have been trying to be both."

She moved closer beside him. "If that is why you're the man you are, I want to live where we do. Then maybe our son will grow up to be like you."

He leaned across the baby and gave her a kiss, so gentle and tender that it proved just what she'd been saying. "All right, then."

Because she couldn't decide whether to cry or laugh and felt like doing both, she stood up. "Come on. Let's get started. We're going home."

About the Author

Barbara Keller was born and raised in Southern California, and despite stints of living elsewhere, again makes her home there. History has always been one of her passions, and with her husband, a chemist, she seeks out the early stories of the places where they travel. She is the author of another historical romance, *The Exiled Heart*, also available from Signet.